Song
of
the Dead

Song
of
the Dead

Douglas Lindsay

FREIGHT
BOOKS

Published by Freight, 2016

Freight Books
49-53 Virginia Street
Glasgow, G1 1TS
www.freightbooks.co.uk

A CIP catalogue reference for this book is available from the British Library

ISBN: 978-1-910449-74-5

Typeset by Freight in Plantin
Printed and bound by Bell and Bain, Glasgow

the publisher acknowledges investment from
Creative Scotland toward the publication of this book

Douglas Lindsay was born in Scotland in 1964 at 2:38 a.m.

Some decades later he left to live in Belgium. Meeting his future wife, Kathryn, he took the opportunity to drop out of reality and join her on a Foreign & Commonwealth Office posting to Senegal. It was here that he developed the character of Barney Thomson.

Since the late 1990s he has penned seven books in the Barney series, as well as several other crime and surrealist novels, written in the non-traditional style.

For Kathryn

1

Friday afternoon. Standing in a queue at the supermarket, staring at the floor, the basket weighing heavily in my right hand. Dinner, milk, wine, water, orange juice.

I've chosen the wrong queue again. We don't always choose the wrong queue, we just never notice choosing the right one. Glance at the old woman fumbling with change, counting the coins out slowly, as though she's still converting from pounds, shillings and pence.

There's another younger woman behind her. Looking at her phone.

Almost dark already. Too late to go for a drive. Tomorrow maybe. I can head off, then get out the car, walk some way up a hill. Nothing major. Nothing that requires a backpack. Up Strathconon, stop long before the end. Sit on the grass, watching the day crawl over the land, the deer mingling at the foot of the hill.

My phone rings. Much too loud. Set on full volume to make sure I never miss it. The three women beside me all glance disapprovingly. Their censure vanishes as I press the green button and put the phone to my ear.

'Need you back in here, sorry.'

It doesn't matter who says it, does it? The voice from the station: *That weekend that you were about to start enjoying is going to have to wait.*

My plans hadn't amounted to much anyway.

I contemplate risking the wrath of someone anonymous at the supermarket by placing my basket on the floor and walking out, but instead I take a minute to walk round, putting my dinner and the drinks back on the appropriate shelves.

* * *

Five minutes and I'm closing the door behind me and sitting down in front of the Chief Inspector. He's on the phone, but he waved me in. He's writing as he listens. When he's finished, he thanks the person he's talking to and hangs up.

'Need you to go to Tallinn,' he says.

Looks across the desk. Humourless. Good at his job, respected. But totally humourless. Which means he isn't joking.

'Estonia?'

As opposed to where, I wonder, as soon as I've asked the question. Maybe there's a Tallinn, Idaho or a Tallinn, North Dakota.

'Yes.'

'I don't…'

'You're booked on the eight-thirty Gothenburg ferry from Aberdeen, so you'll need to get going. Train from there to Stockholm, overnight ferry Stockholm to Tallinn, gets you to Estonia, more or less, for start of play Monday morning.'

He looks at his watch.

'Sorry, Ben, but you're the best man for the job, given your background. They're not intending to do anything with it over the weekend, so Monday should be fine.'

'What's up?'

'There was a case twelve years ago, before your time. It was news around here, but wasn't too big nationally. A young couple went out to the Baltics, aiming to tour around. The chap, John Baden, went missing in Estonia. In the south, in a place called Tartu. It was in the papers for a few days. Then his body washed up on the shores of the lake that forms much of the border between Estonia and Russia.'

'Murdered?'

He pushes a file across the desk.

'Read it on the ferry.'

'Was there anyone here who went out there at the time?'

'Rosco.'

I nod, lean forward and lift the file. We don't talk about Rosco.

'So, there's a new lead? That's why they want someone to go out?'

No dramatic pause. The Chief doesn't do drama, just as he doesn't do humour.

'John Baden, or someone claiming to be him, walked into a police station in Tartu this morning.'

Just as the boss doesn't do drama, he doesn't like to see his officers overreact. I remain expressionless. It was going to be something interesting, or else they wouldn't be sending anyone out there.

'The Embassy are involved?'

'Of course.'

'Is there anyone working there who remembers the case?'

'Doesn't appear to be.'

'They've spoken to the Estonians?'

'Everyone's on board. Baden's been taken to a military hospital.

They're going to keep him there over the weekend, try to get to the bottom of it on Monday. You should arrive just in time.'

'And his partner from twelve years ago? Has she been notified?'

'We're trying to find her. However, at the moment we just want to know where she is and what she's doing. We're not telling her yet. Presumably… presumably this isn't him. Look at the file. He was dead, his body was identified by at least three different people. This was an open and shut case.'

'Except someone just opened it again.'

'Yes.' He nods towards the door. 'You've just got a passenger booking, no need to take your car over. Mary's got the details.'

I lift the folder, and get up. 'You'll let me know if you find out where the partner is?'

'Of course.'

I walk from the office, closing the door on my way.

I'm glad I've got nothing to cancel this weekend, but I'd be lying if I said that there's anything I'd likely be doing that was going to be more interesting than this.

I go back to my office, lift my watch off the desk, and am strapping it onto my wrist as I get to Mary on my way out.

She's ready for me and holds out a few pieces of paper, clipped together, as I approach.

'Have a safe trip,' she says.

'When am I coming back?'

'Open booking,' she says.

I nod and walk out the station without stopping.

2

I was in Goma in 2007. Was supposed to spend six months there, give or take. The kind of operation that some people might find exciting. Me too, probably, a few years previously. By the time I got to Goma I'd had enough. Too many games, too many times looking at myself in the mirror and not recognising the person looking back. Yes, that's a cliché, but it was right on.

Who was that guy? I couldn't tell the colour of his eyes or whether there was any life behind them. I'd shut something down when I joined the security services. I wasn't a natural actor or liar. Could only play the game by being nothing, letting nothing out. Nobody knew who I was. The people who'd known me before wondered who I'd become and what it was I was doing now. Gradually I lost touch with them all.

Goma was the end of it. I'd done two tours in Helmand, been in Kabul and Islamabad, and run some guys in Baghdad for a few months. Goma was always going to be the last. They knew. They knew I needed to be back in London for a few years. At any rate, I was thinking I'd be back in London for a few years; they were probably thinking that they'd wring one last drop of effort from me, and throw me on the scrapheap. At least it wasn't the seventies, when the scrapheap meant a bullet in the back of the head so no one would ever be caused any embarrassment.

Goma was me being thrown into the midst of the Rwanda-DRC border conflict that's been on-going since ninety-four. It was us, the United Kingdom, still trying to be a player. Still trying to influence events.

I don't blame our government, not at all. You think we're just going to screw up everything we touch? You should see everyone else.

There was a night, about four months in, when I was due to meet a couple of guys on the edge of town. A small shack that had once been a teahouse, but which hadn't been much used the previous few years. Now it was nothing. An empty building, home to spiders and insects and small animals. You'd think someone would have moved in, but no one had. Maybe they knew. Maybe it should have been a warning.

I'd met them a few times previously. Maybe as many as five or six. I was trying to groom them to be our guys on the inside of the FDLR. They weren't supposed to know who I was working for. As far as I remember, I genuinely thought they didn't. They probably saw through my lousy South African accent the first time I sat down opposite them in a bar.

Such a stupid game. I mean, really? A fake South African accent? And me as well, trying to carry it off by saying as little as possible.

They arranged a meeting for me about half an hour by plane into the jungle, due north, heading towards Uganda. The fact that they didn't let this get any further was also tantamount to their amateurishness. They could have played me far longer than they did. They could have milked the UK government for far more than they did.

Maybe they were worried that I would get too close. I don't know. Never will.

The plane was a small four-seater, a basketcase, there was no faking that. I took one look at it and wanted to run. Had had my share of horrible flights in war zones the previous few years, of planes that could barely take off, and helicopters taking evasive action under fire.

But what was one more flight?

I could tell there was something happening. They were more nervous than usual. But I'd been in enough tough situations to not doubt my ability to extricate myself from it. Don't second-guess, just play along and deal with whatever happens.

We took off, the two of them in the front, me sitting next to a couple of black plastic bags in the back seat. They wouldn't tell me what they were. Turned out they were parachutes.

Five minutes in, when we'd risen steeply away from the edge of the city, out over Nyiragongo, I had a gun at my head and they were tying me to a chair. They took the money I'd brought along, as though that was it, that paltry sum was all my life was worth, they put on the parachutes, left the plane pointing straight ahead, lodged the stick against the control wheel and jumped.

It was dark. The plane juddered and dipped. I couldn't see anything, and there was no radio to try and contact anyone, even if I'd been able to get my hands free.

Did they intend that I should fly on until the plane came to the Ugandan border, and then it would get shot down? If they thought that might cause some sort of diplomatic incident they could try to exploit, they'd have been wrong. There was no way the British government were going to acknowledge my existence.

The plane never got as far as the border. I struggled with my bonds, but couldn't break them. At some point, the plane started to skirt the tops of trees. I couldn't see anything, but I could feel it. Feel the underside of the fuselage flirting with the roof of the jungle canopy.

I was scared then. I'd been through a lot by that time and something was going to scare me sooner or later. And that was it. Sitting in a plane, no control, knowing that it was about to crash.

The left wing must have caught the top of a tree, and the plane was hurled round. I was thrown into the side wall, still tied to the chair, and then the plane was crashing through the trees, before rudely thumping against a thick trunk and plummeting quickly to the ground.

There was no explosion. Just as well, as I had no way to get out. Someone found me, someone cared for me, and somehow I ended up back in London, sitting in front of one of the DGs, being thanked for my work.

They'd wanted to fly me back from DRC, but I insisted otherwise, and chose to make my way from the eastern border of the country all the way to Dakar, by a patchwork of trains and roads, much of which was likely to be far more dangerous than travelling by air. From Dakar I hitched a boat to France, and then a train back to London.

It took eleven days in all, and I haven't been on a plane since.

3

There's a flat calm on the North Sea. A disconcerting, silent calm. Even the dull throbbing of the ferry's engines seems subdued. Swallowed up by the sea and the dank air and the poor visibility.

Still water beyond the wash of the ferry. How can the sea, so tumultuous at times, ever be this lifeless? As though it's been decreed: today the sea will not move. There will be no waves. There will be nothing.

The mist restricts the view to little more than a few hundred yards. There could be land over there and you'd never know, although the map on the television in the cabin shows that we're in the middle of the sea, edging slowly towards Sweden.

Standing on deck with the smokers. Coat on, freezing November chill in the air, looking out at the grey nothing, impossible to tell, a short distance away, where the sea becomes the sky. There is no sky.

I could imagine, as I did last night on the ferry, that I would spend much of the daylight hours on deck, looking out at the sea. Standing out here now, however, I'm cold and dissatisfied. Slightly bored, even. *How can you be bored looking at this?* I position myself as best I can to escape the cigarette smoke, as though the removal of that annoyance might help. But the disaffection remains, and soon enough I decide to go back inside.

I stand still for a few moments. There's a slight bustle around, the constant movement of passengers, from one activity to the next. Café, restaurant, cinema, floor show, amusements, shopping, a parade up and down, possibly everyone as dissatisfied as me.

* * *

I position myself in the café so that I can look out upon the grey early afternoon. A cup of coffee and a cinnamon bun, another short while in the grey day, and then back to the cabin to read the rest of the file.

'We could be anywhere.'

I turn. There's a waitress standing beside the table, her fingers resting on the saucer of my empty cup, following my gaze out the window.

'There's a timelessness about it. Like we're trapped.' She's not looking at me as she speaks. Almost as though she's addressing the room, or maybe just herself. I follow her gaze back out over the sea.

A ghost ship, looming out of the fog, would not be out of place.

'There's something unsatisfying,' I say.

'You're right.'

'Why is that?'

I glance round at her, but she's still not addressing me, even though we're talking.

'You can't be part of it. You're looking at something that you can't become one with. The same as all views of mountains or... I don't know, a great plain and a big sky. Snow is different, because you can interact with the snow. You can play in it, make things from it, feel it. Same with a beach and a warm, turquoise sea. You can dive in.'

I don't know what to think about that, so I don't think anything. We're not really talking anyway. She's talking, and I'm sitting here, vaguely in her vicinity.

'When you stand out there, leaning on the railing, do you get the urge to jump in?' she says. 'Even though you know it'd be unbelievably stupid. Even though you know you can't. You still want to. It's like there's something calling you, dragging you over the side.'

I nod. She's right.

'That's because you want to be part of it. That's the only way to truly appreciate it.'

'You can climb a mountain,' I say.

In the slight reflection in the window, I see her nod.

4

Papers are laid out on the bed. Ones which I've read and thought might need to be cross-referenced. There's a small pile of one-and-done pieces of information.

The file would have been compiled by DI Rosco. We may not talk about him, but he was a decent enough officer, when the mood took him. Maybe this wasn't one of the good ones.

John Baden and Emily King got together at university. Aberdeen. He was from Dingwall, she was Canadian, from Toronto. They moved in together in Marybank, just off the Dingwall to Contin road, and they set up an internet business. Copywriting. That's what it says, although there's not very much information on it. An incomplete picture, as though Rosco couldn't be bothered with the details, like it wasn't interesting enough for him. The yawn of copywriting.

They took a holiday to the Baltic. Ten days, travelling around. Flew into Helsinki, took the ferry to Tallinn, intending to visit Riga, Vilnius, and St Petersburg, before heading back to Helsinki for the flight home.

They hired a car to drive from Tallinn to Riga. Stopped off in the university town of Tartu. Booked into a hotel called the Centre. The Centre Hotel. From the photograph it looks just as awful and dull as the name suggests. This was still only twelve years after the fall of the Soviet Union, so much of it was yet to change.

Spent two nights in Tartu, which seems odd in itself, if you're intending to do a tour of capitals, and St Petersburg. Maybe it's a fun place. I'd never heard of Tartu until I spoke to Quinn.

The second evening they went out for dinner, walked around the old town square, sat in a couple of bars. The things you do on holiday. Went back to their room. Had sex, went to sleep.

She woke up the next morning and he was gone. Not completely gone, as in he'd taken all his clothes and left a note saying he couldn't stand it any more. Nevertheless, gone, jacket and shoes included.

She presumed he'd been unable to sleep and had gone out for a walk. He'd always been an early riser. She went back to bed. Woke up some time after nine, he still wasn't there. She showered, got dressed, went downstairs and had a cup of coffee and a piece of bread for breakfast, positioning herself in such a way that she'd see him return to the hotel.

He never returned.

She went looking for him. Having just arrived the night before, she obviously didn't know the town too well. Few people spoke English. No one at the hotel was able to help her. By mid-afternoon she went to the police. She didn't find them very interested in the first instance. Who would be? A grown man missing for six hours? However odd it appeared to her, it didn't appear very odd to them. Estonia had opened up to Western Europe, and back then, one of the ways in which it was opening up was by selling alcohol and sex.

She sat in her hotel room the rest of the day, waiting for the door to open. She slept fitfully, and the next morning she returned to the police station. From there she called the British Embassy in Tallinn. They sent someone down.

The story never really captured the imagination of the British press. Even after three days it seems that most people still presumed he was drunk somewhere. Missing children and attractive young women are what the media want to report. A guy in his mid-twenties who was likely still out on the lash was of little interest.

At this stage the British police were not involved. DI Rosco first heard about the case when the Dingwall station was contacted by Baden's father.

About seventy miles to the east of Tartu lies Lake Peipus. The far shoreline was, and remains, Russia. The positioning of the border, through the lake and on either side of it, has not yet been formalised.

A few years ago the two countries reached a border agreement. However, the Estonians insisted that the abuses of the Soviet occupation be acknowledged in the final document, Russia refused, and the precise border was never ratified.

Between Tartu and the lake lie seventy miles of flat marshland and forest. Silver birch and pine trees. Not much else, bar the occasional homestead. No villages, virtually no roads.

Somehow John Baden had made the journey from Tartu, because it was determined that he drowned in the lake and was therefore alive when he got there. He was found in the lee of some trees lying face down on a stony beach.

His body was identified in Estonia by Emily King, and then again, when it was brought back to Scotland, by his parents. With the exception of the bloating caused by immersion in water for forty-eight hours, there were no marks on his face. Identification was not, Rosco writes, problematic.

John Baden went missing, and then his body turned up at the

side of a lake. The questions needing answers were *how* and *why* and *when*. *Who* was never thought to be an issue.

★ ★ ★

Late afternoon becomes early evening. The mist doesn't lift, it just becomes consumed by the darkness. I turn my back on the papers and sit at the cabin window. Mary has served me well for my trip. A double bed, a desk, a small sofa, a stool to sit on by the window.

How many people conduct their lives, watching the world go slowly by, looking at the sea, troubled by this peculiar feeling of dissatisfaction?

Having turned the light off, so that I wasn't just looking at my own grim reflection, the night engulfs the room. Outside there is nothing, any other shipping obscured by the mist.

The light illuminates the dark. The dark conceals the mist. The mist conceals the light. In the end, nothing wins.

5

Dinner in the gourmet restaurant. Gourmet is not a word particularly applicable to the food, nor even the prices. It's more aimed at the people who wouldn't be put off by the name. If you don't like the sound of a restaurant with gourmet in the title, they don't want you in there in the first place.

The place is quiet. Most people must be eating elsewhere. Or not eating at all. I haven't encountered too many other passengers, but I'm not looking, and not exploring the boat, my world is a small triangle between my room, the outside deck and the café/restaurant area aimed at people who don't like the word "gourmet".

Pike perch and sautéed potatoes for dinner, with some indeterminate green. Two glasses of Chilean Chenin Blanc. Crème brûlée. Cup of coffee.

No conversation with the waitress. She's polite, but I'm not in the mood for talking.

I want to find the answer to the mystery of John Baden from the file, to arrive in Estonia with an idea and for it to be proved right. But the papers so far have failed to provide any inspiration. I have another night on this boat, a train journey across Sweden, then overnight on the Stockholm to Tallinn ferry to figure something out.

I want it to happen. Not so that I walk in and instantly produce a stroke of genius to impress everyone. I don't care what they think. I just want to do a good job, and the best way to do that is to be in control.

Always best to control an investigation from the start, which is generally easier than you think. Most of the time you know where it's going right from the off.

So far, however, John Baden eludes me, and the idea of walking into a room and meeting the man on Monday, without any clear idea in my head of what's going on here, is making me slightly nervous.

Nervous isn't the word. But there's something there, lurking; niggling and uncomfortable.

After dinner I go out on deck and lean on the railing for a while. There's no one else out here. Staring down at the water, I find I don't have the usual feeling of being drawn in. On the seventh deck, the dark water, flaked with white, is a hundred feet away.

How long would you survive in the North Sea in the middle of November in a flat calm? Twenty minutes maybe, if you were healthy before it started.

I go up a floor and halfway along to the stern, back to my cabin. Into the dark. Don't turn on any lights, take my place at the window. The bed is clear of papers, as I'd tidied the file away before going for dinner. I won't look at it again tonight. Tomorrow morning I'll grab a pastry and some coffee and come back here and have another couple of hours before we dock.

The night passes by to the low drone of the engines. Eventually I tear myself away from the vacuum of the dark outside.

★ ★ ★

There's no great stretch from the security services to the police. An easy jump to make, and the police are usually happy to take on people with the experience, although often enough the ego gets in the way. I don't think I ever had that problem, although I've heard of others who mistakenly thought the same, so what do I know?

I was offered a job in London, but I wanted to go north. Had been thinking about Inverness or Aberdeen, but there was a post on offer in Dingwall, so I was happy to take it. Rosco's dismissal, after years stuck in the same pay grade – his career going nowhere – had created a vacancy.

My new colleagues were all wary at first, but eventually I began to fit in. Kept my head down, did a good job, the two core principles of being accepted into a new office. They probably thought I was going to be one of those burned-out screw-ups, taking what he could get. Sure, I'd had enough of war zones and getting caught up in fire-fights and spending weeks at a time waiting for the knife in the back, but there's not too much of that in Dingwall. Right from the first day it was fine. No drama, no trauma.

The drama came before I left. The drama with Olivia.

When she found out I was going, she got hysterical. Not for the first time. This time though, it was in public, and she let vent her full fury for an audience. Outed me as a former member of the security services in the process, at least to fifteen people or so in the restaurant. I worried that someone was filming it, and that it would appear on YouTube within a few minutes, but I got some of the guys back at Vauxhall to check. They couldn't find anything. None of the other diners had been inclined to be amused by Olivia's shouting and my painful silence.

It just wasn't that kind of restaurant.

Olivia was one of those people who hid behind the mask. You could never really tell what was going on. A majority of the time things were fine, but sometimes you just couldn't understand what she was thinking. There would be no reason, or if there was, the reason didn't seem to make any sense. Yet you couldn't talk it through.

Of course, I asked her if she wanted to come to the Highlands, but it was in the certain knowledge that she'd say no. Olivia was the kind of London girl who thinks the world north of Regent's Park and west of Sloane Square is some tribal hinterland, where you're lucky to find anyone who speaks English. You might as well be in central Afghanistan.

And so, although she asked me not to go, I said I was leaving anyway. She fought me on it, just out of bloody mindedness – right up until the last time I drove my car away from her front door – standing in the street, shouting abuse at my rear window.

6

DI Rosco was in Estonia for ten days, and somehow things were never the same for him after he returned. The file implies that they welcomed his expertise. Perhaps he looked upon his time there as the halcyon days, the ones he would never get back, the ones that would always be better than what was to come.

Not that his expertise actually got them anywhere.

He and his Estonian colleagues interviewed over a hundred people, none of whom had been able to impart any useful information. No one had seen John Baden leave the hotel, so it was unknown whether his departure had been forced. There wasn't a single sighting of him thereafter. The nearest dwelling to where his body washed up on shore was over five miles away, and naturally they had nothing to add to the investigation. Why would they have had? There are strong currents in the lake, and it was acknowledged that Baden's body could have been dumped anywhere.

Rosco worked on the basis that what had led to Baden's death was in Estonia, and when he found nothing, finally he brought the investigation home.

His colleagues had made inquiries in his absence, but there was nothing to report. It hadn't been much of an investigation. There isn't a police force in the country, even this far north, that has nothing better to do than chase after someone else's case, and one that happened in another country at that.

Rosco came home to a thin file, and had to build on it. He unearthed some strange characters from Baden's time at university, and on that meagre premise, spent another few weeks chasing short leads going nowhere and interviewing people who'd known Baden for ten minutes in Aberdeen.

Eventually the leads dried up and time ran out and he was moved on to something else.

At some stage, back in Scotland – and I don't intend to spend as long in Estonia as DI Rosco – I'll need to speak to Baden's mother – his father died several years ago – and hopefully to Emily King, if we can track her down.

Nevertheless, the reading of the last of the papers in Rosco's file prove unrewarding, and leave me no nearer the desired stroke of genius. That will have to wait.

The boat docks in Gothenburg, I disembark with my small red suitcase and find the bus for the train station. The weather is heavy and grim. The day will be even shorter than normal.

The bus is full, a few people standing in the aisle. The windows are steamed up, obscuring the view of the city. Cars and cyclists and faces flash by, most people hidden beneath umbrellas and hats. The journey is short. Had I realised how close the train station was, I would have walked.

I did a job in Stockholm a while ago. In and out, didn't see much. Back in the days when I could get on a plane without breaking a sweat. I remember the patchwork of islands, but not a lot else.

I had a meet arranged in the *Vasamuseet*, the most frequently visited museum in Scandinavia. The Vasa was a seventeenth-century Swedish warship designed by someone throwing cannons at a piece of paper. Top heavy with artillery, it sank a few hundred yards into its maiden voyage. I'd never heard of it before, which I was slightly embarrassed by at the time, but it stands as the supreme metaphor for political and military hubris and stupidity.

One of those moments when I could have spent a lot longer in the museum reading about it, looking at the salvaged hull, but then I had my quick handover and I was heading back to the airport.

I resolved, then, to read more about the Vasa, but never have done. I think about it again sitting on the train to Stockholm, but I won't have the time to find the museum today. Passing through. Maybe on the way back.

Mary continues to come through for me. There must be money in the budget they're needing to spend, or else lose in the next financial year. A double bed on last night's boat, and now a first class ticket on the train.

I sit alone at a table for four, barely anyone else on the carriage. Sweden flashes by in a series of lakes and trees and glimpses of empty dual carriageways.

7

Another cabin, another window. The boat is moving slowly out of Sweden, past endless tree-covered islands, large and small. Dark already, however, even before we departed, the islands identified by the pale moonlight and the occasional solitary light outside a remote house.

Summer homes, weekend homes, perhaps one occupied by a determined spirit who commutes into the city every day by boat. I see myself doing it, although of course I live in a three-bedroomed bungalow and drive less than ten minutes to the station every day, which isn't particularly adventurous.

There is a knock at the cabin door. Sitting in the dark, watching the evening go by, it comes as a shock. I shake it off, turn on the light and open the door, presuming some sort of cabin service, and that Mary really ought not to be spending so much of the budget on sending her officer to Estonia in this much style.

A young man in a suit.

'DI Westphall?'

They've seen me coming.

'Inspector Kuusk, Estonian police, Tallinn jurisdiction.'

He holds out his hand and I take it.

'Welcoming committee?' I ask.

'I was in Stockholm today anyway. I thought we could get the boat back together, talk things over before you turn up at the station tomorrow, so that I know everything you know and vice versa. We are going to work together, yes?'

He looks about sixteen, which is disconcerting. And one learns not to take offers of help at face value.

'You have I.D.?'

'Of course. My apologies.'

He hands over the card. It seems in order, but of course, we both know it could be anything. I've handed over a hundred fake I.D. cards in my time.

'Just give me a few minutes to get ready, and I'll meet you downstairs in the coffee bar.'

He smiles, takes back his card and I close the door.

★ ★ ★

I sit down opposite him with a cup of coffee and a glass of water.

'Are you happy I should be here?' he asks. He's smiling.

'You really just happened to be in Stockholm today? You got the boat over last night just to take the boat back tonight?'

He's drinking a latte, which is almost done. There is an A4-sized file tucked in beside the arm of the chair.

'Some of us get on a plane, Detective Inspector. I flew in today, I had a meeting with some Nordic counterparts. Yes, normally I would have flown back, but it's always nice to spend time on the boat. We can chat, we can go our separate ways, and by 2 a.m. there will be plenty of drunk young women. If you know what I mean.'

'At least you'll get something out of it,' I say. Then, 'You're young.'

'Twenty-nine,' he says, seemingly unconcerned about my bluntness. I don't mean, in any case, to imply that he's too young to do his job. I'm just curious.

'That's pretty young.'

'We're a young country. We have the youngest Prime Minister in Europe. We have more vigour, more determination to get things done.'

'Not so much experience.'

'We listen to the old and take their advice. But we have the spark to follow through where the older generation will hold back and be more cautious.'

I suddenly wonder if I'm going to find people offering me a seat on the bus, and expecting me to be sage, interesting but largely inactive.

'Am I past it at forty-one?'

He smiles.

'The coffee on this boat is good,' he says, side-swerving the issue of my advanced years. 'That's another reason to be here.'

'You've met this person claiming to be John Baden?'

He nods, although there's a look on his face that suggests he's showing an appreciation of the coffee rather than acknowledging having met the stranger who's crawled in from the past.

'Yes. I spoke with him for several hours yesterday afternoon.'

'That's a long interrogation.'

'Not so much an interrogation. A conversation I should say.'

'What's his story?'

This is the part I know nothing about. The file the Chief Inspector gave me stopped with the end of Rosco's investigation, some twelve years ago. Case closed, nothing to add since then.

'I wonder if I should let him tell you himself,' he says.

'Then you wouldn't be here. What's his story?'

'Very good. I am happy to relate, I just wanted to make sure that you wanted to hear it first from me, rather than the horse's mouth.'

'Your English is very good.'

'Of course. Everyone in Estonia speaks excellent English. Apart from the Russians, who speak excellent Russian.'

He drains his coffee, and then lifts the file, which has been waiting its moment. He hands it over.

'Perhaps you'd like to read my report. The tale is somewhat fantastical, but that does not mean it's not true. Bad things happen to people in the Baltics, as elsewhere. It might be better for you to take that back to the privacy of your cabin. I will be here when you return.'

I look down at my half-drunk coffee, lift it, finish off the rest of the cup and head back to my cabin.

8

There was something else from before. Just a moment, when I was disembarking from the boat in Gothenburg. A covered gangplank for foot passengers with windows along the side. I walked down amongst the mild throng, overhearing some of the conversations; few enough that voices were clear, words could be heard. Trying not to listen to the general chatter of others, no one with anything consequential to say. Glancing out the windows as I went.

There was someone. A woman, sitting against a wall on the dockside. It seemed unusual, as it wasn't the kind of place that anyone would wait. She wasn't wearing the high visibility jacket of someone who was working in the port. A small figure, her head dropped forward, although her eyes were turned up at the ferry.

It felt like I caught her eye, although it's the kind of thing that in retrospect feels ridiculous. She would never have been able to clearly make out the faces of individuals as they walked down the gangplank behind murky windows.

There was no dramatic, and-then-suddenly-she-was-gone moment, like you might expect. Although perhaps she was gone. At the next window my view to where she was sitting was blocked. And then at the next. And then we were off the gangplank and being directed towards a terminal and that part of the dock was lost to our sight.

There was something though, something about her. Every day in a city you catch someone's eye. Most of the time there's nothing there. An awkward glance that just happens to have taken place, and then it's gone and forgotten. Sometimes it means something more. Sometimes it's worth following up.

Or you're walking down a busy street. In the space of a few hundred yards, a hundred people might walk past you in the other direction, maybe more. We avoid each other with the instinct of birds flying in formation, of ants scurrying along a worker's route, of a great shoal of fish, swooping through the ocean creating extraordinary patterns. And yet, every so often, you almost bump into someone. You slow and step to the side, just as they step to the same side. There's a glance, one stands still while the other passes, and the awkwardness passes with it.

Why that person? Was it just chance that your basic instinct prevented you avoiding them, or was there something else drawing you in? And you pass by, and you never know.

The thought of the woman, sitting by the dock, came to me again as I walked up the stairs back to my cabin. No reason. The thought just came and went. I wondered if she was still sitting there, because, strange as that would seem, I couldn't imagine her doing anything else.

★ ★ ★

There's a man claiming to be John Baden. Can we think of him as anyone else until we have proof of who he is?

He walked into a small police station in Tartu at just after nine on Friday morning. When asked why he was at the station, he told the officer on duty that he was a British citizen, that he had been imprisoned twelve years earlier, and that he had managed to escape several days previously. Only on his escape, in fact, did he discover how long he'd been imprisoned, as the passing of the days and years had been lost to him. No television, no Internet, no marks scratched into the walls. Some days he was not even aware of the passing of night.

Why had someone held him prisoner for twelve years? They wanted to harvest him, he said, by whatever means they could. They took some of his blood once every three weeks, and his bone marrow once every three months. At some point they removed his kidney, and at another half of his lung. X-rays taken at the military hospital had confirmed the organ removal. They had shaved his hair once a year, and taken his sperm.

He was kept in a plain, clean room, with a mattress on the floor and no other furniture. There was a toilet and a sink. They would give him books to read in English, but nothing written after the early twentieth century. Society was lost to him. He would be fed once a day, usually vegetables and potatoes, occasionally some indiscriminate meat. At some stage, he relates, he wondered if the meat was flesh harvested from other prisoners – he had no sight of other prisoners, but assumed he was not alone – and stopped eating it. They told him he had to eat the meat or his life, and the lives of everyone he knew, would be forfeit. He went back to eating the meat.

Every so often a young woman would be brought to him, and he was instructed to make love to her. Sometimes very young. Younger than sixteen he presumed. The first time it happened, he refused. The guard who'd brought the girl in began to beat her.

Baden slept with her so that the beating would stop. Thereafter he complied every time.

He had little to say about his captors. If he ever attempted to make closer contact with one of them, he would be instantly rebuffed and, more than likely, he would never see that person again. Some of them spoke better English than others. Some, it appeared, knew none at all. Occasionally one of his female captors would come to him, and use him for sex.

This tale had been written out by Kuusk entirely dryly, as it should have been, giving its absurdity credence by expressing no incredulity. Women using men for sex, as though keeping a guy locked up is the only way to get him to sleep with you.

I stopped as I read, realising that that was the first thing that had given me pause when reading it. All the rest, of keeping someone prisoner in order to harvest their blood and bone marrow, might have been far-fetched, but it's a brutal world. Brutal. People do bad things all the time, and barely a tenth of it ever comes to anyone's attention. Every now and again the media pick up the grotesque stories, but for the most part, they don't want to know or, more likely, they just never find out.

His tale of escape was interesting, relying on suggestions of a woman's weakness. He said he'd fought back on occasion, and every time was brought crashing down. He was kept weak – he said – and they were all strong. Skilled. Every move he tried, every physical move, was rebuffed instantly, and pain followed as punishment.

One time he got the better of one of his captors, just one time, and within ten seconds there were two more at the door and he was beaten. Beaten heavily, and not fed for two weeks. Two weeks, or so, as far as he could make out.

Generally, when one of them came to him for sex, she would be accompanied by another, occasionally a man, who would stand guard. Watching, not taking part. Making sure Baden did not try anything.

In twelve years, he never got as far as the door. Then, one night last week, a woman came to him on her own. She was hurried, he instantly got the impression that she shouldn't have been there. She did not speak. He did not know her name, but she had been several times before. In fact, he realised later as he thought of his escape, she had come to him for sex more than any of the others.

She was wearing a white vest top, and dark jeans. She removed both of them and sat astride him. The women were largely made from the same model. Strong, slim, small breasts, short hair.

Boyish almost.

She kissed him. He responded to her passion, straight away, but realised that he had a rare opportunity. Occasionally there might have been chances in the past, but fear of capture had always cowed him. He didn't know why, but for some reason, the rudeness of her arrival, or perhaps just beaten down by years of incarceration, he took a chance.

He sat up, his lips on hers, his hands on her breasts, feigning passion, and then, when he was in the best position, brought his forehead down on the bridge of her nose. She fell back, and before she could react he jabbed his hand into her throat. He then made a movement on her that he had thought about doing, if ever the situation arose. Grabbed her leg and pulled it hard up, back and to the side. He heard the snap, a sound that sickened.

She cried out, as best she could, given the blow to her throat, and then he pushed her off and ran.

He was in the basement of a large house. He got to the back door and outside without being accosted. There were woods fifty yards behind the house, and he ran for them. He got the impression that the house was not alone, but he did not look back.

As he reached the trees he heard shouting from the house. He kept running. And running. The story of his getting to Tartu involved a lot more running, a long walk through forests, and the not unexpected tales of stealing clothes off washing lines, and digging cabbages out of the dirt. He did not think for a second that he would be able to find the house again, but if the police wanted to accompany him, he'd be willing to try. Not that he knew where to start looking.

And that was the somewhat incredible story of John Baden, whose body had been found dead at the side of a lake twelve years ago.

9

Kuusk is sitting in the same position, another latte in front of him. When I approach, he is looking off to the side. Wherever he is, it's not here. Lost in thought, but a look on his face that suggests he won't even be able to recall those thoughts when I bring him out of them.

I would have expected to find him on the phone. That's what we all do, isn't it, when given a spare few minutes? Maybe you can't get Internet on the boat. I haven't checked.

I announce my arrival by placing the file on the table. And he's back.

'Just going to get another coffee,' I say. 'Can I get you anything?'

'I'm fine, thank you.'

I return a minute later with a cappuccino and a glass of water. He's ready for me this time, the file back where it was, tucked in beside the arm of the chair.

'Do you believe him? Even if he hadn't been pronounced dead, it's pretty far-fetched.'

'Too early to say,' he says. 'I think at the moment we're still at the stage of listening, gathering the facts.'

'You must...' I shake my head. Stupid. Don't go telling anyone they must anything. 'You didn't get a sense of him? His motivation? Some idea of–'

'–He sounded entirely convincing. I know how it looks, and sounds. I would say, at least, that he himself believes it.'

'How did he feel about being taken to a hospital? Didn't he expect to be put in touch with his family? Did he still expect to see Emily King?'

'He barely mentioned Miss King. Indeed, when I asked about her, his replies were short. That was certainly of interest. He was keen to know about his family, and when I saw him, I did not have the relevant information to update him. I believe someone from your Embassy has told him now.'

'He wasn't desperate to call anyone?'

He shakes his head.

'You don't think, if you'd been gone for twelve years, the first thing you'd want to do is get in touch with your family, partner, whoever?'

'Yes, but you must consider the circumstances, Detective

Inspector. Even now, if this is the real John Baden, he's only thirty-five. Two-thirds of his adult life have been spent in a small room. His head must be pretty messed up. What thoughts he must have had, imprisoned all these years, no contact with the outside world. Could you survive by hanging on to thoughts of family, or would it be easier, better, to push them from your mind? And as for his girlfriend, in how many ways had he betrayed her? How many women? How many girls had he been forced upon? Might not some argue that he should have done nothing and faced the consequences? It would be a strong and peculiar man who did not feel a great amount of guilt.'

Good points. Twenty-nine years old, and a better understanding of the human condition than I have.

'OK. You X-rayed him...?'

'Not me personally.'

'If we're going to get along, you can stop being pedantic.'

He smiles.

'He was X-rayed at the military hospital. It confirmed that half his lung, his spleen, his pancreas, a kidney, some liver tissue and a few feet of small intestine had been removed. There was also some evidence of needles being used in his arm, which he claims was for the frequent removal of blood, and also evidence of bone marrow removal. And by the old, painful method.'

Take a drink of coffee. Time to think. Wouldn't be the first time anyone had heard of this kind of thing. People being used in grotesque fashion by others. People will do anything, will fall into anything. Still nothing, of course, to square away the principal fly in the ointment: John Baden has been dead for twelve years.

'There was nothing about how he was taken in the first place,' I say.

'He doesn't remember.'

'What does he remember?'

'Going to bed in his hotel room with Emily King, and then waking up in what was to be his prison cell.'

'So someone came into his room, anaesthetised him in some way, or had drugged him before he went to bed, and then made off with him in the night, without Emily, who was sharing a bed, knowing anything about it.'

'That's what we've got.'

'Does he remember feeling peculiar before going to bed?' Shake my head. 'That's not what Emily said. It all seemed like a regular evening, including having sex, which presumably he wouldn't have done if he'd been drugged and feeling weird. Or whatever.'

'What he remembers is an ordinary evening, making love to Emily at the end of it, and falling asleep with her in his arms.'

He pauses for a moment, and then nods to himself at having decided to voice his opinion.

'I wonder if possibly he blames her. Emily. There's nothing he's said, but it would be another explanation for her not being affected, and him being whisked off in the night. If, in some way, she was part of it. Maybe that's what he's told himself all these years. Although, of course, he doesn't actually know whether or not she was taken.'

'He hasn't asked?'

'No.'

'You didn't tell him that he's been declared dead?'

'No.'

More coffee. Check my watch. Not such a bad time to have a gin & tonic in fact. And then dinner. And then an early night followed by an early morning, and back over the file, re-reading everything that I'd picked out before as being worthy of further consideration.

'The story as he presents it,' he says, 'stands up to the scrutiny that we can currently give it. All except the first and most crucial part.'

'The body.'

He nods.

'I need a drink, and dinner. You want to join me?' I ask.

He checks his watch.

'Sure. The real action doesn't start until eleven thirty.'

10

My first year on the job, first year in Dingwall, we had one of those cases that all police officers hate: the missing teenager.

Teenagers go missing every day of course. They stay out, they come back a couple of days later; they run off, they never come back. The parents come to the police, and what can we do? Sometimes, they won't even come to the police, because they don't want the police to know the reason why their child ran off in the first place.

You make a judgement every time, as soon as the missing person is reported. Sit tight and wait for them to crawl back from the pub; talk with the parents and establish why exactly their child might currently be sitting on the bus to London; or face the music, the instant knowledge that something's happened. Go to the press, let them know, hope they buy into it, because on this occasion you need their help.

Now, just because you're asking the media for help doesn't mean you have to have even the slightest respect for them. The media are like cats. They do what they want, when they want. They might give you the impression that they're on your side occasionally, that you have some element of control over them, but in reality, you're nothing to them other than dinner.

The media will help the police if and when it suits them. I think that time, back in Dingwall, was a slow news cycle. The usual calamities overseas, but nothing much happening in Scotland. Added to that, however, was that the missing teenager was seventeen, female, and attractive.

If you believed nothing but the newspapers you'd think the vast majority of people who go missing in Britain are good-looking teenage girls. The reality, of course, which we all know, is that those are the ones the editors want because those are the ones the public likes to hear about.

Our girl, Abby, fit the bill. And I knew right from the off. She hadn't run away, she wasn't still draped over the end of the bar in the Ceilidh Place in Ullapool. Felt it in the first hour. Walked into the house to talk to the mum, dad and younger brother, and I could feel the crushing weight of sadness.

Not from the family though. They weren't sad. Not yet. They were still at the panicking stage. Panic and fear, coupled with some sense that by reacting this way, hopefully it would turn out to be unnecessary, that at any minute their daughter would be walking in the front door, and they could be relieved and laugh about it and apologise to the police.

The crushing weight of sadness came from Abby herself. I could feel it everywhere. She was still in the house. Some part of her, at least, was still in the house. And if she wasn't actually physically there, then it meant she was dead, and her spirit had come home to be with her family. To mourn her own passing.

I got no more than that. I couldn't ask her what had happened or where we might find her body. I couldn't physically see her. It was just the sense of her, so strong that I was surprised that no one else could feel it.

I didn't ask, of course, but I could tell. No one else looked like I felt. The family were still that stressed, horrible, jumble of dread and hope.

We identified the killer shortly afterwards, and I mean, twenty minutes afterwards. Identifying usually doesn't take long. Building a case is where the time goes.

She'd had one boyfriend in her life, they had split up three months previously. Her decision. I went round to talk to him. He'd already shut down. He had to expect that the police would be at his door as soon as she was reported missing. He'd been dumped, and no matter how amicable the parents made it sound – and not for a second did they implicate him, as the only time they sounded upset with Abby was at the thought of her ending her relationship with this kid they were very fond of – that's your motive right there.

Some seventeen-year-olds might be capable of the cool lie. Not many, I wouldn't think, but some will be. The ones who are due to be true sociopaths throughout their unkind lives. Everyone else though is going to give themselves away, and the only way to avoid doing that is to shut down. Completely.

The boyfriend could barely speak. He looked me in the eye, but his eyes were dead. He gave nothing away, except that he gave everything away. He didn't look like he was in shock, he looked like he was trying not to talk.

There was no satisfactory conclusion, on any level. We found Abby's body in a small burn beyond Evanton. Not concealed particularly well. Bruises on her arms, bruises on her legs. She'd been raped and strangled. We can't say what the boyfriend had been thinking because he never admitted it. He stayed shut down. Never spoke in court, never answered a single question. We had the evidence from her body. We had DNA. We had fingerprints.

We had the e-mails he'd been sending her. There was no question.

The last time I was in Abby's house the place was enveloped in sadness, but now it was everyone, and it was everywhere. So much grief, it was hard to tell if she was still there, seeking solace with her family, bereft.

That's what the rest of their time on earth will be. A time of mourning. Their daughter is dead, and their lives will never be the same. I see these people around town today sometimes, seven years later. They haven't recovered now, and they never will.

11

Standing on deck as the ferry moves slowly past the Estonian coast towards the Bay of Tallinn. Kuusk beside me, a cigarette in his right hand. We're in the No Smoking section, but no one seems to care.

Low, grey cloud. Moisture in the air, but not actually raining. Bitingly cold. I don't have the clothes for this weather. One of the consequences of packing in haste. I thought, we're pretty far north in Dingwall, Tallinn probably won't be too much different. Apart from being a couple of hundred miles out, it was a stupid assumption anyway, Britain being warmer than just about everywhere of equivalent latitude on the continental masses.

Wearing a short blue jacket, three layers underneath, hands thrust in pockets, suitcase on the deck beside me.

The great white hulls of the ferries in dock are the first we see of Tallinn, and then the few towers and spires emerge from the murk.

'Bad day, or is it always like this?' I ask.

Kuusk smiles, takes a final puff of the smoke and then flicks it over the side.

'It's November. The most miserable month. Days are short, weather is cold and wet. The suicide rate soars. Everyone is sad.'

'You're talking it up.'

'It's better when the snow comes. Sometime in December through to April, there'll be snow on the ground. The place looks a little better. At least in the parks and on the roofs. Not so much on the roads. They just get to looking dirtier. Dirty snow is as depressing as this.'

The boat has turned, and suddenly the port is appearing quickly out of the gloom.

'So, what's with you?' he asks. 'You're a tough one to fathom.'

'What d'you mean?'

'I've read the stories. All these maverick British cops. They all have something. Drugs, alcohol, women… What's with you?'

'I don't think I'm a maverick. I'm just a guy.'

'You don't drink?'

'Wine. A little bit. Can quite happily go a week without it.'

'Drugs?'

'Never.'

'Women?'

Shrug.

'Last one was pretty awful, so I've steered clear for a while. Someone'll come along eventually, I expect. Most women I meet seem to be married with kids.'

'Sometimes they're the most fun.'

I smile. He's probably right. Think of Mary, sitting behind her desk back in Dingwall.

'You must have something,' he says, persisting.

'Sometimes I play chess on my iPad.'

'Ah, chess genius.'

'I play on the third level out of ten.'

He takes another cigarette from the packet, contemplates it as though he might decide not to light it, and then puts it in his mouth and cups his hands around the lighted match.

'You have a tortured back story?' he asks, after his first long draw.

'No.'

'Abused childhood?'

'No.'

'You like music, maybe? Opera? Your lot usually like opera, that kind of thing. You know, so you can drive to a murder scene listening to the *Flower Duet* from *Lakmé*.'

'I think you've been watching too much TV.'

'You must like music. Everyone likes music.'

'Turin Brakes.'

'I don't know them. They're a band?'

'Yes.'

Another puff.

'I don't know them,' he says again.

'I can let you hear some on my iPod.'

'Cool. What did you do before?'

'You mean my last case?'

'No. Before you joined the police.'

I wonder about asking him some questions, but somehow it would seem disinterested. Only doing it because he was asking it of me.

'Security services.'

No harm in saying. Not now. Been so long. And the security services don't care. They more or less have photographs of their staff on their website nowadays.

'MI6?'

'Yes.'

31

He nods, the smoke breathed out through his smile.

'I knew it. A spy. You must have seen bad stuff.'

Shrug.

'Some,' I say.

'Traumatised.'

'I don't think I am, but if it makes you happy for me to be, then you can have it. At least it's something. Pretty boring otherwise.'

He nods. He leans forward on the railing, takes another puff and then flicks the half-smoked cigarette into the sea.

'I didn't need that one,' he says.

* * *

John Baden has spent the weekend in a military hospital to the east of the city. We go straight there. Kuusk asks if I want to check into my hotel first, but as it's not much after ten in the morning, there's nothing I would do when I got there. I sling my bag in the boot of his car, and off we go.

We drive round the sweep of the Bay, the ferries behind us, along the path of the promenade towards and past the marina.

'Must be nice in the summer,' I venture at some point.

Kuusk doesn't respond. Lost in thought, or nothing to say. Any place by the sea that isn't nice in the summer must be making a positive effort not to be.

* * *

Baden is sitting at a table in white hospital clothes. He has a cup of coffee and a packet of cigarettes. The air in the room is smoky. A window is open slightly, letting in something of the bleakness of the morning.

He looks thin, distant, detached. If his story is true – and even suggesting that it might be sounds false, because how can it be – then he's going to get to the part where it all becomes too much for him and he has to completely withdraw.

Perhaps someone made him believe he was John Baden, that brainwashing was part of the process of captivity. Why anyone would do that, of course, adds another layer of questions thicker than the meagre explanation that spawned them in the first place.

Face drawn, eyes faraway, cigarette in right hand, hand shaking slightly. Left hand firmly clutching an empty cup.

'Can I get you another coffee?' I ask.

A moment, and then he looks at me, looks at his cup.

'You're the one from Scotland?'

'Yes.'

'You don't sound it.'

'I just work there.'

There's no sixth sense with this guy. Nothing there to latch on to.

'Who's top of the league?' he asks.

Well, there's a question. Safe, neutral, natural.

'I'm sure one of the Estonians could have told you who was top of the Scottish league. At least, they could have found out for you.'

There's a nurse, maybe a kind of security nurse, standing in the corner. She reminds me of Rosa Klebb, which must be some sort of appalling racist profiling on my part. But she does. I wouldn't leave anywhere that she didn't want me to leave.

'I didn't think of it until now,' he says.

'Celtic.'

He nods.

'Rangers went out of business,' I add.

That, at least, brings a flicker.

'What d'you mean?'

'Went under. Got demoted to League Two. Division Three as it was back in your day. Haven't quite made it back to the Premiership yet.'

'Shit,' he says.

Holds my gaze for a second, then lowers his eyes. He's a typical football supporter from Dingwall. Not actually interested in Ross County. I think of telling him about County being in the Premier League, and then decide not to.

'I'll get the coffee,' I say.

'Could I have a cup of tea?'

Staring at the floor as he asks.

'I mean, a proper cup of tea. British. Not the stuff they drink here.'

★ ★ ★

Check the time. Have been in here just over twenty minutes. My coffee finished, bar the dregs. Baden drank his tea in five minutes. Found a guard with some Tetley lurking in his cupboard, two years out of date. How does tea go out of date?

Do they put these overly prescriptive use-by dates on food in fear of the health and safety brigade or because they want you buying their product more frequently than you would otherwise need to? They want the turnover that's at odds with food sitting in your cupboard and fridge.

We're not saying much. There's no rush. He's been gone twelve years, no hurry now. I wasn't despatched with any instruction to get things sorted out and be back in time for Wednesday morning round-up.

'What was your favourite book?'

He glances at me, looks away again.

'You said you were given old books to read. Which was your favourite?'

Pause. Come on, now, that one's not too hard.

'*Pride and Prejudice*, he says'. 'That's kind of stupid, isn't it?'

'Everyone likes *Pride and Prejudice*.'

Another silence. His eyes look off to the side, but there's something there.

'How did the wars go?' he asks, his voice soft, the words placed gently into the room.

'Which wars?'

'Afghanistan. Iraq.'

They would just have started when he went missing. And was found dead. Keep having to remind myself of that fact, so natural does it seem sitting here, with someone saying they've been out of touch all this time.

'Not great,' I say. 'We tried ending the Iraq one and it just came back. Afghanistan, not so different. Anyway, there are other wars now. Lots of wars. The Pope called it World War Three by stealth.'

He doesn't ask where. He lifts his cup, which he hasn't done in the fifteen minutes since he finished it. Looks inside, places it back on the table. Not the time to ask him if he wants another.

'We need to talk about Emily,' I say.

Nothing on his face. He's staring at an indistinct point on the floor.

'We need to talk about Emily.'

'I know. I find it hard to think about her.'

'Why?'

Slight movement of the jawline, teeth pressed together.

'There's too much.'

'Too much what?'

'Too much to think about. I can't go there. Can't think about what's happened to me, and put Emily in the same story. She's not part of it any more. She's not part of my life any more, even if I want her to be, even if by some miracle she's still out there, wanting me to be.'

'How long were you together?'

'From day one of university. Stood in the lunch queue together and bang. Four years at Aberdeen, then three years living in Marybank. Every morning having breakfast, looking up at Wyvis. Thinking it was ours. The mountain was ours.'

Pause.

'Then we came here.'

'Whose idea was it?'

'Emily's. Had been talking about it for a while. Trying to get me to take a break.'

'Why the Baltics?'

'She loved the idea of it. Neither of us really wanted a beach or the sun.'

'You think she was involved in you being taken?'

Furrowed brow, he looks at me. Shakes his head.

'No.'

'You haven't asked whether she was ever taken. Why haven't you asked that? Did you not presume she was grabbed at the same time?'

His face relaxes, he looks away and again loses himself in the indistinct spot.

'I did for a while. Assumed I'd be seeing her. Never did. Over time... I don't know, I thought everything there is to think. I asked myself if she was involved, just as you did. But I couldn't believe it. I don't know how long I considered that, but I never believed it. And the thought that she was being held like me... Maybe she was. Maybe she is. Maybe she was in the next room all the time.'

He looks up, some sort of spark starting to come.

'She was never taken?'

'No.'

'You've spoken to her?'

I shake my head.

'I headed out here as soon as they brought you in. I haven't spoken to home yet. They hadn't located her when I left, but they might have by now. Certainly, twelve years ago, she spent... she looked for you. She was questioned, and no one thought she had anything to do with your disappearance.'

'You hesitated.'

'Yes, I did.'

'Why?'

'I'll tell you later.'

Don't let them start asking the questions. Also worth noting, don't hesitate at the wrong moment.

'Why are you only just getting here then?' he asks. 'Did you take a boat?'

'Two boats. And a train.'

12

Mid-afternoon. Tired. Travelling will do that, regardless of whether there are any time zones and regardless of how much sleep you've had. We're headed back towards town, back to Kuusk's HQ, but I get him to stop along the Bay, so that we can take in some fresh air for a while. Just after three o'clock, already getting dark. Two hours ahead, so UK time I'd just be about to have lunch. I'm not normally tired at one in the afternoon.

Biting cold, but it's waking me up. The air has cleared a little, but the wind is still coming in off the water. The sky is the same flat grey. The cold is the kind that it's hard to imagine any amount of clothing protecting you from. Piercing, slicing. You feel it deep inside, like someone is pouring ice water into your veins.

The sea is calm. I've barely seen a wave since leaving Aberdeen. To the left the port. The bay sweeps away to the right. On the horizon there's a large, low-lying island, barely visible. Everything is grey, making it hard to tell the difference between sea, land, and sky.

'We need to try to get him to find where he was held.'

'Of course.'

'You have any ideas, from what he said, where to start?'

'We know roughly where to start, yes. I don't hold out much hope, but we will try. Tomorrow, naturally, when there is daylight.'

'If you can call it daylight.'

He laughs. He pulls his coat in a little tighter. He seems no better dressed for the weather than I am. He probably wasn't expecting that I'd suggest a walk along the promenade. Looking along the length of it, as far as we can see in either direction, there is one woman walking a dog, and that's it.

'I need to buy a coat,' I say. 'Let's go back to HQ, speak to your boss. I'll call home. Maybe they've found Emily. I don't know how much use it would be if she actually turned up here. You know, if she didn't run a mile first.'

'She might know if it's him.'

'Yes, there's that,' I say, but the idea of that moment, of her walking into the room to see him, feels so bad, so uncomfortably wrong, that I don't want to think about it.

'So, we can go back to the car now?' he asks.

'Yes.'

'Thank God.'

★ ★ ★

Standing at an office window, fourth floor, looking down on the back of a bleak portside scene. Bare trees to the left, a car park, the back of probably empty warehouses, and a view through to an unused dockside. Between here and there a small area of redevelopment, a pedestrian and cycling track, which might look all right in summer, but not so much on a grim November's day.

Have been looking at it for five minutes when the door opens, and I turn to see Kuusk following his boss into the office. Superintendent Stepulov. Again, she seems young for her position. Long dark hair hanging loose, dark rimmed spectacles. Slimmer even than Kuusk, and I'd already regarded him with some resentment.

She smiles briefly, shakes my hand.

'Glad you got here safely. You have a problem with flying?'

I'm not getting into it. Never felt the need to justify myself before, so answer with a slight movement of the shoulders.

She takes a seat behind her desk. Top floor in the offices of the Central Criminal Police. View of the old port area and out over the sea, but not attached to the port. The office is large and sparsely furnished. A lot of dead space. Perhaps she has meetings in here. In the UK this would be an open plan office for about fifteen. I decide the Estonians must still be at the stage where government and the services are expanding, before they hit the part where they have to start shedding people, buildings, and other assets by the hundred-weight.

When was the peak of the British government and civil service? I wonder, but never think of the question when I'm next to a computer. 1914 probably. Thereabouts. The height of Empire. Been downsizing ever since, with no end in sight. Eventually there'll be a few people working in Whitehall calling themselves the government, while the country is run by enormous, corrupt corporations. It'll be the East India Company in reverse.

'I've had a long chat with Chief Inspector Quinn. I don't think he believes you ought to be out here for an extended period. Hopefully we should get this wrapped up very quickly.'

She has a certain tone about her, but I've been warned by Kuusk. She takes a while to warm up and doesn't do small talk. She gets to the point. 'Almost as though she's Estonian rather than Russian.' That's how he put it.

Regardless of whether this is just the way she is, or if there is any real resentment about my being in the country, as her tone suggests, I'll be giving Quinn a call as soon as we're through here.

Kuusk, for his part, seems to be modelling himself on American movies.

'Have they found Emily King?'

'So far, no.'

'They know where she is and can't get hold of her, or they–'

'–They appear to be having difficulty locating her. You should speak to your Chief Inspector when we're done. I believe Detective Kuusk wants to go with you and the supposed victim to try to identify the area where he says he was held?'

'You're sceptical then? About this man claiming to be Baden?'

'Of course, Detective Inspector. I was a junior officer when the case had its previous incarnation. John Baden's body was found, it was identified. There was no question. He was dead. So, how can this man be him? I have seen his dead body. So the question you need to be asking is not, is this man John Baden? It is how does he come to think he is John Baden, or why is he pretending?'

'For the moment, and until proven otherwise, I won't be taking any questions off the table.'

She smiles, which is surprising.

'Of course. You must tackle this as you see fit. Will you be taking Mr Baden back to the UK?'

Genuinely hadn't thought of that. Much too soon. The length of time I think I'm going to be here seems to differ greatly from her expectations.

'Too early to say.'

'Very well. Inspector Kuusk can keep me informed as you go.'

A last look, then she lowers her eyes to her paperwork. The international sign of the dismissal. Not quite ready to go yet, however.

'Regardless of who he thinks or says he is, there's clear evidence that this man has been abused, that his body has been used. Regardless of the historical aspect of the case, you surely must be wanting to investigate the possibility of a group of people, whoever they are, holding prisoners in the forest.'

Her lowered head remains steady. I wait for the glance, the rebuke, the sharp tone telling me it's none of my business. Perhaps she and Kuusk have already had the conversation.

Nothing. I glance round at Kuusk and he indicates with a slight eye movement that it's time to go.

★ ★ ★

Another office window, but now it's completely dark outside and all I'm looking at is my own reflection. Talking Quinn through how I found our man to be.

'Are you convinced?' he asks.

'Much too early to be making any judgement calls. He seems genuine, that's all. But it could just be that he's very well prepared and a damn good actor.'

I can see him nodding at the other end of the phone.

'Right, we'd better press ahead this end,' he says. 'I was trying to avoid going to court to get an exhumation order...'

'But you're going to have to.'

'I'd already started Sutherland on the paperwork anyway. Hopefully, under the circumstances, we can get it pushed through quickly.'

'And how about Emily King?'

'Dropped off the map not long after the affair in Estonia.'

'There wasn't insurance money, was there?'

'Yes, there was.'

God, how mundane, how disappointing. This case seems so far from the normal, so different. How banal it would be if it turns out to have been an insurance scam.

Still, that wouldn't explain the blood harvesting. And the rest.

'Perhaps she sold him off,' I venture, 'and somehow there was another body they could use that she was willing to identify as his.'

'The mother and father would have had to have been in on it.'

'Yes... Yes, a theory too far. But let's play with it, and see where it gets us. With the exception of the mother and father, it's at least something that would explain the anomaly.'

'Indeed. Right, Ben, do what you have to do out there. Try not to be too long about it. Another couple of days maximum if you can. We don't want you going all Rosco on us. We'll keep things going this end, see what we can come up with.'

'Yes, sir.'

Ten minutes later I've said goodbye to Kuusk for the evening, and I'm walking to my hotel, case in one hand a map in the other.

I stop off at a bar in the old town square. An old cobbled area like in a thousand places across Europe, the beer three times the price of what you'll pay two streets away.

I sit at the window, listening to the voices around me. Mostly English being spoken. There's an American couple discussing the effect of the war on Tallinn, and how it changed hands between the Soviets, the Germans, and back to the Soviets. The guy read a book about it on the plane on the way over, or before he got off the cruise ship, and is consequently talking with total authority.

My heart's not in it. I don't really want to be sitting in a bar, drinking beer I don't like and unable to shut out the surrounding chatter.

Rain is falling into the dark evening, as I head out the bar, leaving the beer half-finished, and walk the two blocks to my hotel.

13

We're in a black Peugeot, heading south. Kuusk in the front with a police driver, me in the back with Baden.

I'm not going to interview him like this, sitting in the back of a car, taking him back to the area where he was held captive, taking him back closer to his trauma. I thought he might engage in some conversation, a general what-have-I-missed kind of discussion, even if it was dispassionate and detached. But there's nothing.

I can feel his nervousness, almost a palpable entity sitting beside him. We probably ought to have had him trauma risk assessed by now. If his account is true, then there's no question that the man will be traumatised. I expect there would be a legion of counsellors out there screaming at us for immediately trying to take him back to where he was held. Has to be done, however. It's the only way to take this forward at the moment.

The driver is an interesting chap. He seems nervous as well. I wonder what his story is. He talked to Kuusk in Estonian when we got going, and I didn't understand a word. But Kuusk seems sullen this morning, as though another grey day has finally got the better of him. The driver tried to draw something out of him, but didn't get anywhere. Eventually gave up as we hit the outskirts of Tallinn.

We've been driving, painfully slowly, in silence for the last half hour. The driver scrupulously observes the speed limits. Single carriageway, past woods of silver birch and pine. The Nordic/ Baltic model. Occasionally there are glimpses through the trees of marshland, bogs and wild grass stretching as far as the grey mist of morning will allow.

Daylight, such as it is, doesn't arrive until well after eight. It's early November. One hates to think what it'll be like a month and a half from now.

We're on a long, straight stretch of road. Trees down either side, far into the distance. Grey cloud, so low and suffocating that it seems to be sitting just above the level of the trees. Barely any traffic on the road, but the driver determinedly sits at the speed limit. The energy in the car, the life-force of us four men, seems to be sucked dry, drawn up into the clouds, pulled in by the grimness of the day.

I feel suddenly like I'm part of some awful, low-budget Eastern European film, a road trip, where the producers couldn't afford incidental music, so there's nothing but the sound of the car, and there's no script, just men sitting in silence, and it's filmed in black and white, and you watch this car drive along for mile after mile without anything being said, and it's strangely captivating, yet at the same time it crushes your soul, brings your spirit down to the same level as these four desolate men, going nowhere, thinking nothing, bereft of spirit.

And that's us now. The four of us. The sullen Estonian policeman, the nervous, troubled driver, the Scottish policeman weighed down and feeling like a stranger, and the ghost.

'Can't you drive a little faster?' I ask. Have to force the words out. They don't want to come. No words allowed in this sullen car. Nothing to be asked, or answered.

I wait for him to say something, or perhaps just to speed up a little without actually acknowledging the request, but he does neither. The words disappear in the monstrous claustrophobia.

Perhaps he never heard me. Perhaps I never spoke.

★ ★ ★

Tartu is a university town, bustling, as such places tend to, with the energy of youth. Despite the heavy skies, one still senses the liveliness of the place as we drive through. However, we're not aiming for the centre of the town, the merest glimpse of which we get on our way. We're aiming for the eastern end, the last police station on the edge of town, before it vanishes into the woods and bogs that continue all the way to Lake Peipus.

While he has been sitting absolutely still throughout the journey, now I can see Baden's nervousness manifesting itself in small, uneasy movements. The fingers, the clench of the fist. Feet and toes. A slight judder of the legs.

The blanket of fog over the car lifts. Almost there, we'll be getting out shortly, conversation will be had, the small world of the car will be broken up, escaped from, and others will be drawn briefly into our investigation.

We will announce ourselves at the station: a courtesy to let them know we're in the area, and from then it really is all down to Baden. What he can remember. I wasn't too hopeful starting off, and now, having sat next to him the whole way down, I doubt he'll be able to tell us from which direction he approached the police station, never mind trace his steps back to his starting point.

We park at the side of the station. Having glimpsed the life of the centre of town, out at the edges it returns to the more regulation

Eastern European standard, colourless square buildings thrown together, wooden or concrete or brick, no structure, no life. The roads are poor, the pavements occasionally placed, as though optional. Road signs I don't recognise, arrows pointing towards available directions at every junction.

The station is small and grey. There are three cars parked outside, one of which is marked *Politsei*. A sign over the door, next to a small Estonian flag, marks the entrance. Of the six sets of windows at the front of the building, four are shuttered, two of which have bars on the outside.

Three of us can't get out the car quickly enough. The driver has a cigarette lit and in his mouth practically before his feet have touched the ground. Kuusk and I step out more measuredly, but in all likelihood our desperation to escape was just as great. Baden remains in the car, his right leg now shaking constantly, his hand squeezing his knee.

Kuusk lights a cigarette as he walks round the car. It's cold, I stand with my hands thrust in my pockets. I'd take the cold any day over what we were feeling in the car.

'You want to come in and say hello? We shouldn't be long.'

'D'you think they'll speak English?'

He shrugs, takes a long draw. 'You never know.'

'I'll leave you to it, you can pass on anything you think worthwhile.'

He nods, probably quite happy to be able to conduct the brief conversation in Estonian, rather than potentially struggling through a conversation in English that the other officer might not be up to. He takes another long draw of the smoke and then flicks it casually onto the ground as he walks up the steps.

The driver is stretching, almost as though he's trying to draw attention to himself with the elaboration of movement. Squats, then his leg stretched out with his foot against the car, followed by great movements of his arms, the cigarette in his mouth the whole time. Perhaps he's about to take off running. Perhaps he knows what they're like around here.

I stare up and down the street. Should have had more breakfast. This isn't the kind of trip where you casually mention having lunch before doing what you came here for. We need to get on with it. Unlikely to be more than a few decent hours of daylight left.

I walk round the car and open Baden's passenger door. He jumps at the sound. Hadn't seen me coming. Immersed in whatever narrative he was using to protect himself.

'Can you get out the car, please?'

He glances up at me, looks back at the seat in front. Contemplating the possibility of not moving, but it isn't really a possibility at all. He slowly gets out, stands outside the car, taking vague, darting looks around.

'Can you remember the direction from which you approached the station?'

For a moment he looks as though the question surprises him, then he steps away from me towards the road and points to his right. I walk out onto the edge of the pavement and follow his gaze. Long and straight, the road to nowhere. There are numerous buildings down either side at first, then the main stretch of the road turns sharply to the right. However, a side road goes straight ahead, and it allows a view beyond the end of the town where the buildings run out to scrubland, the trees quickly following.

'You came all the way from there?'

He nods, something I pick up on without really looking at him.

'Have you any idea how long you were walking for?'

This time I have to look at him to see that he's shaking his head.

'But it was two nights?'

'Yes.'

'Would you say you were moving quickly?'

He doesn't answer.

'Would you say you were moving quickly?'

'I don't know. At first, yes, of course. I was trying to get away. Running, running as best I could. I tired quickly though. It'd been a long time since I'd run anywhere.'

'Did you have any idea where you were going, or did you just stumble into the town?'

'Found a small road, followed it.'

'The day you got to the station?'

'The day before.'

'You think you'll recognise that road as we drive out of town?'

Pause.

'I don't know.'

'You have any idea how many miles you walked along it?'

Shakes his head.

I know he's not going to have answers to these questions, but they have to be asked.

'So you were walking for maybe a day and a half before you found the road? What d'you think?'

'I don't know. That sounds about right.'

'Did you have any sense that you were walking in the same direction the whole time?'

'I don't know.'

'Were you aware that you had gone back on yourself at any point? You saw a landmark that you'd already seen?'

'It was just trees.'

'What about the sun even? Did you use the sun?'

He stares at me, and then, slowly, his eyes lift upwards. I know what he's doing, but I can't help myself following his lead. The grey sky lies oppressively on top of us, as it has since my arrival. My sense of direction and orientation is reasonably good, but I have absolutely no idea where the sun should be at the moment.

The door to the station opens and Kuusk trots down the stairs. The second he's outside he lights up another cigarette, takes a long draw, leaves the cigarette on his lips and pulls his jacket in close to him.

'They need us to go into Tartu, the main station. They're expecting us there. They've got like, I don't know, a team of guys.'

'No.'

We both turn to Baden. He's not quite looking either of us in the eye. Staring at the ground, shaking his head. Not sure what he's thinking, but I have to admit I agree with him. I don't want it taken out of our hands yet. I want to spend the day with him, try to make some decision on what's happening with the guy, and then leave the investigation of this apparent band of enslavers to the locals once I'm gone. If they all come on board now, I might as well not be here.

'Did Stepulov instruct you to hand yourself over to the locals?'

'No, I just came here to be nice.'

'Right, we ignore them. You'll be able to handle the fallout.'

'Just obeying orders. Stepulov can handle the fallout.'

Doesn't this have Estonian police turf war written all over it? None of my business.

'Right, let's hit the road. You…' I say, pointing at Baden. He said he was all right coming back here. I need him to start shaping up. I'm not going to start hugging the guy and caressing him towards usefulness. 'I know this'll be tough, but I need you to start buying into it. We're relying on you and we're going to be fine. If we actually come to somewhere that you think you might recognise, then we'll call for backup. We won't just go blindly charging into a situation where we could be heavily outnumbered, but we need to try to at least identify the area.'

He nods, then turns and indicates the road he already pointed me down.

'We need to go down there,' he says, then he shuffles back around the car, his breaths heavy, and gets in.

14

'We came down here when we were children. It's a great area for expeditions, hiking and camping. Dangerous in places, but you learn quickly where you should go, where you cannot put your feet. When you are at school, they send you off in small groups. Missions, we called them, although it is nothing more than getting across the bog in one piece. They say they watch you. They send a group off on their own, children, maybe thirteen or fourteen years of age. They say they'll be watching. You don't know how, and you can't see them, but they've told you that they're watching, so you believe them. That's what stops you being scared. Four nights alone on the marshes, as the hierarchy within the group develops. That's what they're testing of course. To see how the group evolves.

'Nowadays, I think, they send them out with cell phones. They can call when they need help. We did not have such means of communication. I was worried, but they said they were watching, so what was there to worry about? The rain came the second day. Not heavy, but soaking. That misty rain that drenches you in a short time. And it did not go away. The marshes were covered in this. Cold and wet, the air heavy with drizzle. I wondered if they could still see us, but I assumed that they must have moved in closer. Of course they would, we were thirteen- and fourteen-year-old children.

'We had all had enough on the third day. All soaked through, all cold, all miserable. I remember I did not care. I did not care if I received the expedition badge. I knew there would be another chance to do the test, but I did not care about that either. I just wanted to go home. So did most of the others. One or two said no, that we had to go on. There were arguments. One of the boys starting shouting. Shouting for help. Shouting to those adults who were watching. But there was no one. No one came.

'There was an argument and, of course, there was a fight. The boy who had been shouting fell into a bog. He was punched, and he fell back. The bog sucked him down. We hung on to him, but we could not pull him out.

'We shouted. Yes, we shouted for help, but still no one came. There was no one to come, that was the thing. There was no one there. They lied to us. They said we'd be fine, and when we weren't fine, there was no one to help us.

'He slipped into the bog. I can still see the fear on his face, I can still see the last of his fingers as they were swallowed up.

'We walked home. I don't think we even camped that night, just trudged on, each with a torch in his hand. The boy who had punched him did not do what you might imagine, by making up a story, threatening others to go along with him. He was broken.

'We arrived at the camp the following day. One short. No one wanted to tell the story of how one of our number had come to fall in the bog. They asked us, over and over. Finally, when they were talking to us one by one, the boy who had thrown the punch owned up.

'We sat on the bus home, knowing our parents would be waiting for us at the other end. They were all notified, they knew what we'd been through, and those of us who had survived, they knew we were all right.

'I ran into my mother's arms. She cried, she held me. My head pressed into her chest, I looked around the same scene, playing itself out amongst so many parents and children. And there were the two parents without a child. They had been informed of their son's death, but they had come anyway. They stood silently, hopelessly, helplessly. The only parents not crying. No tears, just lost.

'Were they hoping that their child would be on the bus, that somehow the school had notified the wrong parents? Maybe they thought he was playing a game, fooling them all, and that he was going to appear, like magic, from his hiding spot. Perhaps they just had to see for themselves. The confirmation. That he wasn't coming home. That they were never going to see their only child again.'

The driver finally stops talking. It's a long story, a slow narrative to accompany the drive beneath grey sky, between endless forests, the same landscape over and over.

'I don't like coming back here,' he adds, several minutes later.

★ ★ ★

'Stop!'

The driver slams on the brakes. I put my hands up to brace myself against the seat in front, despite wearing a seatbelt. Baden allows himself to be forced forward, and then judders back into his seat as the car stops. We all look at him, although in Kuusk's case it is in the rear view mirror.

He's staring at the seat in front of him again. I wonder if we're

49

anywhere near where he was kept. We've been driving for a while since Tartu, have already changed direction once at his instruction.

That is, of course, if he was kept anywhere. His behaviour seems too rehearsed. I need to keep reminding myself that this could be part of the plan. Someone's plan, somewhere.

'That road,' he says. 'The one to the right.'

He glances back as he says it. We just passed a long, straight side road. Single lane, hasn't been tarmacked.

The driver tosses the car into reverse and brings us alongside the road. Baden looks along it and nods.

'Are we close?' asks Kuusk.

'No,' he says, then, 'I don't know.'

I get a slight feeling of anxiety at the thought we might actually find the house we're looking for, but I doubt the feeling is necessary. I don't see there being much chance of it, and it's not why I'm here, driving into the nether reaches of the country. This is about watching Baden. Gauging his reaction, letting him tell his story. The more he says, the more blanks he fills in, the greater the chance of him stumbling.

Of course, there may be nothing for him to stumble over.

We start driving along the road, slowly now. Baden stares at the floor.

'We need you to look,' I say.

A slight shake of the head, and he remains in the same position.

'Stop the car,' I say, no urgency in my voice so the driver doesn't feel the need to slam on the brakes again.

He stops the car. Baden takes a deep breath, but does not look round.

'We didn't come all this way to not give ourselves at least a chance of finding where you were held. At the moment, you're all we've got, so we need you. You need to look out the window, you need to try to identify... houses, trees, landmarks. Anything that might remind you of where you were.'

He doesn't move. Fingers clenching, unclenching.

'You'll be safe.'

And aren't those empty words? How can I promise him he'll be safe? I think we're so generally convinced that there's something going on here other than Baden and the story he's told, that neither Kuusk nor I have given any thought to what we'd do if we actually managed to locate the building and the people who were keeping him captive. They sound like they'd be up for a fight.

'Look out the window. To me this just looks like any road around here. What is it that reminded you?'

Nothing. I give him another few seconds. The light is growing dim, however, darkness will be here soon enough.

'Why did you instruct us to come along here?'

'The bench.'

'Sorry?'

'There was a small bench at the junction. It was unusual. I remembered it because when I saw it, I was aching to sit down, but I couldn't. I couldn't risk sitting out in the open like that.'

'So it wasn't long after you escaped?

Thoughts are roped in from the outer limits as he tries to put the last few days into some sort of timescale perspective.

'The same day, but a while later.'

'OK, good. At least we're in the right direction. You're doing really well, John, but we're just going to need you to stick at it for a while longer.'

Nothing. I catch Kuusk's eye in the mirror, his face expressionless.

'OK,' I say to the driver. 'Let's move. Slowly.'

The car starts up again.

'I need you to look outside and tell me when it was you joined this road. Was it by another junction, or did you come out of the forest?'

'Don't take me back to the forest.'

'You're not going back to the forest, don't worry. But I need you to look around and think carefully about where it was you joined this road.'

Finally I've got through to him, and his head lifts slowly. He looks along the road, and then turns and looks behind us.

'Did you walk along this road, or did you stay on the edge of the forest?'

'Edge of the forest,' he says. Voice nervous, as though we really might be taking him straight back to his captors.

'Good, John, that was good. Now, d'you have any idea where you joined the road?'

'Came to the road from the woods, looked along... I don't... I chose a direction to go in. Wasn't sure. Came this way, but went back into the trees to follow the road.'

'Will you be able to recognise the spot? The spot where you first saw the road?'

As I ask the question I'm looking along the road. I doubt you could pick a spot on here if you drove up and down it every day.

'While yet,' he says. 'While yet.'

He drops his gaze, looks at his hands. His hands are working, the fingers clasping together, unclasping.

'Think I'll know it when I see it,' he says. He looks up quickly ahead, and then again back down.

I catch Kuusk's eye, then stare ahead. Unless he just happened to come out of the forest next to a monument or a well or a house, I'm not exactly sure how he's going to be able to tell.

I get the sudden feeling that for all the uncertainty and the nervousness, the hesitation and the worried glances over his shoulder, he knows exactly where he's taking us. Right to the very door.

15

We find a track, down into the woods, close to the spot Baden identified. Perhaps it was the track that he recognised. It would have made sense, as he clawed his way blindly through the forest, to attach himself to something that would help guide him, that would, at the very least, prevent him going in endless circles. So maybe it is genuine, rather than part of a plot.

Now on the other side of that patch of woods, and he's indicating another forested area, the other side of an extended patch of damp grassy marshland.

To our right the forests come together again, forming a large arc of trees about half a mile away. The marsh extends away to our left, the trees from which we've just emerged retreating, becoming sparser. The distance is murky, and not far away, as night falls and the damp evening clouds begin to fall ever closer to the treetops.

There's not a road to be seen anywhere, although of course it doesn't mean there isn't one a hundred yards into the next wood. There are a couple of crows, a very slight movement of the trees in the breeze, but that aside, a mostly complete, and unnerving silence.

If there is someone looking out for us, it'd be hard to keep our arrival a secret, especially since we just drove a diesel car through the forest.

'You came from there?' I ask, pointing into the next forest.

He nods. Has that look about him that suggests he can barely speak. Must be getting close, and his fear, or his dramatic performance, is getting more intense.

'Tell me what else you know.'

He looks off into the forest, as if the house might be visible if he stares intently enough through the trees. He lifts his hand and indicates the general area of marshland.

'I came across here. Not long after I'd escaped.'

'You're sure?'

'Yes. Yes. I remember it. I was terrified coming out into the open so soon, worried that they'd see me. But I didn't know what else to do.'

'You could have run that way,' I say, indicating the direction of the main body of the forest, down towards the great arc joining the two woods together.

'I'd come from that direction.'

He points now, indicating his movements up and away from the area to the far left of the arc. Either way, it seems odd. There would always be more forest to run into. On the other hand, it's unlikely he was thinking straight.

'So if we head in this direction, roughly,' says Kuusk, indicating the forest at about sixty degrees from where we are, 'we'll come to this house, do you think?'

Baden gasps slightly. We're coming to it, right enough. I doubt any of us thought that we were coming down here on anything other than a wild goose chase, and yet now it appears that we're pretty close. So, he continues to play the part, or he is genuinely going to be terrified.

I'm not really sure what to do with him if it's the latter. It would be cruel to take him back there, when his captors are very possibly still there, with just two unarmed police officers to protect him.

I hadn't thought of that.

'Are you carrying?' I say to Kuusk.

He shakes his head. The driver, even though I didn't ask him, also shakes his head.

Careless. That in itself is probably proof that we came to observe, not to discover.

'How long d'you think you were running from the house until you got to the edge of the marsh?'

He's staring into the woods. Shakes his head.

'Ballpark,' I say. 'Five minutes, thirty-five minutes?'

'Five minutes,' he says quickly. 'Maybe ten, I don't know.'

'You think you ran in a straight line, do–'

'I don't know,' he snaps, the voice with sudden urgency. 'There were trees, they were flying by, branches in my face, I couldn't... I don't know, I was running. Running, breathing heavily. I told you they took... I can't breathe properly. I couldn't run far.'

As if to provide further proof of his ailing health, his breathing suddenly becomes much heavier, unable to keep up with the pace of his words, the urgency in his voice.

'That's OK,' I say. 'You've probably done enough.'

I move slightly away from him, an indication that it's all right for him to stand down – he's said everything he needs to say – and walk over beside Kuusk. We look into the woods on the other side of the marsh. Evening seems to be seeping out of the trees, crossing the boggy ground, even as we watch.

'Thinking that maybe we should have taken the Tartu police up on their offer.'

He doesn't reply.

It doesn't matter what the time is, the darkness is the thing. Walking into a stranger's territory, holding none of the cards. We might not even have surprise on our side, as they could well have been expecting someone since Baden escaped. Perhaps there's someone right now, on the other side of the marsh, watching us.

I think I've already made the decision.

I can smell the cigarette smoke from the driver, rather than from Kuusk. Must be a stronger brand. Aware that Baden is still standing behind, arms wrapped around himself, nervously waiting to see what's going to happen.

I catch Kuusk's eye. He takes a draw of the cigarette. There's a slight nervousness in his actions, but he makes a small acknowledging gesture. I turn to the others.

'We need to come back in the morning, when we have some sort of daylight.'

Unconsciously look at the sky. Is there ever any proper daylight in this country?

'We can speak to the local police, and return heavy-handed, hopefully. We should...' Pause, turn back to Kuusk. 'What d'you think? Should we just go and find a hotel, or head back to Tallinn for the night?'

'Six hour round trip,' he says.

There's a point. Six more hours in the suffocating awfulness of that car.

'Tallinn,' says Baden. 'I'm not staying down here. I don't trust it.'

'It?'

'The area. The people.' Another wheezed breath. 'Everything. We can't stay here.'

I glance at Kuusk and he shrugs. The driver joins him.

'I'm fine to drive back,' he says.

'Maybe you can go a little quicker,' I say.

'Maybe.'

'And put on the radio.'

'It's broken.'

I turn back to Kuusk and indicate with a look that it's time to go. Baden is straight into the car, the world-weary driver takes his seat. Kuusk and I walk round to the other side of the car.

'You look sad,' he says.

'Sorry?'

'That's what it is. I've been wondering about you. Trying to get a handle on you. And that's it. You look sad.'

'We'll come back tomorrow, it'll be fine.'

'No, I don't mean now, about this. This is a business decision. No one would look sad about this. I mean, generally. Since you arrived. You have an air of sadness.'

I say nothing. I wouldn't be surprised if, in fact, I look even sadder at the thought that this is how I come across.

We get in the car. Baden seems to retreat into himself. Not quite curling up into a ball, but I can feel his energy withdraw into a tight knot somewhere in the middle of himself. Both the driver and Kuusk flick their cigarettes away, although the smell of the smoke from their breath quickly infects the car.

There's so little cigarette smoke around in the UK one becomes even more aware of it when it's there. There should be smoking areas, and then smoking decontamination areas where smokers have to use mouthwash, because there's really no difference between smoking, and not smoking ten seconds after you've stopped.

Some smokers would probably see decontamination areas as a step too far.

'What about you?' I say, asking the question that I didn't ask the previous day. 'What's your quirk?'

Even though there are three others in the car, the driver and Baden both know that I'm speaking to Kuusk.

He shrugs. The car turns in the small clearing, and then starts back up the uneven track we came along fifteen or twenty minutes previously.

'I like to have sex with the animals,' he says.

I smile and shake my head. The driver glances at him and in the mirror to see my reaction. Kuusk laughs quietly, although I'm not entirely sure he's joking.

We start the long drive through the early night back to Tallinn.

16

Chief Inspector Quinn's is an interesting story. Said to me once, maybe five or six months after I arrived, that he'd been married for a few years back in the eighties. No children. His wife left him in the end, because he spent so much time at work, and he never seemed to want to spend time with her. When she left they hadn't had sex in over two years, and they were still in their twenties.

He told me this over a drink in the Mallard. I thought he was giving me a valuable lesson in not putting your job first if you want to hang on to the girl. And then he told me he was gay. That he'd always known, but he'd also known that there was little chance of him progressing in the police force at that time if he'd been an openly gay officer.

The way he spoke, I was the first person to whom he'd come out, but I didn't ask if that was the case. He said he'd asked one of his female friends to marry him, without telling her the truth. He just used her as cover. He didn't then particularly mind when she left, because as far as he could tell, she never knew. The marriage fell apart on the story of him always being at work, which isn't so different from so many other police marriages. Thereafter, he never had to get married again. He was the officer who'd been married once, but it hadn't worked out because he was married to the job.

'One day I'll tell her,' he said.

I wonder if he has.

It was a confessional, but I'm not sure why he told me. Maybe, finally, he had to tell someone as he was carrying the guilt around with him, like all guilt, strapped to his back, weighing him down. I was new, not from around Dingwall, didn't know his past. Perhaps at the time he didn't think I'd stay around for long. The memory of my parting with Olivia still being so strong, I didn't judge him at all, I just thought, here's another man who's treated a woman badly, even if the reason was different. Join the club.

In retrospect, his was much worse, and not just because Olivia was married to someone else within the year, and now has two children in private school and an Aston Martin.

I never asked what his ex-wife is doing now and how much he'd screwed up her life. I didn't want to know.

★ ★ ★

'I know it's going to be tough for you, but I need you back tomorrow evening.'

'I don't think I can make it back that quickly.'

I look at my watch, although the time right now is of no significance. Quinn has that tone in his voice.

'There's been a death on the High Street. A hit-and-run, possibly. We don't know yet, but we're having to investigate. And also, of course, as with any hit-and-run, the possibility that it was murder. Add to that, two assaults at the Caledonian last night, three different domestics in the last three days, and a woman walked in off the street, attached to a lawyer, with an historic rape claim against a councillor. Suddenly it's like downtown LA around here. I'm sorry Ben, it's just the way it goes. Last Friday you going out there wasn't entirely unreasonable. Four days later, and we look foolish. I'm not in a position to go crying to Inverness on this, and I just can't afford to have you on the other side of Europe.'

As he talks, the timings run through my head. I've already looked at the various routes back, to try to avoid taking the sixty hours or so that it took me to get here. Google Maps has a direct route driving back, through the Baltic states, Poland, Germany and on through the low countries, of thirty-seven hours, Tallinn to Dingwall. That would be insane.

Just after eight... no, just after six in Dingwall. Give me an hour to hire a car and sort things out this end, then hit the road. Live on coffee and Red Bull, I'd be in Dingwall by eight on Thursday morning, maybe earlier if I could make up time through Germany.

Do they really need me for the raid on the house east of Tartu, if that's what it's to be? Of course not. Way out of my jurisdiction. Regardless of the nationality of the alleged victim here, I'm going to be nothing more than an observer. I've already told Quinn about the plan for the morning, and the usefulness of my being there, but I could backtrack from that easily enough.

'If I left now...' I begin, but that's as far as he lets me go.

'You're booked on a flight out of Tallinn tomorrow evening at six. Change in Amsterdam for Heathrow and then onto Inverness. You'll be back here by ten at the latest.'

'But–'

'–Ben, I'm sorry. I wouldn't have sent you out there if I'd known I was going to put you in this position.'

'But–'

'–You are not driving for a day and a half without a break, on official duty. It is not happening. And I need you at the raid in

Tartu tomorrow morning. You said you were starting early. You need to get down there, get your own car and driver if you have to, and then get back to Tallinn in time for the flight.'

'But–'

'–It's an order, Detective Inspector. You will be observing the raid in the morning, I want that information first hand, not through the eyes of an Eastern European police force we know nothing about. I don't care if they're European Union. And I want you in the office first thing on Thursday morning, fresh and ready to get to work on the case at this end. We're exhuming Baden's body early tomorrow morning, so by Thursday we should have been able to do the DNA testing.'

The arguments are still raging in my head, but he knows how to have an argument with a junior officer. Never cede the floor.

'Mary will have your flight details in your inbox in the next twenty minutes. I'll see you on Thursday.'

He hangs up.

★ ★ ★

I get another call not long afterwards. Maybe twenty minutes. I've spent the twenty minutes thinking about sitting on the plane. I'm sweating. The evening stretches before me. All I'm going to be doing is thinking about the plane. I need to stop thinking about it. Do that thing. The thing, which I'm usually so good at, where I can simply put something out of my mind. Dismiss it. Just plant the phrase, *stop thinking about it*, in my head. Stop thinking about it.

It usually works. Not this time. And then the phone rings, and it's Superintendent Stepulov, inviting me out to dinner. I'd rather spend the evening alone, but the invitation puts me on the back foot, unexpected as it is, and I accept. At least it stops me thinking about the damn plane.

★ ★ ★

She talks about the case for a few minutes. She's received the download of the day's events from Kuusk, so I presume she just wants some sort of confirmation. She lets me tell the story, rather than relating to me what he said. I don't think there's anything to hide. Perhaps she doesn't trust him.

We're in a small, basement restaurant called Salt, a little away from the centre of town. Unassuming décor, wonderful food. The place is packed, which I thought was good when we arrived, as I assumed there would be long silences between us. Long silences are always worse in quiet restaurants. As it turns out, Superintendent Stepulov is a talker.

She has the sea bass, I'm eating squid. Tender squid, not the kind of thing you usually get in the UK that you could roll up and use as a squash ball.

'My family came here during Soviet times,' she says, in reply to a question about her Russian ethnicity. 'The late 1950s. My father was young.'

I don't ask why. The Soviets used to move populations around on a whim, mixing ethnicities, spreading the Russian population to the occupied territories. Not that they actually considered the Baltic states to be occupied. They just considered them theirs.

'What does your father do?'

'He makes puppets,' she says.

My mild surprise probably shows on my face. I don't know what I'd been expecting, just not something out of the seventeenth century.

'A puppet maker?'

'Yes.'

'He still makes puppets?'

'Yes.'

I wonder if she enjoys the reaction of people on telling them that her father is a puppet maker. Having said that, from what I've picked up so far, Estonians probably don't react at all.

'That seems very Hansel and Gretel,' I say.

'Pinocchio perhaps.'

'Of course. Do people buy his puppets?'

Does anyone buy puppets any more?

The troubled shadow crosses her face. She dabs the corner of her mouth. She's not finished her meal, but I can tell there's a story coming. I wonder how often she tells the story.

'The Soviets gave him a small shop. The late nineteen sixties. People used to still buy puppets back then. At least in the Soviet Union. And then time moved on, and even with us, puppets were less and less desired. But father worked on, sitting in his small shop every day, making his puppets. He would sell one every so often, but never as fast as he made them. And so the shelves filled up...'

She shakes her head, a slight smile returns. The tumult of the small restaurant seems to ease a little, as a party of eight or ten noisily leaves, the door is closed, and a more subdued atmosphere settles over the room.

'It was a sight, a wonderful sight. He didn't mind, he didn't need the money, and those shelves, so full of his work. So colourful. Walking into that shop, it was beautiful.'

'Your English is very good,' I say. I don't know why it seems a surprise. Her English was good earlier.

'Thank you. I studied for four years in Manchester.'

'Manchester University?'

'Yes.'

'Nice. The shop, sorry. You were talking about the shop. Is it in the old town?'

It sounds like it should be. Any old town in Eastern Europe, in fact; pitching to the tourists with their traditional artefacts and designs that have been around for centuries. Or maybe such places are just marketed like that. Maybe they've only been around since the beginning of the era of mass tourism.

'Oh no,' she says. 'And a good thing. If the Soviets had given him a shop there, the Estonians would have taken it back by now. His shop is in Kalamaja. Not many people go there. It's coming though, it's coming. Every area is being redeveloped, made into the image of the west. Shopping malls and cinemas showing American films. It will come to Kalamaja soon enough. And then someone will find a piece of paper that says that so-and-so used to own that building, and it's now been sold to some property development, and he needs to get out in five days.'

She shakes her head, as though trying to shake away the bitterness that has crept into her voice. I'm not sure what to say to all that, but she waves away the subject and continues talking.

'And then one day, I don't know, maybe fifteen years ago, when his shelves were full, and his shop was a treasure trove, and he was refusing to let any of those trashy tourist shops around the town sell his puppets, a film star found his place. God knows how.'

'A film star?'

'American,' she says, disdainfully.

'Who?'

'Her name will not pass my lips,' she says. 'I forget her anyway. I put her out of my mind. She is a bitch.'

I'm not going to find out who the film star is, but it doesn't really matter. Just the thought of it, of this senior police officer badmouthing any film star in this strange little basement restaurant seems comical. Can't help smiling.

'What did she do?'

'She bought three puppets. *For my adopted daughters*, she said, as though Father was supposed to be impressed.'

'Doesn't sound so bad.'

She snorts.

'Then she told everyone. Told everyone about her puppet maker, as though Father had made those puppets personally for her. She tells everyone about the shop, and she tells them all where to find it, and that they should buy puppets. Father sold virtually all his puppets in a matter of a few weeks, and the shelves were empty. He was on the news, he was in magazines.'

'That doesn't sound so bad either,' I say, although even as I say it, I realise I'm speaking for someone else. I'm speaking for those people who would want that to happen. If you didn't want to sell everything you'd ever made, if you liked things the way they were, you're not necessarily going to want anything to change.

That part of the conversation is exchanged in a look.

'He loved them all. I like to think there's a little piece of him in every one of those.' She makes an exasperated noise. 'The story, where does it go...? The usual. People picked him up and they dropped him. Women. He should have known better, but he was just a man. Typical Russian. Head turned by the fame and the glamour, as though it was actually at all glamorous.'

She pauses, coming to the wretched part. Coming to the part that's still relevant today, the part that still causes her pain, the part that kills her every time she thinks about it.

'For a while he couldn't make puppets fast enough, spending all his time at the shop. But it turned out, he wasn't always at the shop. Started wearing new clothes, started talking about new things, started spending time with new people. Foolish man. And where was Mama all this time? At home, feeling abandoned, waiting for him. Waiting for the phone to ring. Waiting for the front door to open.'

She's staring at the floor. This isn't going to end well. While the words seem scornful, slowly her voice is getting lower, slowly her tone becoming more resigned.

'And then people realised they were just puppets. They weren't phones, they weren't some new kind of American or Korean device. Just puppets, that's all. Nothing special. And father was dropped again. Pfft! Off you go, you pointless little puppet maker.

'But that was him. He'd seen the other side. He'd had his fifteen little minutes of fame. He didn't care about Mama any more. He still wore the clothes, and he continued to chase after the dream he'd been shown. The fantasy. He wanted a sixteenth minute. He even said it to me one day. *I just want the sixteenth minute.*'

The memory of the conversation seems to hurry her to the end of the story, makes her straighten herself a little. She glances at me, shakes her head a little.

'He came home one evening – yes, he actually came home – and Mama was hanging by the neck from the beam in the bedroom.'

Her eyes drop, she makes a funny little noise, before straightening herself again. Forgetting that she's learned to deal with this. Forgetting that this is a story she can let lightly trip from her lips.

'And so, where was this film star then? Where was she? We all know, don't we? She was nowhere. None of these people, none of them cared. Why would they? Who cares about the puppet maker?

'And father was broken. Of course he was. Mama had always… she'd always had trouble. You know, with depression. Drinking. Ha! She is not alone. And now… dead. No more depression, eh? Maybe we should be thankful.'

She takes another small piece of fish, then places her knife and fork in the middle of the plate, and pushes it slightly away from her. Less than an inch.

'Your father still makes puppets?'

She said that already, didn't she? At the start of the conversation, which seems a while ago.

She's staring at the plate. Takes a sip of wine.

'He sits and makes puppets, and no one buys them, and slowly the shelves fill up again. But you cannot replace someone who loves you with puppets. You cannot replace someone who loves you… with anything.'

The waitress stops beside the table. Just a second, and then she picks up on the moment. She catches my eye, smiles a little uncomfortably, and walks quickly to the next table.

'I'd like to see his shop,' I say.

Seriously? Who am I going to buy a puppet for?

'You won't have time,' she says.

17

Back on the road early. Stepulov remains sceptical, yet she knows she has to act. She can't risk there being some kind of thing that she chooses to ignore for no reason other than her gut instinct. She has to do something.

Last night she called down, dragged the Chief of Police in Tartu out of some sort of reception, listened to his general outrage at being stood up by her officers earlier in the day, and then forced him to cede to her authority and supply the necessary backup for this morning.

I doubt we'll find them particularly helpful, but it doesn't really matter. We just need them there. Feet on the ground, that's all. Weight of numbers.

Leave early enough that we drive all the way in darkness. Get to Tartu as the sky is turning a lighter shade of grey. Almost eight fifteen.

Our car remains the same as yesterday. No conversation on the way down, yet the silence is of a completely different texture. There's a nervousness this time, the energy of it coming from the driver and Baden. I doubt Baden slept. Not happy to be going back.

Last night, for the first time, he mentioned returning to the UK. We still haven't told anyone back there that he's come in. How can we until we know more?

I cut him off by telling him I'd need to speak to the Embassy, something which I've still not done. I'll need to squeeze it in on my way to the airport.

And that, of course, is the thing that bothers me. That's where my nervousness comes from. It doesn't matter what happens when we turn up at this house, assuming that we can actually identify the right one when it comes to it. That will take care of itself. And I am, entirely, an observer. If there really is some kind of human farm, it's a matter for the local police. I'm here to try to sort out the curious case of John Baden, and later today I'll be getting on a plane out of the country and, more than likely, never coming back.

The thought of the plane is the plague.

Never liked flying. Maybe when I was eight and it seemed a big adventure. When turbulence was fun. When you never thought about what could happen. When bad things were what happened to other people.

In adulthood, however, it has gradually moved – through

experience – through different levels of discomfort, before ending up in absolute terror. And that's the decision I came to, seven years ago, when I sat on the train heading north out of the DRC. I never have to get on a plane again. Those people, the ones who think nothing of flying, the ones you hear chatting casually while the plane shakes and rattles through awful turbulence, I don't care if they don't understand. I don't care if they feel contempt. I don't care if they mock me, to my face or behind my back. It's my life, and I need never get on a plane again.

What had I been thinking when I'd allowed Quinn to send me over here by boat? That it would be such a leisurely trip, that things at home would be so relaxed, that in the end I'd be able to spend six days travelling, not including whatever time I was going to need to spend in Tallinn attempting to unravel the mystery?

I will never have to get on a plane again. And if anyone tells me I need to get on a plane, there will be nothing so important that I can't just tell them to forget it. I'm not going.

That was what I told myself. And here I am, about to get on three flights in quick succession.

I look out the window at the dawning of another bleak November day. There is a nervousness in the car right enough, but my own comes from somewhere completely different.

I try to think logically about the situation, but my attempted logical thoughts aren't about flying and how safe it is and how you're more likely to die using virtually any other mode of transport.

What have I told myself the last seven years? No one can make me get on a plane. What can anybody do if I choose not to? Shout at me? Sack me?

The boat to Stockholm leaves at a not dissimilar time to my flight to Amsterdam. My thoughts are all about how it will play out if I get on the boat and not on the plane.

* * *

No one is speaking English to try to make this easier for Baden. I expect the real reason they're not speaking English is in order to exclude me, but I already feel, quite happily, on the outside, so they needn't bother. I suspect Baden feels the same. In fact, he possibly likes the fact that discussions are taking place and he has no idea. Almost as though all this is happening to someone else. None of his concern.

Kuusk tried speaking English when we arrived, but he didn't get a word of it from Inspector Lippmaa.

Twenty minutes now we've been waiting in the car park. Dawn is creeping over the town, cold and grey. There might actually be some patchy sun this morning, if those few breaks in the cloud that are evident manage to hold up. I've got some coffee, handed round in small plastic cups. Bitter and strong, not enough milk. I drink it quickly, try not to let the sharpness show on my face.

Baden refuses, the driver takes a cup, downs it in one, and then lights another cigarette.

There is agitated discussion, although it's impossible to tell whether or not there's a real argument taking place. We're about to raid an alleged body-harvesting prison. If there wasn't tension, then it would be strange.

We get back in the car, leading the way, trailed by four cars from the Tartu force.

'What was the discussion?' I ask, as we leave the town and start to head off into the backwoods where Baden directed us the previous day.

Trying not to think about the plane. I put myself there for a short time. I put myself in the plane. I imagined strapping myself in. The other passengers. The safety announcements. The noise of the engines. The take-off. I imagined the turbulence, imagined how I feel when a plane is flying through it. I rationalised the turbulence. I thought about the fact that when a plane passes through turbulence so bad that people get injured, it makes the news. That's how rarely it happens.

The rationalisation didn't help. I was starting to sweat, so I stopped. I asked the question.

'They didn't want you here,' says Kuusk in reply.

'That makes sense,' I say.

'It's your case.'

'John's my case. Potentially though, what we're going to find here, it's all for your guys.'

He doesn't reply. Baden makes a strange little noise, like a tiny explosion of nervous gas. We drive off towards the woods, the day meeting us reluctantly, tension settling nicely over the car. It reminds me of working for the security services, rather than anything I've had to do in the Highlands.

'There's something you should know about Lippmaa,' says Kuusk.

I ask the question with a look in the mirror.

'He's an asshole.'

* * *

And so we come to the operation. Baden and I remain at the back, for now, with nineteen others ahead of us, as we cross the marshland. Baden tried to hang back, cross as slowly as possible, but we had to keep up with the others, to follow in their tracks.

The driver is just ahead of us. He argued, through Kuusk, that this was not in his remit. I said I wanted him to come, so that he could then get Baden out of there once he had identified the house. I didn't want to be the one left with that job. If we're entering a building, observer or not, I want to be there.

The driver, who I come to like more and more in his sullen, smoke-filled silence, seemed even more unhappy about babysitting Baden than storming the house, but Kuusk used whatever powers of persuasion were required. Maybe he just ordered him to do it.

Orders. Orders. Do I really care so little about my career that I'm going to defy the Chief Inspector this evening? Or is it that, while I suppose he might well be angry about it, ultimately what is his sanction going to be? Demotion? Six months on traffic? Will it really be a charge of insubordination followed by dismissal?

Into the woods on the far side. Boots soaking. Cold seeping up from my damp feet. Now the pressure is on Baden. Will it be worse for him if we fail to find any potential buildings for his human farm, or if we find it and he faces his trauma head on?

We stand at the front of the small crew as they begin to spread out to either side. Some of the men have already drawn their guns.

'You have to try to ignore them all,' I say. 'Take your time, don't worry about them. Now, you said you thought you approached the marshes roughly at this angle?' I ask, pointing to our right.

He shakes his head. Looks incredibly nervous, like me getting on a damned plane.

'That was what you said last night,' I add.

'I don't know.'

Turn away. Maybe he's going back on what he said because he's just making the whole thing up. I'll choose to assume the nerves are jumbling his brain. If it's all true, then why wouldn't they be?

'Come on,' I say, and start walking in the direction I'd indicated. He makes another small tense ejaculation and follows. We're also followed by the sound of the others dropping in around and behind.

I wonder what action these woods saw in the war. I don't know much about Estonia in the war. Occupied by the Russians, the Germans kicked them out, then obviously the Russians came back.

Did they fight over Estonia the way they fought over Poland? I don't know.

But that's what it feels like now, at the head of a group of twenty or so men. Like troops marching through the forest, like they might well have done over seventy years previously, on the lookout for enemy combatants.

A few minutes in we come to a small track. Probably just about wide enough for a car, but it doesn't look as though cars are ever driven along it.

'You remember this path?' I ask.

Baden nods.

He hasn't quite walked fully out onto it, as though fearing it would give away his position. The fact that everyone else around him has happily walked onto the track, has probably already done that, however.

'Which way?'

He points to the right.

'Not far,' he says.

'Not far along the path until we turn off, or not far to the house?'

He shakes his head, eyes darting in the other direction, then back again.

'Which don't you know?' I ask. 'You have to help me out a bit more here.'

Another shake of the head. 'Not far along the path, but I'm not sure about the house.'

'You didn't walk on the path for long?'

'No.'

'Ten yards? A hundred?'

Another head shake.

'Come on, lead the way. You can see you're perfectly safe, you're surrounded by people on your side.' Not that that's something I'm entirely convinced about. 'We'll walk along the path and try to see if there's anything that rings a bell about where you emerged from the woods. If you can't see anything, we'll just pick a spot not too far along and go in.'

Deep breaths. I can see him taking them, fingers nervously clicking. The others are waiting, spreading out along the path, none of them looking at Baden, everybody looking into the trees. Then he starts to move, everyone gives him space and he heads along the path to the right, pine trees on either side, me following closely behind.

He stops. Studies the trees. Walks on a little further. I think I'm going to be suspicious if he suddenly says, *oh, here we are, I recognise this pine tree, quite distinguishable from all the others.*

'I think it was here.'

I stop beside him and look into the woods. He's got to be kidding. If not kidding, something more sinister.

'Why?'

He glances at me, stares back into the trees.

'You wanted me to find the spot,' he says. 'The spot where I found the path.'

'How can you tell?'

'I'm not sure, I don't know,' he says, the words edgy and uncertain.

I turn and look at Kuusk, who's been following closely behind. He shrugs. What else can we do, his shoulders ask? We've trusted him this far, we can't now say, we don't believe you, so we're just going to go back.

'Right, lead on,' I say.

He nods, his head a series of nervous twitches, and walks into the trees. The ground is soft, the air heavy with the scent of damp pine, as it has been since we stepped away from the cars.

He walks for a short while, not far, maybe less than a hundred yards, then stops, his head shaking slowly.

'Not sure.'

'Sorry?'

'Not sure. I might recognise it, but I was running at this point. Everything was a blur. I was quite disorientated.'

'That's OK,' says Kuusk surprisingly and he pats him on the shoulder. Then he walks past me a few yards, away from Baden, and I come alongside him.

'I think it's time to spread out,' he says. 'He might have given us everything he's going to.'

'I'd still want him to make a visual of the outside of the building. I know it's going to be sketchy, but–'

'–Of course.'

He turns back to Lippmaa and they have a quick exchange in Estonian, following which the local police commander, in a series of low, barked instructions, sends his men in a fan out across the woods, at something like twenty yard intervals.

And on we go, walking slowly.

The plane is still there, in my head. That's stupid. I should be able to get rid of it, for now at least. But I can't. I'm sitting in it, I'm buckling up, I'm in the air, I'm being served a drink as the cabin rocks, I can't enjoy any food because of the shaking of the plane, and my own nervousness. My own all-consuming nervousness.

Concentrate!

Walk forward, occasionally taking a look along the fan of police officers. Mostly keeping an eye on Baden. Would I be surprised if he suddenly took off in the opposite direction?

A ripple suddenly carries along the fan. Someone on the far right of the line has passed the message, and everyone stops. Lippmaa indicates for Baden and I to follow, and Kuusk joins us as we run along the line, on attempted quiet footfalls, to the far end. As we go, the policemen are all ducking down onto their haunches, following the lead of those on the right, so that we, as we run, start to duck down.

We can see it before we stop running. A building through the trees, the slight glint of a couple of SUVs parked outside. We come to a stop, and Lippmaa waves for complete stillness along the line. Crouching down low, we try to make out the building. Some do, at any rate. I think Kuusk and I are more interested in Baden. Is this where he ran from?

'What d'you think?' I ask, voice low.

He looks terrified. That's something, I suppose, something he was going to have to go through when he got near here.

'I don't know,' he replies, his voice breaking.

'We'll get you a little closer.'

'No.'

'You need to. Just you and me. The others will hold back for a moment, and we can just go another few yards.'

What are we? Seventy yards away perhaps. Another twenty closer maybe. It's not really about the distance anyway, more about getting a good, clear view.

I start to move forward, keeping as low as possible, indicating with no more than a glance for him to follow. His reluctance is a palpable presence in the forest, but I'm aware of him moving behind me.

I move from side to side, as much as forward, trying to get a clear view, dropping lower down every time I change angle. And then I get the better view of the house, and I look behind at Baden, a few yards back, and indicate for him to catch up. This is the spot.

I pull back and usher him into the clear line of sight with a nod. He closes his eyes, braces himself for it, then inches forward into position without opening his eyes. There's a laugh there, somewhere, in my head, although it doesn't come out, at the childlike thoughts that must be running through Baden's head. *If I can't see them...*

He opens his eyes. Focuses. Strains to see through the trees, and then he's backing off. Suddenly I can hear his breath, his body seems to be about to burst. Recognise the signs straight away. Panic attack.

Bad place for it.

'John! John! Look at me!' My voice a strained whisper.

Grab him by the shoulders, as he looks as though he's about to run.

'Did you see anyone?' I ask. I know he didn't. If he had, he'd already have been running.

Shakes his head. His body is straining against my hands, but I'm not sure he'd actually jump away if I let him go. Not risking it though.

'We're good, John, we're good. Look at me. Look at me, take a deep breath.'

I can smell him, his warm breath in my face.

'It's all good, John. Now, tell me. Were you held in the main house, or in one of the outbuildings?'

He swallows. Words seem impossible, but he manages to say, 'Main, I think,' and that's all I'm getting.

'That's good, John. It's all we need. You've done everything we asked, so it's all good. We're going to turn, we'll walk back to the others same as we walked here, keeping low, quiet footsteps. And then they take over, and you are out of here. You all right with that, John?'

Closes his eyes. Grips my arm with his right hand. Deep breaths, the warm air back in my face again. Try not to breathe in the scent of him.

'Right, come on, nice and easy.'

I'm talking in clichés. Dear God. I let go of his arms and turn back to the others. I can see a few of them, but really only because I know to look for them. They have done a good job of natural concealment.

We walk back towards them, bent low. I nod at Kuusk, and he finds the driver, who's made it this far at the back of the group, and again, a nod is enough to give him his instruction.

As Baden walks past me to the driver, I notice Lippmaa pass the same nod of instruction to one of his men to follow them, and he turns as they go, and then the three of them disappear into the trees, back in the direction from which we came.

'What did you see?' asks Lippmaa, coming towards me and speaking English for the first time. Maybe he really didn't trust Baden.

'Looks like a farmhouse, at least two more buildings to the side. Could have been a lot more. Didn't see any more cars, but there's some sight of the road leading away to the other side.'

Lippmaa takes a look over his shoulder at what he can see through the trees, then turns back to me.

'Your work is finished. I would prefer if you would go back with your man, but if you don't want to, then keep out of our way. I don't want to see you following us into the house.'

I nod. He surely knows that I have no intention of paying any attention to him.

He turns, looks both ways along the line, tosses his hand forward to indicate the start of the approach, and then the small police team begins to quickly advance through the trees.

18

If I die here I won't need to get on the plane tonight.

That thought passes through my head as we emerge from the trees. An honest thought; one that genuinely makes me feel better. I'm happier at the thought of death than at the idea of sitting on a plane that may, or may not, experience a little bit of turbulence.

That's the moment I decide I'm not getting on the plane, and that I'd better do a decent job here to compensate. If, that is, there's any sort of a job for me to do.

★ ★ ★

There's a maroon Land Rover and a Dodge of some sort. The Dodge is huge, a cab with a large platform at the back. Neither of them has been cleaned in a while. Lippmaa indicates to one of his men with a slight wave of the gun in his right hand. *You stay out here, make sure there are no getaways in these vehicles.* Another wave, and the men start to flank out around the house and the outbuildings. I get a warning glance from him, but pause only briefly before moving forward.

Round the side, to the front of the house. There's another car parked, this one an old, small Toyota. Men staying in position as we go past, others running silently ahead. I wonder how often they do this kind of manoeuvre, or if they've trained for it and this is the first time they've had to implement the moves they've learned.

Lippmaa, leading the way, gets to the front door, a couple of his men, and Kuusk, still at his back. There's a small bell on a chain to the right of the door. I think for a moment that he's going to ring it, but instead he lifts it in order to inspect the handiwork, then he lets it gently down into place.

He glances around at the set-up of his men, making sure those that he can see are in the places he'd want them to be, and then, with a dramatic chopping movement of his right hand, he puts a giant boot to the front door and strides forward as it bounces off its hinges.

The signal goes instantly around the buildings from corner to corner and within a couple of seconds there comes the sound of other breakages, and then a couple of windows getting put in. Men disappear from view as they enter the house. The last person I see enter is Kuusk, a gun in his hand.

There is loud shouting, and then from round the back a single gunshot.

I get the feel of it now, with the opening of the door. This place, this wretched place, so full of sadness and horror, as if all this negative energy was waiting for a breath of air to escape.

I don't get the sense of evil however. There wasn't evil here, it was just business, bastards doing brutal things for money. Like a grand metaphor for every government and large conglomerate that put wealth first without a thought for people or workers. Faceless and nameless individuals being sucked dry.

The wave of sorrow has me standing still for a moment, as though it has physically manifested itself in lead boots. I'd been intending on going in behind them all, but I find myself frozen. And regardless of the innate feeling of horror, the show of force followed by the gunshot is enough to make me stay my hand. This kind of thing doesn't scare me, but if I've learned anything from my time in the security services, it's don't go into a gunfight without a gun.

I back away behind the solitary vehicle out front, the blue Toyota, and decide that if I can make myself useful, it'll be in stopping someone making a break for it. I look round for the guy that Lippmaa ordered to wait outside and can't see him.

The shouting continues. There's another gunshot, then a woman's voice, loud, screeching. One of our men runs around from the far side of an outbuilding and in through the front door. Another gunshot.

I don't know what they're doing. It seems so bizarre, so alien to anything we'd do. Up until now I've had nothing but scepticism bordering on downright disbelief for what John Baden has said, and yet on his word, and as far as I know, nothing more, they're launching a full scale assault on the place, putting in doors and windows and firing shots. Perhaps they sensed the misery of this place long before I did.

What would I have done? Men in reserve in the trees, and a knock at the door.

A couple of quick gunshots and then someone falls through the window at the front of the house. The loud crash of the glass, then moments later the dull thud onto the ground, with the sickening crunch of bones breaking.

A face appears at the window – one of our men – and then quickly backs away.

The shouting continues, there is no more gunfire. Someone else runs past. I walk round the car to the man lying on the ground. I bend down beside him, put my hand needlessly to his neck. There's a handgun lying just to the side. I lift it, check for rounds, put the safety catch on and stick it quickly into the back of my trousers.

He's in his early sixties, maybe. Grey hair, grey complexion, old clothes. A farmer's hands. Neck broken, two gunshot wounds in the chest, brutal head wound from where he hit the ground. Any of those could have been the thing that killed him. I doubt there will ever be an autopsy to find out.

The shouting has quietened down, there's a sudden air over the place like the brief burst of action is over. The event, such as it was, has passed, and suddenly I realise that, in fact, I'd better get in now while there's still uncertainty over everything. If I wait, the place will be locked down, and it'll be too late.

Pause at the front door, a wall of sorrow before me, then push through it. The sound of heavy boots all over. Pass a couple of our men, who pay me no attention. From the barked voices, I can hear that Lippmaa is upstairs, which is good, because I want to go in the opposite direction.

Along the central corridor, and just before I get to it, I hear voices coming from a door which must lead downstairs. Squeeze past another couple of guys, and then down a narrow flight of steps. Down here there's a long corridor, doors off either side. There are a few men going along, having not quite finished the check. The corridor, white and dirty, extends away some ten doors on either side.

I take a look in the first door, a small dank office. Chair and desk, there's a window high up on the far wall, allowing in virtually no light. A few pictures on the wall, a calendar, a phone on the desk, a few papers strewn around.

Along to the next room. I'm glancing in – this one looks like a holding cell, a mattress on the floor, a toilet in the corner, of the type that Baden described – then Kuusk emerges from a room further down the corridor, sees me, and indicates for me to follow him.

The two men who have been checking all the rooms have finished now, and they shout out loudly as they push past us, back towards the stairs.

Kuusk holds the door open for me and lets me walk into the room first, following closely behind. It is a very rudimentary surgery, a gurney in the corner, an operating table in the middle. A couple of lights, a monitor against the wall, a sink, a small table with a silver tray of instruments.

Like the office at the start of the corridor, but unlike the holding cell I'd just looked in, there is a window high up on the wall, long, narrow and dirty. The thought that you'd really want your surgery to be a sealed room flashes through my head, but is instantly dismissed. The room is grimy and squalid, much more so than the cell. What difference would a window make? The air from outside can hardly be any worse than the fetid air of filth pervading in here.

Down here the feeling of grim misery is thick, but I do my best to shut it out. Need to shake it off and not think about it.

'Perhaps your Mr Baden was not making up so much after all,' says Kuusk.

I take my phone out and, out of courtesy, make a small gesture. Kuusk nods, and I quickly start taking photographs around the room. I doubt I'll get much more time before Lippmaa turns up to eject me from the premises.

'Just remember that John Baden's body was identified by his girlfriend, mother, and father,' I say. 'Whoever he is, and however much truth he's telling, it's too early to be calling him my Mr Baden. Or anyone else's for that matter.'

'So you won't be taking him back to the UK with you this evening?'

I stop for a second and look across the small, unpleasant room. There's a thought. I could hire a car, and he could share the driving.

Must be getting desperate.

'I'll leave him with you fellows,' I say.

'We will need to question him some more, certainly, but soon enough it will be time for him to go home.'

I take another couple of photographs, then place the phone back in my pocket. Find myself smiling at him.

'We're all European Union. He can stay if he likes.'

Kuusk smiles ruefully, and then follows me back out into the corridor. Another look along. A couple of Lippmaa's men at the far end outside the office, but the boss himself isn't down at this level yet, and we turn and walk further along, looking in rooms as we go. More cells, one ill-equipped storeroom.

'So, we presume the operation, whoever they are, cleared out after Baden escaped,' I say, but I'm shaking my head as I speak. 'Who did they shoot?'

'They found three people in the facility. They all resisted arrest.'

'But how did they know...' Pause to get my thoughts clear, because when you think about it, it feels wrong. 'Surely the point of anyone being left here was to attempt some cover of normality should the authorities turn up?'

Kuusk makes a small gesture, indicating the corridor and

everything around us.

'How was this ever going to look normal?'

Turn away from him, look along to the two men at the far end. They have visibly relaxed. One of them has lit a cigarette.

'The people in the house… they just went straight to confrontation without any attempt at artifice? The only reason they were here was to attempt artifice.'

'We just burst in with twenty armed men. There was never going to be a lot of conversation.'

There, I must admit, he has a good point. Although they weren't from his station, I don't like to say that I found the instant use of heavy force questionable too. Although the old guy falling out the window with a gun in his hand, does seem to speak in Lippmaa's favour. As does, of course, the fact that the farmhouse was indeed hiding something.

I don't trust it though.

'Doesn't it feel weird?' I say, then pause as I hear Lippmaa approaching through the house, loud footsteps identified as his by the accompanying barked commands. 'Doesn't it feel weird that we're here at all? Baden fled in a panic, running past trees, barely stopping to look over his shoulder. Not to mention it was the first time he'd seen daylight in twelve years. Yet he leads us back to this place with barely a step out of place.'

'You're very British,' says Kuusk, clapping his hand on my shoulder. 'Always cynical, always trying to see behind the curtain. Perhaps this is just what happened. Perhaps one thing they did not manage to remove from Mr Baden was his sense of direction.'

He laughs and then walks ahead, just as Lippmaa appears at the bottom of the stairs, still shouting instructions and asking questions at a hundred miles an hour.

He finally pauses when he sees me. Takes a moment, briefly considers his options, then says, 'You, leave!' jerking his thumb in the direction of the door.

I walk past him, holding his gaze as I go. Up the stairs and back out into the grey morning. The fresh air.

The weight of desolation begins to lift, although it will not be gone until we are far away from this place.

I turn and look back at the house for a moment, wondering if it will ever feel normal again. Hard to imagine. Then, turning away, I take the gun from the back of my trousers and toss it onto the ground beside its former owner.

'I won't be needing it,' I say to him.

19

Back in Tallinn, I stand at the window of the office of the Deputy Head of Mission at the British Embassy, looking out over a small park. The full cloud cover has rolled back in from the Baltic and darkness has come early. There are lights on in the park, a few people around.

My flight is in two hours. My certainty of earlier about not getting on the plane has gone. I don't know what to do. Considering getting blindingly drunk, but that's not terribly professional, seeing as I'm here in a professional capacity, and anyway, if I was to try to get blindingly drunk in the next two hours, I'd likely just throw up.

The door opens behind me, and he appears with a couple of mugs of tea, hands mine over with a smile, and stands beside me looking down onto the trees. He's in his early fifties, slightly overweight and refreshingly normal. Ten years working overseas with the security services left me generally wary of the cocky twenty-five-year-old Foreign Office, Oxbridge grads determined to change their little part of the world in two years. It's nice when you come across the regular ones.

'Your hand's shaking,' he says. 'Are you all right?'

'Got to get on a plane, three planes in fact, before I get to go to bed.'

'Ah. Not a lot I can do about that, sorry. You can't get the ferry back?'

'Supposed to be back tonight.'

Don't take a drink of tea yet. Catch his eye in the reflection in the window.

'Don't suppose you have anyone just about to drive back to the UK that I could share a car with?'

'You mean with a diplomatic bag and a secret telegram for the Foreign Secretary?'

I nod at the gentle mockery, and he smiles.

'Would be nice if I could beam over,' I say.

'They have that technology, you know,' he says.

'Who?'

'I don't know. People. The Americans, probably. But they're keeping it under wraps because it would put all the airlines out of business, and the cars and the oil corporations. Think of the hell it would play with the world financial markets. The entire infrastructure of the western world would be destabilised.'

'Foreign Office recommendation to keep the technology hidden away?'

'Definitely. Think of the terrorist implications. Anyway, if you don't want to get on a plane, I'm not sure why you'd want to be broken down into your constituent atomic parts and reassembled a thousand miles away.'

'There's that.'

'OK, Detective Inspector, where have we got to? Where is Baden now?'

'He's back at the military hospital. The police are giving him another day, and then they're going to be questioning him further. At least they don't seem to be in any rush to kick him out. Maybe they're keen on not letting him go.'

'They think he might be involved? That doesn't make sense, does it?'

Take a sip of tea. Tetley, I reckon.

'Nice,' I say. 'It's not Lipton Yellow Label then.'

He smiles. 'No, thank God.'

'How did that stuff get to be in every supermarket in the entire world outside of Britain?'

He laughs. 'Blame the Victorians, I think.'

Another sip. Not too hot.

'The whole thing's messed up,' I say. 'Not sure what to think. They know, the police I mean, the police down in Tartu at least if not the ones up here, they know far more than they're telling me. And what can I do? It's fair enough. It's their case, it's their illegal body-harvesting operation. All we've got is this one guy claiming to be British, with absolutely no proof that he is. Did you meet him?'

'No. It was one of our local staff members. She found him convincing. Scared even.'

'Can't argue that. He's definitely scared.'

'Have we got any family notified yet?'

Shake my head. 'As far as we know, they still haven't found the girlfriend. Maybe they did today, I haven't been in touch yet. I'll go and speak to his mother when I get back, but she's in a home with dementia, so...'

'Father's dead.'

'Yes, and no siblings. There must be aunts and cousins or something, but I've not been involved in that. We'll see when I get back.'

I'd been beginning to relax, but there it is again, just the thought of having to return, and the fear comes sweeping in.

Take a large drink of tea, but it doesn't really help. He catches my eye in the reflection again, then steps away and places his mug on the desk.

'When do you need to be back?' he asks.

'In work, tomorrow morning, 8 a.m.'

'Realistically you're going to have to fly.'

'I know.'

'How long would it take to drive?'

'I'm thinking, twenty-four hours to get to Brussels, get the Eurostar to St Pancras, the sleeper to Inverness, be at my desk on Friday morning.'

'A day late.'

'Pretty much.'

'What's your boss going to think about that?'

Make a small gesture with the tea. Even as I explain it I relax a little. Not driving the whole way makes a difference, at least in my head.

'How much sleep did you get last night?'

'A few hours.'

'And on the back of that you're going to drive for twenty-four hours non-stop? Those time of travel numbers on Google Maps don't include stopping for a cup of tea and using the bathroom, never mind sleeping for several hours.'

Another check of the watch. The idea's sounding good in my head. The last thing I want is some kindly middle-aged chap talking the sort of sense that usually gets inflicted on you by your parents.

'You're a dad, right?' I say.

He smiles.

'Look, I might be able to help you.'

He heads for the door, throwing, 'I'll make a call, be back in a minute,' over his shoulder.

I look at the open door and out into the office, catching the eye of a young woman, who smiles and then looks back down at her work. I turn again to the window and try not to stare at my reflection.

20

In the modern world, where everyone is brave and heroic, and life is conducted in superlatives, I expect there would be plenty of people who would have blindly charged into that farmhouse, when shots were being fired and the place was in a state of confusion, to do their bit. Good sense, in that narrative, would be seen by many as pusillanimity. I just saw it as good sense. However, where I was, without question, pusillanimous, was in not calling Quinn and letting him know I wouldn't be in work tomorrow.

That was gutless. Equally so is the fact that I've turned my phone off. I'll put it back on at some point along the way, the middle of the night, to make sure I don't miss anything they really need to tell me. Other than, that is, the condemnation of my actions and whatever sanctions that Quinn is intending to lob at me.

Maybe I'll speak to him tomorrow when he might have calmed down. Little to be gained from him shouting at me, and me growing entrenched in my decision not to get on a plane. Or, my decision not to come into work when told to, as he will no doubt put it.

I called Mary. Pretty craven. Getting the woman on the front desk to deliver the news. At least it was in the knowledge that Quinn isn't a shoot-the-messenger type of man. Mary sounded concerned for me, rather than concerned about having to deliver the news. I didn't feel I deserved her concern. I just wasn't getting on a plane.

The DHM found a solution, and I'm sitting next to her right now. I'm driving the first leg, she'll take over somewhere around about Riga. That means I get the bang-in-the-middle-of-the-night shift, starting around 1 a.m., so I'll need to make sure I sleep while she's driving.

Her name's Dorothy. That's all either of them told me. Works in the Embassy, but I've no idea what she does. UK-based, I presume. We don't need to talk about it. So far, in fact, we haven't talked about anything.

The DHM gave me a five-minute explanation of why he thought what he was suggesting was a good idea for everyone. Dorothy is having a hard time. Needs a break from work, but is refusing to take it. I formed the impression that she's suffering from depression, but he didn't go that far. He can't force her onto a plane, particularly since her job performance isn't affected, but this way he's getting her to help out the police – or me, as it really is – and she obviously agreed to it. Perhaps there's some other problem being solved by this. I immediately assume it's some sort of romantic entanglement, but quickly dismiss the thought. I haven't a clue, and I don't really need to know anyway.

He was aware that Dorothy had a friend in Paris she'd been to stay with a few times, so this would give her the perfect opportunity to visit. The Embassy would arrange a car hire and Dorothy could leave it in Paris, stay for a few days, then fly home. This was all suggested with the usual caveat that, of course, the Embassy didn't actually have any money, because no government department does these days, so that I'd be paying for the car hire. He didn't explain who'd be paying for Dorothy's return flight, but that wasn't really my concern. I'd have gladly done it if he'd said it was the only way the whole thing was going to happen. By that point I'd already made up my mind that I was hiring a car to drive to Brussels, so it made sense to have someone to share the driving.

So now, here we are, sitting together in a car driving south through Estonia, Dorothy and I. We haven't got past hello yet. I don't know what she was thinking, dragooned into this journey at little more than a half hour's notice.

She's not trying to sleep. Eyes open, staring straight ahead. No music on, no radio, but hardly the suffocating atmosphere of the car trip to Tartu. Eventually, presumably, one of us will say something. Perhaps then conversation will develop. Perhaps not.

★ ★ ★

She took over at a service station south of Riga. Glad to see we're already a little ahead of the game. Ultimately it doesn't matter, as I'm getting the sleeper to Inverness, so arriving at King's Cross two hours early probably won't help. But it's good to make up time, in case at some point we lose it.

Just after nine thirty our time, seven thirty back at home, sitting in the passenger seat, I finally crack. Feeling bad about not speaking to Quinn. Time to man up. So much for my bad intentions about not speaking to him until tomorrow.

I doubt he'll still be in work, but it's possible. I'll never get the switchboard through to him, however, so I call his mobile.

'Where are you?' he says by way of answering the phone.

'Just south of Riga, sir.'

'Latvia?'

'Yes.'

'You'll be here on Friday morning.'

'Yes.'

'Any further fallout from the raid this morning?'

I already spoke to him, sitting in the back of the car, on the way home from Tartu. A mistake, I quickly realised, as I should have called him without the others in earshot.

'Not so I heard. I didn't have much more contact with the police on getting back to Tallinn. Spoke to the DHM at the Embassy...'

'The what?'

'The Deputy Head of Mission. The Deputy Ambassador.'

'Right.'

'They're going to get someone along to see Baden tomorrow, start talking to him about coming home. See if there's anyone he wants them to speak to. He hasn't asked them to contact anyone yet. The DHM said he might go himself.'

Pause.

'We'll need to talk when you get back,' he says, and we both know he doesn't mean about Baden.

'Of course, sir. Any luck finding Emily King?'

'Sort of,' he says.

I don't say anything, waiting for the explanation.

'She's dead. We tracked her down to Anstruther. She'd been living there more or less since Baden died in Estonia. Natterson went down to see her yesterday. When he got there, the police were at her house. She'd been strangled and badly beaten. Hard to say right off, but the pathologist reckons it was two or three days ago. Waiting for his final results.' Pause. 'You can get into it when you bother coming into work.'

There's another pause, which I don't immediately fill and he hangs up.

Stare at the dashboard for a while, still holding the phone to my ear, even though it's dead, then I slowly lower it.

'Crap.'

So John Baden, or someone claiming to be him, appears after twelve years, and the next day the woman who had perhaps been waiting for him all that time is murdered. And I'm in a car driving across Europe, feeling stupid.

I glance at Dorothy, but she's staring straight ahead – which I have to say is a positive, given that she's driving – and I close my eyes and rest my head back against the seat. Not at all tired, but I'm going to be driving in the middle of the night, so I can't stay awake all that time.

'They're not happy with you.'

I open my eyes. I wonder if it was Dorothy who spoke. *They're not happy with you.* Was I asleep? Look at the clock. Just after midnight. How did that happen? Just like that, a flick of the switch, a snap of the fingers. Two and a half hours have vanished.

Lick my lips, blink. Aware from both the taste in my mouth and from the feeling in my eyes that I've been sleeping for a while.

'Where are we?' I ask, as we pass a signpost with names and a language I don't recognise.

'We're not far from Kaunas in Lithuania,' she says.

'How are you doing? You all right?'

'Sure.'

'OK to keep going for another hour or so?'

'Sure.'

'But if I fall asleep again, you'll stop anyway, and get me to take over. That's the point of this.'

'Of course.'

The brief conversation falls into disuse. I think about her tone of voice, what she said. They were at odds with one another. She sounds tired.

'Would it help if we talked?' I ask. Waking up now, might as well make the effort.

'Sure,' she says, unexpectedly. 'What d'you want to talk about?'

She glances at me this time, then looks forward again. The road is quiet, only three or four other cars in sight along the stretch of motorway in either direction.

I smile, make a small gesture.

'I guess it might be a little forced if we approach it like that,' I say.

'Tell me why we're sitting in this car,' she says.

'I don't want to fly.'

'Why not?'

'Some bad experiences.'

'Does everyone who's had a bad experience on a plane refuse to fly again?' she asks. Hint of disapproval in her tone.

And so I don't answer, sliding into the familiar self-doubt. She's right, of course. How many times have I told myself to get over it? Get on the damn plane. Well, not so often, as it happens, because I usually never put myself in a position where I'll need to get on one. Until now, when someone else put me in it.

The road stretches ahead. A BMW overtakes on the outside, the driver switching to full beam as he eases in front. I move another inch or two down in the seat and close my eyes.

21

We're nearing the final stretch, still beating Google Maps by a couple of hours. Stopped three times, just had a good few hours' sleep, eyes closed, in the passenger seat, through the middle of Germany. Now the Rhineland, before cutting through the bottom of the Netherlands, into Belgium.

The fitful conversation of the middle of the night dries to nothing through Germany. The autobahns are insane. Where there are three lanes, things aren't too bad, but then there are all the two lane sections, with someone driving at fifty-five in the inside lane, and the procession of Mercedes and BMWs on the outside doing a hundred and thirty.

Everything calms down coming into Holland. We're both awake, the cars and the afternoon flitting by. Low cloud, but bright. Melancholy sits on the car. I can feel it from her, as I did when we were introduced last night. But this close, after this much time, it's painful. A painful sorrow.

I wonder... I wonder, when they sent her off across Europe in a car with me for company, if they realised how consumed she is. Consumed by misery. Did they do it because they think she can be cured by a little distraction, cheered up by having something to do?

Try not to worry about her. I need to process what's happening with Baden and what the news about Emily King could mean. Realise, every time I start thinking about it, that I have too little information; and as soon as I think about that, I start kicking myself for being in the car, rather than at home getting on with the investigation and filling in the gaps.

I'm hoping I'll be able to get an earlier Eurostar, by at least a couple of hours, although I doubt even that will give me any better options upon arriving in London. Even if there was a train that got me into Inverness at two in the morning, it doesn't actually get me into work any earlier. I just need to be at my desk when I said I would be, and take it from there.

'I went back in time.'

Her voice comes slowly across the car. *I went back in time.* I don't immediately turn to look at her, the words seem so strange, then I give a quick glance to my right. She's awake, eyes wide, slightly glazed expression, her head back against the headrest, staring straight ahead.

'How do you mean?'

We come to it at last. The root of her sorrow. I thought that we'd get to the end and she'd never say, and all that would be left was an image of this person who I met once, so full of sadness, this strange young woman I'd barely remember.

'There was this moment in school. High school, just before A Levels. I always remembered it. A warm afternoon. Early May. We'd been somewhere, into a museum in town. Bath. We were on our way back to Chippenham, the sun was warm. I was sitting on my own, didn't have any friends on the trip. There was a lazy, sleepy feel. Hard to pin down, but something peculiar. It felt... there was something about the moment. It felt liquid. Time itself felt liquid.'

She stops talking for a while. I don't turn and stare. She's not waiting, with some conceit, for me to show interest. I can tell. She's never told this to anyone. She's working out how to tell the story, having never put it into words before.

The sun flashes for a brief moment, showing that the cloud is not impenetrable, and is gone before I can lower the visor.

A small movement of her hand.

'I had a normal kind of life. University, work. Got married, had a kid. That was all. Like everybody – maybe not, maybe not everybody – I thought about all the things we'd done wrong, all the opportunities that were missed or that came too late. I didn't live in regret or the past, I just had these moments. I used to wonder about going back, having it all again. I'd still have married Jonathan, we'd still have had Gabriella, but then there'd be everything else. The chances we could grab.'

Another pause, the story coming in painful chapters, as she assembles the narrative in her head. I glance at her again. Maybe making sure she's not crying, although there's nothing I'd be able to do about that. But there are no tears.

'And then it happened. I can't think. I can't think what it was about that moment. Why then? I was dozing on the couch, Gabriella sitting next to me watching *Scooby Doo*. That ordinary a day. And it just happened. I went back in time. I was asleep on the sofa, and when I came round I was back sitting in that minibus, on the way home from the museum in Bath. Snapped out of it, like I'd fallen asleep, and I was there. Me. Sitting in my own eighteen-year-old body.'

Of course I don't know what's coming, but it's obviously not good. I don't really want to hear it, but she has her audience captive.

And this is her, talking for the first time, choosing me. How can I not listen?

'And there was the future, all in front of me. I knew what was coming. I knew… I knew everything. Except, what I didn't know.'

Another pause. I could think ahead and try to work out the story, but I'll leave her to tell it. You never know where people and stories are going to go.

'The first part of the story was that Jonathan and I met at Cambridge. A couple of semesters in, just as he was getting in with the wrong crowd. The money crowd. The coke crowd. He always said I saved him from them. Except, this time, I was thrown back just ahead of my A Levels. I had a week to study and remember everything that I hadn't studied for fifteen years.'

A pause, but no deep breath, no tears forced back.

'I never got into Cambridge. I had all those exams to do, and I could barely study. Just spent that week confused, trying to concentrate, barely able to think. When it came to it, I did all right, but not good enough. I… I had options to think about, and in the end I chose to go to Nottingham. Studied there two years, got back in the groove, went down to Cambridge to do my third year.' Slight shake of the head. 'It was too late, but of course I tried to tell myself it wasn't. I'd worried he'd have found someone else, but he hadn't. At least not the one person. He was the centre of them, all these rich pricks with their money and their drugs. Money, drugs, and sex. I got to know him. I tried, I really did, but I couldn't compete.

'I thought, it's not about Jonathan. Or me. It's about Gabriella. What if Gabriella never gets born? So I slept with him. I mean, that was easy enough, he was sleeping with everyone. But in the end… it was only a couple of times, and the others didn't want me there. I tried sticking with him, but they all painted me as some kind of obsessive crazy, following him around. So he stopped seeing me.'

Full stop. Pause. Then the moment of harsh violence.

'He died. Heroin overdose. I took a pregnancy test the next day, just in case. But what was the point in that? Even if I had been pregnant, it wouldn't have been Gabriella, would it? Gabriella wasn't going to be born for another three years. This kid wouldn't have been her. It would just have been another child born to a single mother without a job, whose dad died of a drug addiction…

'I wasn't pregnant anyway. And that was that. I was stuck at Cambridge doing my final year, and my husband and daughter were gone…

'I was never optimistic. I mean, when this thing, this thing that happened, and I don't know why, this thing that sent me back, I was nervous right from the off. By the end of that bus trip back home, I'd already thought it all through. Had it figured out. The trouble I'd have with my exams, how it would go with Jonathan again, because there'd been bumps along the way before. And then, how could we ever possibly replicate Gabriella? Even if we had sex on the same evening at exactly the same time… there are sixty million sperm to choose from. It could be any one of them…

'So, I'd had this dread, right from the start, and everything I thought happened. All my worst fears. And looking back, if I was sitting on that bus again, there was nothing I could do differently. I had to be at Cambridge from the start, more or less. Maybe I could have gone there as a cleaner…

'I had a husband, and I had a daughter, and now they're gone. I didn't do anything, I didn't touch anything. No one did anything. It just happened.'

I notice the small movement of her hand to her face, but I don't turn and look at her. I don't look to see if she's wiping away a tear. Her voice is steady though. This is it, she's told her story, it's out there. Will it being out there make any difference?

A long pause. I don't think she's quite finished, but eventually I say, 'Maybe there'll be another moment.'

'Maybe.'

Her voice is small suddenly. How am I supposed to leave this woman in Brussels? How can I leave her to drive the further three hours onto Paris? Except, this isn't new for her. She's not any more miserable now than she was this morning, yesterday morning, at any time in the last fifteen years.

Her sadness soaks through my skin. Infects me.

'Maybe there'll be another moment,' I say. 'If the last one just happened out of nowhere, maybe it'll happen again. Maybe you need to wait…'

I suddenly know what it is, I suddenly know why she is so afflicted even before I make the suggestion and she answers. Her story, however far-fetched to some, sounds utterly credible. And I know why it's worse now than it ever was before.

'You already passed it, didn't you? In the past month. You were holding out, holding out hope for the day that you were sent back, the day your life changed. You thought, when that day comes again, maybe I'll revert. I'll doze off and suddenly I'll be sitting on the sofa next to Gabriella…'

'I even sat and watched *Scooby Doo*. The exact same episode on

Boomerang. Not that I was ever going to fall asleep.'

I look over at her. A single tear has run down her left cheek, the drop at the bottom not heavy enough to fall from her face.

'When was it?'

'Three weeks ago last Friday.'

Cars speed by on the outside. I realise I've slowed to just over fifty, so I start to build speed again. The atmosphere in the car feels heavy and thick. Peculiar.

'I'm sorry,' I say.

She doesn't reply at first. Her eyes are staring straight ahead, seeing nothing. I move into the outside lane for the first time since we started talking.

The mood has become one with the car. More tragic, more terrifying than that first awful drive south to Tartu. I will leave the car in Brussels, she will drive on to Paris and leave the car with the people at Hertz. Later on today, or tomorrow perhaps, someone else will get in the car, and they will notice it as soon as they get in, they will feel it, as much as if the inside of the car was covered in cobwebs. Except they won't be able to see it and they won't know what it is, and they won't quite be able to bring themselves to ask for a different vehicle because they don't think they'd be able to understand why. And they'll drive away, and they'll feel like their world has fallen apart.

Some time later, when we're in Belgium, and the mood hasn't lifted, and some part of me can't get out the car quickly enough while another never wants to leave her, she finally speaks again. A few small words.

'I don't even have a photograph.'

We get to Brussels a short time later. I kiss her goodbye, my hand lightly touching the top of her arm.

22

On the Eurostar. Need to check in with Dingwall, but will wait until we're the other side of the tunnel. Could have called from Brussels, but didn't feel like it. Needed time to recover.

Darkness comes as we speed towards the tunnel. This train goes a little too fast for me, but that's not something I'm ever going to openly admit. I sit on trains sometimes and imagine, if this was a plane, with this level of movement and juddering, I'd be freaking out. Of course, it's not 30,000 feet in the air.

There's a lot of banging on in Britain about the pace of the rail network, and how so many other countries in the world have high speed, and won't it be great when we've spent several billion pounds we don't have so that we can have intercity tracks where trains can travel at three hundred miles an hour. I think, why is everyone in such a rush? Why do they need to go so quickly?

So, I don't really like Eurostar, but it's a vague kind of discomfort. I was on this train when it started, twenty years ago, and it's apparent the rolling stock hasn't been updated since then. So we're sitting on a twenty-year-old train that was built by a company struggling against bankruptcy and doing everything as cheaply as possible.

There's no fear. I am aware, however, that I used to have a vague discomfort about flying and that developed into fear. Hopefully I won't ever have the same experiences on a train as I did in the air.

Nevertheless, I'm looking forward to getting on the slower Highland train out of King's Cross.

The train disappears into the tunnel and I'm looking at my own reflection even more than I have been. I look into my eyes, the same old eyes look back. Unchanged.

What does one make of Dorothy's story? Most people wouldn't believe it. Why should anyone believe it? Conventional thinking, I imagine, would have her suffering from some kind of neurosis. A storyteller. Schizophrenic perhaps. I doubt many would not think that she absolutely believed the story she'd told, but they wouldn't for a second believe it themselves. Except I did. I believe her. I know she's telling the truth. Maybe it doesn't make sense in our conventional narrative of how life and time work, but the very existence of life at all in all its extraordinary forms is incredible in itself, so this is just one more remarkable story in a world full of them. And, like many of the other remarkable stories, crushingly heartbreaking.

I never asked her if she did anything outwith her own little circle of interest, during all these years of waiting to get her life back. Did she put money on Tony Blair to win three elections? Did she bet on Spain to win the 2010 World Cup final 1-0? Did she call someone before the 7/7 bombings and warn them? If she did the latter, they didn't listen to her.

I suspect she thought she couldn't risk changing anything.

She's just waiting to commit suicide. Just waiting. For the right moment, the opportunity, the day when she wakes up and feels, down into the pit of her soul, that all hope is lost. Then she's going to take some pills. Or cut her wrists in the bath. Something where at least there's a moment. A moment in time before she slips away, for time to revert. For time to realise it's had its fun, that it has messed around with her quite enough. That it's gone too far, and she can get her life back.

★ ★ ★

I call Quinn when we're out of the tunnel and I've set my watch to UK time. 1607 hrs. Early enough, unexpectedly, to get to King's Cross and catch a train that'll get me into Inverness tonight. Of course, I won't be able to transfer the ticket, but that's all part of the scam of British trains. *Those are the terms and conditions* they will say, as though the terms and conditions are laid down by a higher authority – Zeus perhaps – and there's nothing they can do about them.

'Where are you?'

He needs to ask, I think, largely to make the point that I'm not where I'm supposed to be.

'Kent,' I say. 'On the train into London, then I'll get the next one available up to Inverness. Will be in work first thing tomorrow morning. What's happening?'

'Natterson's taken over the investigation. He'll fill you in in the morning.'

Well, there's a rebuke. Didn't really see it coming, but I could hardly expect less. Natterson is the other DI at the station, my junior officer by several years. It's the use of the words 'taken over', as well as the reproach of refusing to let me know what's been happening.

'You've had Baden's corpse exhumed and identified?' I ask.

'DI Natterson will fill you in in the morning,' he repeats.

There's another one of those brief silences.

'Very good, sir,' I say, 'see you tomorrow,' managing to get the farewell in just before he hangs up.

So, I really am in the doghouse then. Well, fair enough. He didn't order me back to Scotland so that I could spend twenty-four hours in a car.

I call Natterson. He's a decent guy, we have a good relationship. I don't have the ego to care that he's been put in charge of a case that was mine, especially under these circumstances.

'Hey, Nat, how's it going?'

'Ben, where are you?'

'On the train. Will be in first thing tomorrow. How's it looking?'

'Weird,' he says. 'Look, I'm sorry about the thing. I don't know what's…'

'It doesn't matter, don't worry about it. How d'you mean, weird?'

There's a slight pause, and I wonder if he's driving, then he says, 'Look, you couldn't do me a favour, could you?'

'If it's to do with the investigation, you're the boss.'

'Could you get off the train in Perth?'

'What's in Perth?'

'Baden's mother. She's in a care home. I've spoken to the head of the house, and it sounds like she's not the most coherent. Well, consistent perhaps, just not on the same page as everyone else. Nevertheless, we need to at least try. If you could get off there, maybe spend the night in a Travelodge or something, it'll save one of us having to go down there in the next day or two.'

'Sure,' I say. 'E-mail me through the details, I'll pick it up somewhere along the way.'

'Cool.'

'And what's weird?'

'Where to begin… There was no corpse. In the coffin, in Baden's coffin. All the paperwork on the file suggested that he'd been buried, that the body had been buried. We dig it up, there's a coffin, but inside the coffin there's an urn.'

'And the ashes in the urn could be anything, I suppose. A cat. A block of wood…'

'Well, now we go to the crematorium in Kilvean, and sure enough, they have the record of Baden having been cremated twelve years ago. The body was cremated.'

'So why did we think he'd been buried?' I ask.

'Because that was what Rosco wanted us to think.'

Rosco. 'Ah, OK.'

'Anyway, although we can't get the body DNA checked, there was a DNA sample on the file, taken from the body when it was returned, so we have those details. And they match the DNA sample that was just sent back from Tallinn, and taken from Baden this week.'

'So the DNA tells us that both the corpse and the living victim are the same person?'

'Yes.'

'Well, that is weird. Not the weirdest thing I've heard today...'

'Isn't it?'

'No, but I'll grant you, it's weird enough.'

And this one has documented evidence to support its weirdness.

'It just doesn't make any sense whatsoever,' he says. 'Unless, of course, there was something else suspect going on with that original DNA sample.'

No, it doesn't make sense, not without us having more information. I'm not going to think about that at the moment, though. I need to see some sort of proof to be able to move on from general disbelief to actually trying to think about what might be going on.

'Anything else happening?'

'Had a long chat with the lead officer in the Emily King case. She lived a quiet life, on her own, on a small scheme at the back of the town. Never spoke to her neighbours, and we haven't been able to pin down any family or friends so far. She'd been strangled, beaten, but her house hadn't been touched. They're thinking it was a robbery, burglar was interrupted, killed her but then fled.'

'Rape?'

'Nope, just beaten. And she didn't get to fight for very long. Thumbs pressed forcefully into her windpipe, and it popped.'

'Popped? That the word the pathologist used?'

'Yep. And some of the facial beating was after she'd stopped breathing.'

'Where did she work?'

'Didn't. Like I said, so far they haven't been able to establish her as having any connection with anyone. She went into local shops, went to the chippie sometimes, a lot of people recognised her from sitting on a bench down the front, but she never spoke to anyone. Ever.'

'Online?'

'Waiting to hear.'

'And have we mentioned to them about the connection with

Baden?'

Slight pause.

'Not yet.'

'Quinn's orders?'

'Yes.'

The pause being because he thought we should have done. I would too. That's Quinn playing his cards close to his chest, worried maybe that the investigation will get away from him.

'OK. And what about the hit-and-run on the High Street?'

'How much d'you know?'

'That it happened.'

'Couple of witnesses saw a white car, but no number. One of them thought it was a Land Rover, the other said it was a saloon of some sort.'

'Great. Who was the victim?'

'Local guy. Andrew Waverley. Well, lived in Cromarty. Local enough.'

'Known to us?'

'Not to us, but down south. And when I say local, he's from London. Came up a few years ago. Worked as an artist, had a few pieces in local shops and galleries around the place. Very dark. I mean, his paintings were dark.'

'How'd he make his money?'

'In the city. Made a shedload, got busted for some sort of business thing. Insider trading. Spent six months in one of those jails in the south-east where they more or less lock you up in a room in the Hilton. Came north when he got out.'

'They never took his money off him, then?'

'He might have used some of it to upgrade to a suite.'

'OK, thanks, Nat. I'll give you a call after I've seen the mother.'

'OK, cheers.'

We hang up. I didn't ask him if he'd looked for connections between Waverley and our case. There needn't be, just because it happened on our patch – after all, one aspect of the case happened a thousand miles away and the other in Fife – but we're involved because those two people were from around Dingwall the last time anyone knew they existed, and now, as they emerge strangely and darkly from the woodwork, someone else is killed. It needs checking.

We can talk about it when I get into the office tomorrow.

Rest my head against the seat. Tired. England passes by, under cover of cloud and almost dark. I think about Dorothy. I should call her. I could call her now, but I didn't get her mobile number. Next week, I'll call the Embassy. I won't be calling to make sure she's all right, because she won't be. I'll just be calling. She trusted me with her story, so I'm the guy. From now on.

Thinking about her troubles me. I'm not sure why, and it's not because of the peculiarity of her narrative. There's something else. Something else bothering me, just out of reach.

The train starts to slow. Specks of rain show on the window.

23

I catch the 16:35 from King's Cross, gets into Glasgow at 21:57. Decide I'll stay in Glasgow for the night, then head up to Perth early in the morning. Book a room in the Central Hotel, arrange a car for 7 a.m. Spending money like I have plenty of it to spend. Guilt money. Guilty because I ought to just have got on the plane and come home.

Now that I'm back here, the plane doesn't seem so frightening. Now that I don't have to get on it. All I would have to do though is imagine it again, sit and feel it, surround myself with the sensations of taking off, being in the air, but I don't even want to put myself through that.

Asleep within thirty seconds of getting into bed.

* * *

I blindly head off towards Perth, even though I'm going to be far too early. Spoke to the home, asked if I could be there at eight. They said ten. We compromised at nine. Mrs Baden is always up before six anyway, they said, but give her a few hours to get herself together.

Nevertheless, approaching Perth well ahead of schedule, wondering what I'm going to do with myself, when I notice a garden centre with a sign advertising a full Scottish breakfast served from 8 a.m. Already past the entrance before I make my decision, make a U-turn, pull into the car park, and settle down to a large plate of grilled breakfast, two fried eggs. Several cups of tea, too much toast.

As I sit in the usual bright and airy garden centre café, in the company of two other customers, the sky begins to brighten to a pale blue and weak late autumn sunshine. I begin to feel my mood lighten, on the back of breakfast and the sun, and it's not until it happens that I realise how dark and melancholic I'd been feeling. Not just these past few days. Been a long time.

There's no reason to be so unhappy. Up and down, that's not unreasonable, everybody is up and down, but not this consistently despondent, so steadily miserable that I don't even notice. It doesn't make sense.

When was the last time I felt like the sun was shining? In my head, and not just out there? I don't remember.

I leave the café and take a few moments before getting in the car. It's a beautiful morning, fresh and cold and clear. Not quite the sharp crispness of a perfect autumnal day, but close enough.

A door closed, briefly, on the eternal bleak November.

★ ★ ★

There's a large common area at the back of the care home, overlooking a lawn which is surrounded by trees. Large, broad pines, mostly, a few deciduous trees amongst them, their leaves yellow and red and brown in the morning sun. I pause to look around the room, the nurse beside me.

Care homes can be depressing. Everybody knows. Money, as everybody also knows, can buy separation from the norm, and this is a care home for people with money.

The room is quiet, five people in all. The woman at the reception desk called them guests. They're all guests. One of them, an old fellow in a wheelchair, is reading the *Scotsman*; there are a couple of women sitting together in silence, impossible to tell from a quick glance whether it's companionable or a silence they don't even recognise; there's another woman talking to herself, rosary beads in her hand, her fingers working the beads, words tumbling softly from her lips; and at the window, looking out, is Mrs Baden.

'This way,' says the nurse, having given me my moment of evaluation.

'Who pays for Mrs Baden to be here?' I ask, as we weave our way over between velvet-backed chairs.

'You'd need to ask the director,' she says. 'Sorry.'

'Does she get many visitors?'

She pauses, concerned we're getting into earshot.

'Just the one, I think. A woman. Younger. I think it might be her daughter, I'm not sure.'

'She doesn't have a daughter.'

'Oh.'

She looks at me for a moment, a look that says we don't quite understand each other.

'Perhaps don't mention that to Mrs Baden, I'm not sure she realises.'

I glance over at her. She's looking out of the window, not appearing to have noticed yet that we're approaching.

'But *you* realise, though, right? She doesn't have a daughter.'

'I... no, I didn't know. I'll need to look at our records.'

'So, who do you think it is that comes to visit her?'

'I'm not sure then. I got the impression, like I said... she said it was her daughter.'

'What's her name?'

'Mrs Baden seems to call her a different name every time. Thinks it's funny. They both do.'

I hold her gaze for a moment, look over at the old woman, her back straight, her gaze steady out over the lawn. On the table before her there's a small pot of tea, a cup and saucer, a jug of milk. It doesn't look as though she's poured any yet.

'She's waiting for the deer,' says the nurse. 'There's one, the same young buck, passes through the lawn every morning. He always stops and looks at the house. She thinks he's looking at her. She thinks they're communicating.'

'Maybe they are.'

We look out over the lawn, as though this may be the moment that the young buck chooses to appear. The nurse touches my arm, her voice drops even lower.

'She calls him her son.'

She walks over to the table and I follow.

'Mrs Baden,' she says, and she doesn't speak slowly and loudly, as you so often hear. 'This is the policeman we told you about.'

The old woman looks at the nurse, slightly confused, and then she sees me and a smile comes to her face. A broad smile. As if she's been expecting me. As if she knows who I am.

'Of course, of course. Sit down, Detective Inspector.'

I nod at the nurse, the nurse looks vaguely curiously at me, as if she's suddenly got the impression that Mrs Baden and I have met before.

'Don't take too long,' says the nurse, inevitably, as she leaves.

As I sit down I hear her say to the man with the *Scotsman*, 'How's the cricket going, Mr Jarvis?'

'I'm waiting for John,' says Mrs Baden, by way of a conversation opener. 'Perhaps today you'll finally get to see him.'

'The deer?'

'What? Of course, who did you think I meant?'

She smiles, but then suddenly there's a shift and a note of agitation crosses her face, and with a shake of the head she looks back out over the lawn. She briefly taps the middle finger of her right hand against her thumb. A slight twitch of the head.

I think of Dorothy again. Why did I do that? Why now? I

have an image of her, sitting alone in a hotel room, consumed by unimaginable sadness. Where did that come from?

I shouldn't wait until next week to call her. I should call her in Paris. I'll get her mobile number from the people in Tallinn.

She shouldn't be in a hotel room, though. She should have gone to Paris already and be with her friend. Why did I picture her in a hotel? She shouldn't be alone. She should be talking to someone. Perhaps, ever so slightly, starting the long process of trying to move on.

She's never going to move on. Who could?

I'll call her tonight. Why did I even get out the car and say goodbye? She spoke to me. After all this time, all these years, I could tell. That was the first time she'd ever said anything to anyone. The strangest thing imaginable happened to her, and for a decade and a half she never mentioned it to anyone. Why now? Why me, now?

I shouldn't have got out the car. I need to call her tonight.

I realise Mrs Baden has placed her fingers lightly in mine.

'You look distracted,' she says. I leave my hand where it is for a moment, then finally withdraw it, shaking my head.

'It's all right. I just need to make a call later.'

'Yes, you do.'

Somehow I feel if I could get Mrs Baden to speak plainly to me, I could get answers to virtually everything in the world in the next ten minutes. She seems so wise. Yet, she's sitting here in a care home, looking out a window, waiting for a deer, who she thinks is her son. That, as Terry Jones said, doesn't seem very wise to me.

'Do you know why I'm here?' I ask.

Her eyes drop slightly, but she doesn't reply.

'I don't know anything,' she says. 'Ask anyone. They'll tell you.'

She's not what I'd been expecting, although there's a strangeness about this entire business which dictates that I should have come with no expectations at all. Indeed, that's a good philosophy to take into every police investigation.

More and more, in the public services, as in life in general, we come across people with dementia. A natural result of an ageing population. There's always something there, something that says there's no mask. There's no artifice, because the ability for artifice has been lost. It doesn't mean there are no lies. There's something deeper than that, more intrinsic.

I'm not picking up the usual signs with Mrs Baden.

'Who is it who comes to visit you?'

Another lowering of the eyes, and then slowly they're lifted back up and she looks into the trees.

'Who do you suppose comes to visit me, Detective?'

She gives me a quick glance. Venomous in a way that I don't quite understand either. Four sentences into the conversation, and already I feel like I'm getting rings run round me.

'I don't know, Elsa, I'd like you to tell me.'

The middle finger and thumb tap together again, another slight movement of the head.

Suddenly her head lifts, her face lightens. I watch her closely for a second, the life and brightness in her eyes, and then turn to confirm what has obviously happened. The deer has emerged from the woods.

A young male, he stands on the grass staring up at the house. It really does look, for all the world, like he's staring straight at us.

Her hands clap silently together, as though she's sitting in an audience in a church, silently letting her child know her approval of his performance in the choir.

We watch the deer, the deer appears to watch us. I glance round the rest of the room. Another couple of people have come in. No one else seems interested in the deer. I wonder if only Mrs Baden and I can see it, but dismiss the notion. There may be a certain peculiarity to events, but it's not a ghost deer.

When I look back, the deer has bowed its head and is eating the grass. Elsa is watching him with a kind of parental concern and pride.

'What's the connection with the deer?' I ask.

'We're friends,' she says.

'How long have you been friends?'

'He's been coming here every morning since I arrived. He says hello, we exchange a few morning pleasantries, and then he goes about his business.'

'You've been here three years?'

'That's correct.'

'He seems young. Younger than three.'

I say this last one with a soft voice. The truth-hurts voice. The *I-just-need-to-break-this-to-you-gently* voice.

'You don't need to be embarrassed pointing that out, Detective. It's not as though I don't know. But I'm only telling you what I'm seeing. He hasn't aged a day in three years.'

'Maybe it's not the same deer.'

She turns to look at me full on for a moment, her face softens from the look of outright disdain with which she turned, then she shakes her head and looks back at her friend, whose head remains bowed, eating grass.

I don't think I'm going to get anywhere talking about the deer. After all, it's not about the deer. Unless the deer is also, as one might suppose from the way she's looking at it, her son.

'Tell me about John,' I say.

'What?'

'Do you remember he died twelve years ago? In Estonia?'

She doesn't immediately answer. The deer looks up, and they're staring at each other. Maybe they're talking. A few moments, and then the deer turns its head and walks slowly away across the lawn and into the trees. It seems to disappear before the trees completely surround it, just as it appears to leave a space where it's been.

She watches the space for a while, then turns back.

'That wasn't him,' she says. 'That person who died in Estonia. It wasn't him.'

'You identified the body.'

'No, I didn't.'

'I've seen your signature on file. One of my colleagues spoke to the coroner of the day. He remembered the case, he remembered you coming in to confirm the identification, albeit he said it was just as much about you seeing your son for the last time.'

'I'm not saying that someone didn't go along and look at that body and identify it as my son. However, it wasn't my son lying on the table, if that's where the body was, and it wasn't me who looked, because if it had been, I would never have identified him.'

Total denial. Tough to argue against.

'We have DNA evidence to support the fact that it was your son.'

'It's wrong.'

I watch her for a moment, and then follow her gaze out to the trees. So assured, so measured. She catches my eye. We share a forlorn glance over the table, as though neither of us is getting from the discussion what we wanted.

'Can you pour me a cup of tea, please, Detective. I don't really have the strength to lift the teapot. Just a splash of milk, thank you. I'm sorry there's only one cup, shall I get you another?'

She goes to press the small alarm that's hanging around her neck, but I wave her off.

'Just ate a huge breakfast, drank a lot of tea.'

'Of course.'

I pour a little milk into the cup, add the tea.

'Not too much,' she says. 'Half a cup.'

It looks cold and stewed, befitting tea that must have been sitting here most of the morning.

'It's the way I like it,' she says.

'Who was it, then? If it wasn't you who identified the body, who was it?'

She lifts the tea. Her hands are shaking so much I think the cup will fall from her fingers, or that the tea will spill, which explains why she wanted the cup half empty.

She takes a drink. I wait for the slurp, the old person's slurp at a cup of tea, but there's no sound.

'Yes, it's vile, but I can't drink it hot any more. Shame. A crying shame.'

'Who identified the body?'

Was it really not her? Or am I sitting here pushing a mad old woman, who can't even remember her son dying, into naming someone who doesn't even exist?

'Roger got a woman to go along with him,' she says. 'Pretended it was me, got her to sign in my name. He was embarrassed that I wouldn't go. He was embarrassed by me.'

'Why wouldn't you go?'

'Because I knew it wasn't John. My son wasn't dead, I knew he wasn't. I wasn't wasting my time going to look at the dead body of someone else's son. Anyway, it would have been disrespectful.'

'Why did your husband think it was John, then?'

'Oh, he didn't know him, did he?'

'Your husband didn't know your son?'

'Well, you know, not really. They'd lived together for eighteen years, but he didn't know him. Not the way I did.'

'He knew him well enough to recognise him, surely?'

She'd been engaging for a few moments, but at that I can see the shadow cross her face again. She looks away, back out towards the trees, a slightly forlorn look on her face, as though she'd been hoping the young deer would have returned.

'You know better than that,' she says. 'You know better, Detective, I know you do.'

Her eyes are now fixed on the trees. I doubt she will look at me again.

'Who was the other woman?' I ask.

A slight head twitch, the barest movement of her fingers.

'Who was the other woman?'

'Might have been my sister, I suppose, I don't know. It's been so long since I talked to her. Perhaps she died. I don't know.'

The words are drifting away. There's no point in enquiring after her sister, I'll need to find out elsewhere. I glance over my shoulder, having felt the presence of the nurse, and there she is, just inside the door, indicating that I should leave.

I turn back to Mrs Baden, stand, put my hand on her shoulder.

'Thank you, you've been very helpful. If you think of anything else that might be of use, let one of the nurses know and they'll get in touch with me.'

She stares straight ahead, her shoulders do not move, her mouth does not open. She barely appears to be breathing.

I leave the room, stopping at reception on the way out to enquire after the sister.

24

Come into Anstruther on the Leven road, pull into the car park down by the harbour. Plenty of spaces. Could have gone straight to the police station, but wanted to get a feel for the town again. I can't remember the last time I was here. Twenty-five years maybe. Been a long time. So long, in fact, that I don't really know how much has changed. The harbour, of course, is still as it was.

The sun remained behind in Perthshire, as if it wasn't wanted on the east coast. Patchy cloud became thick cloud, and now, flat, grey, low, oppressive cloud, the sea and the sky indistinguishable. Seems the same, everywhere you look.

It's a classic harbour, with two walls a couple of hundred yards apart, arcing round towards each other and leaving thirty yards or so in the middle, for the tide and the fishing boats. There are another couple of short piers in the middle, in between the two, creating a further, even calmer, harbour to the right.

Not so many fishing boats any more.

I walk out along the right-hand wall. There's one old trawler moored up. Looks like it still might be in use. Not much else. An old wooden cruiser, a couple of modern plastic yachts, a couple of rowing boats.

There's a guy walking a dog, a couple out for a walk, three teenagers sitting in a little group, passing around a single can of McEwan's.

I called Natterson earlier. There was a pause there, a definite pause, when I said I had the car and that I wanted to go to Anstruther, and then, like the good team player, he said that'd be a great idea. Felt bad, like I'm stepping on his toes, but I wanted to check it out.

I walk along to the end, step up onto the higher wall and look out over the water. Can see a couple of boats, but there's not much out to sea. Flat and grey and dull, until the water meets the sky. No wind, but the air is cold. I realise the teenagers were sitting in t-shirts. Turn and look back at the town. I recognise it now, the basic shape of the seafront.

Shops and ice cream and afternoons spent on the small beaches start to come back to me. Look round to my right, up to the golf course. Nine holes, very short. Used to go there, play a couple of rounds, made me feel better than I ever really was.

I become aware of the cry of the gulls. It used to be such an evocative sound, a noise that could take you to the seaside in an instant. Maybe not so much any more. Seagulls are everywhere, always scavenging for food. Nobody likes them. The noise and the faeces and the general tumult, as if it's their fault. As if it's the fault of the gulls that they've had to come inland looking for food.

The seagulls cry and swirl, and as I stand and look over the harbour, I realise how empty it is, how dead. It never used to be like this. Maybe I just came in the summer, that was all.

There's someone on the far side, down near the bottom of the other arm of the harbour. We stand still, her and I, and I feel like she's looking at me, like we're looking at each other, although we're really far too far apart to tell.

Then she starts walking up the harbour, her gaze directed north, along the shore to Crail.

I don't wait to see if she looks back. Suddenly the place feels full of ghosts. A harbour full of ghosts. Fishing vessels that no longer ply their trade, and fishermen who are now dead or doing something else, or doing nothing at all, except sitting in a small room lamenting the passing of the years and the passing of the old trades.

The feeling I had sitting in the bright garden centre café while the sun shone suddenly feels like it was several months ago. As I walk back down the harbour, the dog walker is gone, the couple are gone, the three teenagers are gone. The empty can of McEwan's lies in the middle of the wall.

I stand and look at it for a moment but don't pick it up.

* * *

And so we come to Emily King's house, revisiting another part of the tragedy of Tartu from twelve years previously. Me and a police sergeant from the Anstruther office.

I need to get back to the station and get into the old investigation. Never had the chance, of course, leaving so quickly in the first place. That's what needs to be done, because whatever is happening to these people now, it started twelve years ago, and something has occurred, some event, to make the story relevant again.

Maybe it starts with Baden escaping from the house in the woods. The timing of Emily King dying certainly ties in with it. Whoever those people were, they evacuated that house very quickly. Maybe now they're tying up loose ends. Maybe that's all

Emily was. A loose end. Lucky, perhaps, that she lasted this long.

The house is small, detached. A couple of rooms and a kitchen downstairs, two bedrooms and a small bathroom upstairs. Taking a general walkthrough to start.

'You haven't tipped through the cupboards and such yet?' I ask.

The sergeant shakes her head. In uniform, no jacket. Hair clipped back. I find her very attractive, nice voice, lovely laugh the one time I say anything remotely funny. So I know how it will play out. I'll barely look at her, and she'll think I'm rude, our business will be concluded at some stage, and that will be that.

Seven years and I can still imagine Olivia seeing right through me, as if it matters. How stupid.

'We had a basic look, but haven't had the time to get down to the bottom of underwear drawers yet.'

'Correspondence?'

'None. Of course, these days we hardly ever find correspondence from anyone, unless it's online.'

'How's that looking?'

'She had an old laptop. Surprisingly little on it, for anyone. She was still using some antediluvian internet connection, very little history. Watched some porn, looked at YouTube. Never downloaded anything. By modern standards, just not interested.'

I turn away from her and look at the meagre collection of items in the front room.

'You got time to help me look through the house now? Shouldn't take too long.'

I'm not looking at her as I ask. I could do it myself, but I feel I really need to get back to my own station at some point. It will already look like I'm delaying the rebuke from Quinn, which I'm not. Not trying to avoid anything, just following a sensible course of action. Still, it's time I went home.

'I can give you thirty minutes,' she says, after a short pause. I turn and give her the merest of smiles.

'What are we looking for?' she asks.

Good question.

'Anything to do with Estonia...'

'Estonia?'

'They still haven't told you?'

She shakes her head. 'I presumed there was more to it.'

Stare at the floor for a moment. Quinn obviously has his reasons for not yet passing on the full details of this along the chain, but I can't think of any that I'm not going to find absurd and petty.

'OK, me telling you this is probably a bit above both our pay grades, but here it is. And feel free to pass it on up the chain when you get back to the office. I'll take the heat when I get back to Dingwall...'

'If you're sure.'

'Already due a trip to the naughty step. One more thing...'

We share a smile. A moment. One of those moments that always feels so utterly hopeless.

★ ★ ★

Natterson's a decent kid. I don't think he has a story. Perhaps, in its way, it's the best story of all. Nothing dramatic, nothing untoward. A normal life. He was a kid from Inverness who always wanted to be a police officer. And now he is. Nothing outstanding about him, just a decent kid doing his job. Working his way through the ranks, but without any ego attached to him. Does his job, goes home to his wife and kids in their house in Culbokie. That's all.

There will probably be something, somewhere. Everybody has it. Everybody has something, don't they? A secret. A trial. Something that weighs them down. Something that consumes them in the dark moments.

I don't know what it is with Nat. His wife is great, the kids don't seem as annoying as most other people's kids.

It's kind of weird to witness a life that seems so untroubled – I had Sunday lunch with them a few weeks ago, and it felt like walking onto the set of one of those happy family fifties US sitcoms – but then, Nat has to do police work. His own life may be all right, but he's still being presented with this ongoing tale of drunken, drug-addled woe on a daily basis. Messes with you in one way or another. Perhaps Nat's way is to surround himself with family, and make sure it's as good as it can be.

Or maybe he just got lucky.

25

Back to Perth by the same route, and then hit the A9. Long ago gave in to the flow of traffic. No point in getting annoyed. No point in thinking that you can get to the other end any faster than you're ever going to. No point in imagining that you're going to be able to overtake all the trucks and caravans on the meagre stretches of dual carriageway, or that there's not going to be another one just around the corner on the single carriageway if you do. Accept it, take your time.

Hungry, so stop in the Shell garage on the way out of Perth. Buy a prawn sandwich, a bag of Kettle Chips, a KitKat, bottle of water and a coffee. Use the bathroom.

She asked me if I wanted to have lunch before I headed off. Sergeant Edelman. Maybe she didn't find me as rude as I'd thought I came across. I said no. I said I had to get on the road. In that, at least, I wasn't lying. I hope I wasn't rude in saying no, but I wouldn't put any money on it.

I said I'd be in touch. I think she might have been embarrassed about the lunch suggestion.

I get a clear run largely to the end of Drumochter, then everything slows up. A Tesco lorry. That's all it takes. Big fellows to get past as well. Only one person tries. Horns blare. This time no one dies.

They should give out patience at either end of the road. Or perhaps upgrade the whole thing to dual carriageway. Then again, it doesn't go directly to Edinburgh, so why would they?

★ ★ ★

Phone starts ringing around Daviot, not far short of Inverness. Dual carriageway by now, the traffic flying. Down the hill, the big sweep back up. I lift it to see who's calling. No name. It could be some crappy junk voicemail on a subject I know nothing about, as I always cut them off before they get anywhere near the point of what they want me to buy. But I get that feeling. The one that insists I pick it up, just in case.

There's a parking spot fast approaching, check of the mirror, foot on the brakes, and swerve quickly off the road. A guy blares his horn at me as he goes by, but he wasn't even close. Just one of those people, doing it because he can.

'Westphall.'

'Inspector…'

It's the DHM from Tallinn. He could be calling about anything. Baden is still out there, and very soon the Estonians are going to tire of him, and they will release him and it will be up to the Embassy to help get him home. There could be developments around the body harvesting farmhouse. There could be developments on any aspect of the case coming from the Estonian police. But that's not it. I can tell from his tone. One word, three syllables, that's all it takes, and I know why he's calling.

'Kenneth,' I say.

'I'm afraid I've got some…' he begins, but stops himself, words catching.

He looked like he cared. He'd obviously been troubled by what to do about Dorothy for a few weeks, and then I walked into his office, and he thought, here's a chance to give Dorothy something to do. Get her to take a break, visit a friend, but combine it with doing the police, and the Embassy, a favour.

Maybe it never even seemed like a good idea to him at the time. It was just an idea, and he took the chance.

'Dorothy never went to Paris. She called her friend, said she was exhausted after the drive, and that she'd spend the night in Brussels in a hotel… She said she'd go on to Paris this morning.'

I know what's coming. I've seen the hotel room. I know what happened. I know what went through her head. And now, sitting here at the side of the A9 on the approach to Inverness, I can see her sitting in the bath, the water turned red.

And there it is, that thing that was just out of reach, the reason the thought of Dorothy had been troubling me. That was why she told me her story. It doesn't matter how fanciful it was. It doesn't matter if it was true. Perhaps the whole thing was a fabrication of a deluded, ill mind. That she told me, that she chose her moment to finally let it out, showed that she'd made her decision. It was time to go. It was time to give up.

Her telling me was her last act. The passing on of her narrative. Making sure her story was known, and that it would not die with her.

I should have known. Should have seen it coming, and not just as a quiet, troubled voice at the back of my head.

And what would I have done?

* * *

Knock on his door, wait for the call, and enter. He's sitting at his desk, music playing quietly on an iPod. As is usually the case with him, it's film music. I sometimes wonder if he intends it to be scene appropriate, appropriate to the act that he imagines is about to play out in the office, although of course he always turns it off when he's talking to someone, in person or on the phone.

He clicks it off, just as I was beginning to recognise it. The music is gone, the tune leaves my head and instantly I've forgotten it.

He looks tired. I wasn't fearful of his reaction, but I have been constructing some sort of argument in my head to defend myself. Sitting down across the desk from him I realise I likely won't need it.

'I'm going to send you on one of those courses,' he says.

'What courses?'

'Overcoming fear of flying.'

'No.'

'Yes. You're booked on it two weeks today. As long as this is cleared up by then. If not, we'll get it pushed back.'

'I can't.'

'You can. The courses are aimed at people like you.'

'With all due respect…'

'You can go on the course, or you can face a charge of insubordination and disobeying an order, with a potential suspension and loss of rank. If you'd prefer to go in front of the police tribunal then we can arrange for that to happen.'

Steady look across the table. I know which one I choose. I'm not going on one of those courses. They're not for people like me, they really aren't. Is there a section, for example, where they address the fear you feel as a result of being in a helicopter that was fired upon and hit by the Taliban?

They might point out that that's unlikely to happen to your EasyJet flight to Marbella. But I know which I'd rather take. I'm not getting on the flight. I'd take the suspension. I'd take the demotion. I'd take dismissal.

It's a pointless exercise. I know, he knows. I might never have to get on a plane again in my police career, and if I do, it's liable to be in the next week to return to Estonia. He thought of a compromise because he doesn't want to discipline his senior officer. This is his way out. I appreciate that's what he's trying to do.

And it's not that I don't want to give him his way out. I can't, that's all.

It's not for now, however. There's a case to be solved, a strange one at that. He doesn't really know me well, not yet. It's only been seven years. If I refuse, he might well imagine I'm playing a game, trying to call his bluff. I don't mean to, I don't want to.

'Yes,' I say.

'You'll go on the course?'

'Yes.'

'I can't have you doing this. It was round the station in minutes. If they see you doing that, how do you think it makes them feel? What message does it send?'

He's not looking for me to answer. So I don't. There's a pause. A long-held stare across the desk.

'You've got nothing to say?'

'I thought the questions were rhetorical,' I say, trying not to sound glib.

'Yes,' he says. 'Yes.'

'You know my history, sir.'

'It was seven years ago, Inspector.'

'Not so long.'

With fear, a lifetime isn't so long. He knows that. He has nothing else to say. If at some point he imagined a great dressing-down because he'd ordered me to face my greatest fear and I cracked, it's vanished over the previous forty-eight hours. Over the time it took me to make my convoluted way home.

'And you told a Sergeant Edelman in Anstruther about Baden?'

'It seemed preposterous not to, sir.'

And so it was. I'm not letting him go anywhere near that one. He can be mad at me if he likes, he can find some spurious reason to mark down my annual report if he wants, when he's really doing it because of this. It's up to him. But keeping cases to yourself is just plain stupid.

He presses the intercom. 'Is Natterson in the station?'

'Yes, sir.'

'Send him in.'

He finally breaks the stare, looks down at the file that's open in front of him. Lifts a pen, taps it a couple of times. I spoke to Natterson earlier, before and after going to Anstruther. The care home acknowledged that at one time there had been a sister who came, but that Elsa always refused to see her. They said they couldn't give me any contact details for her. I put Natterson on to the task of locating her, while I went to Anstruther. Not that I quite couched it in those terms.

Natterson comes into the room, nods at me, sits down.

'Nat,' says Quinn, with a nod, 'I know it might be awkward for you, but I'm going to leave you in charge of the case. The Inspector will do what you tell him. It's the way it's going to be on this one, as a result of what happened in Tallinn.'

We both nod. *What happened in Tallinn.* Like some black and white, tension-filled spy movie from the early sixties, starring a couple of guys you've never heard of before, and a cameo from Orson Welles, mailing it in and owning every scene. That all it amounted to was me hiring a car rather than getting on a plane doesn't sound so terribly exciting.

The part of the story with Dorothy doesn't really belong in a movie from the early sixties. I'm not sure where it belongs.

I need to examine it. I need to think about every minute I spent with her, every word that she said. I need to hear it again in my head, play it back over. That's for later, however. For the moment, I need to concentrate on the peculiarities of this case. And I need to remember my place.

'We'll discuss where you've both got to, and then you can bring it together, Nat.'

'Yes, sir.'

'You've already brought each other up to speed?'

We both nod, although I haven't seen Nat since I got back.

'More or less.'

'Are we any closer to explaining why we have two sets of identical DNA from two different people? Answer that, it seems to me, and we'll be a long way to explaining this ridiculous situation.'

Ridiculous. Nice way to put it.

'There's the possibility that they were twins,' says Natterson.

'Yes.'

'You've got the request for further examination of the DNA, so we'll need to see how that plays out.'

That's an interesting way of putting it from Natterson. How it plays out. The DNA of identical twins seems to be just that – identical – unless you want to spend a lot of money getting a month-long test run on the two sets to pare them back to the most basic level possible. Seeing how it plays out will mean Quinn being persuaded that it's worthwhile doing, and spending what might well be a quarter of the station's annual budget on one case.

'Without that, though, we're not going to know whether the DNA, if it contains minor discrepancies, shows the men to have been twins, or whether, if it's exactly the same down to the sub-microscopic level, we're looking at the DNA of the same man.'

'Is it possible there was a twin?'

He looks at us both.

'Absolutely no sign of that whatsoever. If there was a twin, he was a secret.'

'We need to explore that nevertheless,' says Quinn. He takes a moment, taps a finger on the desk. 'Any other possibilities?'

'The most obvious is that the DNA we have here, on record, was somehow taken from the man who is currently in Estonia, twelve years ago.'

Quinn grunts.

'Or that someone in Estonia is sending us duff gen,' adds Natterson.

Duff gen. There's really no excuse for that phrase. Game face.

'Intentionally false, rather than duff,' I venture, although I immediately kick myself as it feels a little like competing with him.

Quinn nods and looks back at Natterson.

'That's what I meant,' he says. 'Under this scenario, the Estonians still had Baden's DNA on record from twelve years ago. Someone in their police force wants us to believe that this man is Baden, so they send this DNA.'

'Why would they want us to think that?'

He shakes his head. They both look at me. I'm the one who's just been to Estonia after all.

'The detective... my contact, Kuusk, seemed like a decent guy. His boss was a little passive aggressive, but she seemed to know what she was doing. There was definitely something going on down at that farmhouse, though. I mean, other than what had been taking place. There are layers of stuff that I don't know about, and didn't get close to investigating. And of course, I don't know the language, so who knows what they were saying to each other.'

'All right,' says Quinn, 'anything else? Any other possible explanations? You double-checked against a basic mistake?'

'Triple,' says Natterson. I know him. He probably octuple-checked against a mistake.

'So, what else?'

Quinn opens his hands, inviting in all possibilities. Natterson has nothing. He shakes his head. I don't really have much either, but my head is full of Dorothy's story, the absurdity of it. The notion that anything is possible.

'Maybe there really were two John Badens,' I say.

They look at me.

'How d'you mean?' asks Quinn.

'There were two of him. One of him died. The other was kidnapped.'

'But how could there be two of him?'

'I don't know, sir, and I know it doesn't make sense. Maybe he split into two in some sort of strange metaphysical way. Some sort of psychosis, schizophrenia maybe, that manifested itself... that somehow manifested itself physically.'

I don't seem to be getting much enthusiasm for that suggestion. Staring curiously, they're making me feel slightly uncomfortable, although probably because I made them feel uncomfortable first.

Perhaps this is the lasting impact of my twenty-four hours with Dorothy; an openness to accept the possibility of the implausible.

'Maybe something happened with time,' I add, with a slight movement of the hand. 'Maybe one of him walked in from a parallel world.'

Quinn isn't entirely looking at me like I just arrived from a science fiction convention dressed as a Klingon, but there's not a lot of credence behind the eyes.

'Or maybe we can keep it grounded in reality,' he says curtly.

'Either,' says Natterson quickly, to move the conversation on from my brief excursion into a fantasy netherworld that clearly doesn't exist, 'we're looking at the twin angle, or there was some duplicity taking place twelve years ago, or in Estonia today. I think that's where we should be concentrating for the moment.'

Quinn nods.

'Yes. Spend a little more time on Baden's younger self, his life leading up to his death. We need to know if there was the slightest hint of some other brother who was never recorded. Maybe we even need to go back to his birth. Look at his birth certificate, check the hospital where he was born. Perhaps the parents wanted to keep the twin off the grid for some reason. People do the most peculiar and criminal things, so you never know.'

'One of us should speak to Rosco,' I venture.

The usual Rosco shadow crosses his face, but he nods all the same. A dark, grudging nod. Talk of Rosco is as liable to be uncomfortable for everyone as talk of the physical manifestations of a split personality. Rosco, at least, is grounded in the real world.

Quinn stares at an indistinct point on the floor between me and Natterson. We wait in silence. No one talks about Rosco around here, at least not when Quinn's around. Nearly cost him his job.

'You'd better handle that,' he says looking up at me, eventually. I can feel Natterson's relief.

'I wondered, also,' I begin, 'if I shouldn't try to speak to my old crew. Still got a couple of connections in London. See if there's anything on Estonia that the DHM at the Embassy didn't tell me, or that maybe he doesn't know.'

'Yes, that makes sense.'

The thought of Rosco, and at what he sees as a troubling case, is still showing on his face, the creased brow, the lugubrious downturn of the lips.

'Yes, yes, that's how we'll split it. Nat, you continue to follow the current events. Speak to anyone who knew Baden and Emily King. Ben, you look into what happened twelve years ago. And, you know, do the other thing with your old lot.'

I like how people can't even say SIS sometimes, as though just acknowledging the name is breaking the Official Secrets Act. I mean, seriously... They have a website! They use their actual building in James Bond movies!

'Yes, sir.'

'Yes, sir.'

A nod and then Natterson and I rise and leave the room, closing the door quickly behind us. Out into the small, open-plan office at the heart of the station. The usual quiet bustle, seven or eight people, a mix of police and civilians, going about their business.

'Right...,' says Natterson.

'Sorry about the intentionally false rather than duff line,' I say. 'Didn't mean to sound that pompous.'

He smiles. 'That's OK. Just thought you were being a bit of a douchebag.'

'A fair call... Did you find the sister? Elsa's sister?'

'Yes, she's in Inverness. Going over there to speak to her now. You want to come?'

'I should get on. Let's cross-check later, although I'm not sure anything Elsa said is going to be cross-checkable.'

Checks his watch.

'Conflab at six?'

'Sure. Meet you back here.'

26

Rosco was married for a couple of years at some point.

A couple of years.

I've never been married, but that barely sounds long enough to get to know what your wife likes to have for breakfast, never mind make a decision that you don't want to live with them any more. Everyone, it seems, just assumed that she didn't realise that Rosco lived on a diet of pure alcohol, although how could anyone have missed it? She came out of nowhere, she married him, and then she left. Must have been something in it for her. Something more than his exorbitant Detective Inspector's salary.

Whatever her reasons, whatever went on in that sad little relationship, once she left, Rosco's drinking became worse, and his life tanked. There was a litany of mistakes, and then finally, when he'd screwed up one case too many, and the inevitable disciplinary proceedings had revealed just how frequently Quinn had covered for him and tried to keep his officer's head above ground, Rosco was gone, nearly taking Quinn down with him.

I arrived several months after Rosco left, although the investigation into his conduct was still ongoing. I was the guy to trust around the station, because I hadn't been tarnished by association.

As far as everyone knew, Rosco's story was as old as modern law enforcement. He worked long hours, he drank too much, he drove his wife away with unusual haste. However much drinking Rosco had been doing before, it upped a notch or two. The station had to watch an officer in free fall. Quinn innately liked him – everybody did – so tried to help him through it, rather than suspending him or making efforts to kick him out.

Then one day, could have been any old day, Rosco went to interview an assault victim, accompanied by a female constable. Constable McDonald. Aly McDonald. Had a good career ahead of her, until that day.

She could see that her Inspector was drunk, but couldn't force the issue. He was the boss. She tried to talk him out of going to the victim's house, but failed. So she went with him in the hope that she would be able to mitigate any damage he might do.

To cut a painful episode in police history short, he more or less accused the girl of asking to be assaulted by the manner of her dress and through her actions, and then when her father, who was present, took issue with him, he ended up in a fist fight with him, causing several hundred pounds' worth of damage in the living room, and ending with Rosco making a drunken arrest.

From there on it didn't play out well. He was suspended, and the internal investigation raked over everything he'd done in his career. Well, I daresay, no one looks good under that kind of scrutiny. Rosco's career, certainly, did not survive the intimate inspection.

He was ejected from the police force, and Quinn was left calling in favours to not go down with him. Managed to cling on to his job, but that was it for his career. He was left needing to maintain a good, solid presence in Dingwall, keep his head down and try to hang on to his post as long as possible, because it was more or less certain that he wouldn't ever be getting offered another one.

Rosco is still around, living in the middle of Dingwall, like some sort of lingering effect of an STD, just to remind the police of their problematic past. He has a job working security at the timberyard over behind Evanton. He's been stopped for drink-driving, driving without insurance, and driving without a licence. He's been in a couple of fights. He's been convicted of causing a public disturbance on three occasions. If there was a three-strikes law, he would have been in prison several years ago, and he wouldn't be getting out.

Yet plenty of times you see him, trudging through town, obviously sober. Lost a lot of weight, cheeks drawn, coat closed and held tight to his body with his hands in his pockets, regardless of the weather. He says hello, even though I was the guy who eventually got his job. Still calls me 'newbie'. That doesn't get old.

There's something about him, though. Something that separates him from the clichéd figure of the drunk ex-policeman. An air of tragic melancholy, rather than bitter recrimination.

He was cast off into the ocean and allowed to sink. The fact that he didn't die and is still wandering the streets of the town is a cause of embarrassment to Quinn, but he faces that embarrassment by pretty much never talking about him. A classic case of washing your hands of the problem, and doing your damnedest to pretend that it never existed. However, knowing how much effort he put in to try to save Rosco in the first place, perhaps Quinn is the one who deservedly owns the bitterness now.

I decide to first talk to the former Mrs Rosco. She turns out, like so many of the players, to no longer be anywhere near Dingwall, having moved to Aviemore. I call, I speak briefly to a woman who claims to be the cleaner. She says Debbie Rosco is working and won't be home until later. Tells me, rather glibly, that she doesn't know her employer's work phone number, where she works, or even what she does. I choose not to pursue it, perhaps because it was always going to be an uncomfortable conversation that was liable not to get me anywhere in the first place.

★ ★ ★

Don't even have to get in the car, Rosco has stayed so close to the centre of town. A small apartment, just back from Tulloch Street. The light is grey, heading towards early evening, but the sky is mostly clear.

There's a slight warmth in the air, even though it's November, preventing there being any crisp, autumnal feel to the late afternoon.

I get to the door of his block just as he's emerging. The door closes behind him, he pulls his coat in close, as he always does. Nothing passes across his face as he sees me.

'Newbie,' he says, as he starts to walk by.

'Need to chat, Inspector,' I say.

He stops, glances back at his house, then looks at me.

'Something going on in there?'

'About one of your old cases.'

His eyes drop, he seems to consider whether or not that's something he wants to do, then he shrugs.

'I'm on my way out to Evanton. Shift's starting in half an hour. You can sit with me on the bus, or give me a lift if you like.'

Evanton's not so far, it's not like I'm going to find myself in the car in the middle of nowhere.

'I'll drive,' I say. 'Car's at the station.'

Not a flicker of discomfort at having to go anywhere near there, or at seeing any of his old colleagues who turned their backs on him. He just doesn't care.

'How are you doing?'

He gives me a glance, maybe gauging the level of my concern.

'All right. Been dry two months, if that's what you're asking.'

'You going to meetings?'

Shakes his head.

'Weren't you supposed to be?'

'At some point. My obligation ran out. So I don't go. Never did me any good anyhow.'

I try to remember when his obligation would have run out. I was sure from the file that he was still under court orders to attend. I notice that he's watching me, as if reading the thoughts unfolding in my head.

'You've been reading my file,' he says.

'Yes.'

A curious look, but he doesn't chase it any further. I'm not going to start the conversation about Estonia until we're in the car, because I'm wary of him not getting in the car at all.

'I drink, Newbie. Go on benders. Sometimes I do stupid stuff. I've got this, I don't know, this inner voice. This other person who lives inside me. Like that, you know, that thing in *Lord of The Rings*. That's me. A bit psycho. That other guy, that voice, he tells me not to. He tries, he really does. And I go for these periods. I don't know, months sometimes. Six, seven months. Then something sets me off, and I know. It's not even a desperate lunge at a bottle. It's just something inside that tells me. Something says, now, now you have to go down to the supermarket and load up. You're going to go home, and you're going to drink everything you've bought. Might be over a weekend, or it might be that I'll take the days off work that I think I'll need.'

'Why don't you... when you know it's going to come, why don't you speak to someone? Go to a meeting then.'

'I don't want to.'

We walk on in silence for a while. A couple of people say hello to him.

'What kind of thing sets it off?' I ask.

He shrugs. Getting close to the station.

'Anything. Nothing. There was a girl once. Knew each other in school. Had a thing for a while, but it didn't work out. If anything it was like a Springsteen song, rather than some romantic love affair that one of those eighteenth-century poets would've written about. Anyway, we were young, went our separate ways. But you know, I always had that first love thing about her. The thought of her always made me smile. Inside, at any rate, smile inside. Still, didn't think about her much, hadn't even seen her in fifteen years.

'One day I hear she's dead. Cancer. Forty-three. Three kids under ten and a husband. How's that for life kicking you in the face? I went to the funeral. Watched those kids, watched the husband trying to keep it together. I thought, that could have been me. I mean, it probably couldn't, or at least, not any more than any other guy she went out with in her life. But that didn't matter. Her death, the awfulness of that afternoon, the sad kid, and the slightly younger confused kid, and the youngest, the youngest of all, just not getting it, running around, enjoying seeing everyone, having fun in her new dress...

'Got back to Dingwall, had to work that night. So I did. Didn't miss a minute. I got home the next morning. Sunday. Too early for the supermarkets to be selling booze. I had a cup of tea, a bit of toast. Hands were shaking. I was there, on the dot, when they opened up the booze aisle.

'I was wasted for five days. The following weekend, back on the night shift, no problem. Didn't miss a minute. All I had to contend with was the disappointment of that other guy who lives inside my head.'

Sitting in the car on the way out of town. My heart sank as he talked, and now I'm down there again. I'm with him, as I was with Dorothy, in that lonely place. I can feel his misery, and what makes this much worse is the knowledge that asking him about the Estonia story is liable to set him off. Whatever happened over there, I doubt it will transpire to have been a great moment in his career.

Do I want to throw him back into the alcoholic pit just for the sake of a chance at some sort of resolution in this case? He's liable to not tell me anything anyway, so I'll be left empty-handed and he'll be in the gutter. You can't keep going on benders all your life. Eventually it knocks you down, then it knocks you out. And then you die.

Or should I accept that it will happen anyway, so I might as well make the most of what Rosco can tell me now?

How callous do you want to be today, Detective Inspector?

'Out with it, Newbie,' he says after a few moments' silence. 'I'm getting out the car in under ten minutes. What d'you need to know? That idiot Harlequin back on the scene, is he?'

I came across the name Harlequin while going through the file – a petty complaint from a petty criminal over a petty business. It barely registered.

I'm going to sound stupid and weak if I don't just get on with it. We've all got our crosses; I need to ask the question, and he needs to deal with it however he sees fit.

'I have to ask you about the case in Estonia,' I say.

Clear bit of road, no cars in the immediate vicinity, I take the opportunity to look at his face as I ask. There's a flinch in the eyes, a betrayal – like he knew all along that was what I was going to ask about – then the blank expression resumes.

'Can you talk about it?'

'Always have,' he says. 'Doubt I'll have much more to say than what's written in the report.'

'Can you talk about it truthfully?'

The words initially met with silence. I wonder if anyone questioned the veracity of his report back in the day. It wasn't really our case, after all, we wouldn't have had the resources to spend much time on it. When an officer returned, did some more work on it, and then more or less said that the case was closed with nowhere else to go, they probably couldn't take him off it quickly enough. The Estonians would have been happy too. A dead Brit on their patch could be problematic, but if the officer leading the investigation into it wasn't interested, that was nine-tenths of the battle.

'You read my report?' he asks. Like a politician. Even though we know the report is a whitewash, he'll keep banging on about the report, as it supports his story.

'I don't believe it,' I say. The *Evanton 2* sign flashes by before the headlights. Need to get on with it. I could speak to him tomorrow, of course, but I have a feeling that tomorrow will find him flat on his back, or kneeling over the toilet bowl. Depends on how his body takes to occasional bouts of heavy drinking. Everybody's different.

'Reading your file, there's a clear pattern. Despite what the tribunal said, you were a good officer when you started out. Now, I know you can't look at it and say that you went downhill directly after, and as a result of Estonia, but you had your moments before you went, and didn't have many after you got back.'

He doesn't speak, although I give him the space. Not much space, though, as we don't have the time for it.

'What happened over there, Inspector? What aren't you telling me?'

'There's nothing,' he says. 'The guy disappeared, then he turned up dead. I spoke to, I don't know, a bunch of people. Spent a couple of weeks out there. Didn't get anywhere. I mean, big surprise, I usually didn't get anywhere.'

'Do you watch the news?'

Nothing. Driving in a car isn't the best place to interview someone, especially when you want to look in their eyes to get some idea of what they're thinking, but I know that he wouldn't be sitting in my company at all if he actually had the choice. I can hardly arrest him for that.

'There was a woman murdered in Anstruther a couple of days ago. Emily King. The wom–'

A small noise escapes his lips, but when I look round his face is still as expressionless as before.

'Everybody dies,' he says.

'Had you any idea what happened to her?'

Pause.

'Thought she hung around Dingwall for a while. Then she left. That was it. I wasn't going to keep tabs on her, was I?'

At least he's talking for a moment, albeit just talking at the edges. It's a start, but when he stops, another quick glance shows him staring at the dashboard, his eyes glazing over.

'John Baden turned up last week.'

He barks out a laugh.

'Walked into a police station in Tartu. Said who he was. Didn't seem to have realised that he was already dead.'

'Where'd he been all these years?' he asks.

The fact that his first question does not question that Baden was who he said is noted.

'Held captive in a farmhouse, where his body was harvested and he was used for sex.'

I glance at him, catch his curious look, then he turns away again.

'If John Baden's dead, who's this new guy?' I ask.

'I don't know,' he says. 'Maybe Baden isn't dead.'

'You brought back his body before.'

'I did.'

'You stated in the file that he was buried.'

'He was.'

'We disinterred the coffin.'

Nothing. I give him a quick look. Face blank, staring straight ahead.

'There were ashes in the coffin. No one buries ashes in a coffin.'

'I must have made a mistake,' he says.

Approaching the Evanton turn-off. I briefly contemplate continuing to drive. Along this stretch of the A9, the roundabout at Nigg excepted, I won't need to slow down enough to let him jump from the car for over a hundred miles. And I can take the roundabout at Nigg fast enough if I choose. Still, I'm not there yet. I'm not about to kidnap the guy. I'm not about to make him late for his job. For all he says, it's hard to imagine that it's not already on a shaky peg.

I slow down, turn off the main road. 'Half a mile, take a right,' he says.

'You need to tell me something I don't know,' I say. 'You need to tell me what wasn't in the report. You need to tell me why the body was cremated.'

'Everything was in the report, Newbie. Everything. If there was anything to say, I would have written it down. That's what we do. We're police officers.'

'Then why did your career go down the toilet afterwards?'

'Same old same old, Newbie,' he says, and his voice has lost the previous edge.

He was getting agitated, into a state where maybe he was going to blurt something out. Not now, however. The moment is gone. I moved the questioning on from Estonia to his life. He's happy to talk about his life. He's an expert on his life.

'I made a mess of it. Got married, threw it away, wife left me, I made a bigger mess.'

A tired, sad, resignation. A voice that knows that this time tomorrow he's going to be sitting alone in his house with a bottle.

'Here.'

I turn off to the right. Into a car park, large storage buildings illuminated in the gathering gloom.

I pull in close to the entrance, and turn the car so it's not facing where he's going. As though that might distract him for a moment.

'Tell me one thing from Estonia twelve years ago that I'm missing.'

He laughs ruefully, a slight shake of the head, head bowed.

'It's too late, Inspector,' he says. 'Now, if you'll excuse me, I need to get in a bit early so I can ask for the next few days off.'

27

Walk back into the station. Need a cup of coffee, tiredness having swept in. Despite the decent night's sleep in Glasgow last night, it'll take a day or two to fully recover from the drive through the night with Dorothy.

Dorothy, and her sad story, comes and goes. The guilt sits upon me. Stupid guilt. Like there was anything I could have done. If I spoke to someone – did she want me to speak to someone, was that why she told me – what would they think? What would they think of her tale? They would think she was making it up, telling stories. If they thought she actually believed it, as I am absolutely sure that she did, then they would think her ill.

So why then am I so unquestioning? And does my credulity make me more open to some incredible explanation for the mystery of Baden and the two men with identical DNA?

Sit down across from Natterson. He's on the phone, although he hangs up as soon as I appear. Detective Sergeant Sutherland is sitting beside him.

'Ben,' says Natterson. One cup of coffee in my hand, I'm immediately aware of my selfishness.

'Sorry,' I say.

Sutherland shakes his head.

'It's fine,' says Natterson. 'Had one earlier... You spoke to Rosco?'

The civility of Natterson. He probably had a coffee six hours ago.

'Yes. On his way to work.'

I imagine Rosco the following day, drunk and hopeless, and have to forcefully remove the image from my head. Take some coffee, shake my head, as though the physical act will help dislodge the picture of despair.

'You look tired.'

I wave it away.

'He's not talking. There's something there, but I don't know what. Rosco... I don't know if there was anything particular to that investigation with Rosco, but there's some all right stuff on his record beforehand, and nothing after it. I feel like we need to get to the bottom of it to help with this.'

'Speak to his ex-wife?'

'I called, didn't get her. I'm not sure though. The fact that she left him… Maybe she was just part of the problem. Maybe she was an escape, and then she realised that's all she was to him, and wasn't committed enough to stick around.'

Like I would know anything about commitment. Natterson doesn't say anything to that. Maybe he's thinking about himself and Ellen. Maybe he's wondering if I just read that in *Cosmopolitan* while waiting at the dentist's.

'But we should talk to her tomorrow. I'll try to get hold of her in the morning. We can imagine all sorts, because this seems like a complex business, but maybe all that happened was that he was drinking from day one, and she mistakenly thought she could stop him. Maybe he slept with someone else. Maybe she knows nothing about the Tallinn business and what it did to him, even though they married shortly afterwards. Presumably they were together when he went out there.'

'You'll talk to her, or d'you…'

'I'll do it.'

Look at my watch. I shouldn't leave it until tomorrow.

'We didn't talk about our hit-and-run with Quinn,' says Natterson.

'Where are we with that?'

Natterson looks at Sutherland.

'Analysis of the paint left on the clothes of the victim indicate the car was a Ford vehicle. Although we've had differing eyewitness accounts of the vehicle, the consensus appears to be that it was most likely a Mondeo. White. We've no number plate. Waverley was walking along the High Street, the Mondeo left the road, took him out at a pace, then headed quickly up Park and turned left onto the eight sixty-two. There was one guy who decided to try to follow him, rather than stop to help the victim, but he lost him out of town, over the hill on the Ullapool road. We think maybe he took the Marybank turn-off, then went who knows… possibly back through Beauly to Inverness. Could have gone anywhere. We've been looking at what CCTV we have for the area, but as you know, it's not especially extensive.'

'Is it possible the car just lost control? The driver was using their iPod or spilled their Starbucks mochaccino?'

'Possible. If you want to kill someone, hitting them with a car isn't the best option, if you're only going to hit them once,' says Natterson nodding. 'More liable just to leave them hospitalised.'

'Maybe that's all that was intended,' says Sutherland. 'Basically, though, we don't know. With a lot of accidental hits the car will slow down, there'll be that moment of *oh crap, what have I done, should I stop?* before the panic sets in. This guy was gone, like hitting Waverley and escaping were all part of the process.'

'Where have we got to on a possible connection between Waverley and Baden?' asks Natterson.

'Thunderbirds are go,' says Sutherland, with no affectation at all.

Everybody at the station likes Sutherland. Decent man, honest, always has time for people. More than anything, just damned good at his job. And he says things like *Thunderbirds are go*.

'They were at Aberdeen together.'

'Same time as Emily King,' says Natterson, and Sutherland nods.

'All three of them together.'

'Was he doing the same course as the other two?'

'No, he wasn't. Waverley was doing economics and philosophy. But they were all in the Young Conservatives Association.'

'There was a Young Conservatives Association at Aberdeen?'

'Still is,' he says.

'Anything further?'

'Not much. I was thinking we need to go there tomorrow, speak to a few people, see what kind of records there are.'

'The main thing, though, is that there's a definite link,' says Natterson. 'It means the hit-and-run stops looking like a coincidence and becomes part of the story.'

'Rosco's wife is in Aviemore,' I throw into the mix. 'We could combine that with going to Aberdeen.'

'Yes,' says Natterson, 'that'd be good. OK, OK, what else do we have?'

'Did you speak to Elsa's sister?'

'Didn't manage to have much of a chat, but I did arrange to go by and see her in the morning. I'll go to Inverness early, then Aberdeen, come back via Aviemore. That should work out all right.'

I almost point out that Quinn's instructions had been for me to tackle the historic aspects of the case, and the investigation in Aberdeen is just that, but that would be getting into something incredibly petty, so I don't go there. It just points to the fact that this whole thing is a bit messy and directionless. My fault for taking the car rather than the plane.

Have to stop beating myself up about it.

'Room Two's clear at the moment, isn't it?' I ask.

Natterson looks at Sutherland for confirmation and nods.

'We should set up the room. This thing is getting pretty broad, we need to try to bring it all together. We need to be able to look at the big picture.'

'Of course. I'll...'

'I can do it if you like.'

Natterson hesitates a moment, then says, 'Of course, that'd be great. Thanks, Ben.'

So Natterson does the historic stuff, and I try to pull the current investigation together. In complete contradiction of instructions from the top.

I feel like I'm stepping on his toes, and I have no idea what he's thinking. Is he worried about stepping on my toes by making the Aberdeen trip? It's all monumentally stupid, and would probably be overcome by talking it through, but then I don't feel it's my place to start the conversation, and I'd be worried that he'd take it the wrong way.

Time to stop overanalysing. Check my watch. The tiredness has cleared at just the thought of setting up a whiteboard. That's all it took.

'Right, I'll get that going. Come in when you get the chance and we'll go through things.'

'You should go home and get some rest,' he says.

'I'll just do a couple of hours,' I say, getting up.

Stop after a couple of paces. It's not his place to tell me to go home and get some rest. Rest? Seriously? I don't have to leave, just because he wants to go home to see his kids before they go to bed.

Hesitate, mainly because Sutherland is there, then turn back and decide to say what's on my mind.

'You have the case, Nat, you have the lead, but don't tell me how to do my job, or how much I should be doing my job or when I should be doing my job.'

'I just...'

He starts, but the sentence vanishes beneath his insecurity. The insecurity that I've just helped perpetuate. He was probably only trying to be nice.

And he's right. I am tired. I catch Sutherland's eye, then turn to go.

'I'll get Fisher to come in and fill you in on everything you've missed,' says Natterson to my back. I pause for a moment, and walk through the open plan to the currently vacant Room Two.

28

Setting the boards up twenty minutes later when Constable Fisher knocks and enters.

Fisher is the kind of policewoman who, if she was ever killed on duty, would, without doubt, be on the front page of every newspaper in the country. Young and attractive, just like all those white, male, middle-aged newspaper editors like them.

She has a story, of course. Everybody does. I'm not saying that without the story she'd be some shallow airhead, married to a Premier League footballer and living in a mansion in Cheshire, but it's a shallow world, and people who look like Constable Fisher get on in it without too much effort.

Her father abused her up to the age of sixteen. Her mother knew what was going on, hated it, didn't do anything about it. Fisher finally went to the police, the police didn't want to know, or at least, they didn't want to believe her. No good was going to come of believing that the local councillor, who'd been popular in their little part of Angus for over twenty years, was committing incest, rape, and child abuse.

She might have turned against the police. She might have hated them. She might have hated everybody. But she's strong. Kept her nerve. Left home for a while, kept at it, didn't let the naysayers get in the way. And then she found a sympathetic ear. A police sergeant willing to take up her case. One brave man. That was all it took.

Finally, after months of her father denying everything, and going so far as trying to get his daughter sectioned, the mother finally came to her rescue. It was two against one, and then the father crumbled. His world fell away from him. Was prosecuted and convicted. His wife stood by him nevertheless. As far as anyone knows, she's still living in the same house waiting for her husband to get out of prison.

And young Fisher joined the police, determined that she would be the same kind of officer as the sergeant who'd helped her. That she would listen to every complaint, and not brush people off because what they were saying was going to be inconvenient.

She put her father in prison, and he deserved it. Strong woman, Constable Fisher.

'Inspector Natterson thought you might want these details, sir,' she says, holding a thin report.

'OK, thanks Fish,' I say. 'Hey, you got a few minutes?'

'Yes, of course.'

'OK. Just need to talk this through. You can sit down if you like.'

She knows I don't want her advice or necessarily her input. Just someone to call me out on anything obvious that I'm missing, or spurious that I'm suggesting. I hear her sitting down, although I've now got my back turned. It's about the boards.

On one, headlined Aberdeen, there are pinned pictures of Emily King and John Baden, taken from the original file, and the name of Andrew Waverley. King and Baden were studying biology. I need to find out what that involved in Aberdeen twelve years ago. This is where it starts, and this is where our knowledge is at its weakest.

'You know something about this case?' I ask. 'You've looked at the files?'

'Yes, sir, Inspector Natterson has me on the team.'

'Was there anything, from twelve years ago, was there anything about Waverley? I mean, I don't think there was, I don't...'

'Nothing, sir. We only made the connection after going back through Waverley's life following his death.'

'OK, OK. So, we'll get that looked into tomorrow. This is a big empty hole that we need to fill. The next hole is here.'

Next board along. Estonia, twelve years ago. Once again we have John Baden and Emily King, which starts as a holiday and ends with King sitting alone in her hotel room and Baden dead in a lake. Something happened here, beyond what was in the files, and that's the large hole we have to fill. The largest. Without filling it in, I don't know that we can truly fill in the current hole.

'Do we know if Waverley ever travelled to Estonia?' I ask.

'I'm not sure, sir. I saw somewhere that he'd travelled in Europe, so obviously that could have been it.'

'We need to get on to that. If he's dead now, it's because of something he knows or something he did.'

'If he's dead? He's definitely dead, sir.'

'Yes, you know...' and I finish the sentence with a wave of the hand.

Then we come to the third stage. Present day. Two of the three have been murdered, and the one we thought was already dead, comes back to life.

'OK, tell me about Waverley. Was he married?'

'Yes.'

'When did they meet?'

'Four years ago through an online dating site.'

Pause, turn round.

'He met his wife online?'

'Yes. She's Thai.'

'OK. The Inspector spoke to her?'

'Yes, I was with him. She was a little upset. Just a little.'

'Did she have any idea–?'

'–None,' she says, cutting me off.

'He didn't...?' I start, then shake my head, because it's hardly like I need to be politically correct for Constable Fisher's sake. 'He didn't, like, go to Thailand and buy her, did he? Not that that would make any difference, I don't think.'

'She was already in Scotland. It would appear, from what she said, that her previous husband did just that. Brought her back from Thailand having gone through an agency. He died, his family cut her off. She said she was lonely and went looking for someone, but it might just be she needed the money.'

'Have we checked out her story? It's possible she got all the money, and now she's looking for more.'

'I think Sergeant Sutherland is on that, sir.'

'OK, good. Right, the big question here, the head scratcher, is how the same DNA result could show up from two different people. D'you know where that initial DNA test was taken, and what it was taken from?'

'I'm not sure, sir, I'll need to check.'

'Please do. You have any theories on how the two men could have the same DNA?'

'Must either be twins, or there's something dodgy happening, sir. Something from twelve years ago more than likely.'

'Yes, that's about the size of it.'

Look back at the boards. Tap a contemplative marker pen against one.

'The holes in the first two are dwarfed by the gaping holes in the third. Two murders, and the curious instance of the matching DNA.'

Fisher doesn't say anything, but I'm more or less done with her anyway. As usual, at this point in a case, the first job is in understanding where the gaps are in your knowledge. After that, you systematically start trying to fill those gaps. In some ways, even though I've been on this for a week now, it still feels like we're at the beginning. Just getting to understand the gaps.

Suddenly I see the woman standing at the far end of the pier in Anstruther. The woman who I felt was watching me. The vision flashes across my head and then goes.

I turn and glance at Fisher, who is sitting on the edge of her seat, waiting to be dismissed, I think, rather than in excitement.

I stare at her, while I think about the woman on the pier. It was likely nothing. Why wouldn't she have been looking at me? There were two of us on the pier. I was looking at her, after all.

Of course, I'm trying to be in denial about what's in my mind. There seem to be two John Badens, why then wouldn't there be two Emily Kings? Maybe one of them killed the other. Maybe one of them was standing on that pier watching me.

I'll keep those thoughts to myself. Quinn might be pedantic, but he's right this time. Let's keep it in reality.

Suddenly realise that I'm hungry, and the tiredness is coming back. I need to call it a night, get some food, and get some sleep. I should call Vauxhall Cross, but I can do that in the morning. While Natterson's on his way to Aberdeen.

'Can I go, sir?'

* * *

I stop off at the supermarket on the way home and buy a meal for two for ten pounds. Two salmon *en croute*, potato wedges, two pieces of cheesecake and a bottle of Chilean sauvignon blanc.

I walk into the house, for the first time in over a week. It's cold, and I remember that just before I left it had been mild for a couple of days and I'd turned the heating off. There will still be hot water, however.

I turn the heating on, put the food in the oven, and then go and stand under a warm shower.

When I eat dinner, I stack up the plate with both of the *en croute*, and most of the wedges, pour myself a large glass of wine, then go and sit at the table by the window, with the lights off. I eat in the dark, *Dark On Fire* on the CD player, looking out over the lights of Dingwall and what I can see of the Cromarty Firth.

The weekend is here, but it's going to be a working one for many of us at the station, while we try to make progress on this. I need to speak to Tallinn again in the morning, to see if there have been any further developments. Somehow I doubt Baden will have said anything, but hopefully the police will have progressed a little further. I'll call Kuusk and the Embassy. At some point, presumably, Baden is going to want to come home. Not that he'll find anything, or anyone, when he gets here.

We need to follow the money. Baden's money, from twelve years ago. That's another thing to add to the list. Might help us get somewhere. Fearful I'll forget that by tomorrow morning, I take out my phone and leave myself a note for 9 a.m.

I'm aware that it's not out of the question that I might have to return to Tallinn. We don't really know where this thing is going yet, so it could happen. I need to guard against trying to steer the investigation away from there, if it happens to be naturally moving in that direction. If I need to go, then I need to go. Perhaps Quinn would just save everyone the trouble and send Natterson.

I've driven, taken the train, taken the ferry. There aren't really any other ways to go that would get me there inside of a week and aren't the plane. Even if I lived in London it might not be so bad. The extra length of Britain really adds to it. I start, absurdly, thinking of getting a ferry to Bergen and driving through Scandinavia, as though that might be quicker than speeding through Germany.

I take out my phone and start to look on Google Maps, but there's no point. You end up needing to get the Stockholm – Tallinn ferry or take the enormous drive round the Gulf of Bothnia between Sweden and Finland. It's so long that I get fed up trying to persuade Google that I actually want to drive all the way round it and not jump on the first convenient ferry.

If I have to go, the quickest way would be to drive back the way I came. I think of Dorothy, in her hotel bathroom, the water in the bath running red.

29

Into the office just before eight. Several calls to make, starting with Kuusk and the Embassy. They're two hours ahead, so I won't be waking anyone up or catching someone before they've kickstarted their day with coffee.

Get through to Kuusk, after being passed around four different sections. Everyone I talk to speaks English.

'Inspector, how are you?' he says. Sounds happy to hear from me. 'You got back to the UK all right? I hear you went by bicycle.'

'Funny. I got here, that's all that matters. How's it going out your end? Will you need me to come back to sort everything out for you?'

He laughs lightly.

'I think you might find it is all sorted out by the time you got here, especially if you were going to walk.'

'Tell me.'

'Your Mr Baden does not tell us much we do not already know. Nothing new to add. But we find many things at the farmhouse. The main thing being a mass grave of young men. They'd all had their bodies harvested in exactly the way Mr Baden describes. They are being examined now, the ones that had not decomposed so much. They had surgical scars in the same places that Baden has them.'

'So you think he was telling the truth?'

'There are many truths, Inspector,' says Kuusk unhelpfully, 'but he certainly believes it to be true, and so it may well be.'

'You know who these people were?'

'Russians,' he says, more or less spitting out the word.

'Come on,' I say, blundering into a centuries-old Eastern European feud, 'really? Russians? Is that not just who you all want it to be?'

'Remember who you are speaking to, Inspector. There are divisions in this country, definitely, I do not argue. But we know right from wrong. And if these people were our people, had they been Estonian, they would still have been hounded down, and they would have lived in shame. They would deserve nothing from us, regardless of their ethnicity. However, we know they are Russian. Many have told us about these people. They came into the nearest towns for food, various other supplies.'

'No one suspected anything?'

'We do not know exactly how long they have been there. Your man, Baden, he remembered being moved once, under blindfold. The place he ended up, the room he was in, was not so different. He wondered if they were just playing with his head, and had driven him around before taking him back to where he was before.'

'How long ago was that?'

'He was unable to say. The local police do not say much, Inspector. That is their way. If they had suspicions, if anything had been reported to them, they obviously did not act upon it. Perhaps they are embarrassed and are covering their tracks.'

'What about Stepulov, what is she saying about it? I can't imagine her letting them away with being embarrassed.'

'She is spitting chickens,' he says. I can't stop myself laughing. Like one of those perfectly placed moments of slapstick in a serious drama.

'Feathers,' I say, followed by a quick apology. My Estonian isn't so great after all.

He laughs ruefully.

'She is angry,' he says. 'But this is political now. We must balance these things. We decide who we accuse of what.'

'You don't want to pick a fight with the Russians?'

A pause. No need to go there, although having thought of what he's going to say he finally fills in the gap.

'We are happy to pick fights, we just need to pick the right ones. They may decide that this is not the right one. We shall see.'

'Of course.'

The conversation drifts on. We get back on to the matter of body harvesting, and whether it's ever really going to be that worthwhile keeping someone alive once you've taken the valuable parts. Indeed, wouldn't it be more valuable harvesting all their organs and disposing of what's left? Perhaps they did that with some, kept the others for bone marrow.

There are no more answers, just speculation. I feel that the matter of the body harvesting farmhouse is going to be swallowed up in internal Estonian police politics. And I know that if I need their help to further our investigation at this end, I'll only get it if it really suits them.

* * *

On to the British Embassy. Get straight through to the DHM,

working on a Saturday morning, stressed and tired. Not even ten thirty their time, and he sounds like he's had a long day already.

'The place is reeling about Dorothy,' he says. 'And... well, of course, I'm going to have to answer questions about putting her in the car. Just couldn't... felt like I had to come into work today. There's always something to do.'

'You did it for the right reasons,' I say. 'As you said to me yesterday, there's nothing anyone could have done. She was lost to the world, for whatever reason. She was just... lost.'

A pause. Gathering himself. He must be feeling awful. Stupid and awful. Even though I'd met him, I still had him down as a faceless government official. By that standard, I'd be the faceless police officer.

Nobody's faceless.

'We should talk about Baden,' I say to move the conversation on. 'We need a strategy.'

'Yes, of course... Has anyone come forward at your end? Does anyone even know?'

'No, there's been a complete lid on it. Very impressed that nothing's leaked from your end.'

'A small miracle in itself.'

'The only family we've found is his mother. I spoke to her, and she was convinced he hadn't died all those years ago...'

'I thought she identified the body?'

'She said it wasn't her who made the identification. I chose not to tell her that he'd turned up. She's constructed a nice world for herself, and I made the decision not to put too much strain on it just yet.'

'Probably a good move.'

'So, what would you people usually do with someone like this?'

'Normally, we get the family to take care of things. We do have to tell people we don't run a travel insurance company. Under the circumstances, though, I think the British taxpayer might understand us putting Mr Baden on a plane home. It's where he's going to go when he gets there, that's the question. And the media.'

'Why does there have to be media?'

'There usually is,' he says, 'but then, we've got this far. Maybe we can get lucky. He might want the attention, sell his story, get him started back on his feet. I'm speaking to London, coming up with a strategy. Either way, he's likely to be coming home tomorrow. My vice-consul's going to fly with him.'

As the DHM is talking, Constable Fisher stands across the desk from me, beside Natterson's chair. She looks pale. Troubled. Not the usual sign of some emergency development in a case.

I hold up a couple of fingers, and she nods, but does not move away. Stands still, staring at the floor.

'OK, Kenneth, thanks for everything. We can speak again later today when you've got a bit more of an idea how things are going to play out.'

'Will do, Inspector. Goodbye.'

He doesn't hang up straight away. The silence seems to exist so that words can be dropped into it.

'Kenneth,' I say, after a few moments.

'Yes?'

'You did what you could. All you're guilty of was trying to help her. She was going to do this, regardless...'

I can hear him swallow as my words run dry, stuck in my own remorseful throat. I can picture him, his head resting heavily on his right hand, and then the phone goes dead.

I lay down the receiver with a great sense of unease. Then I look at Fisher, and realise that the awful feeling that has just enveloped me is not just because of the forlorn conversation with Kenneth. Fisher is lost somewhere, doesn't look round when I hang up the phone.

'Fish, what's up?'

She lifts her head. Swallows.

'Inspector Natterson.'

'What happened?'

'There was an accident, just outside Nairn. Not far from the airport rou–'

'–Is he all right?'

'He's dead, sir.'

Her voice breaks. We stare at each other across the back-to-back desks. I realise the peculiar sound coming from the office is almost total silence. This time in the morning it would usually be bustling, and subconsciously I'd noticed it as I spoke on the phone. I glance round, see the shocked faces, look back at Fisher.

Natterson. What age was he? Mid-thirties. I think of the last time I spoke to him, getting tetchy, walking away from him, him still being polite, as he always was, and me not bothering to turn round. A slight shake of the head to remove the thought, throw it away.

As he always was... The thought was right there in my head. How quickly someone moves into the past tense.

'Has anyone been to tell Ellen?'

'Sergeant Sutherland thought the Chief Inspector might want to do it. He's in with him now.'

Swallow, deep breath. I thought that Dorothy had hit me hard, but this is much more real. Dorothy was a strange experience that came and went from my life. Nat was there every day, smiling and slightly awkward. Always helpful, always diligent, always good at his job. And always home in time to play with his kids before they went to bed.

'How did... do we know, do we know what happened?'

The thought finally starts to form. There's already been a hit-and-run. He's investigating a double murder – at least a double murder, for there's so much we don't know here – and now he's dead in a car accident.

'It wasn't...' she starts, then has to swallow and catch her breath. Takes a moment, swallows again, composes herself.

'It was a student. The Nairn police have him now. He was coming the other way, was looking at his phone, changing the music, looked up to the blare of the Inspector's car, as he'd drifted over onto the other carriageway. The Inspector swerved, the kid swerved the same way at the same time. Says he panicked. The cars hit each other head on. His airbag worked...'

Another moment, another swallow, another couple of breaths to compose herself. The next sad horrible line speaks itself, words softly echoing through the dreadful, hollow space of the office.

'The Inspector's didn't.'

30

Driving through to Aberdeen. Wasn't this what I wanted? To be the guy investigating the historical aspects of the case? The thought of that, and of the death of Natterson, sits like a dead weight in the pit of my stomach.

A couple of people to see at the university, but first I'm going to doorstep the former Mrs Rosco in Aviemore. I don't know whether Natterson called her, and neither did Sutherland. There's a fifty-fifty chance she'll not be there, but if I call to say I'm coming, I'd think the odds would drop dramatically.

I'm glad I'm not taking the A96, through Nairn and Forres. I don't know whether the road's been cleared or not, but can't bear the thought of going past the spot where Natterson died. His car might well still be there, one lane cordoned off, traffic filing by in mournful, rubbernecking procession. Can't stand the thought of it. Fortunately I'm on the low road, south to Aviemore.

I keep thinking about Quinn turning up on Ellen Natterson's doorstep. Her in the kitchen, baking with the kids. Having a laugh. In my head, every moment in that house was happy. How would I know otherwise? So, there would have been no shouting, no tense words, just a regular domestic scene, mother and daughters amusing themselves, not even a TV playing in the background, and then the doorbell goes.

Ellen goes to answer it, flour in her hands, wiping them on her apron, or maybe in the nearest dish-towel she could grab, and she opens the door, blowing a loose hair off her face. And there he is. Quinn. The Chief Inspector. The face of Death. And she knows. He doesn't even need to say anything.

There's the moment of shock, and then immediately her maternal instinct kicks in. She glances over her shoulder. She can see into the kitchen, where the younger of the kids is playing with flour and making a mess, while the other is very studiously stirring the eggs into the mix, her tongue sticking slightly out of her mouth.

That's the moment. The moment that will never leave her.

She steps forward, she closes the door behind her, and she hears the news from the Chief Inspector while standing outside on her front step.

* * *

Get out the car, look around. An estate of new houses, tightly packed together, like commuters squeezing onto a platform, though the houses are big. Whatever she's doing now, whoever she lives with, Mrs Rosco is a hell of a lot better off than her ex-husband. I wonder if she still insists that he pays her some meagre alimony.

Up to the front door, ring the bell. Look back over my shoulder. This visit is, of course, entirely speculative, and I really doubt that I'm going to get anything useful from it, but if I am, then it'll be as a result of keeping Mrs Rosco onside. Have to be straightforward and non-confrontational.

The door opens, and I turn back. A woman in her late thirties, long dyed blonde hair, thin face. Something unattractive about her, made all the more unattractive by the make-up and the hair, which are a vain attempt at something that isn't naturally there.

Listen to me; Gok Wan. I hold out my ID.

'Inspector Westphall, from Dingwall.'

She stares at the ID for longer than is necessary, possibly contemplating telling me where to go, then finally looks up.

'Rosco dead, is he?'

It had occurred to me that that was going to be her first thought.

'No, saw him yesterday. He was fine. Sober.'

She nods grudgingly, stands for another few seconds as though contemplating closing the door in my face, then says, 'Suppose you'd better come in.'

She steps back, lets me enter and closes the door behind me. The house is big enough that it has a small central hallway, with stairs up the middle and rooms off either side. She nods to me to go into the sitting room, then follows behind. A large, bright room, can see through to a dining room behind. Television on the wall, a couple of sofas and a single chair. Not much decoration. It all looks sleek and simple and expensive.

If I ever have this kind of money, I think I'd spend some of it on not living so close to other people.

'Cup of tea?'

I usually say no, but have decided that this is an interview that will go better if it's eased into.

'Milk, no sugar, please.'

A few minutes later, we're sitting opposite each other, a sofa each, both of us with a mug of tea in our hand. I noticed the complete lack of sound while I was waiting for her. Total silence. Barely a car outside, not a clock ticking, if there's a plane overhead or so much as a bird, the noise is excluded.

She was safe leaving me alone in the room, as there was literally nothing for me to look at. Not a book, not a DVD, not a magazine, not a photograph.

'So what's Rosco done this time?' she asks.

'I wasn't lying,' I say. 'I spoke to him yesterday. He was fine. On his way to work. Dry...'

She makes a small rueful noise, puts the mug back to her mouth.

'You look miserable enough that you might be here to tell me he's dead,' she says, 'although presumably you wouldn't presage that with how well he was yesterday.'

'I know this was round about the time you got married. Just before it, so maybe you knew each other already.' Feel like I'm rambling. 'I need to ask you about a case Rosco had in Estonia.'

Watch for the expression, but there's nothing more than a slightly guarded shadow in her eyes.

'It's come back in one way or another.'

'Why don't you ask him?' she says, then she nods in answer to her own question. 'Of course, you already did. That's why you're here. He's not talking.'

'No.'

'I never knew anything about his cases, so I'm not sure what I'll be able to tell you.'

'I don't need to know about the case. It's more about Rosco. Maybe... I mean, it's a long shot, in case there's something you can remember that strikes a chord in some way.'

'OK, go on. What do you know?'

Think again about how to put it. I should have been thinking more as I drove down. Basically I'm asking a fairly personal question about their marriage, and I've no idea how it still affects her. Some people, ten years later, would have moved on and wouldn't care. Others, not so much. Not so much moving on.

'Looking at his file... he seemed to change after that case in Estonia. That's how it looks. Pretty decent officer before then, not so good, sliding into... becoming terrible over the ensuing years. I need to know what it was about that case. Although the tribunal found a variety of things to say about him throughout his career, it was bogus. A lot of it... you know, it's like when the press discover one story, and then suddenly find all these other stories that are similar to try to make some sort of a thread.'

She's nodding, so I bring the press analogy to an end. She doesn't need me to explain the workings of a police tribunal that knew what its findings were before it started.

'So the narrative around the station–'

'–Had you met him before yesterday?' she asks.

'Seen him around town, spoken to him a few times. He calls me "Newbie".'

She smiles.

'The narrative around the station is that something happened to him in Estonia. It made him, I don't know, rethink things, made him... did he marry you as a result of it? Was that it? And then it didn't work out, he started drinking more, it affected his performance, it became a downward spiral where it all intertwined, and eventually...'

Nodding again.

'Yes, the latter part's about right.'

'What about the case in Estonia?'

She takes a deep breath.

'Can I ask when you first met him? Where was he on the downward spiral?'

'I'm not going to be much use to you, you know,' she says.

'Anything.'

'I met him a month before we got married.'

Crap. One of those.

'At an AA meeting. We were both dry. We had so many stories. It was going to be great. Except, of course, I'd been dry for three years and he'd been dry for three minutes. He stayed dry until, I don't know, about a week before the wedding. I should have known but I was in love. Horrible, isn't it? To think of it? Me and him, a pair of losers. So I had my doubts, but I loved him. Pushed through it. Got married. He celebrated by getting hammered. Think he was drunk for the rest of the time we were together. And then I left. Sounds terrible, but I didn't love him any more. It came and went, like I was fifteen or something.'

'So what made him drink?'

'Apart from being a police officer?'

'We're not all alcoholics.'

She shrugs, follows it by taking a loud slurp of tea.

'You knew he'd been in Estonia?'

'Think he mentioned he'd been there not long before we met, but I never asked him about it. Don't suppose I cared much. Never thought it was that big of a deal for him.'

'He didn't mention it as being some sort of moment?'

'Some sort of moment? No, no he didn't.'

'Did he ever mention the names John Baden and Emily King?'

She laughs. 'Did he ever mention names? Are you serious? It was twelve years ago!'

I've got nothing else. She shakes her head, and seems a little guilty that she was openly laughing at the line of questioning.

'Maybe he did talk about it. I mean, seriously, maybe he did, but how am I going to remember? He was drunk! I could barely make out what he was saying most of the time, never mind remember any names.'

Well, it's not like I'm surprised. I didn't come out here thinking she was going to suddenly reveal the truth behind Rosco's part in the great John Baden mystery. Not that it seemed like so much of a mystery at the time.

She laughs ruefully.

'Thought I was done with that loser. Can I just say, see when he does kill himself, or ends up dead in a ditch somewhere, you lot really, really don't need to come and tell me. I don't care.'

And that is pretty much that from Mrs Rosco.

Sitting down by the front at Aberdeen, looking out over the beach. The tide is midway, the sea is flat. The same flat sea that stretches all the way to Scandinavia, working its way past Denmark, and into the Baltic to Estonia. Away to our right a ferry moves slowly from the port. The sky is unremarkable, grey and neverending. There is that fluid quality to the light that is so wonderful in the Highlands and north-east. Maybe you get it everywhere, but it seems so clear, so special up here. You can let yourself go in it, like pushing yourself into the water from the edge of a swimming pool. Float away.

The guy sits down next to me, and hands me the coffee. He sets his own down beside him on the bench, then pulls a packet of Gauloises from his pocket. Well, there goes the perfect sea air.

'D'you mind?'

I shake my head. How terribly polite of me. He's all movement, like a spasming fish in the bottom of a boat. Wired. Yet, this isn't speaking to the police nervousness. This is constant nervous energy, his hands always on the move. Fingers rubbing together, a scratch at the ear. But steady, very steady as he lights the cigarette, and blows the first puff of Gallic smoke out the corner of his mouth, away from me. I still, of course, get the full scent of it. Not awful, in its fresh state, but still. On a clear day by the beach, the light smell of the sea in the still, cold air, he might as well be breathing death.

He's thin, early fifties, a slight moustache, hair starting to thin and go grey. Anyone who uses this much energy just sitting still is never going to be anything other than slim.

'So, I get a call to meet Inspector Natterson from Dingwall, then it's on the news that a police officer died on the Aberdeen road just outside Nairn, and now you're here and you're not Inspector Natterson. Does two and two make four on this occasion?'

'Yes,' I say. Need to work, need to focus. Can't think about Nat now.

'I'm sorry. You must have worked with him.'

'Yes.'

'You're involved in the case that he was working on here, or are you asking questions from his notes?'

'It was my... We were working together.'

'He wanted to talk about the Young Conservatives from just

after the turn of the century.'

I spent too long with the turn of the century meaning the early 1900s for it to ever mean anything else, so I take a moment, and then say, 'Yes.'

'I've been involved since the eighties. We had our day back then, but it was coming to an end of course. Dear old Margaret saw to that. Well, actually, you know, they say that Lady Thatcher did for the Tories in Scotland, but in eighty-seven we still had eleven MPs, and in ninety-two we had twelve. It wasn't until the end of the Major years, and until the lying Blair came in and seduced everyone, that the MPs vanished. It wasn't like the mining industry didn't need tackling head–'

'–Is that some sort of default position?'

'What?'

'When you meet someone new, without prompting you immediately start defending Mrs Thatcher?'

He smiles. Rubs his hands along the top of his thigh, takes a draw, lifts his coffee. If you were to study him, you could probably work out a strict sequence in which he makes all his little movements. Like a batsman with a hundred little ticks and affectations before each ball.

'What's your attachment to the Young Conservatives?'

'Kind of a senior adviser. Obviously there's a constant turnover of students, and the new ones in first year learn the ropes by the time they're in fourth year, and they have some idea of what's going on. But it's still good to have an old head around, just to keep everyone grounded, to reign in the craziest of the ideas – at least, I try to – and make sure that relations with the wider party in general are relatively smooth.'

'You have a good memory of everyone?'

'Of course. There have been fewer to remember in the last twenty years, but we keep going. There haven't been any years when we didn't have enough for a committee, and to play a full part in campus political life.'

'You remember John Baden? Emily King?'

Another drag, another small smile. The smile goes quickly, as he obviously remembers what happened to Baden.

'Yes, of course. They were great. A great little group we had going for a couple of years. Very energetic. The Four Musketeers, we used to call them.'

'Who were the other two?'

'There was Waverley. Thomas. He was the plutocrat, the free

marketer. He was going to be driving Aston Martins and living in Mayfair by the time he was thirty. Oh, we had to keep him in check. He was happy to have a health service, but that it should only treat people whose ailments and illnesses weren't self-inflicted. Heart problems because you eat too much junk food? Lung cancer?'

He laughs, as he blows out another plume of smoke, having already given up the pretence of blowing out the side of his mouth away from me. The slight breeze is in my direction in any case.

'Bad legs due to diabetes? Broken leg walking in the mountains? Skin cancer from too many holidays in the Algarve? Anything alcohol-related? All of the above, you'd better have medical insurance. I mean, to be fair to him, he practiced what he preached. He smoked and he drank, and he had very good medical insurance.'

He laughs.

'Emily and John were the go-getters, the ones who were going to change things, the ones who believed in old-fashioned Conservatism. Caring Conservatism. God, I hate the way people just laugh at you now when you mention that. And the bloody SNP... what d'you suppose they are, eh? They ran their bloody referendum pretending to be, God, I don't know, Socialists or some such, but give them five minutes in real power, give them five minutes, and they'll be further to the right than us, or they'll go down fighting in the attempt, as broken and busted as New Labour.'

'Who was the fourth?'

'Ha! There was the joker in the pack. Jason. Jason Solomon. He was the bright one. He was the boy, he really was.'

He scuffs his feet on the ground, takes a last puff of the cigarette then drops it at his feet and grinds the butt into the ground. There's something childlike in his constant movement, back and forth, a tug and a pull and a scratch.

'There are so many students that pass through here,' he says. 'You see them all, don't you? You see them all.'

He stops for a moment, suddenly it all stops. The movement. He looks sadly out to sea, and I follow his gaze. There really is an hypnotic flat calm. The cry of the gulls, the meagre sound of the wash on the beach. Inevitably, there is also the sound of the cars behind us.

The fingers start working again.

'So much hope. Some you know are destined for nothing, and they rarely surprise you, but those who are destined for something, you never know. You never know if they'll live up to their potential.

'I didn't think any of them really had a future in the party. They were bright and brilliant, but they weren't going to be politicians. I saw Emily and John going off and building wells in Africa or something, and although they never quite got around to it, they were going to. I'm sure they were. Waverley went off to do what he'd always said he would. It was just Solomon, the dark devil. It could have gone any way with him. He could have been Prime Minister if he'd wanted. Could have been Judas too. The betrayer. Could have been anybody he wanted. He played them all at the time, that's what I thought. But, you know, it was university politics, nothing more. In the end, what did any of it matter?'

'What did he do? Solomon?'

'Went to Sandhurst. I honestly did not see that coming.'

'Is he still in the military?'

He shrugs theatrically, the full range of movements and curious little habits having returned.

'Couldn't tell you. I don't usually chase them up. I just thought, I'll be hearing about you again. Yet I never did. I don't suppose I would if he's off somewhere, in Afghanistan or wherever, killing ethnics.'

Ignore that.

'What about Emily and John? They were a couple right from the off?'

That's what he'd told me. Gibson makes a noncommittal movement of the head.

'I think that's how they played it, but she was much freer than that, Emily. A free spirit. She and John were close, always the closest, but she had the other two as well, I've no doubt.'

'She had relationships with them...?'

'Oh, you know, it always seemed so complicated. She was probably just fucking them. I don't know, I really don't.'

'Did you think there were tensions between the three guys because of her?'

'Oh, yes. Tensions. That's the word. All in all, however, they were a great team. I didn't mind the tension. Tensions stop things becoming stale. Look at the Beatles.'

'Did you ever witness the guys falling out, ever see them fight, anything like that? Punches thrown?'

He takes another long drink of coffee, then lifts the packet of cigarettes out of his pocket and pulls one out with his teeth.

'I don't remember. They probably did simmering resentment and petty squabbling rather than actual fighting. We're Conservatives, not Neanderthals.'

That makes me laugh. He smirks and then settles back, seems to make a conscious effort to stop fidgeting. We sit together, in sudden silence and silence of movement, and look out over the grey sea. I stare away in the distance. I try, as I seem to do every time I look at the sea at the moment, to work out where the water meets the sky, and once again, despite the liquid clarity of the light, I can't decide.

'Why d'you ask, by the way? John back from the dead?'

* * *

He gives me a few more names to talk to, others who were involved in the club, who knew the main four. The big four, as he refers to them at one point. I decide I ought to ask the others about Gibson, with his greying moustache and constantly moving hands. If I can find any of them alive, of course.

I call Sutherland before I get back in the car, and ask him to find out everything he can about Jason Solomon.

We don't talk about Natterson.

32

I drive back along the A96. Might as well face it. I presume the road will have been cleared by now, and I can hardly go through life not driving along it. What if something takes me to Nairn? Am I going to go via Aviemore and the Dava moor? A road's a road and Natterson is dead and not coming back.

It's dark by the time I'm through Nairn and on the Inverness road anyway. There's nothing obvious to see on the approach to the roundabout. What would it be anyway? Turfed up grass. A lone, damaged tree. The spirit of Natterson, smiling at me, telling me not to worry. *Of course I don't begrudge you your slight show of annoyance. Tell Ellen that everything's all right. I'll see her and the kids in sixty years, give or take a decade.*

I feel it, though, as I go past. I don't need to look. There's a weight that descends. The car doesn't slow down, but suddenly it's like driving through something tangible. Some indefinable part of me feels like it's passing through fog. A thick fog of sadness.

I wonder if anyone else feels it. Would I have felt it anyway, or is it just because I know it's there? But then, I'd been assuming it was the Nairn side of the roundabout. I don't know why. I can't remember exactly what Fisher said. I get the feeling on the other side though, after passing round, and pulling away again on the way to Inverness. I'd already thought, there it goes, the site of Natterson's death, I couldn't see anything, and I didn't feel anything. And then it comes to me.

Natterson isn't standing by the side of the road saying everything is fine, but his spirit is there. His spirit hangs over this place. Forlorn and bereft, clinging desperately to the last place he will ever be on earth.

In the dark there's nothing obvious to mark the spot. No flowers, no tyre marks, no small pieces of car. The accident was ten hours ago now. Long since cleared away. They didn't even need to leave the constant reminder of road traffic collisions that are visible around the country; the yellow board, detailing the date and time, asking for witnesses. They only needed one witness, and it sounds like he owned up on the spot.

No duplicity, just guilt. How long it stays that way will likely depend on whether or not he has rich parents and a good lawyer. One can easily imagine the dead Natterson being held up in court as a reckless driver, the police officer in too much of a hurry, a police officer thinking he's above the rules, the police officer who owned the road. Was the defendant guilty of looking at his iPhone? How can we know? He confessed to it in the immediate aftermath of a terrible accident. The police had no right speaking to him on the spot. Those witnesses who were held up on their way to the airport? They too were traumatised. Perhaps they were angry. They didn't care someone was dead, they just cared that they were going to miss the 0935 hrs to Gatwick. They were quick to blame someone, so they blamed the one who wasn't dead. They blamed the one they could see. How can we trust what anyone saw?

Maybe the kid will just take what's coming to him.

The traffic is heavy around Inverness and onto the Kessock Bridge. I sit in slow-moving silence, the death of Natterson sitting heavily on the car.

* * *

Get back into the station just after six. The place is dead. Slightly fewer people than normal at this time, and everyone quiet. Just doing what has to be done. Sutherland is eating a doughnut. Drinking a cup of tea. Young Martin's still here, also PC Campbell and PC Wright.

'How are things?' I ask, sitting down opposite Sutherland.

'Been comfort-eating all day,' he says, indicating the last of his doughnut. 'We've all been. Hasn't made any difference.'

'No.'

'The boss went round to see Ellen. Said it was horrendous. Like, after she heard how it happened, you know.'

'Somehow makes it worse,' I say, nodding.

If it had been in the line of duty, not exactly normal up in the north, but the possibility is always there, it's somehow expected. A car accident that could have happened to anyone on any given day, however. Of course you're not going to see that coming, you're not in the least prepared for it.

'The boss still in?'

He nods, I glance over at the closed door.

'He sent a couple of people home early.' He indicates the seat in which I'm sitting. 'Bernie went home to be with his wife and kids. Me…?'

He shrugs, puts the rest of the doughnut in his mouth. Sutherland had a wife, but no longer. Fortunately, by some measure, there were no kids, so all they were left fighting over was the CD collection.

Place my hands on the desk, by way of moving things on.

'Sadly...'

'Yep, yep,' he says, trying to shake off the maudlin air. 'Interesting stuff about our Solomon guy.'

He searches around for his notepad. 'So, yes, sure enough he went to Sandhurst. New recruit, February 2001, after leaving Aberdeen Uni the previous summer with Honours in Physiology.'

'What did he do in between?'

'Went to work in an archaeological dig in Syria. Some sort of site of ancient Roman remains.'

'Wonder what state they're in now?'

'Oh, totally destroyed. I checked.'

'Well, if you're going to be slaughtering people, why would you care about Roman remains?'

He shrugs.

'He went to Sandhurst, did the eight-month officer training course, passed... and then left.'

'That sounds strange.'

'Yes. Spoke to Army Records, albeit not anyone who knew him there at the time. His file has a record of his CO and training officers at the time being completely bemused. Didn't make any sense. He was bright, he was good, he was fit. He didn't pass out as top of the class, but he was in the top five. And he left.'

'Then what did he do?'

'I spoke to his mum. They live near Glasgow. He came back up to Scotland, they heard from him less and less. They weren't even sure what he was doing. He never gave them an address or a home phone number. And then they stopped hearing from him altogether. They'd been used to the gaps, so time went by, and then, nothing...'

'When was the last time they heard from him?'

'Late 2002. About nine months before Baden and King go to Estonia.'

'Was he reported missing at any point?'

'His parents did, but it was several months after they'd previously talked to him. And she said the police weren't particularly interested.' Another shrug. 'You know yourself, guys like that. We don't go chasing up people just because they haven't given their mum a call.'

'When was the report made in relation to Baden being found dead?'

'Several months before.'

'But it wasn't made up here, I mean, to Dingwall?'

'No, Aberdeen. That was where they thought he'd gone.'

'OK, well this fits into things as much as all the rest. Did his mother ask why you were calling? She didn't suddenly think we'd found him?'

He nods. 'I had to manage expectations on that front.'

I don't ask how he did that. 'How about Waverley and his Thai bride? Black widow, or lonely in Bangkok, looking for love?'

'Went round to her place, had a cup of tea,' he says.

'Very civil.'

'I'll say this. However she was when the Inspector went to see her, she's not upset. And their house is amazing. Big thing, out past Cromarty, up on the hill above the Sutors. Brilliant view. I mean, really. That guy had some serious money.'

'So, what's your assessment?'

'I'm not going to say she had him killed. Reading further into the death of her first husband, that looked above board. The guy was a drunk, and he had zilch. She got nothing. I guess she faced having to go home or find someone else. I don't know, not sure about residency rights in that case.'

He asks the question with a raised eyebrow, I shake my head.

'Anyway, she meets Waverley online. She says that the women up here weren't good-looking enough for him. He wanted someone sleek, Asian and beautiful.'

'He could have married a Mazda.'

'Funny.'

'And is she beautiful?'

'God, yes.' He shakes his head, as though it shouldn't be allowed. 'Anyway, it looks like a marriage of convenience. She was good-looking enough for him, and he had money. Doesn't seem they got on that well, but he travelled a lot, she had her big house and expense account, and all she had to do was sleep with him every few days or so. Said he was pretty good, but his dick was uncomfortably large.'

'You really got all the details.'

'Oh, yes.'

'So, how does she feel, stuck in a house on the Black Isle looking at the rain? Isn't she desperately homesick?'

'Says she loves it. When I got there I could see her from the driveway. Curled up in a big fleecy jumper, a mug of tea in her hand, looking out over the water.'

I can see her as he talks. A vivid and clear image. Despite the recent death of her husband, and the fact that he's not even buried yet, there's no sadness about her, there's no sadness about the house.

'So we need to consider everything. With all that's going on with the others in this quartet from university, it's easy enough to presume that Waverley's death is tied in with that. But it could be the widow, and it's completely unrelated.'

'I didn't get that impression, sir.'

'And that's not just because she wooed you with her feminine wiles?'

He smiles. 'You get a feeling,' he says.

'I know, I know. Still, let's not lose sight of it. Keep digging, see if they have any friends up here. They must know someone. There might be a story or two about them fighting, or, I don't know...'

'I'm on it.'

'Right.'

Stand up. Take a look around the beleaguered station. I wonder, as second most senior officer, if I should say something. It crosses my mind. Yet, we're not in some American TV show, and whatever I said it'd likely sound forced and awkward.

'I'll go and talk to the boss.'

Another look around the room, tap my fingers on the desk, walk through to Quinn's office.

Knock and enter. Open door policy with Quinn, even though he keeps his door closed. He's standing at the window, his hands behind his back. No music playing. Turns as I enter.

'Ben,' he says. 'Come in.'

I contemplate going to stand by the window with him, but he's not looking at anything, other than the reflection of the room and a few raindrops on the glass. He waits for another few moments and then comes and sits behind his desk.

'How was Ellen?' I ask.

A slight shake of the head. He stares off to the side, one hand resting lightly on the desk, the other on the arm of the chair. His look is slightly lost. Suddenly get the feeling that, unlike his staff out in the station who have had to get on with the job, he has spent the bulk of the day beneath a cold blanket of sorrow.

'We need to look out for her,' he says.

'I'll go and see her tomorrow.'

'Yes, please do.'

'Does she have anyone coming to stay? Her mother maybe?'

'I wasn't there long. She didn't want me in the house, didn't want the children to see. She said she'd call someone. She said she'd get her brother to help out with everything.'

'Did she get hold of him?'

He looks up, almost as though he's suddenly aware that he's actually talking to someone.

'I don't know. I called a couple of times this afternoon, but there was no answer.'

Look at my watch. Not long before seven.

'I should go round now,' I say.

'Yes, that'd be good. You should. If you see her, call me later.'

'Will do.'

I'm waiting for him to ask about Aberdeen, but I get the sense that it won't be happening. He's not asking about anything this evening. He's lost an officer and he's spent the day allowing it to consume him.

'We still have a case to address, sir,' I say. 'It still needs to get done. We need to make sure it's staffed properly.'

'Yes, of course, of course.'

He waves something of a hand, a gesture like he's telling his staff to order in as much wine as they want at the Christmas dinner.

'Take who you need. It's your case now, obviously.'

Pause. I give him the moment to see if he has anything else to add, but it seems he's said everything he has to. I wonder whether I should force the conversation, but what would I be doing it for? I don't need the direction as such. I'm the detective, not him. If it comes to it and we need cooperation with Fife, or anything else that's obviously above my pay grade, then I can take it to him.

Get to my feet.

'I'll go and see Ellen and give you a call later.'

'Please. I'll be at home.'

'Right, sir.'

Out the office, close the door behind me. Take a moment. Deep breath. Head back over to talk to Sutherland. He's eating another doughnut. He holds his hand up.

'Don't worry about it,' I say. 'Do we know, I forgot all about it, do we know if Nat saw Baden's aunt in Inverness before... if he saw her on the way out this morning? It would have been pretty early, but...'

'I don't know if he did, but yes, he'd arranged to see her very early.'

'We need to get in touch with her again. Whatever she said, she's going to have to say it again. I'll go and speak to her tomorrow.'

'I'll call her, set it up.'

'Thanks. And what else… PC Fisher still around?'

'Shift finished a couple of hours ago. She'll be in at eight.'

'We need to know, you know, about that DNA sample from twelve years ago. When was it taken? Who took it?'

'You'll need to speak to Fish, sorry.'

'Sure. And, d'you know if Nat had been following Baden's money?'

'What money?'

'Sorry, insurance money. Baden died, as far as anyone knew, twelve years ago. There was life insurance. Where did it all go?'

'I think he was, but he hadn't said if he'd got anywhere. I'll look for it.'

'OK, great.'

Suddenly feel stressed, which I haven't done in a long time, and certainly not during the course of any of this, those brief few hours of contemplating getting on a plane excepted.

It's because of Ellen. It's because of walking into that house. It's uncomfortable, but this is what life is, isn't it? You can keep as few people around you as possible, but life in all its awfulness still intrudes, from the least likely of places sometimes.

'I'm going to see Nat's wife, see how she's doing. Might come back here later. Don't know. If I don't see you, catch you in the morning.'

'Yes, boss,' he says, his eyes dropping at the mention of Nat, and of his wife, widowed and alone.

Turn, stop, take a last look over the station, then walk through the main room, down the stairs and out into the wet dark of early evening.

33

It doesn't take long to drive from the station up to Nat's house. Fifteen minutes, if you're not in a rush. I force myself to think about the case. I don't want to think about what to say to Ellen. Anything planned will be as awkward as some pointless little pep talk to three or four people at the station. Although, having seen the dead weight that was enveloping Quinn, someone's going to have to grab the station by the shoulders and haul it off the ground.

Four people in some little clique in the Conservative club at university. The fact that they were Conservatives I don't think makes any difference, and Conservatives aren't quite as rare in Scotland as the jokes and the media would have you believe.

They were overseen by the twitchy guy with the moustache. And there are the other names to check out. One must always keep one's eyes on the periphery. If the genesis of this is twelve years ago, then that's where we should be looking, and those people, the players from back then, could have dispersed far and wide. Doesn't mean they haven't been making trips to various areas to take care of old business. Or what has become new business.

How did it become new business, that's the question? It became new when Baden turned up out of the blue in Estonia. Baden hasn't requested any contact with the UK, nor has he been given the opportunity to make it. He might have now, I'm not sure, but he hadn't when I was there. He was held in a hospital room without a phone, so they would have known that he had no means to make the call.

There is the possibility that he made the call before turning up at that police station, and neglected to tell anyone about it. That aside, there's been an embargo on the information, and yet someone in Scotland found out that Baden was back, and was busy taking out the old crowd. It can only mean that somebody in Estonia passed on the information, either from the Embassy or from the police.

The British staff at the Embassy would have been long gone, but perhaps there was someone from the locally engaged staff with contacts from the previous time. Will need to speak to the DHM again, although I can't really ask him to do detective work on my behalf. As for the police, there's no real way to find out.

However it happened, it seems there's no doubt that Baden turning up started off the killing, and if it was so much of a deal that his re-emergence on the scene was enough to spark murder, then isn't it reasonable to think that, yes, this is the actual Baden. This is him! Why else would there be a fuss?

There could be a hundred reasons!

I'm having the conversation with myself, partially speaking out loud. I should have had it with Sutherland back at the station.

You can't follow a hundred scenarios at once. You have to pick the most likely, the one that fits what you know; and the most likely, it seems, is that this is the guy. This is Baden. And someone doesn't want him back.

It's always about asking the right question. It's not about how two bodies, one alive one dead, can have the same DNA, it's how the pathologist who checked the corpse's DNA came to believe that he was confirming Baden's identity.

I need to get on that. There's not going to be anything metaphysical. I'm happy to accept strangeness if that looks like the most likely explanation, but not this time. This isn't it. This doesn't feel right. Baden turned up and people have started dying, because someone, somewhere, doesn't like it. That's not weird, it's not metaphysics, it's not supernatural. It's criminal, that's all.

Will speak to Fisher first thing in the morning and see how far she got. The fact that she hadn't taken anything to DS Sutherland, doesn't suggest too much progress.

There's a basic peculiarity about the case, that was heightened by the slight otherworldliness of Baden's mother, and heightened in my own mind by Dorothy and her melancholic demise, but what we have here is just plain murder and I need to focus and start treating it as such.

I start thinking about Rosco and if there really is anything he can help us with, and I wonder if he's lying face down on the carpet in his front room, choking on his own vomit.

Concentrating, I drive along the A9 towards Inverness, missing my turn-off, and not until I'm going round the roundabout at Tore do I realise that I missed my left turn several miles earlier.

★ ★ ★

The lights are on, there's the sound of voices from inside. I don't need to lie to myself. I hope that the place is busy, the family surrounded by people, and that I end up standing on the doorstep for two minutes talking to one of Ellen's relatives, who's telling me that she's fine but she's getting some rest with the children.

As I start to walk up the garden path, the front door opens. Ellen and another woman. They embrace on the doorstep, then part, both with tears in their eyes, noticing me as they pull away from each other.

Ellen smiles weakly, but can't speak.

'Hey,' I say. Find that I have trouble speaking myself. There's a slightly awkward moment that the friend breaks.

'I really need to get going. I'll call in the morning, Ellie.'

Ellen nods. Smiles. Wipes away the tear.

'You'll be OK, sweetheart. Just remember to breathe.'

They're smiling supportively at each other, hands clasped.

I lower my eyes and wait my turn in the line of condolence, the queue of platitudes. *Remember to breathe*. That's what people say now, isn't it? I wonder where it came from. I don't think people would have said that in the 1930s. *Remember to breathe*. Hollywood probably. One of those phrases that a scriptwriter thought would be a great line, and then it became an actual line that people say.

The friend smiles at me, turns and is gone. The baton is handed over. One last wave, and she's jogging off down the pavement. Must be late for something. Stayed much longer than she was intending, which likely means there's no one else here.

I walk up the steps, not entirely sure how this will play out. I don't really know Ellen that well.

When it comes to it, I take her in my arms and hold her until she decides she's able to let go.

★ ★ ★

Fortunately, or unfortunately, depending on which way you choose to look at it, the children are young enough that they don't quite get it. The younger one not at all, the elder is old enough to care, to get that daddy won't be home tonight, but not to feel the full force. Not the full force of horrible stomach-wrenching grief that comes with death.

Here I am sitting in a comfy seat in the sitting room, an empty cup of tea on the floor beside me. No one else here, the phone hasn't rung. Ellen is upstairs putting the kids to bed. Reading them a story.

Sitting in silence. I could go back over the case, but find myself too distracted. When I came in the lights were on full. Every light in the room. Once she had left me alone, I turned off the main, left a couple of side lamps on.

The usual small front room of a modern house. TV in the corner, DVDs scattered on the floor. *Thomas the Tank Engine* and *Winnie-the-Pooh*. There are a couple of Jack Vettriano prints on the wall. There's an open fire that looks like it hasn't been lit since last winter.

Footsteps on the stairs, and then they pad around in the kitchen, before Ellen comes into the room holding a glass of white wine. She sits down on the sofa, staring at the carpet. Takes a sip of wine. She looks tired and drawn, beyond tears. The first night of the rest of her life.

'How am I going to cope?' she says. Her voice is small.

I don't know what to say. A hundred different things come into my head, but they all sound so trite. They're all from the same movie script as the woman and her breathing instruction.

'Nat did everything. I mean, literally, everything. Some days...' She stops to laugh ruefully, shaking her head. 'Some days I wouldn't change a nappy after about midday because I knew he'd be in eventually and could do it. Seriously. Seriously... I'm that bad of a mother.'

'How d'you get on tonight?' I ask.

'Look at me drinking, and I didn't offer, sorry,' she says, ignoring the question. 'Are you sure you don't want something?'

'I'm good, thanks. Got to drive.'

'Stay the night?'

'I don't think that'd be a great idea,' I say.

What do I mean by that? That I think we'll end up in bed together? Really? I could just have said no! She shakes her head and looks slightly puzzled as if she wasn't sure what I'd just said, but doesn't really want to think about it.

'When will your mum get here?'

Deep breath. Another moment sweeps over her. Her mum is coming. Why is her mum coming? The realisation sparks across her face. That's the thing with grief. It won't leave you alone for long. If, for some reason, you manage to think about something else for even the briefest of moments, the grief swiftly comes hurtling back in.

'Her flight gets in at eight. She's got a car hired, so I don't need...'

She lets the sentence go. We sit in silence. I wish it was comfortable. I wish I was better at this.

'I don't want to go to sleep tonight... When I wake up... when I wake up I'll have that moment. I remember it from Dad dying. That moment where you don't remember. You wake up and there's a second, maybe two, that's all, where your mind is getting going and you haven't quite realised yet that your world has just collapsed into nothingness… And then you remember, and it's like finding out for the first time all over again.'

★ ★ ★

In the end I stay until she falls asleep on the couch. I find a small blanket from somewhere, one she uses for the kids, and lay it over her. I stare at her, making sure she's not about to wake up. I don't run my hand through her hair, or kiss her cheek. I can't show her any affection, even though she's asleep, a little bit drunk and probably wouldn't notice anyway.

I walk out into the hallway and look up the stairs. She's forgotten to close the gate at the top. I feel duty-bound to go and check on the children. Someone should, shouldn't they?

They share a room, and they're both asleep. The baby monitor is on, but I didn't see one downstairs. I find it in Nat and Ellen's bedroom – where the sheets are ruffled, the bed unmade – and take it downstairs and place it on the floor beside her. Then I leave, clicking the Yale lock behind me.

Sudden death, the total carnage of the spirit.

I stand on the doorstep and look up at the sky. There's nothing to see, no moon, no stars. Across the road a curtain moves, there's a brief wink of light, and then it's gone. I walk to my car and drive home, deciding that it's too late to let the Chief Inspector know that Ellen Natterson is alive and well and utterly devastated.

★ ★ ★

Dorothy comes to me in the night. I suppose it's a dream. Maybe it's the actual Dorothy, or what's left of her on earth. Her spirit. I feel her pressed against me in the bed, her right arm wrapped around me, her face held lightly against my shoulder.

Her hand finds mine, and our fingers entwine. I don't know what she's wearing, can't sense clothes on her, yet it doesn't feel like she's naked.

'You don't mind,' she says.

Her voice sounds small. For a moment I think it might be Ellen, her voice was small too, she was equally sad. The moment passes though, as I come out of sleep – at least, it feels at the time that I'm coming out of sleep, but maybe I'm sleeping the whole time. The middle of the night, surrounded in darkness. How would I know?

'No, it's fine,' I reply.

I realise that there was a different quality to Ellen's sadness. Perhaps she just hadn't got used to it yet. Dorothy had had fifteen years getting used to the fact that her husband and daughter were gone. A long time to become entrenched in and consumed by her sorrow. It was still fresh for Ellen. She still hadn't become accustomed to it. As she said, she still had to wake up and not realise. She still had to turn and ask if he wanted a cup of coffee, she had to buy his favourite pasta sauce at the supermarket, she had to look to see what time he'd be watching the football, she had to have a conversation with him in her head that she might have later; she had to think and do all of these things, the instinctive things that come with living with someone, before being struck by the crushing sucker punch of realisation.

'Why are you here?' I ask. 'I thought you'd be free.'

There's no reply. Her face presses against my shoulder a little harder. I feel the dampness of a tear.

Her sorrow seems to seep into me, the osmosis of pain. Why is she here? Because her spirit cannot find what it's looking for. In that spirit world, wherever it is you go when you die, her child isn't there either. How could she have been when she was never born? Not in this life. And perhaps her husband was nowhere to be found, or his spirit was as dismissive of her spirit as it had been before he'd died of the heroin overdose.

'I won't come every night,' she says. 'You understand, don't you?'

I squeeze her hand. I don't think we talk any more. I feel like I fall asleep again, although perhaps I was never awake in the first place.

She's not there when the alarm goes off at 5.45 a.m.

34

Walking into the station at just after 8.30 on a Sunday morning. Mary is there, which seems strange, but I could tell from the car park that more people than usual had come in. Yesterday was tragic. Yesterday the station had been brought to its knees by an unexpected death. Today we get on with the job, regardless of what damned day of the week it is, we do it well, and if it makes it easier for some people, they can imagine they're doing it for Nat, and that somewhere, he's watching.

'Call for you,' says Mary.

'Right now?' I ask. I start to look at my watch.

'The Embassy in Tallinn. I saw you coming, he's holding.'

I glance at the stairs up to the main room and then lean on the counter.

'I'll take it here.'

She hands me the phone.

'Kenneth,' I say, making the assumption.

'Inspector,' he says.

'It's early.'

'Already 10.35 here.'

'Of course. Any news?'

'Mr Baden will be on a plane this morning, indeed our people are already taking him out to the airport. He'll be back in London by early afternoon. He'll be met by the Foreign Office, I suspect someone will take him to the office and he'll be further debriefed, and then they'll put him up in a hotel for the night. Maybe you could help coordinate from there, and I presume you'll need to get the social services involved etc. Wouldn't look good if the government just dumped him on the streets.'

'OK, cool. Can you e-mail me his flight details and a contact in London, and we'll start getting it sorted this end?'

'Of course.'

Having not been expecting to speak to him so soon, I haven't quite gathered my thoughts. Race through them to remember what it was I'd decided I needed to be asking him.

'Can we talk?' I say. 'I mean, how secure is this?'

He laughs. 'I'd say not very. I mean, we're probably all right, as long as we don't say anything we don't want the Russians to hear.'

'It's not the Russians I'm worried about.'

Silence, although I can tell it's neither frosty nor uncomfortable. He's nodding.

'Go on,' he says after a moment.

'I don't have any confirmation, but I want to work on the basis that this man, this really is John Baden. There's no brainwashing, there's no question of him being someone different but somehow being made to think that he's Baden.'

'OK.'

'And here, in the UK, as soon as he'd turned up in Estonia, people started dying. People started getting murdered.'

'Someone got the information back.'

'Yes, they did.'

He thinks about it for a moment.

'Someone in the police, or someone here at the Embassy?'

'Either that or it was Baden himself.'

I need him to ask a few questions, but I pause, waiting for him to offer.

'OK, leave it with me,' he says. 'I'll speak to some people.'

'Thanks, that'd be great. Appreciate it.'

We say our goodbyes, I hand the phone back to Mary, it's 8.37 a.m. and that's already the first item of the day chalked off the list.

* * *

Standing in the front room of a new house, up the hill in Inverness, overlooking the city, the Kessock Bridge and the Moray Firth. Clear day. You can see every contour on Wyvis. I could stand here all day. Wish I had a view like this. I live in the Highlands, and I thought at the time I bought the house that the view doesn't matter so much, you can walk out your door, you can get in the car or on your bike and see the view in a couple of minutes.

Stupid thought. Tried selling my house a couple of years ago, but didn't get anywhere. Waited and waited, then picked a really bad moment to go to market. Gave up after having to keep the place permanently tidy for six months. Might try again in a little while. Sure, you can see a little of the water from my dining room window, but no one's chasing me out of there for the view.

She comes back into the room, two small mugs of tea in her hand.

'Sure I can't get you a bacon sandwich?' she asks.

I would love a bacon sandwich, but have already decided to stop in town and get one before heading back to the station. The view won't be as nice, but I won't have to ask questions with my mouth full of food.

'I'm fine, thanks.'

She stands beside me and we look down the hill, out towards the Firth.

'Don't suppose you can see the dolphins from up here?' I ask.

'I like to think so,' she says, smiling, 'but I'm probably just fooling myself. I go down, often enough, to North Kessock.'

We stand there, in comfortable silence, Margaret and I, for a few moments. I get the sense of her, have had it since coming into the house. No sign of a husband, or of there ever having been one. She's a couple of years younger than her sister, and there's the same dreamy, slightly detached quality about her.

One of those houses you walk into and there's a feeling of a lack of fulfilment hanging over the place. Impossible to pin down, but there's something.

'Never married?' I say, although I hadn't intended to. The words just appeared.

'Is it that obvious?' she asks, smiling.

'Sorry, not really relevant,' I say, immediately feeling slightly embarrassed.

'That's all right. There was a chap... there's always a chap, isn't there? Never quite happened. We were in Sri Lanka together in the sixties. Ceylon, of course, as it was then. He got posted to Germany, and that was rather that I'm afraid. We hung on to each other for a while, but in the end he married an American girl.'

She takes a sip of tea. Glance at her. She's looking out at the view, but her mind is somewhere else. She's in Sri Lanka, with her chap, in 1963. Probably sitting on a veranda at sundown, drinking a gin and tonic, listening to the cicadas.

'Moved to Michigan,' she says. 'Don't know what became of him after that.'

I almost ask about Sri Lanka, how long she was there, what she was doing. But we're a man down in this investigation and I need to be getting on with it. Don't have time for the idle chitchat.

Look back out over the view. It's glorious, in its way, but I wonder how it looks compared to the colours and warmth of Sri Lanka?

'Tell me about the time you pretended to be your sister and identified your nephew's body?' I say, deciding just to go straight for what I'm beginning to presume is the truth.

I glance at her. She's looking impassively out at the view, but I can see that her hand, previously steady, has started to shake a little.

'Is that what she told you?' she asks.

'Tell me how it happened and how it played out,' I say.

'What makes you think it didn't play out... that Andrew and Elsa didn't go and see John's poor body?'

I pause just before dropping the news on her. You want to shock people sometimes, because that's when their guard is down, but that hand of hers is shaking a little more, and we could end up with a cup of tea on the floor, and while this investigation is more important than her carpet, the distraction could be enough for her to regain her composure, to retreat to the lie.

I put my tea down on a small table, and then take her mug away from her, laying it down beside the other one.

'Seriously,' she says, 'I don't know why you would...'

'I know Andrew and Elsa didn't see John's poor body, because the body wasn't John's. He's still alive.'

Hand to the mouth, she takes a step back. I put my hand on her back, so that she doesn't walk into a piece of furniture.

'You want to sit down?' I ask.

I don't entirely have the confidence of what I'm saying. There's a certain amount of bluff, of course, given that I don't know any of this for sure. But maybes and mights are easier to fend away. I need to start making serious headway.

She slumps into a large comfy seat, which is turned towards the TV, rather than towards the view.

'Tell me what happened,' I say. Her hands are fretting away, she's staring at the carpet. Head shaking slightly now.

'Margaret, I need you to talk to me,' I say. 'I know you did something wrong, but there's unlikely to be any comeback for it at this stage. We just need to know the truth so that we can press on with our current investigation.'

'Where is he?' she finally says, looking up.

'In a minute,' I say. 'Tell me about the identification.'

She stares in my direction for a moment, her gaze going right through me, her lips moving slightly.

'She always said. Elsa. Elsa always said. It can't be him. He's not dead.'

Another pause. Another long stare into the depths of the past. Her head starts moving, slowly, from side to side. She seems to have aged, suddenly. Now the younger sister looks about ten years older. I wonder how much younger Elsa will look when she learns her son is still alive, if that's what he is. Perhaps she will just smile and say, of course he is.

'The police asked his parents to come along. Andrew couldn't face it on his own, and Elsa refused to go. Point blank refused. She'd already... Andrew was worried, he'd spoken to the doctor, they were worried that she had the first signs of dementia, and her refusal to accept the bad news, they just thought it was part of it.'

I didn't see that, even twelve years later. Not dementia. I could imagine a twenty-year-old having the same, dreamy, detached view on life.

'I went with him. He told them I was John's mother. I'm not sure why, or what he was thinking. They didn't know any different, they'd asked for John's parents... The body was awful. Blue and bloated. The face was badly beaten. It was horri–'

'–The face was beaten?'

'Yes, I could barely look. Andrew stood over him, stood over John, looking down. But his eyes were closed. He couldn't look. He couldn't bear to see his son like that.'

'Didn't the police notice? Someone? Someone must have seen him standing there with his eyes closed.'

She shakes her head. If she were younger I'd think she might be about to start crying, but her eyes are dry.

'I don't think so. They were to the side, behind him maybe. I was standing across from Andrew. He was in a terrible state. I felt so bad for him, the poor man.'

'But you looked at the face?'

'Yes.'

It shouldn't have been badly beaten. There was no mention of that previously. The face must have been beaten to cover up the identity, and the body was then cremated. And all of it done on Detective Inspector Rosco's watch.

'And you couldn't tell it wasn't your nephew because of the state of his face?'

The head is still shaking, she looks up, bemused.

'Actually I could.'

'What?'

'I could tell it wasn't him.'

The eyes drift away, and suddenly I can see the shock and the nervousness bleed from her, as she is made to face up to the long-forgotten and long-denied truth.

'Why didn't you say?'

'They told me it was John. They'd told Andrew and Elsa. The police had gone to their house and said to them that John's body had been found. They said Emily had identified him. It had to be John... The body... the body was so puffed and horrible... the skin stretched, that frightful colour. I hardly looked. I thought, it doesn't look like him, it really doesn't. But, who would look like himself in that state?'

Not sure what to say. At last, however, we're getting somewhere. The real John Baden is coming back from Estonia today, while someone else died twelve years ago. It also raises a substantial question about Emily King, although those questions have been growing. She, too, surely couldn't have identified the body with her eyes closed?

'And the policeman said, he said even before he pulled the sheet back, don't worry if you don't think, if you don't think it looks like him. His face is... different. He used the word different. I wasn't even sure that Andrew hadn't just done what I did, looked quickly and then closed his eyes. So I just thought, it must be him. It must be John. And the little voice that doubted, I was able just to ignore.'

'But what about Elsa, didn't you listen to her?'

Her head moves slowly from side to side, the eyes glaze over again, the stare is directed at the carpet, off into a vague distance.

No, of course she didn't listen to Elsa. It was hardly as though Elsa was providing evidence. What Elsa had would have been considered little more than a feeling in her water. But Elsa knew right enough. Elsa knows things. Elsa can sense things.

I need to go and see Elsa again. Still considering dropping Baden on her and watching what happens, or whether to prepare her.

'What about the policeman, do you remember him?'

The look on her face doesn't change. She heard the question, probably, but it's of no interest to her. It's a pedantic question. Why, under those circumstances, would anyone remember the policeman? Except, some might, some might remember every detail. Margaret isn't one of them, however.

'Don't call your sister yet,' I say.

She comes back from far away, looks up at me.

'John's back, you said?'

'Yes. Not back in the country yet, but he will be soon.'

'She wouldn't speak to me anyway. Hasn't spoken to me since that day. She thought Andrew was foolish, but me, me she saved the real contempt for.'

'Don't tell anyone. I'll come and see you in a day or two and let you know how it all lies. Until then I need to ask you just to keep this to yourself.'

'Of course.'

She looks so guilty, so distracted and confused, that I have little doubt she'll keep to her word.

'I just thought… I never believed that it wasn't him. Even though he didn't look quite right, I just thought, it must be him, it simply must be. Why wouldn't it be? Why would Emily have said it was John if it wasn't?'

★ ★ ★

I decide to go where the tourists go on my way back to Dingwall. It's a Sunday morning in November, there aren't many tourists anyway. Over the bridge, and rather than turning left into Dingwall, take a right and nip along to the Storehouse of Foulis. Get a bacon sandwich and a small pot of tea, take a seat at the window looking out over the Cromarty Firth.

The sea is the same flat calm that it seems to have been for weeks, all across northern Europe. The tide is out, and the grey sand stretches far out. There are a couple of small motorboats gliding through the water, but not much other activity. A few oil rigs in for servicing at Nigg sit at the head of the Firth, miles away to the left.

I come here often enough that they all know how I like my bacon without my having to ask. Lean and crispy. Again, as ever, this is cooked to perfection. Again, as ever, I finish it and contemplate having another one, then decide against.

Pour a second cup of tea. A sharp drone begins, growing in volume, and then a large speedboat, its bow raised, accelerates up the middle of the channel on its way out towards the Moray Firth.

35

I know that the police officer in question, at the viewing of Baden's body, was Detective Inspector Rosco. The day after he returned from Estonia. The battering of the face described by Elsa's sister contradicts the report, but it's inconceivable that it hadn't been noticed in Estonia. The only possible explanation is that Rosco got to that body and made sure that identification was going to be a lot more difficult. Hardly a fullproof plan, but perhaps that was just because he was no master criminal. He was just a drunk cop trying desperately to cover for himself.

He's not even particularly covering up that he was more involved. I don't see any deceit or artifice from him. He's just not talking. The effect is the same, nevertheless. Rosco, inevitably under the circumstances, knows more than I do, and he's unwilling to share.

Back into the office, time to get to the root of another issue at the heart of the case. Suddenly it feels like I'm in a groove where things are starting to fall into place. All there's been, however, is some logical thinking on my part, and one aspect of that logical thinking backed up by Margaret Williams. I need to guard against pieces of information seemingly going my way, when it could just be me fitting them into the narrative that I've carefully constructed around the available information.

Take a seat at my desk. Opposite, where usually sits Natterson, is Sergeant Sutherland. He's eating a bacon roll. He nods, his mouth full of food, and shrugs an apology.

'That's OK. How are you getting on?'

He slurps some tea, wipes the corner of his mouth with his shirt cuff.

'Sorry, the boss said I should sit here since we're working the case together. Feels a little...'

'Makes sense, don't worry about it. What have you got?'

'This guy, Solomon, can't find any mention of him. He really did just disappear.'

'When was the last time his passport was used?'

'Didn't have a passport.'

'That's pretty unusual in itself, I'd have thought. I mean, he sounds like he was quite well off, they were generally a well off crowd.'

'Aye. Wonder what he did with himself while all the others went to Verbier for skiing in February.'

'Last official mention you can find? Last bill paid, last anything?'

'Well, bill paid, you know, there are direct debits, so the bills are still getting paid. Still got a house.'

'You've been round?'

'Aye. Got someone in Aberdeen to have a look. It's locked, there's nothing to see. They said it's pretty apparent, even without breaking in, that no one's been there in a long time. I would have thought that his parents might have done something about it, but they didn't even mention it.'

'Last credit card bills, last bank withdrawal? Last time he used the phone?'

'This is where it gets interesting.'

'Good. Interesting's good.'

'He last used his phone and made a cash withdrawal from a UK machine on the same day that Emily King and John Baden left the country for Estonia. He was in London.'

'So this was several months after his mum had heard from him?'

'Yes, but I think we can take from what she said, that he didn't care much for contact with them. The long gaps in communication were just part of his relationship. And–'

'One of those people who just thinks–'

'–And the last use of his credit card was four days later in Estonia.'

Having imparted his main piece of information, he then takes another large bite out of the roll. Ketchup oozes out the other side.

'You're right, Sergeant, that is interesting. But why… why didn't the police find that out at the time?'

'At the time his parents filed the initial report, he definitely wasn't missing. He was just a guy who hadn't called his mum. Then later, when the parents tried to ramp it up, they brought the complaint up here.'

'To this station?'

'Yes. It would have landed on Rosco's desk.'

'Seems like everything landed on Rosco's desk,' I say.

'Doesn't everything land on your desk?' he asks, with absolute common sense.

I nod. He's right. Every potentially criminal case passes across the desk of the Detective Inspector, and it's his or her call on how high it will be staffed. Rosco could have kept anything to himself that he felt like keeping.

'I think the more we get into this case, the more we're going to find that every time we have a question on why something was done in a slightly peculiar way, the answer is liable to be Rosco.'

'We should go back and speak to him,' he says.

I nod. That's certainly what we need to do, but I'm wary at the moment, since he's so liable to be inebriated.

'So, where d'you think Solomon is?' asks Sutherland.

I wave a slightly dismissive hand.

'I think, by a not too outlandish stretch of the imagination, we can assume that his body was wrongly identified twelve years ago as John Baden, and then cremated to make sure no one was able to prove otherwise.'

Sutherland smiles slightly, nodding the whole time. He takes another bite of roll as he looks down, his eyes flitting between two pieces of paper.

'I can see it,' he says, then he lifts them both and hands them over.

Separate photographs of Baden and Solomon, placed side by side.

'They were of similar build,' he says. 'Solomon's hair looks longer here, but that doesn't mean anything.'

Pause for a moment, to try to formulate, rather than speak. Stare at the two photographs. If they were bloated and discoloured and beaten, would you really be able to tell the difference? Well, a parent would. And a lover, you'd think. But there will be no bringing Emily King in for questioning.

'We need something… we need to speak to the mother. Where did you say she lived?'

'Some part of Glasgow. Don't really know it.'

'Everyone's just dotted around Scotland, aren't they? It'd be so much easier if they were all in Inverness or something.'

I look up. Sutherland takes another bite of bacon roll, a bite which ends up with him stuffing the remainder of it into his mouth.

From nowhere I suddenly think of Nat, and of Ellen, at home with her two children. Should I go and see her again? Her mother ought to be here already, and she also mentioned her brother, but even so. I'm the face of the station in this, and I shouldn't just forget her because I already went over there once.

Mind on the job.

'It'd also be easier if we still had the body. Rosco, and presumably Emily King, knew what they were doing. We need to speak to Fisher about how the corpse's DNA ended up being Baden's DNA. See if she's got anywhere.'

'Think she was out on a domestic this morning,' says Sutherland, finally finishing his mouthful and draining his mug of tea. 'Saw her briefly. Ultimately, though, it kind of tells itself, doesn't it? Rosco must have been in on it. The most straightforward explanation is that Emily King gives Rosco a piece of Baden's hair. Could have been off a brush. Rosco sends it off to the lab. The DNA goes on the file as having come from the corpse. Rosco might have had to play a few dodgy cards to pull it off, but it's hardly inconceivable.'

Nodding, long before Sutherland has finished talking.

'Likely bang on,' I say.

Last look at the photographs, which I realise I'm now just staring blankly at without taking anything in, then pass them back across the desk to Sutherland. Sit for a few moments, contemplating how this will work out, but it's impossible to tell.

Shake my head, decide that the brief period of prevarication is over.

'Right, we need to bring Rosco in. I'm going to go and speak to the Chief. Can you call Hunter's in Evanton – he works there as security – and see what his shifts are this week? Then we need to spend some time looking over the paperwork from twelve years ago, making sure we know where we can pin him down.'

'Yes, boss.'

And off in to see the Chief.

36

Quinn was better today. More focused. Asked relevant questions about the investigation, didn't just blindly stare off into the far distance of the office. He tends not to form opinions on cases, when the facts such as we know them are presented to him. Happy to act on the word of his detectives.

As ever, the shadow crossed his face when Rosco was mentioned, and he no more than I likes the idea of him being brought in for questioning on a matter that isn't just drunken behaviour. The police tribunal went over Rosco's career and pulled it to shreds already. Why wouldn't they have found this?

Still, it doesn't really matter whether he's guilty of something or not. The events that are taking place now are a reaction to what happened twelve years ago, and he's one of the people who we need to ask questions of in an attempt to break down the walls.

Met Fisher on the way out of the station. She said exactly what Sutherland had just surmised. The DNA came from Baden's hair. Simple as that.

Worryingly Rosco had done just what he told me he usually did when he knew he was going on a drunken binge. He'd booked time off work. The entire week, on this occasion. He must have thought this one would be particularly bad.

Sutherland and I head out the station, on the way to his house. It's a short walk, but we take the car, as maybe we'll have to bring him back here in a drunken heap to sober up.

* * *

We seem to spend our lives as police officers knocking on doors that won't open. It's a metaphor probably. We didn't really expect to get in. I don't expect anything other than to find Rosco exceptionally drunk. Indeed, our best hope is that he's unconscious, then we can drag him into a cell, and feed him liquids while he sobers up.

That was the main reason we called the estate agent from whom Rosco rents his house. Used our police powers of persuasion to get the guy to come into the office and give us the key. So much easier than bursting a door in. It's a small town, everyone knows the score. We didn't say it, but they know that if the police are looking for the key to Rosco's house, then Rosco is more than likely drunk. We got the key.

'I'll take this as a good sign,' I say, as we stand with our backs to the door, looking between the buildings to the sliver of the Firth that's visible.

'Why?'

'I hate the thought of him drunk and aggressive. I really don't want you to have to wrestle him to the ground.'

'Me?'

I give Sutherland a bit of a glance.

'I didn't bring you along so you could get lunch in.'

Sutherland rolls his eyes and turns back to the door. He knocks again, but it's been over a minute. It's not like he's living in a mansion and has to walk the length of a couple of football fields to get here.

'Come on, let's go,' I say.

Sutherland opens the door and in we go, me first.

Stand for a moment. Stairs lead straight up in front of us. To the side a short hallway, two rooms off, then the kitchen. Upstairs, the estate agent told us, two small bedrooms and a bathroom.

'Rosco!'

We pause for a second, but no reply is expected and none comes. Walk into the dining room. There's a small table, with one chair. The unpleasant smell is much stronger, and sure enough, there he is, like he could have written it himself. Rosco, face down on the floor, and from the smell and the discolouration on the carpet, face down in a pool of his own sick at that.

'Crap. Sergeant, see if you can haul him up. I'll go and get him some water, and get the kettle on.'

I walk through to the kitchen. A few empties beside the bin, vodka mostly. One dirty plate in the sink. Two mugs waiting to be washed, a few glasses.

The window looks out onto a small yard, surrounded by a wooden fence. The only things in the yard are a green council bin and an empty plant pot. Behind the fence, and blocking any outlook, is the end of another block of terraced houses, running perpendicular to this one. There's one window visible, small with a net curtain.

No wonder he drinks. I'd go and live in a tent in the Cairngorms rather than this.

I hear footsteps and I know. I know already. I knew even as the words were coming out of my mouth. *See if you can haul him up.*

Why did I even bother? He's dead. Knew it as soon as I looked at him. But it was as though I'd been expecting to find him face down, unconscious through alcohol, and that was what it looked like we'd found. So I followed that narrative, knowing that we'd found something much worse.

I turn and look at Sutherland. He realises from the look on my face that I know already.

'How long?' I ask.

'I'd have to say at least twelve hours, sir. Quite possibly longer. The smell isn't just the vomit.'

Poor bastard. And there he goes, more than likely taking his secrets with him. Which is a thought. If he had secrets, isn't it possible that someone else wanted him dead. That just because he had a self-destruct button, and he had foreshadowed his own demise when talking to me the other day, it doesn't mean that someone else didn't kill him.

'Any sign that it was anything other than how it looks?'

'You mean…? What do you mean?'

'People have been dying because of this Baden case, Sergeant.'

'I don't think he was murdered, sir. At least, there's nothing obvious. Looks like… it's almost a cliché, sir. Looks like he drowned in his own vomit.'

'Aye, OK. Sanderson can check it out. Put the call in, please.'

Sutherland nods, takes out his phone and walks through into the hallway. I stand at the sink and look out at the pale, fading blue fence, no more than three yards away, the curtained window of the house above it. All he could see from his kitchen window. Trapped.

The same as anyone here, there would have been nothing stopping him getting on his bike and being at the top of Wyvis, or halfway up Strathconon, should he have wanted to. But Rosco wasn't that kind of man. Rosco was trapped looking at his fading fence, and he was never going anywhere else.

* * *

I leave Sutherland behind to deal with the estate agent and the beginning of the post-death wrap-up. Stand for a moment at the end of the street leading to the station, then decide I need more space to think.

Walk through town along High Street, take a left down past the old houses and across the railway tracks. Heading towards the water.

There's an air of gradual decline about the town at the moment.

Maybe it's the same everywhere. Austerity Britain, slowly fading away, like a seventeenth-century painting, losing its colour over time.

Along the path by the old canal, behind the football stadium. There are a few players out at the back, being drilled around a single small goalmouth. I stand and watch them for a minute, listen to the shouts and the cajoling, a coach standing to the side, a whistle in his hand, barking instructions.

Move on, get down to the water, where the River Conan meets the Firth. Stand watching the tide slowly making its way in, hands in pockets.

Cold November afternoon. No one else around the park, the same few number of boats out on the water, although the only one making a sound is the gentle putt-putt of a small motor boat. The air smells wonderful. Crisp and clean, a mixture of the Highlands and the sea. Often enough it's not like that down here, but sometimes on the good days, like today, the atmosphere gets it just right.

I'm in no rush to get back, but I don't really have any choice. Too much to do. Too many people to speak to. I need to call my old office just for general Tallinn information, and I should make contact with the Foreign & Commonwealth Office to establish their exact plans for the return and questioning of John Baden.

Start to walk back towards the station, reluctantly turning away from the still of the day.

If Baden is who he says, and Solomon was killed in Estonia, how did that play out? Emily King, presumably, knew what was going on. Could she have killed Solomon and sold Baden off? Did she collude with those people? Maybe she drugged Baden, and then they took him away in the night.

But why was Solomon there undercover, which effectively he was, as whatever name he was travelling under, it wasn't his own?

Undercover. That thought, those two words, start a whole new ball of thought rolling. Another completely different possibility, another theory that might fit what facts we know, but which could quite possibly be miles off track.

Solomon did eight months of military training and then abruptly left. Thereafter, barely heard of, hardly ever contacted his family, went long periods without making contact with anyone at all as far as was recorded in the police files. The police at the time, for their part, were not terribly interested. We can assume that was another fault to be placed on Rosco's shoulders, but what if it was something entirely different? What if the reason Solomon left the military when he did was because he was recruited by some other government department?

It's exactly the kind of thing my old organisation would do. Yes, they have a website these days and they do open recruitment, and it seems that hardly anything they do any more is a secret. But of course it is. Of course most of what they do is secret.

I stand at the road, waiting to cross, lost in thought. Cars go by. Gaps appear in the traffic. A woman with a pram moves around me and crosses the road.

Is it possible that Solomon was recruited straight from military training as an operative? Yes, it is. Would they then have set him up on some assignment tagging Baden and King, people with whom he went to university? Not so likely, but not out of the question that he was asked to get involved as he would have had an automatic in.

That then would be a whole new bag of nails. It might explain, however, why it was all so sketchy from before. It wasn't just Rosco covering his tracks, but a covert government operation, not so much covering its tracks, as just not leaving any in the first place.

I finally move. A car horn blares.

37

'So, let me see if I have all this in order,' says Quinn.

I'm in his office with Sutherland, having just given the boss the full catch-up, including much that amounts to little more than speculation at this point. I had to tell Sutherland to wipe some sugar from his cheek before we came in.

'We need to tell Mrs Rosco in Aviemore about the Inspector. You also want to talk to this man Gibson in Aberdeen again, you want to go to Glasgow to see Solomon's mother, you want to return to Perth to see Mrs Baden, you want to go to London to see MI6 and the Foreign Office and... are we done, or do you need to return to Anstruther to follow up on Emily King?'

'The latter isn't out of the question, but you're right, we do need to prioritise.'

'I'm glad you agree with me. Tell me what you're going to do first?'

'We should get the locals to go and see Debbie Rosco. I'm thinking I ought to go down there out of some sort of duty, like I'm avoiding delivering the bad news. But we don't have time, and I doubt she actually cares anyway.'

'What about Gibson?'

'I want to go back to him once I've spoken to my old lot and the Foreign Office. I don't think he told me nearly as much as he could have done, but I need to be armed with more before I go back.'

'So–'

'–Mrs Solomon needs to be told that her boy has been found, but not until, obviously, we have definite news. I'm not sure, yet, how we get that.'

'Which leaves London. If you got on a damned plane you could be there before COP today,' says Quinn, allowing his eyes to drift to the clock on the wall above the door.

'I was thinking I might get the sleeper,' I say. 'Do more on this today in the office, will be there for start of work tomorrow morning.'

That one makes a reasonable amount of sense, so there's a certain grudging quality to the nod that he directs across the table.

'Suppose you think that's coming out our budget, do you? You can get the bus.'

'I'll pick up the tab for the train, sir, just the same as I got the hire c...'

'Yes, all right. It doesn't really do the rest of us any good when you substitute your ability to get on a plane with piety.'

Quinn takes a moment or two, letting those words linger in the room, and then nods at the door. Class dismissed. We get up, we walk from the office, close the door behind us.

One day I expect we'll get to stopping outside Quinn's office and telling each other what we think of him, but I don't know Sutherland well enough yet to think that'd be a good idea.

'We haven't had anything from Sanderson yet about Rosco?' I ask.

'I was going to give him a call now, get his initial impressions.'

Take a moment. What do I actually have to achieve today before heading down to London tonight? Mostly reading files, making sure my thoughts are in order, that I'm asking everyone the right questions.

'Let's go and talk to him, we can get something to eat when we're out.'

Sutherland nods, a man who invariably looks positively upon any mention of food.

'Excellent,' he throws at my back as we head to our desks to grab a jacket.

We'll need to go into Inverness, so on some level we're basically taking an hour out the office when we could make a two-minute phone call, but as ever with these things, it's not just about the interaction and seeing things for yourself, it's taking the time to talk through the case. Sutherland and I can do that in the car without distraction, the blight of the mobile phone notwithstanding.

I stop at the front desk and smile at Mary.

'What are you after?' she says.

'Can you book me on the sleeper to London tonight, please?'

'Very fancy,' she says. 'Business or pleasure?'

'It's business, but the boss wants me to get the bus.'

'He does not!'

'Well, he wants me to get on a plane, and in light of the fact that I won't...'

'He wants you to get the bus.'

'Exactly. Nevertheless, I'm not. Book me a single cabin please, and if I need to pay it myself, then we'll do that.'

'First class on the sleeper?' she says.

I smile.

'I think you might be paying for it yourself.'

'I don't care, I'm not sharing.'

'Good for you. When are you coming back?'

'Let's say tomorrow night. Don't want to be rushed. I can always grab an earlier train if it works out.'

'Single cabin on the way back too.'

'That'd be lovely.'

She shakes her head, and says goodbye with a slight nod as the phone rings.

★ ★ ★

'Are you going to see Ellen today?' asks Sutherland, as we pass the road end.

Have barely thought about it, and now I've booked myself a trip to London. I was going to, wasn't I? I shouldn't let it pass.

I wonder if perhaps we should pop in on the way back from the city, but that's not right. That's not the way to do it, turning up two-handed. I should at least call to make sure that her mother arrived, and that she's not on her own with the children all day. Look at the time. Too late for that, really, too late to be checking. Should have called when I had the thought earlier.

'I'll try to drop in,' I say.

Glance at him. He's staring at the road, has a distracted air about him. He called her Ellen, and I wonder how well he knows her. And then I get the feeling, and I know there's something there. Something beyond passing concern in his colleague's death and the widow's well-being.

Suddenly the sense of it fills the car, and I realise that Sutherland has been up and down since Natterson died. It made sense, of course, because everyone has been up and down, everyone at the station. For the first time though, I get a little more than that.

'Maybe you can go later,' I say. Choosing to force the subject.

'I can't,' he says quickly, and then shakes his head.

Past the Newton Kinkell turn-off. So much for sorting out the case.

'I mean, I don't think it would look good,' he says. 'The Chief Inspector yesterday, then you last night, then me. Like we're working our way down through the pay grades.'

There he has a point, although that's not the real reason for his reticence.

We get to the roundabout in silence, then continue along the A9 towards the bridge, unusually high levels of traffic speeding around us. I suddenly wonder if the bridge is going to be congested, as it so often is, and this quick trip to see the pathologist and discuss the case en route, will be neither quick nor involve any relevant discussion.

'You want to tell me about it?' I ask eventually.

I feel the quick glance.

'Tell you what, sir?' he says.

One of those slight feints in a conversation, working our way around a subject, when he knows what I'm talking about, and I know he knows.

'There's something with you and Ellen, there's a reason you're not comfortable going to see her.'

We drive on in silence. The dual carriageway and the traffic flash by. The bridge comes into view, and as we get closer it's obvious that the traffic is not backing up. We're on the right side of town, and it should be a quick in and out.

'I mean, you're right,' I say. 'It wouldn't look great. *This is all we can afford to send today. Tomorrow there'll be a couple of constables.* So... it doesn't matter. It doesn't matter why you can't go. I just need to fit in time for a visit. I'll take the files on the train with me and make sure I've got plenty...'

'I slept with her.'

Oh, God. I was afraid of that. I mean, I pushed him into saying it, yet I didn't want to hear it. A slight discomfort over another officer's wife? Life is rich, right enough, and it could have been a hundred other stories. A thousand stories. Look at Dorothy. No one would ever, ever, be able to work out why she was unhappy. That's a story out of the blue. Even if it wasn't true, and it was all an invention of her tortured, crazy imagination, it doesn't matter. No one would ever be able to work it out. There are lots of stories, and always another one to surprise you. And always another one to make you realise how sad the world is. How much unhappiness there is out there. How many bad things happen to good people.

'Sorry,' I say, 'I shouldn't have forced that out of you.'

'I...'

'It's all right, Sergeant, you don't have to tell me.'

I glance at him, catch the back end of a scowl. That's unusual.

'What?'

'Nothing, sir.'

We're all the same, I think. Essentially, we're all the same. If that was me sitting there, would I be annoyed? And if so, why would I be annoyed? I got it out of him. I got him to tell me why he couldn't see her. But there's more. There's a story, it's not just some desperate tale of drunken sex at New Year, or behind the shed at a summer barbecue. There's more. And he was about to tell me, and I told him not to. And now he's worried that I'm left with the impression that he and Nat's wife did something stupid and wrong and maybe a bit filthy, when it was more than that.

'You were in love with her,' I say, not questioning, just kind of resigned. Because I am. 'Sorry, Sergeant, I just kind of pick up these things. Did you know her before Nat did?'

'No,' he says.

Voice low. He knows we're almost there, past the football ground and along Shore Road, so he won't be talking for very long.

'Met her not long after they'd had their first kid. Well, I don't know, six months. They had a thing at their house.'

'I remember,' I say.

That was the first time most of us met her. She'd been eight months pregnant when Nat arrived at the station and they moved into the house in Culbokie.

'Yes,' he says, remembering I'd been there. 'It was just like... I don't know, I've never known anything like it.'

His voice is low, the words coming slowly. I struggle to hear as a motorbike accelerates by in the right-hand lane.

'Caught her eye in the kitchen. Just felt it, straight away. Right inside... What do I sound like?' he says, after a moment.

'What about Ellen?'

'Yes,' he says, his voice light. 'Yes. It was one of those moments, one of those moments in life when... when there's nothing else. No other sound, nothing. Like everything in your world is concentrated in that feeling in the pit of your stomach, and you know you're looking at the person you need to spend the rest of your life with. And yet... it's painful. It hurts, right away, it hurts. You know something like this can't end well. No two people can feel that for each other and it be all right. It's almost like... you know someone's going to get hurt, probably both of you.'

I pull into the car park, turn off the engine. I don't move. Sutherland is staring at the dashboard, his eyes blank. This big hulking man, usually to be found with doughnut sugar on his lips, brought to this by the thought of a woman he very possibly hasn't seen in several years.

'My soul was crushed, in that first second, even before I realised I was looking at Inspector Natterson's wife. It didn't really matter that she was married, there was just this awful realisation that for me to be… whole… I needed someone else. I needed her. And it's impossible to imagine being happy when there's that level of intensity. Nothing would ever be the same.'

'What did you say?'

Eyes don't move. Head doesn't move. He's lost in the thought of her, in a way that I've never noticed him before. It must take some effort from him to put her out of his mind.

'We never spoke,' he says. 'We didn't need to. It was like looking at someone… like I'd spent all my life with her, yet I was seeing her for the first time. And then I noticed her ring and I realised who she was and why she was in the kitchen. I don't know how long it was, maybe only a few seconds. We just stared, and I knew everything about her and she knew everything about me. And I turned and walked away.'

Another car draws up beside us, a silver Citroën, and a woman in a trouser suit gets out and walks quickly in through the front door, the car locking with two sharp bleeps behind her.

Suddenly it seems almost painful to look at Sutherland, like his agony is scolding to the touch.

There's no rush. I don't prompt him. You can't rush personal agony. All we're going to do now is find out about someone who's already dead. Rosco's own agony might have been great, but there's little to be done about it now.

'I left it as long as possible, but every time the Inspector left the office and I knew he was going north or into Inverness or further afield, I thought, this is my chance. I can go round there. And I did. I have no idea how long it was. In moments when I'm kinder to myself, I think of it as being two or three months. It was probably less than that.

'I had someone to see in Cromarty. Left the station, went straight to their house. Rang the doorbell, full of certainty. I presume the baby was sleeping. I never thought about the baby. Ellen answered, and stood there for a moment, and it was the same moment, the exact same thing as we'd had in the kitchen. She held the door open, I walked in. There was just a second or two when one of us could have said something, but I know… it was never likely. There were no words. We held each other, we kissed. We barely moved from the spot. We had sex right there. I can't… I don't know how to say it. It was brutal in its intensity, but so complete, so… blissful. And then it was done, a long time later it was done, I don't know how long. And there was nothing to say. Nothing happened then. It wasn't that Nat called, there was no baby crying. There was Ellen in her house, and there was me, the lumbering fool who'd just walked into her life, and there was no place for me. There never was.

'She could have got in my car, and we could have driven off, and no one would have ever seen us again. But she wasn't going to do that, and I wasn't going to do that. And what we had was no more a thing of furtive meetings and desperate sex than it was about driving off into nowhere...

'We never spoke. Not a word. I got dressed, I stood at the door. That was it. The itch, if it was so inconsiderable that it could be called an itch, had been scratched, and though it hadn't even touched the surface, that was all there was. My eyes dropped at exactly the same time as hers, and we haven't looked at each other since.'

Silence slowly fills the car, like it's being squeezed from a tube somewhere beneath the glove compartment. Silence filled with sadness. Silence complete with its own personal tragedy.

I'm not going to comment, just like I didn't comment to Dorothy. Everyone has a story. Not for me to judge. Perhaps there's something to be done now, now that Ellen is a widow rather than a wife. But not the day afterwards. Not *now*. And perhaps not ever. The decision has already been taken, the agony already faced, irrespective of circumstance.

We sit for a while, staring at the entrance to the mortuary. The story is out there, nothing else to be added. Eventually, like a ball of wool slowly unravelling, the silence exhausts itself and it's time to move. We feel it at the same moment. His story has been given the right amount of respectful silence. With no words, I put my hand briefly on his arm, and then we're out into the cold afternoon, the clouds are gathering and threatening an early evening, and the weight of despondency is lifted slightly with the first hint of rain.

38

Here lies dear old Rosco, taking his secrets with him. After this we can go back to his house for a closer look than we had earlier but, from what we saw before, it didn't seem that there would be too much to find.

He looks happier lying there than any time I've ever seen him before. Hint of a smile on his lips? I don't think so. I don't really think like that. But maybe Rosco, wherever he is, has imparted some little measure of control over his corpse to slightly turn up the edges of his mouth.

Nevertheless, it's a look that says, you should see it here, people, you should see what's waiting for you, you're going to wish you'd been drunk as often as I had.

'Liver's not as bad as everyone had been expecting,' says Sanderson.

There's music playing, there always is. Apparently – though I've only got this on the back of general office chitchat – he requested a PA system, so that it could be played from speakers inserted in the ceiling. That was refused, so he has a small CD player, with in-built speakers, sitting in the corner.

Sanderson likes fiddle music. Laments, usually. Indeed, I don't think I've heard anything else, although Nat said he'd been in here once when there was a jig playing. I think Nat was just being nice to him.

Not that a lament isn't always suitable, an appropriate soundtrack to the events that slowly unfold in this room. The deceased dissected.

You know, I don't know what it is that Sanderson does most of the time. Life in the Highlands is hardly an episode of CSI, we're not constantly coming up against random murder, where Sanderson has to unearth strange toxins in the blood or weird objects inserted beneath fingernails. Not yet anyway.

Maybe he just sits around, waiting for the phone to ring on a Sunday afternoon, alerting him to the latest corpse in town.

'If I'm honest, I've got to say that I thought dear old Rosco's internal organs were going to be new to science. I might even have got a paper out of it. But… he still had some way to go before his liver was going to kill him.'

Dear old Rosco. That's what I just called him. In my head. Funny.

He was the same age as me, probably a year or two older than Sanderson. It's like we all had this strange affection for him, rather than finding him an embarrassment, and wishing that, since he obviously was never going to be alcohol-free, that he'd just go and live somewhere else. Take the awkwardness with him.

I never really thought like that, I suppose, having not known him previously, but clearly Quinn did, and he wasn't alone.

Dear old Rosco. Dead now.

'He binged infrequently, was dry the rest of the time,' I say.

'That what he told you?' asks Sanderson, but not in a way that implies doubt.

I nod.

'When?'

'Two days ago.'

'He was sober two days ago?'

'Yes.'

'Why were you speaking to him? It's not like you people. You weren't offering him a drink were you?'

I give him the required glance, and he nods.

'No, no doubt you questioned him about something which then set him off. None of my business.'

Sometimes Sanderson is direct enough that you just want him to stop talking.

'So, where are we?' I ask. 'Drowned in his own vomit?'

'Bang on the nail,' he says.

'Any possibility that he was held face down in the vomit?' asks Sutherland, the first time he's spoken since we got out the car. As though he's taken ten minutes or so to recover. Now he's found his voice.

'I'm looking for that, but haven't found it yet. There's no doubt that the levels of alcohol in his body are such that he could very well have been completely unconscious, or at least, completely unable to move.'

'You got a percentage?'

'1.027.'

Sutherland lets out a low whistle.

'He'd be struggling to survive that, regardless of the vomit,' I say.

'Quite.'

'What are you looking for?' says Sutherland. 'What signs are you looking for to suggest he'll have been held down?'

'Oh,' says Sanderson, waving his hand over the body, 'signs of pressure on the back of the head, on the shoulders, maybe on his arms.'

'He's lying on his back,' says Sutherland, 'how can you tell?'

The music stops, as the fiddles fade off into the distance. Sanderson looks unhappily over the corpse, the stomach cut open, the viscera revealed.

'I've already done it, Sergeant,' he says, as a harp starts playing and a lone fiddle comes in desolately over the top. 'I couldn't find anything. When I'm done doing this, I will turn him back over, making sure not to spill anything, and have another look. I don't think I'm likely to find anything because I do think I checked rather well before. However, I'll need to shave the back of the head because it's quite possible, given his level of inebriation, that all it would have taken would have been some pressure applied to his skull. Even then, perhaps all they had to do was gently hold his head, in which case, I'm not going to have an answer for you, other than that he likely died alone. Of course, in a case such as this, one can never absolutely rule anything out.'

All that was directed at Sutherland, with a little bit of acerbity.

'Any possibility he had sex in the previous twenty-four hours?' asks the Sergeant, not daunted by the tone.

'I also checked for that, because I know it's one of the first things that you always ask, Sergeant. Absolutely none whatsoever, not in his state. In any case, there is no evidence of ejaculation, of any activity in the genital region, or of any sexual stimulant in the bloodstream.'

Again, all directed at Sutherland, then he turns to me with a look that demands any further questions.

'Thanks, Peter,' is all I give him. 'We'll let you get on with the job.'

'Thank you.'

I turn away, Sutherland follows.

'You'll send the report over when you're done,' I throw over my shoulder, receiving a vague, grudging grunt in response.

Out into the corridor, start heading back towards reception and on out into the late afternoon. I wait for a comment from Sutherland, but nothing comes.

39

Sitting in the restaurant car of the night train, trying to see out the window in the dark. Occasional lights flashing by, sometimes the line of a hill etched against the sky, fitful raindrops smeared across the window.

Waiting for a lasagne. I don't usually order pasta dishes anywhere, they're so easy to make at home, but I didn't fancy anything else on the menu. Have a half bottle of Pinot Grigio, and some bread. Sitting at a table for one.

It feels like we're coming to it, the great disentangling of the knots. It doesn't mean we'll have the answers at the end, but I sit and stare at my own reflection in an attempt to see the Highlands flit by, and wonder how many more people could possibly die because of this. Something that happened twelve years in the past. The story that I'm finally hoping Baden will tell.

He's going to have to be careful, that is certain. His confederates of old are dying, one by one. King and Waverley for certain. Rosco, it's hard to imagine, was ever his confederate, but perhaps he was. And while ultimately we found nothing incriminating in Rosco's house, and neither was Sanderson able to report anything suspicious about his death, and even though I was more than half-expecting to find Rosco face down in a swamp of vomit, there can be no ignoring the possibility he was helped on his way to death.

Without knowing what happened in Estonia twelve years ago, and who the main players were, it's impossible at this point to predict who, if anyone, might be next, and who might be responsible.

Perhaps it's all over. This little burst of excitement that occurred as a result of Baden crawling from the woodwork could be done. The work of Emily King and Thomas Waverley's killer is at an end, and we've seen the last of them. I'm due to spend my next few weeks chasing a ghost; one that has disappeared back into the netherworld of everyday life, lost in the melee of society.

And then there's the other possibility. This whole thing, this whole damned thing, is me trying to squeeze explanations into a box. Into the one box that explains everything, ties together all that's happened.

Maybe there was something twelve years ago with Solomon, but that story could be another one. A completely different story. Waverley could have been killed in a regular hit-and-run. Emily

King could have been killed in an attempted rape or robbery that went too far. And dear old Rosco died face down in his own vomit because I'd been to see him and told him that the past wasn't just crawling out the woodwork, it was screaming blind fury from the woodwork and was coming to get everyone involved.

The steward stands over me and places the plate on the table, smiling as he does so. He pours a little more wine into my glass.

'Can I get you anything else, sir?'

'I'm good, thanks.'

And off he goes. There are three of us dining in the restaurant car. Maybe it will get busier later. I certainly came along here as soon as they announced it was open. I like sitting in the dining car as the train goes through the Highlands, although the dark certainly detracts from the experience.

Having been unable to ask it of Sutherland, I went in to see Ellen on the way back to Inverness. Only had ten minutes. Her mother was there, playing on the floor with the children. Ellen was making them dinner. We spoke briefly. Her brother is coming tomorrow to help out with all the arrangements. I said to coordinate with Quinn.

She was drained. Getting by. Existing one breath at a time. She walked me out into the small hallway.

'Ben, I hope...' she began. 'Sorry, I didn't come on to you last night, or anything, did I? I thought there was something...'

'No, not at all.'

Almost let slip the words, *I was quite disappointed actually*. A stupid joke, and completely inappropriate under the circumstances. Fortunately my brain kicked in and overruled my tongue at the last second.

'I said something that made you think that was what I was thinking, but I wasn't thinking it, I just said something that I can't even remember any more.'

'Oh, OK,' she said, smiling a little, shaking her head.

I gave her a hug, kissed her cheek, said I'd be back in a couple of days. Again words were in my mouth and I stopped them. Was going to ask if she'd like to see Sergeant Sutherland. That would have been foolish. I kept those words to myself too.

I cut into the lasagne. Outside, the Highlands at night flash invisibly by.

★ ★ ★

Dorothy's in my cabin when I get back. It's not late, but I'm tired. I like lying in bed listening to the sound of the train, the rhythm of the wheels, so I'll go to bed early. Let the train put me off to sleep.

I go back with the intention of getting ready for bed, but she's there, I can feel her, so I don't do it straight away. There's no reason for Dorothy to be on the train, so she must be here to see me.

I can't actually see her, of course. I just feel that she's here. It's sad that she has nowhere else to go, no one else with whom to be. The only life she has is the one she had just before she decided to commit suicide. Spending time with me, travelling. That's all.

The cabin feels melancholic in a way that it didn't when I came in here two hours ago. It's not frightening. I might have thought it would be, going to a small cabin in a train whistling through the darkness, with the spirit of someone so recently dead. And yet, if I could see her, I know that she would be sitting at the window, staring sadly out at the night, looking slightly lost. She would have an air about her of a girl in a café in Paris, her coffee long since finished, but with nothing to leave for, nowhere to go, because everywhere reminds her of her lover, and her lover is gone.

Would someone have described me in similar such terms, as I sat at the dinner table, looking out at the night, the dregs of a cup of coffee spun endlessly out over the evening?

'Hey,' I say, to the empty room, feeling not at all self-conscious, 'how are things?'

I don't know what else to say, but it must be wrong. Perhaps anything at all was wrong. As soon as the words are out my mouth the feeling is gone. Dorothy has gone. I wasn't supposed to speak.

And although she has gone, she leaves behind her sorrow and, lying awake in the bed some time later, listening to the relentless click of the tracks, slower by half in the middle of the night, that sorrow rests upon the room and upon me, heavier than the meagre blanket.

40

I walk into the building at Vauxhall Cross for the first time in seven years. Photograph taken, temporary pass around my neck, sitting in the small reception area waiting for my old boss. Alec. In keeping with the way things are done around here, I never knew his second name.

The walls haven't changed, the carpet the same dark blue. Nothing has changed, or so it seems. The practices will still be the same, the feeling in the office will still be the same, the senior managers still won't have the kind of technology that they have in the Bond films, because it doesn't actually exist, or would take their entire budget for a decade to supply. Probably the latter.

The last head of the department was brought in from the Foreign & Commonwealth Office. That couldn't have been very popular. He's gone now, replaced from the inside by one of those gentleman spies, the kind who don't receive a salary, and who hark back to some imagined halcyon time in the fifties or sixties.

Perhaps, as the Cold War has returned and the Middle East has tumbled ever further into the abyss, things are a bit different now. It's like the post-war period combined with the Bush/Blair period. Threats all over the place, combining and contrasting, tugging at resources.

Alec appears in reception, hand immediately extended, great smile on his face.

'God, Ben, good to see you. Look at you. Lost, like, what, twenty pounds since you were here?'

I smile and follow him out the waiting room, across the main foyer towards the elevators.

'Almost exactly to the pound,' I say.

'That Highland air must be doing you good.'

'Can't beat it.'

'Yes, Marcie is always wanting to go back, but it just never seems to bloody happen. Three please.'

The young woman by the panel presses three and four, the doors – as ponderous as they always were – slowly shut, and we wait to see if someone is going to grab the lift in that interminable period.

'So, you're not thinking of coming back to us?' says Alec, his voice still brimming with the same good-natured enthusiasm that it always did.

'No, I'm not,' head shaking, smiling at the suggestion.

'I mean, there's a job there for you, Ben, you know that. There's always a job. And I know there's the flying thing, but you can be based here, you really can. Not out of the question that we could get you up to Cheltenham. It's lovely up there. Course, the locals are barking mad, but it's part of the charm.'

The doors ping at the third floor. Slowly they open, and out we go, my head still shaking.

'Look, come and say hello to a couple of people, and then we'll talk.'

And off we go, walking through these corridors and open plan offices where I used to belong.

★ ★ ★

Standing by the window in a small side office, overlooking the Thames. A great location, right enough. Alec doesn't have his own office, not many people do, so conversations such as this one tend to take place in offices like this. Usually reserved for more classified business, but in this instance, I feel like he's just doing me a favour, getting me away from everybody. Or perhaps, as I'm hoping, he's intending on telling me more than he should, and doesn't want anyone else to hear.

'It's not really our territory, of course,' he says. Mug of tea in his hand. His hands are as huge as I remember them, so that it's almost as though he's holding a child's cup, 'but at the time the Estonians were worried about illegal Russian activity along the eastern border, including on the lake.'

He laughs, makes a broad gesture with the mug.

'*At the time* they were worried? Ha! They'll be worried right up to the point when the Russian flag flies over their parliament building.'

I'm staring out the window, tea at my lips. There's little need for me to say anything. I can tell Alec is settling into a narrative. And he's right, I certainly got the feeling that it was something the Estonians are permanently worried about. And why wouldn't they be?

'There was all sorts, of course, smuggling in and out. Then there was the more serious stuff. This organ and blood business.'

Shake of the head, loud slurp of tea.

'You knew about it before Baden turned up last week?' I ask.

'Of course. Come on, Ben, we know everything.'

'I was here then.'

'Were you on the Estonia desk? You didn't know about it. Your people, this Baden and the King woman, they ran some spurious dotcom, claimed they made a stack of money online. Copywriting? Seriously? No one makes money copywriting. In truth, they were fencing organs back to the UK, on the black market obviously.'

'Black market organ donation?'

'It's huge. Still is. There are seven billion people on the planet, that's a lot of available organs, that's a lot of people to keep tabs on for society. A lot of those people just disappear, and no one can ever find them. Chances are, any time someone vanishes – especially in Eastern Europe – they're being sold as traffic, or dissected.'

'But Baden said he was kept prisoner and used–'

'–As I said, we usually leave this kind of thing to Interpol to sort out, it's their bag. But back then young Solomon had come on board, and Interpol contacted us about King and Baden – and it was a bigger operation than just those two, let's not forget – and asked if they could use Solomon to infiltrate them. We agreed… never saw him again.'

He shakes his head, takes another slurp at the mug. He must swallow every mug in about three goes.

'How did Interpol know he was here?'

'Oh, you know, we do occasionally speak to other departments. Down to chance to be honest. Happened through the FCO.'

'We think Solomon's dead,' I say. 'Sorry, the body that was identified as Baden twelve years ago…'

'We know.'

'Sorry?'

He drains the mug, tipping his head back as he does so, then settles it on the ledge after wiping the bottom on his trouser leg.

'We worked it out at the time. He disappeared, a body turned up.'

'Baden disappeared as well.'

'Solomon knew they were onto him. Oh, he was good Solomon, he really was, but they were onto him. They knew their racket was coming to an end. So, they planned to kill Solomon, pass him off as Baden, Emily King would claim the life insurance, and then Baden would disappear. They would meet up at a prescribed time and place, and off they'd go and live happily ever after. So, we had one of our people in the area check out what was supposed to be Baden's body. He knew it was young Solomon. But, you know how it is, it didn't suit us straight away to say anything. We let them think it had worked. We thought we'd leave it a day or two. And then, we don't know how, but Baden's parents also identified the body, so suddenly everybody *knew* it was Baden. We decided to just let it run, see what happened.'

'What did happen?'

'Nothing!' he says, and barks out another laugh. 'Bloody nothing. We didn't know where Baden had gone. We watched King to see what would happen, and nothing did. She collected the insurance money, that took some time, and then we presumed she'd fly. I don't know, we kind of lost track after that. Iraq was in full swing, all kinds of shit started flying around, you had 7/7, and suddenly we weren't so interested in Eastern Europe. Terrorists and extremists, that's our game. That nice little period, when we had the time and resources to get up to all sorts, was suddenly over. Far as we knew, Emily King bought some abject little house in some depressing former ruddy fishing village in Fife and, I don't know, waited for him. Absurd.'

He shakes his head.

'All those years waiting, and then, when he finally turns up, someone kills her. Extraordinary.'

'And you never said anything all those years. Solomon's mother never knew.'

He nods.

'I know. I felt bad about that.'

And that's all he says, as though there was nothing that could have been done about it.

'We need to tell her now.'

'Of course. Just, you know, maybe don't mention the Service. That's all.'

He turns and gives me a vaguely remorseful look, as some sort of acknowledgement that this is the kind of thing that makes people despise and distrust us.

'You know how it is, Ben, things get in the way, time moves on, etcetera, etcetera…'

I know exactly how things are around here, and depressingly, I know that I likely wouldn't have done it any differently.

'So, I don't understand about Baden,' I say, moving the conversation on, as the thought of Mrs Solomon, and the moment she receives the final, crushing blow, starts to eat its way into my head.

'No, we didn't either. At the time we wondered if perhaps King betrayed him as well, all part of the package, but she didn't go off and live the life one would have expected if that had been the case. So, maybe someone else made the betrayal. Sold him down the river to the organisation they were working with, and Baden ended up in the middle of the forest in one of their basement cells. He can consider himself lucky, if that's what it is, that they didn't kill him. I presume that someone there, and I have no idea who that would be, knew him and made the decision to at least give him some sort of life, even if they weren't prepared to let him go.'

'Have we got enough to charge him now?'

'I think we can hand over that kind of information.'

I nod, but of course, that won't be my decision.

'Interpol coming down?' I ask.

'You've got dibs,' he says, like we're in the playground. 'We're certainly not interested any more. Too much going on over here these days. This kind of business...' and he dismisses it with a slight shake of the head. 'I knew you were coming, so thought I'd give you another stab at him if you wanted.'

'Does he know you're onto him?'

'He's fairly impassive, from what I understand. But he can't have been surprised, despite the fact that he would've given you a fair amount of misinformation when you saw him.'

'Do we think he escaped or was let out?'

'Definitely escaped, no one involved in this wants anyone knowing it's happening.'

'Why didn't he just run in the opposite direction? Why come in at all?'

Alec takes a contemplative thumb and forefinger to his chin.

'Speculation on my part, but I suspect he was scared and had had enough. Just wanted a soft pillow under his head, even if it was for one night at the expense of the British Embassy, or whoever. And now, possibly, he imagines he can buy some sort of amnesty by implicating all those who came before.'

'Not knowing they're all mostly dead.'

'Or so we think,' says Alec.

'Do you know how many people we're looking at in the UK.'

He waves another one of those desultory hands.

'It's kind of moved on from us, I have to say. Was never really our business in the first place, of course. I suspect it moved on from everyone. There were another couple of people up there that they had names for. I had a look at the file before you arrived, of course. Thomas Waverley, now dead. And an Andrew Gibson, works at Aberdeen. Was a kind of mentor to them all at the ruddy

Conservative club or something.'

'Gibson,' I say nodding. That makes sense. He was either going to be a victim or he was going to have been the one doing the killing. 'Talked to him a couple of days ago. He's on my re-interview list.'

'I think you might want to get someone to bring him in.'

'I'll speak to Baden first, but, yes, that seems likely. What d'you know about Rosco?'

He's staring impassively out the window, then turns slowly, looking quizzically at me.

'Rosco?'

'Rosco.'

'Name rings a bell.'

'He was the policeman from Dingwall who went out to Estonia as liaison at the time. Seems more or less to have helped Emily King cover it all up, to make it look as though Baden had died. Went downhill afterwards. Ruined his career. Died this weekend.'

'Interesting. I remember there being a policeman. Murdered?'

'He was an alcoholic. Drowned in a pool of his own vomit.'

'Oh dear.'

'Nevertheless, impossible to say that someone wasn't holding his face in the vomit when he died. No sign of a struggle, no sign of force, but he was likely unconscious from alcohol when it happened.'

He looks at me while I'm relating the demise of poor Rosco, and then he turns away, staring out the window. I follow his gaze.

The weather is reasonably bright, the day in the south-east unseasonably warm. Although, since that appears to be a phrase used more and more often, especially in the south-east, perhaps it's time to adjust our expectations of the seasons.

A tour boat is going by, and we watch it, knowing that the eyes of the tourists will be looking up at us while the guide tells them that inside the building are the real-life James Bonds of the British Secret Service.

'Don't you feel,' he says after a while, 'that every day you wake up, the world seems a little sadder than it did the day before?'

41

Walking through the corridors of the Foreign and Commonwealth Office, on my way to see Baden. Accompanied by a junior officer from EU section. I was expecting to be taken by a security officer to some basement room, tucked away somewhere in the bowels of the establishment. Instead, he's taking me to one of the most decorated and written about rooms in the whole of British government.

'You're holding him in the Map Room?'

The kid, because he cannot be more than twenty-two, and possibly younger, doesn't even look sheepish.

'I don't think we're actually holding him, as such. We're not the police, we don't actually have the resources to hold anyone. We were told by Vauxhall Cross that the police would be coming to interview him, but that he's not a threat as such.'

'So, he's been free to walk out the front gate if he wanted?'

'Yes, of course. He stayed in a hotel last night.'

'Which one?'

'I think, I'm not sure, might have been the Dorchester.'

'You're kidding?'

'I know, but orders from the top. They're worried about it getting out, that, you know, a Brit was held prisoner for twelve years by some crazy gang of Russians, he finally gets home and we put him up in the Travelodge or an EasyJet hotel or some such. Would look terrible in the press. The Minister gets really pissy about those British-hero-treated-like-dirt-by-the-establishment stories.'

Hero? Who do these guys think they've got? Then again, it's a fair point. There's no doubt the press could make this guy out to be a hero if they wanted to. His survival, whatever the reasons he was there in the first place, has been pretty heroic.

Up a flight of stairs. A couple of people walk by, and I think I recognise the guy in the suit. A junior minister. I've seen him on the television explaining why we're giving aid to such and such and doing nothing about somewhere else.

He'll have a career for a while, and then he'll be caught overseeing the supply of weapons to some group that are now using them against us, or he'll be found in bed with someone he shouldn't have been, or he'll actually say something honest on social media, and his career will be over.

'But why the Map Room?' I ask.

I've been in the Map Room. It is as it suggests, where the FCO keeps all the old, extraordinary maps, from the days of Empire and before, many of them so old they can rarely actually be brought out.

'It was free,' he says.

'This guy hardly deserves the Map Room,' I say. 'A small cubicle somewhere, with a chair and a desk and nothing on the walls.'

He shrugs. We're walking along a corridor hung with pictures of old Foreign Secretaries, men of weight, Lords and Earls, in ermine robes. Designed to intimidate visitors. *Look at us. Look how old we are. Look how long we've been doing this. You can't possibly know as much about running things as we do.*

'No one said. Anyway, there was nothing else free. Hardly any space left now that most people are back in London.'

'Why are most people back in London?'

'Cost cutting. Most overseas jobs are locally engaged now.'

He stops at a large wooden door, opens it, steps inside, checks that Baden is still there, and is where he's supposed to be, then ushers me in.

The Map Room. I've been here before. Large table, maps at one end, Georgian fireplace at the other, against which Napoleon and Wellington once leant. One of the great rooms refurbished when the Foreign Office was given a makeover and returned to its previous glory. Soon enough, in order to fund government, they'll be charging tourists. They'd make a bomb. In fact, they could probably get about a billion from selling this room alone to an Arab prince or a Russian oligarch. Not that one billion would make too much difference to the national debt.

'Please don't touch the maps,' says the kid, 'and don't leave the room until I come and get you. You can't walk around unaccompanied.'

He hesitates a moment, as though expecting me to thank him for talking to me like I'm five, then he leaves, closing the door behind him.

* * *

'Do you suppose I'm going to be able to believe anything you tell me?' I ask.

I left Baden briefly to go and find a jug of water and two glasses. The twenty-two year old would probably consider that I went rogue. No one stopped me as I walked the corridors. Anyway, I couldn't find any water, and in the end I stumbled across a Costa Coffee, which definitely wasn't in the building the last time I was here. I bought two bottles of water, and returned to the Map Room.

We're sitting across the table from each other. He has his hands clasped in front of him. Hasn't touched the water.

'Why would I lie?'

'You weren't entirely truthful when I saw you a few days ago.'

'I didn't tell you any lies, and I took you to where I'd been held in prison.'

There's the word. It stands out right away. There's his story, there's the narrative his lawyer, when he gets one, is going to tell in court, should this ever come to court.

Yes, he did things he shouldn't have. Yes, he was involved in some illegal trade. But he's already been punished. He's already served his time. He's already done twelve years. There are murderers and paedophiles who get less than that. And ultimately, how many people in the UK benefited from what he was doing? How many people got a new kidney or a new liver? And the operation – of which he was but a minor cog – never once harmed any British citizen. (The lawyer, I suppose, would make some value judgement on the judge and jury before making that last argument.) He worked on the margins, he worked in the black market, he may have profited from it, but what he did was provide a service for people who were dying, and as a result he helped save lives. He knows that what he did was wrong, but look, he's been in prison for twelve years. And not some cosy British prison, regulated to death by human rights lawyers. His was in a dungeon beneath a miserable and bleak farmhouse in a forest on the far edges of Eastern Europe. He helped people in the UK, and for his trouble he was treated barbarically.

Lawyers...

'How do you see this playing out?'

'I don't understand why I was just left to wander the streets,' he says. 'I mean, I actually walked here this morning from the hotel. And I'm not in the papers. No one seems to know about me. Didn't the Embassy report me turning up? Isn't this a story?'

Some reasonable questions there, from the ex-prisoner, which I won't be answering.

'Someone appears to know about it.'

'What d'you mean?'

'Emily King is dead. She was murdered.'

Barely a flicker. Blinks a couple of times. Finally he breaks the stare and looks to the side. I don't go in for all that, looking to the left means he must be lying nonsense. Like you can't give it some aforethought. Look them in the eye and work it out for yourself. And then, if they're good, it doesn't mean anything anyway.

'Thomas Waverley is dead. He was also murdered.'

Eyes stay steady off to the side. The fingers grip the bottle.

'Who's going to have been killing them off, John? And how did they know you were back on the scene? And, actually, why weren't you on the scene in the first place? What's the story, John?'

He looks rueful for a moment, or he plays the part of looking rueful, as those questions and the information are added to what he knows about the whole thing, which is, of course, far more extensive than what I know about it.

'I didn't know Emily was dead,' he said.

Doesn't look up. He's either good at this, or he's genuinely upset by it.

'Don't you think Emily betrayed you?' I ask, albeit I don't actually think Emily betrayed him. 'I presume it wasn't part of the plan for you to spend twelve years being forced to have sex.'

That was cheap.

He looks at me now, the first sign of anger in his face, then he quickly lets it go.

'Tell me how it played out,' I say.

A slight head twitch, the one I've seen before. A shake of the head, lips move soundlessly for a moment, another twitch. He opens the bottle and drinks half of it without removing it from his lips. In the quiet of the room, the noise of him drinking is very loud.

He tightens the lid of the bottle, puts it back on a mat on the table. He adjusts it a millimetre or two.

'I'm not talking to you,' he says.

This will be the first mention of the lawyer.

'People are dying, John,' I say. 'They're dying because you appeared again from nowhere. They thought you were dead, and now you're back, and people are dying. As soon as you get your lawyer, we're screwed. Us, the police, are screwed. Now, look, look at me. I don't have a notebook, I don't have a microphone. I have nothing. Nothing you tell me now will be of any use to anyone in court. If I try, you will have one hundred per cent deniability. And anyway, I can promise you I won't. I won't be in court. You're not my case. My case is the people getting murdered in Scotland. I need to stop that. We need to stop it. You can help. I need to know if there's anyone else in the firing line, and I need to know who you think...'

'OK.'

He fires it out, the two syllables bursting from his mouth, intended as brakes to stop me talking. I'd been quickening my pace, getting under his skin. Not lying either. I need him to talk, and will say anything to get him to do so, but I more or less don't care what happens to him, and whether he can convince some judge that he's done his time. I just don't want any more murder. There's been enough already.

I'm just about to mention his mother, who will obviously be able to positively identify him, and who therefore might be under threat as well. It's a stretch, and I don't actually believe she is, but I'm willing to throw anything at him. Mentioning her could backfire, of course, so it's good that he cuts me off before I get that far.

'We got into it through the biology classes at Aberdeen. There was an exchange student who Emily started having a thing with. A guy from Ukraine.'

'I thought you and Emily were an item right from the beginning?'

'We were, but you know, it had its rough patches. Andrei was one of them. He... these things come out. He knew we were in it for making money. It was a weird group, the lot of us, I don't know what was going on. We were young. There was sex, some drugs, a lot of alcohol. Andrei was this magnetic guy. You know, he attracted people.'

'Did you sleep with him?'

He gives me the look, then dismisses the question with a slight shake of the head.

'It was all a bit crazy, but ultimately we all had plans and those plans involved making money. It started the last year of uni. Andrei had all sorts of schemes in play, and we were just sort of on the periphery. But then this organ thing came up, and he was going back home to Ukraine and asked us if we wanted to get involved, to run our end of it. You know, it was all through this end of the former Soviet Union. Ukraine up through Belarus, the Baltics. All over. We thought, I guess at first, you know we thought the organs were removed maybe from people that were already dead, something like that. You know, classic donor situation, except rather than going to people in the country, there was this slightly suspect situation where money was changing hands, the organs would come here, and there was this whole black market thing. I mean, it was huge. There's this whole subculture, like a netherworld, that people don't know exist.'

'I'm in the police.'

'Yes, of course.'

'And you were but a small part of the entire operation.'

'Yes.'

There's a moment when you can see that he feels like he's been talking too much. The words die in him. Getting too involved, going back to thinking about something he doesn't want to think about, even though he knows he has to. I'm not going to get many details of what was going on and how it all worked, but I don't actually need it. I need names, that's all.

I give him the space, but it looks like he really might have shut down.

'Tell me about Estonia,' I say. 'I don't need the details of the operation in the UK, that'll be for others. Just tell me how you ended up in a basement in the middle of a forest.'

Eyes close for a moment. Taking himself back there. Then he shakes his head again and comes up. We should get him counselling, sooner rather than later. That'll be something else his lawyer will use, more than likely.

'There was always something funny about Solomon, and the fact that he turned up. He wasn't in on it at uni, then he came back... said he'd made a hash of things down south, wanted to be part of the show. By this time, we were already thinking that it might be time to get out. Emily and I. We wanted out, had been making plans. Didn't realise that they knew everything. Andrei's people, they told us that Solomon was working for the security services. We had to go out to Estonia – which was part of it, but just as much stuff was being brought in through the other Baltic states – and we thought maybe it was just him, just Solomon, who was going to get taken out. Then we realised how much trouble we were in. Solomon was onto us, the Ukrainians were pissed off, the Russians were pissed off. At me. Em wasn't such a big part of it. You know, there was this really sexist thing going on. She was just the girl. It was me they were pissed off at. You don't want to get on the wrong side of these people. We hit on this plan. Emily killed Solomon...'

'Emily killed him?'

No honour among thieves.

'Yes, she was always much more brutal than me.'

'Of course.'

'She killed him, we dumped his body in the lake. Then I disappeared. When Solomon's body was discovered, she identified him as me.'

'How did she think she was going to get away with it?' I ask.

Apart from the obvious, that she did.

'There was some policeman in Dingwall that Em knew. Rosco. He used to hang around her like a dog. I mean, puppy love. It was kind of embarrassing. He'd do anything for her. Fucking lovesick retard. I just stayed away from him.'

'So he was involved all along, it wasn't just that he came out?'

'He came out? When did he come out? When I went missing?'

OK, that was cheap as well, and he didn't fall for it.

'Yes, he did. And he covered for Emily all the way through, and it was helped by your father not actually looking at the body when he went to identify you.'

He blurts out a small laugh, the kind that sounds like it might be about to be followed by tears. In doing what he did, he more or less decided to never see his parents again, and to let them think he was dead. That, in itself, is the action of a very particular type of person.

'Presumably if he had, none of it would have worked,' I say.

'Rosco said he'd take care of it, that's all. We just needed out of the situation we were in. Emily was going to come home and wait for me.'

'And you never came.'

Shakes his head, head low. He must have done a lot of facing up to his past in the last twelve years, but here he is, sitting four feet from a copper while doing it, and it doesn't really bear close moral inspection.

'So, what happened?'

'I was going to make my way south, through the Baltics, and into Poland. From there I was going to head home, somehow find my way into the UK without going through an airport. It's not like the entire coast is guarded, and anyway, if I did happen to be onboard a yacht or something, the coastguard wasn't looking for someone like me.

'I walked out of the hotel in Tartu in the middle of the night, and disappeared into the forest. I couldn't be seen leaving on a bus, God knows, I couldn't get a taxi. Had to be the forest.'

'How long were you in the forest before you were taken?'

'Ten minutes,' he says, then he laughs, bitterly, lowers his head again. 'Really, I don't know. It was that night. That first night. When Em was reporting me missing to the police the next morning, well, as far as I know, you know, that was the plan, I'd already been dumped in a basement.'

203

'You'd been betrayed?'

'I presumed it was Em at first. She was the only one who knew, who knew the plan, knew the specifics, knew the timing. No one else.'

'And then?'

'I don't know. A week or two later a couple of guys came to see me. Checking me out medically, seeing what I was good for, I guess. I didn't know them, but I could tell. One of them knew me. He knew me. I thought, maybe this is my way out. I start speaking to him in, like, the worst Russian anyone ever spoke. He looks at me for a while, he looks at me in a way that just shuts me up without him having to say anything. Then he says, in English, heavy accent, he says, 'I do you a favour.''

He's not looking at me as he speaks. He shakes his head, a bitter smile on his lips.

'His favour being that they didn't kill you?'

He nods.

'And you got lots of sex.'

Objection your honour, prosecution is goading the witness!

He closes his eyes. Nothing to say to that.

'So if it wasn't Emily, it was just chance? Seriously?'

Another movement of the head, an airy hand waved vaguely at the bottle.

'I had a lot of time to think about it, and I never could make up my mind. Either it was Em, or she told someone what we were doing, not realising what they'd do…'

'And given her relationship with this Andrei character, surely that's not out of the question?'

'They had moved on, it really wasn't like that any more.'

'What about Rosco?'

'Rosco… That guy wouldn't tie his shoelaces unless Em told him to. So if he did anything, it was because Em wanted him to do it. Rosco being involved is the same as Em being involved.'

Well, that could be significant. The kind of thing that doesn't point to anything specific, but which speaks volumes all the same.

'What else? What else could it have been? *Who* else could it have been?'

'In all those years of thinking, I didn't come up with any other explanation. It was either Em or it was an accident.'

I smile at last and laugh lightly. He looks sharply at me and I take a drink of water.

'What?'

'It's just kind of ironic,' I say. 'I mean, that is some serious irony going on there. You have a part in some awful illegal organ importation business, and then you end up on the receiving end. That is some major karma.'

'Thanks.'

I let the smile go. It wasn't like I was actually laughing at him. But that is biblical revenge. An eye for an eye, a kidney for a kidney.

'That's why I should not go to prison,' he says.

'That's not for me,' I say. 'I need names, and no Andrei whoever and Sergei something-or-other. I need names in Scotland. Emily's dead. Waverley's dead. I don't need to know what their parts were in this thing all those years ago. I need to know who would want them dead now, and if you have any idea how word got back to someone that you're alive, because we kept it out of the press.'

'Is Emily really dead?'

His voice finally sounds small. That's been a while coming. Had he hung on to a belief in her this whole time? That she might still be waiting for him? Quite possibly. What else do prisoners hang on to? Everyone needs something. Despite the possibility of betrayal, despite the possibility that he's telling the truth about being forced to have sex, what else did he have to hang on to?

And there she is, killed as soon as he's released. That potentially comes high on the irony stakes, except there's nothing ironic about it. She's dead because he escaped, pure and simple.

'Yes. She was attacked in her house. Badly beaten. Hands round her neck, fingers into her windpipe. They were good. It didn't last long.'

He swallows, his fingers drift up to his neck and he touches it lightly.

'She didn't deserve that,' he says.

'You just said she killed Solomon. I know we don't operate capital punishment, but she chose to play that game, she put herself in that world.'

'Was she married?'

'You know, I can't be sure but I'd say she was waiting for you. She had no life. I mean, literally, she didn't do anything. Like she was just waiting for something to happen.'

'Where was she?'

'Anstruther.'

Another blurted noise from his lips, he leans forward, eyes closed, resting his head in his hand.

'What?'

Head shakes. 'That's where we arranged. Twelve years ago...'

That was careless. He's either upset or acting tremendously. Either way, I should have let him tell me Anstruther, not the other way round. Seriously, how long have I been interrogating people?

'So, now, you need to let me know who else was involved in Scotland. Who thought that this was all over? Who would have built a nice life for themselves and who suddenly had to clear up all the old mess when it became apparent that you were coming back? And who, in Estonia, would have let them know that that was what they had to do?'

He lifts his head, and then he sits back. Slumps against the chair. Looks like there are tears in his eyes.

'Waverley's really dead too?'

'Yes.'

'I don't know many others.'

'Go on.'

Another shake of the head. Feels like he's constantly moving, constantly going through some motion or other.

'Gibson. He was... he was a bastard.'

He laughs. More head shaking. Sit still!

'No scruples. He's there to help students, just kids really. Advise them. All he did was get in with those who he thought would help him make money once they left. And then there was the sex too, of course. And the great thing about uni, I mean, against a school, is they're all over eighteen.'

'Did he sleep with Emily?'

'Ha!'

I guess I'll take that ejaculation, coupled with the withering look thrown off into the far distance, as a yes.

'You think the whole thing would have folded after you left?'

'I don't know!'

'But the authorities investigating at the time. If they knew enough to have Solomon on the case, they surely didn't just give up because he vanished. That doesn't make sense. They would have come back looking. Even with you gone, surely they would have come back.'

'Why are you asking me?' he says, annoyed now. 'Why don't you ask, I don't know, the people who were working the case back then?'

'Because you know more than they ever did. You know what the connections were. You know where the breaks were. Maybe Solomon just knew about you and Emily. Maybe, with the exception of you two, not one person knew what anyone else was doing, who was involved, what the lines of communication were. That's how these kinds of things work best, we all know that. You're never in a position to implicate anyone else.'

He's nodding now. The anger given away – slightly – to some sort of mocking incredulity.

'Now you get it, eh?'

'What?'

'Seriously? You ask me to tell you everyone involved, suggesting that I know all about it, while at the same time implying that I probably didn't know all about it because that's how these things work.'

'I'm suggesting you were in charge, John.'

'And I'm telling you I wasn't.'

'Who was in charge, then? Gibson, Waverley? Emily?'

'I don't know who was in charge.'

'Who sent you to Estonia in the first place?'

'Gibson.'

We hold a stare across the table. I look at my watch. I can easily be back up north by this evening, rather than waiting all day for the night train. I think I'll do that. I need to speak to Gibson, but this way I can be on my way early in the morning. Or I could get the train straight to Aberdeen now.

Either way, doesn't matter what I do, it'll be too long. If Gibson is the killer, then we should be bringing him in. If not, then he may well be on the list. Either way, he's been implicated in a serious historic crime, and shouldn't be whiling away his days at the university Conservative club.

I need to put a call through to Sutherland. First of all, however, I need to get something done with Baden, so that his life is a little more uncomfortable than it currently is.

I take out my phone and call Scotland Yard, getting up and walking towards the door as I do so. I'm going to need help getting him home, because he's not going anywhere other than into custody back in Scotland.

'I want to see my mother,' he says to my back.

I turn round as I get through to someone. He's not looking at me. Head down, staring at the table.

42

Sitting on the train out of Euston. Changing in Glasgow, will arrive in Inverness not long after seven. That's pretty good going. A useful trip all round. Feels like we're slowly closing in. You never know, maybe it has nowhere else to go. Some cases are like that. Some cases just stop, when they seem to be going full throttle.

Perhaps Gibson is all we're going to get. It feels like there must be someone in the Estonian police involved in this. It might be that Gibson tells us, something he can use as a bargaining chip. It's not really our business, but it would be good to be able to pass something back to the Estonians. Well, I say, good. It would depend, of course, on who it was we were selling down the river. If it turns out to be some long-serving, highly-respected, law enforcement officer, worshipped by everyone in authority, then we might not be very popular.

There's no dining car on the train, but I buy a ticket in first class, and the steward walks up and down, constantly dispensing drinks and food to the four of us in the carriage. The woman across from me is on her third glass of white wine. The time is three minutes past one. I wonder if she always drinks this much, or if it's just because she's paid for the ticket, and there has to be some reason, other than a slightly bigger seat and fewer children, for it being one thousand per cent more expensive.

I want to say, I hope you're not driving at the other end, madam, and I probably would have done at some point in the past, but these days I sensibly keep my mouth shut.

I'm drinking water and eating a prawn and rocket salad. Sitting with my back to the direction of travel, watching the world rush away from me. Been on a lot of trains in the past week, which is good. I like trains. Perhaps, when Quinn notices I haven't had any holiday for about two years and forces me to take a couple of weeks off – although with Nat's death, plus Quinn's general lack of ability to pay attention to such things, it's unlikely – I could travel around Europe by train. Stay in nice hotels. Paris and Vienna, the Swiss Alps, the beach at Barcelona, the Amalfi coast, the Danube. Or the train that crosses Norway, the one people say is the most scenic in the world, and then cut down through Denmark.

My phone rings.

'Sergeant.'

'Gibson's dead,' he says, getting right to it.

'Crap.'

I lower the phone, heavy breath. Look out the window. The train has its full speed up, the flat landscape, low grassland leading away to the North Sea, racing by, the occasional spot of rain on the window, streaking across the glass before stretching out into nothingness.

I don't want to hear about Gibson dying. It's not one of those, wanting the world to stop moments; wanting to pause time and not step into the next second. There's just been too much killing, that's all.

The press haven't really got hold of it yet, as it's been here or there, and one of the murders was a hit-and-run. They haven't made the connection, and we haven't given it to them. They might have done in the old days, when all the papers had thirty guys running the police and court beats. But now, when they've cut their numbers to the bone and fill their pages with Associated Press stories and celebrity flimflam, they miss so much.

Phone back up to my ear. Sutherland is talking.

'Sorry, Sergeant,' I say, cutting him off, 'didn't catch all that. Can you start again, please?'

'Gibson was beaten to death. Head pummelled in. To a pulp. The beating continued long after he would've died. Whoever did it really didn't like him.'

'What'd they hit him with?'

'A large crystal ornament – amethyst – that Gibson had in his living room. You know, like you get in these crystal shops. The big chunks of the stuff.'

'He had that in his house?'

'Yes. We've spoken to a few people already. They identified it.'

'So the killer didn't necessarily turn up with the intention of killing him.'

'Or if they did, they were always going to pick something up and hit him with it. Maybe they knew the crystal was there. Maybe they thought they'd just get a knife from the kitchen.'

'Either way, he must have happily let them in.'

'Certainly no sign of the door being forced.'

Pause to think, to watch the world. At the far end of the carriage, the attendant, or whatever her official job title is, starts another walk through the carriage. Might be time for coffee.

'Anything else? Anything from the neighbours?'

'Not so far.'

'OK, stay on it. You working with Aberdeen?'

'Robertson.'

'Good. Right, let me know if something else comes up. I should be back in the office before eight.'

'How'd it go with Baden?'

'We're getting there. The Met have got him in custody, and they'll bring him up in the next day or two. We'll see how it plays out once he's spoken to a lawyer.'

'Custody?'

'Admitted his part in an historic body parts smuggling operation. Ultimately the procurator might decide not to pursue it, given that he's been locked up all this time, but we need to bring him in. Will just have to handle any crap from the press once it starts.'

'Right, boss.'

I hang up. A spot of rain sprints across the glass at eye level. I turn at the arrival of the attendant.

'Coffee please, just milk.'

* * *

I wonder about Gibson. Who has he left behind? Who's going to be upset by his death? There's usually someone. Who's going to be happy about it? If Baden is telling the truth, then it sounds like Gibson might well be a divisive, contradictory character. Using people, playing with people, helping some, casting others aside.

Spend a couple of hours on the Internet getting into his life, as much as it reveals. He'd published a couple of papers on political party financing (seemingly of no particular use to the investigating police officer, but then, the things he said would have been at odds with big business, and he might well have been in dispute with money and power, so these things have to be checked out), there was some old stuff written by him relating to the Young Conservatives (again, seemingly of little use), and then there were the comments from students on Facebook (potentially very useful). Spend the longest amount of time on that, although ultimately all it does really is confirm the thought I'd had when I'd started, like an exit poll revealing the precise result of a vote. There's some disgust at him, there's a lot of love for him. Two girls in particular had a nice Internet slanging match two weeks ago. I note their names, and they will be on the list of people to be interviewed. We can make the assumption that Gibson's death is related to all the others, but you can never rule anything out.It's the first time that someone I've spoken to in the course of an investigation has subsequently been murdered. I know, happens all the time in television series. Just not to me. Unless we count Rosco, of course, in which case Gibson is the second.

The train continues up the east coast, running on time, running through the rain. I have a hot sandwich and a can of Diet Coke just before arriving in Glasgow.

43

It doesn't take much sometimes – maybe it never does – to get your mind working. This time, it's a family of Asians walking through the carriage. They get on at Perth, bundling past, all luggage and enthusiasm and chatter, and then park themselves at a table for four near the end. Amongst them, two women and a young girl talk incessantly, a silent teenage kid, headphones on, stares at a small screen.

I wonder what nationality they are. Feel like I ought to know. Feel bad, on some level, for not knowing. Like there's a part of my brain that looks at Asians and thinks they're all the same. I don't think that, but then I wonder why I can't work out which country they come from.

And it has me thinking of Mrs Waverley, the serene Thai woman, sitting at her window in the house beyond Cromarty, looking out at the waves on the Moray Firth. I hadn't been thinking about her much, but now that she's in my mind, now that the thought is there, I have to examine it.

What made me think about her? The Asian family, that was all. But I've just been in London. I've seen lots of Asians. What made me think about her right now, at this moment? There must be something. Thoughts don't present themselves out of nowhere without reason.

Back online. Different train, have to pay for the privilege this time. Just get on with it. Don't get very far, as I don't have her previous name. Get on the phone to Sutherland, as I don't have notes.

'Sir?'

'Mrs Waverley,' I say. 'Anything further with her.'

'Sorry, sir, not so far. Haven't really had th–'

'–You said she'd been married before. Can you remember her name?'

Pause, and then, 'Yes, yes. It was Cameron, sir. Calls herself Melanie, but her original name was… Just a moment… Those Thai names, sir…' Hear the rustle of paper.

'Charoenrasamee. I think she still uses it for some things. Not too sure.'

He spells the name out for me, then says, 'On to something?'

'Don't think so, just sitting on the train, looking for things to check up on. You got anything else of note.'

'The pathologist in Aberdeen–'

'–Maxwell?'

'Maxwell. She's done a preliminary. She thinks the heavy beating inflicted on Gibson might have been done to disguise any indication of the direction and strength of the blows. But there were another couple, high up on the neck, that remained distinct from the general mishmash.'

'And?'

'And she thinks the blows were struck by someone considerably shorter than Mr Gibson, possibly a woman.'

'OK, that's good.'

'Good?'

'Good to know. Any further thoughts on that?'

'The people around there, they just assume… they say he was something of a Lothario.'

'Yes, I got the same from Baden. Would appear the years never changed him.'

'Obviously they don't know any of the past stuff, so they're assuming he's been killed by some girl that he's pissed off. Or a jealous boyfriend.'

'Any suspects in particular?'

'Got a couple.'

'OK, good. Make your enquiries, fill me in when I get back.'

'Already back at the station, sir. The Aberdeen guys are handling things.'

'K. See you shortly.'

Hang up, and then back onto the Internet. Melanie Waverley. Melanie Cameron. Charoenrasamee Waverley. Charoenrasamee Cameron. Cross-checking, ploughing through endless pages, linked from Google. The trouble is, of course, that there's no reason why she should rank particularly highly. She's just someone staying in Scotland, whose name has changed a couple of times, and who hasn't done anything particularly memorable. Unless, of course, she murdered both of her husbands. The Thai name doesn't show up at all, at least, not with either of these surnames.

At this stage, I'm not as interested in her as I am in her husbands. I don't know anything about her first husband. Where he worked, even what he did for a living.

Despite the fact that it took several minutes for the phone to finally connect to the Internet, I quickly cut it off and call Sutherland again.

'Sir?'

'The original husband, Cameron. What was his first name?'

'David,' he says.

'You're kidding, right?'

'Straight up.'

Suppose it can't be that unusual a name, but it's liable to make it hellish tracking him down on the Internet.

'Date of death?'

'Just a moment.'

I can hear the rustle of paper again, a slight muttering beneath the breath.

'Sixth December, 2009,' he says. 'Alcoholic. Had eviscerated his liver by the time he was forty-five.'

'God... OK, thanks.'

Hang up again, and back onto the Internet. Even slower to connect this time, as though it's saying, you had your chance. I find a mention of him pretty quickly, by looking for him and his wife together, but it doesn't give me much. Keep searching.

Another mention, another dead end. The night flies by, now through the Highlands, but there's nothing to see outside except the dark hills, an occasional light. There's more noise in this cabin, but I'm not paying any attention. Glance out the window and see little more than myself looking back. Another link, click on it and wait.

'Would you like anything to eat, sir? Or drink?'

Look up. The steward, who's been on this train since Glasgow, is smiling down at me. He's kept up the smiling the entire time, even though I ate and drank a tonne on the first leg of the journey and have taken nothing from him so far.

Look at my watch. It'll be easier to eat now than stopping off on the way back to the office, even though I'm not that hungry yet.

'You got a sandwich?'

He continues to smile, even though he's explained to me before what kind of sandwiches there are, and he must have told the tale of the sandwiches several times now, up and down the carriage.

'There's a ripe French brie, with Spanish merlot grapes on organic Italian ciabatta, and there's a roasted Mediterranean chicken with spring vegetables and original Speyside onion marmalade on wholemeal bloomer.'

We stare at each other for a moment. The smile begins to waver.

'Can I have the chicken, please? And a still water.'

'Of course, sir.'

'Thank you.'

He turns to walk back to the end of the carriage, satisfied that he's finally enticed me to take something, and I look back out at the night, as we begin to slow on the approach to Kingussie. Facing forward now, on this second train, and I watch the station approach, the lights of the town bright in the dark, Highland evening.

Get lost in the night for a moment. The arrival at a station. Would be nice to finally be getting off, going to stay in some hotel somewhere. Getting up in the morning, a large breakfast, and then out onto the hills for the day.

The sandwich and water arrive as the train comes to a stop.

'Can I get you some wine or beer? Or a hot drink, perhaps?'

Maybe they have to keep asking until they get a no.

'I'm fine with this, thanks.'

'Very good.'

The carriage seems a little quieter, almost as if the passengers are waiting to see if anyone else is going to get on, someone who could ruin the atmosphere. No one does.

I look back at the phone. The link to another, longer obituary of Melanie's first husband, David Cameron, is there, and the obviousness of the connection leaps off the small screen, and I wonder how we managed not to find this before.

The same reason we miss anything. Understaffed. Although, on this occasion it might have something to do with the death of Natterson.

I contemplate calling Sutherland again, but decide to wait until I get back to the station.

44

Almost soaked walking from the car to the front door of the station. When I walk in, Constable Andrews is on the front desk.

'Good evening, sir,' she says.

I nod in reply, head up the stairs and into the office, taking off my wet jacket as I go. Not many people around. 7:47 p.m. Sutherland at his desk, on the phone. We acknowledge each other as I put my jacket over the chair. I glance at Quinn's door, but there's never any way to tell whether he's there.

Sutherland shakes his head slightly to indicate that the boss isn't in, and I sit down. Computer on, will get online quickly, and take another look at what I saw on the train. See if there's anything else to be established, and then we're heading back out, to see the serene widow, who will more than likely be sitting at her window in the dark, watching the rain fall, skirling in the wind.

He hangs up, shakes his head again.

'Aberdeen,' he says. 'Still nothing from the neighbourhood. No one saw anybody arrive or leave, nothing suspicious. No one heard anything. Then again, Gibson lived amongst a young crowd, most of whom would have been out at work.'

'Why wasn't he at work?'

'Not sure. Possibly took a call. He didn't have a lecture this morning, but he was usually in his office. We don't know why he went home.'

'So, he returned home? He'd been in the office?'

'Yes.'

'Someone must have called him. Do we have his phone records?'

'Already checked his mobile, and there's nothing significant. We're waiting on the university. It's possible that it had been pre-arranged, of course.'

'OK. When are we expecting the university phone records?'

He shrugs. 'We're on it.'

He looks at his watch and I nod. We're not getting them now. Need to get back to it tomorrow morning.

'When you were looking into Mrs Waverley's background, and you found out about her first husband, how much checking did you do?'

He pauses for a second, sensing that there might be some sort of rebuke in the air.

'Mainly around the circumstances of his death,' he says. 'I thought that was what was important, and it seemed all above board.'

A slight hesitation, then he adds, 'What did I miss?'

'It's OK, you'd really have had to dig. Anyway, take a guess at where Mr Cameron, Melanie's first husband, was working twelve years ago?' He looks confused for a moment, and then he shakes his head. It's fair enough. It only seemed obvious to me after I'd read it.

'Aberdeen University,' I say.

He looks confused again for a moment, then, 'Seriously? How did I miss that?'

'Don't worry about it. It was four or five years before he met his wife, so there's no reason why it should have been of relevance.'

'So, what do we think?'

'At the moment, we don't think too much, but it places her two dead husbands in the same establishment at the same time. I know, it's a big place, but this isn't a coincidence we can ignore.'

'If only everyone wasn't dead, we could ask someone about it,' he says.

'Funny. We need to dig deeper. Speak to the engineering department, there must be someone who was there twelve years ago, see if they remember Waverley.'

'Do we go and see her?'

'I was driving from Inverness thinking that, but it's too early. Let's see where we can get. Much better turning up at her place armed with some facts, rather than some vague link that she can easily laugh off. Work on it tonight, make some calls in the morning, take it to Quinn. Maybe then we go over there with a full complement. We'll see.'

Sutherland nods, then tosses over a photograph he's got sitting at the top of his in-tray.

'Found this at Gibson's place. What did he say to you he called them? The Four Musketeers was it? Not very original.'

I look at the photograph. Baden, King, Waverley and Solomon on a beach. The beach at Aberdeen presumably, although there's nothing in the background to indicate where it is.

I realise I've hardly seen any photographs of them. These people we've been investigating have been largely faceless, apart from the couple of photos we have pinned to the board. Even Baden, who I've met, seems so detached from this young smiling man on the beach. And now, he's the only one of the four left alive.

* * *

As it is, after a few hours online and making calls, we probably have enough to bring Mrs Waverley in for questioning. Eleven o'clock in the evening, and we have Waverley and Cameron, who would both ultimately be married to the same woman, as friends. Not as part of the Conservative gang, and in completely unrelated departments, but they knew each other. Played rugby together. The rugby was the clincher. Always the same with teams. Shared experiences and the number of people who are aware of things that were going on, suddenly get much larger. Waverley and Cameron were tight, even though there were ten years between them, and at least a couple of people knew of them keeping in touch.

Another check of the clock. Turning up on someone's doorstep at eleven at night is the preferred approach of many a police officer around the country.

'What d'you think?' I say to him.

Sutherland is currently staring at his screen. He looks exhausted. Looks like I feel. Neither of those is a reason not to go and speak to someone who may be a suspect in several murders. Neither is the fact that it's eleven o'clock in the evening. 'You're the boss,' he says.

'I don't think she's going anywhere, and there are a few more people we can contact in the morning, so...'

Long sigh, wave an undecided hand.

'If she's not involved, it hardly matters; if she is, we get her in the morning, and it could be we go there with even more than we have now. At the moment we have a piece of circumstantial... whatever. Circumstantial whatever, that's all we've got. But then...' Wave the hand again, then continue talking. 'What if she's involved, but not the killer, and she gets murdered? Tonight. Or, worse, she's not involved at all, but someone takes her out the game anyway.'

Stand there nodding at my own words. Look at my watch again.

'Nah, we can't think like that. We're not bringing her in tonight, because we hardly have enough to do that. So, what then? We go and see her, talk to her for a while, then likely leave and she's still alone in her house. And then someone, if they're going to, can kill her anyway. We've got nothing on which to base putting a watch on her house. No, no, we'll forget it. Go home, get some sleep. If, you know, if she gets killed in the next twelve hours, it's on me.'

That doesn't sound great. Shake my head. 'You know what I mean.'

'I was recording that on my phone,' says Sutherland smiling, 'so we're good.'

45

Set the alarm for six. Wide awake about ten seconds before the alarm is due to go off, a voice in my head. It happens. Waking up, as though someone is speaking to you. Seems so real. It's a woman's voice that I don't recognise. Young. A slight accent I can't place.

'It finishes today.'

That's all. I wake up with someone saying those words to me. Bolt upright in bed, in the way that people wake up in movies. A quick glance around the room in the dark. Look at my phone, check the time. Quickly turn off the alarm, so that it doesn't blare out into the darkness. Swing my legs over the side of the bed. Straighten my back.

The voice is still in my head. *It finishes today.* That's what she said. That's what who said? Try to remember what I was dreaming about, but there's nothing there. No dreams. Or, if there were, they are instantly gone.

Into the bathroom, cold water on my face, brush my teeth, step into the shower. Water as hot as I can stand for five minutes, and then full-on cold for thirty seconds.

Dressed, into the kitchen. Two fried eggs on toast, cup of coffee, glass of water, glass of orange juice. Put the dishes in the sink, contemplate washing them, then decide to leave them until later. Tie on, out the door, and I'm in work before seven.

★ ★ ★

'What's the latest on Baden?'

Sutherland and I are back in Quinn's office. The superintendent is thinking a lot. There are long silences, but at least it's better than its opposite; not thinking at all. You can hear the cars on the road outside. The clock is unusually loud. There's something about the tick today that seems jarring. Perhaps its battery is running out, and the hands are struggling to keep up.

'They're bringing him up to Gartcosh this morning. I thought I'd go down there after lunch. I want to take him to see his mother.'

'At the home in Perth?'

'Yes.'

'You've cleared that?'

Hesitate for a moment. 'No, not yet. I need to make a call.'

219

He holds my eyes for a second, understanding that getting them to release Baden might not be particularly straightforward.

'If you need me to intervene,' he says.

'I have someone I can speak to.'

'Very well.'

He nods, glances down at his notes.

'And you're bringing this Asian woman in?'

'Not sure yet. Just about to go and talk to her. I'll make the call when we're there.'

He taps his fingers. Right hand. Often has a slightly distracted air about him. Just his way. He's not at all distracted.

We've been in here twenty-five minutes already. Been through it all. Death by death, murder by murder, what we know of the case from twelve years ago, what we know now. The answer to the murders in the present lies in the past, on that we have so far agreed.

'Gentlemen,' he says, breaking the silence, 'go and speak to her, and do what you have to do. I hope, however, that this speculative dart will not become the sole avenue of investigation.'

'Of course not, sir.'

We stand up, quick glance between us and out the door, closing it behind.

★ ★ ★

And there the widow sits, just as Sutherland had previously described her. The sofa in the front room is placed with its back to the window, and she is sitting side-on, resting her arms on its back, resting her head in her arms, looking out to sea. As I get out of the car, I follow her gaze. Fresh morning, something of a wind, clouds flitting across the sky, sunshine and rain promised in equal measure. It must be like this most days up here. And if I had this house, would I ever be able to pull myself away from the window?

She turns to watch us as we approach the front door, waits for Sutherland to ring the bell, so that I've almost begun to think that she must be expecting someone else to answer it, and then, after leaving us standing for half a minute or so, she's there before us, dressed all in white. Slim, tight-fitting jeans, a woollen top, her long black hair hanging straight around the shoulders.

She is beautiful. Catch-your-breath-in-your-throat beautiful. If the bereaved Mrs Waverley wants to find another husband, I can't imagine she'd have too much trouble.

'Sergeant Sutherland,' she says. 'And…?'

'Inspector Westphall,' I say, automatically showing her my card. She looks in my eyes, doesn't look at the card.

'Come in.'

Sutherland closes the door, and we follow her into the front room, the room with a view, looking out directly over the mouth of the Cromarty Firth to the cliffs opposite, and away over the large grey expanse of the Moray Firth. All three of us stand and stare at the scenery for a few moments, then she moves, sits back down in her spot, and resumes her position.

'I find it hard to drag myself away sometimes.'

I recognise her voice, but not her face.

'Can we talk to you about your first husband?'

She turns, a slight look of surprise on her face.

'David?'

'If he was your first, yes,' I answer.

Maybe she was married in Thailand. Maybe she's been married to others, and we missed that as well.

'Yes, David was my first.'

'Did you know that David worked at a university before you met?'

'Yes, of course. Aberdeen.'

'And did you ever meet any of his friends from his days at Aberdeen?'

A slight pause. Whatever she is, she's not a professional liar. We can see her quickly thinking this over.

'That was how I knew Andrew,' she says.

'Your second husband?'

'Yes.'

Shakes her head slightly.

'Of course, there was an element of chance about it. There are, sometimes, elements of chance. We'd met a couple of times. He was at David's funeral. Then… then I signed up to an online dating site, and we…'

'Why?'

She stares straight at me for a moment. Really, where am I going with that question? Am I going to tell her that she's preposterously beautiful so why did she feel the need? Am I just going to dismiss questions of confidence and self-assurance and personality, and suggest that everyone's actions are entirely based upon their looks? Am I living in the 1970s?

'I was lonely,' she says.

'Of course.'

'How long did you see each other before deciding to get married?'

'He asked on our first date.'

That's not surprising. Andrew Waverley presumably was going to want to get her off the market as quickly as possible.

'Are you going to judge us, Inspector Westphall?'

'Did you say yes?'

'Yes, I did. We knew each other, he seemed like a nice man. It felt like fate that we'd both signed up to the same site. It suited us at the time, there was no point in waiting.'

'Was it working out?'

She holds my gaze for a moment, and then turns so that she's looking over the back of the sofa, out to sea.

'No, not really,' she says.

'Were you both unhappy, or just you?'

She doesn't turn back. We sit in silence. Sutherland is staring at her, his expression hard to read. The silence is somehow special. A silence quite beyond explanation. A silence that can be waited out, no one in a rush to fill it. Melanie staring at the view, Sutherland and I looking at the back of her head, the stark, attractive contrast between her dark hair and the perfect white of her top.

It was one of the great differences between Olivia and I. One of the things that defined us, that separated us. The silences. I was happy to exist in the silences. The silences that are conducted with music in the background, or the clatter and hubbub of a busy restaurant. The silences like this one, that are absolute. The silences that are ultimately a silence of two people with nothing to say.

Olivia hated those silences. She filled them. Or worse, she chose not to fill them and instead she judged them.

'There was a book once,' she says.

I don't know how long it takes her to speak. That kind of silence has no time. Time is irrelevant.

'You know Mr Wakamoto, the Japanese author?'

'I've heard of him,' I say.

Sutherland nods, although she's not looking at us, her gaze still directed out to sea.

'I was in a bookshop. Last year. I was looking at Mr Wakamoto's books. I've read some of them, but not all of course. There was one I had not heard of. *The Song of the Dead*. I started reading the book. It was the story of a young woman who is lost. Lost in her life, and in time. She loses her family, her husband and her young daughter, and cannot get them back. It seemed such a sad story.'

A young woman, lost in time, who cannot find her family. She's talking about that? How can she be talking about that?

Her voice is part of the room, part of the scenery. We need to get on with this day, and yet I get the feeling that when we leave here, we're unlikely to have been in the house for more than a few minutes.

'I wasn't... I didn't buy the book. I don't know why. A few days later I was back at the bookshop, and this time I thought, this time I will buy this book. I want to know what happens. So I went back to the section with Mr Wakamoto's books, and I look. But there is no book with this title. No book titled *The Song of the Dead* by Mr Wakamoto. I think at first that someone must have bought it. I go to the counter and ask if they have another copy. They look on their system for the book. They say they have no book with that title, nor have they ever had the book.

'We argued for a moment, but the lady was adamant. I checked the list of his books inside his other titles, but there was no mention. I went home and I looked online. There is no book with this title, by Mr Wakamoto, or by anyone else. A short poem by Mr Kipling, but no book, and certainly not by Mr Wakamoto. How is one to explain this, Inspector? I picked up the book. I can see the cover, now, in my head. I read the first few pages. I know there was a book. And yet... I cannot find the book. The book does not appear to exist.'

Slowly she turns and looks back at us. There are mundane explanations in my head. The book is by someone else. She got the title wrong. It's an advance copy that somehow found its way onto the shelf. But I doubt it's any of those.

Is Dorothy listening? Was she just a character out of a book?

That's absurd! She was an officer in the FCO! It's not like I sat in a car with her, and no one else even knew she existed!

'What did you learn from the first few pages of the book?' I ask.

'There was nothing to learn from those pages, Inspector. The question is, what will I learn from the radio? I heard this story...'

She pauses, her eyes lower. Sutherland and I glance at each other.

'I don't know what made me turn on the radio. I don't usually listen to the radio. Maybe I was lonely again, maybe I needed another voice in the house. And there it was. My strange story was on the radio. My lonely, lost girl.'

The room and the view and her voice and her looks, they all kind of swallow you up. Mesmerising. I suddenly think, I should have brought Fisher with me. Would she be telling this story if there was a woman in the room? Did she tell stories before when Fisher came?

I don't pick up on any artifice in her voice. This doesn't feel like the conversation of evasion. Nevertheless, I probably ought to be somewhat more focused, as Quinn will be asking, and we can't say that we spent the entire time discussing mysterious Japanese literature and its otherworldly connection with the woman who is now haunting my dreams.

'Did you know anyone else from David's time at Aberdeen?' I force myself to ask. 'Ever meet them, get to know them, anything?'

She seems slightly curious that I've interrupted her narrative, stares at the carpet for a moment, then there's a slight movement of her shoulders.

'A few. I don't think I remember their names. Maybe if I tried. But Andrew didn't want anything to do with them. He said he'd moved on from those days, wanted to leave them behind. Leave the people behind. I thought it was sad.'

'Did he talk about them? Was there a reason why he wanted to leave them behind?'

'There was definitely a reason, but as to what it was…'

Finally glance at my watch. Needing to get on with the day. One last person to ask about.

'Did you know Detective Inspector Rosco in town?'

She turns back, smiling. 'Everyone north of Inverness knew DI Rosco, didn't they? Poor thing.'

'How did you know him?'

'When I came up here with Andrew. He was one of the ones he knew from the old days. I'm not sure why, what context. Andrew didn't want anything to do with him.'

Hold her gaze for a moment. Look at my watch again. There's more to be found out here, I think, but it'll take time.

'We might need you to come down to the station,' I say. 'We're trying to piece together the story of what went on at Aberdeen back at the time when your husbands were friends.'

'Just call and let me know,' she says. 'I'll be here.'

She smiles, a slightly sad, almost affectedly hopeless smile.

'I'll be looking at the view, listening to the radio later. Listening to my sad story. They haven't said, but I have a feeling it finishes today.'

And that was how I'd recognised her voice.

46

'I didn't tell you what Baden said about Rosco, if we could believe him.'

Back at the station, sitting at our desks. Now that we're here I am, inevitably, questioning myself over the decision not to bring Melanie Waverley straight to the station. Did I not bring her because she's beautiful, a beauty increased by her air of melancholy? Was it her strange story that somehow mirrored the other strange story of the last few days? Or because Quinn told us not to make her the sole avenue of the investigation? If it was any of those, I don't deserve to be in the job.

It didn't feel right, that was all. Like we'd be wasting our time. Another road slowly explored with nothing to show for it at the end.

'He knew him?' asks Sutherland, looking up.

'Said he was all over Emily. Lovesick. Would do anything for her, which would explain why he helped her with the false identification. We could do with finding out if there's more to it, or if there was even that much.'

'You mean, if Baden's telling the truth?'

'Yes.'

Look at my watch. Have already called Gartcosh and arranged to meet DCI Meadows just after three. Meadows owes me a favour, a pretty big one at that. Slightly disappointed that I'm calling it in over this, although I'm not sure what I'd consider worthwhile, if this isn't it.

Not that he was particularly gracious. Be there at three or miss your chance, he said, so I ought to be heading off in the next few minutes.

'Money? Maybe there was money.'

'Money, certainly, has got to be a possibility. We need to chase down his banking records. You know who he was with?'

'Clydesdale.'

'OK, get on to them, see what we can get. I'm sure you'll get the usual raised eyebrow about information that old, but you know...'

Phone rings.

'And we need to imagine it's not money. Let's think about other things... Westphall?'

'Sergeant Edelman.'

Anstruther calling. Another neglected strand.

'Beth, what have you got?'

'You sound business-like,' she says, a smile in her voice.

'Got that, you know, got that feeling. It's coming to an end, one way or another. What do you have?'

No time for idle chatter, I think, although I seem to let Melanie Waverley get away with rather a lot of it.

'We've been looking at Emily King's bank account. Basically she was being paid once a month for the past nine years. Not clear yet by whom, but we're chasing the money.'

You should always chase the money. At the root of nearly everything.

'How much?'

'One thousand.'

'A thousand a month for nine years... One hundred and eight thousand. Had the amount changed at all?'

'No. You're bang on. A hundred and eight thousand paid into her account, give or take a month or two. Seems she paid her mortgage and her bills, and saved several hundred a month. Had nearly thirty grand in there.'

'You think she was saving for something? Waiting for something?'

'I think she was. But then, we knew that anyway.'

'Yep.'

Pause. A curious, slightly awkward pause, as though one of us is supposed to say something else.

'OK, thanks, Beth. Can you let me know if you manage to trace the money?'

'Of course.'

'When are you working 'til today?'

She laughs lightly at the other end. Am I thinking I might stop by after dropping Baden back to Gartcosh? Like it's anywhere near.

'Not sure,' she says. 'Evening.'

'OK, thanks. We'll be in touch.'

Hang up before there's any more awkwardness. Stare across the desk at Sutherland.

'Well, Emily King was getting paid money from somewhere. Things come together for a reason, Sergeant. We were just talking about Rosco, and we hear about Emily King's bank balance.'

'Loaded?'

'She was doing all right, although more through frugality than any individual large payments. Rosco similarly didn't look loaded, but I really don't think he was waiting for anything.'

'Maybe he spent it all,' says Sutherland.

'Or maybe he gave it to someone.'

Sutherland has a moment and then nods. Mrs Rosco.

'You know, people keep getting murdered and distracting us, but so much of it comes back to Rosco. What was he doing? Why did he do it? If he was as besotted with Emily King as Baden implied, why then marry someone else?'

'Maybe Emily just blew him off, finally, and it was a knee-jerk thing. Your classic marriage on the rebound.'

'That's got a solid ring to it.'

Look at the clock. I really do need to get going but I think there might well be time for a quick stopover in Aviemore.

'If I leave now I'll have time to stop at her house on the way down the road.'

'You want me to call ahead and make sure she's in?' he asks.

'No. She doesn't like talking about her husband. I'll need the element of surprise.'

★ ★ ★

Almost as though she knew anyway, as I arrive she's locking her front door. I park my car across her driveway, to stop her leaving. It's not that I think she has any reason to run, but there are plenty of people all too willing to be rude – who see the police investigating crime as an intrusion – regardless of whether or not they have anything to hide.

'Can you move that, please?' she says.

'Just got a few more questions.'

She stands beside her car, staring blankly at me. We are very familiar with this stare. The one that covers the internal debate on whether or not they should tell us where to go. It's a wide driveway, and I can see her judging whether or not she'll be able to squeeze past. I really don't think she will, and hope she doesn't try. The paperwork for the car repairs would be a pain in the neck.

'Can I make an appointment for later?' she asks. Unexpected. 'Or tomorrow, if that suits you.'

'It shouldn't take long,' I say.

It finishes today. Why are those words still in my head? I've already established where they came from. Melanie Waverley and her strange little story. There's no reason why I should have dreamt about it before having the conversation, but it happened, and that's all.

'I've got a doctor's appointment. You know what it's like these days. Miss one, and you don't get another for six months.'

I don't answer straight away, but she's got me. It's not like I've got a huge amount of time anyway, and if I insist on it, it's more likely to make her clam up. I had to catch her off guard and willing to talk, rather than just about to go somewhere and annoyed at being interrupted.

'I can see you in an hour,' she says.

'Needs to be now or tomorrow.'

She smiles, which is something I haven't seen before.

'Look,' she says, her tone softening, 'another day would do me good anyway. I know you want to talk about Rosco, and I know he was the biggest arsehole on God's earth. But he was my husband, for a while at least, and I am allowed some mourning period, aren't I?'

I'm not sure why my gut instinct is telling me not to let her go. She's not accused of anything. As far as we know, she hasn't done anything. This is a background check, another one, that's all. Yet, when you come to talk to someone and they immediately want to leave, it's innately suspicious.

Of course, she had started to leave before I got there.

'Very well,' I say, 'tomorrow afternoon. Early.'

She nods.

'Thanks, Inspector.'

She opens the car door and gets in. Starts the engine straight away, although she doesn't do anything so crass as rev the engine. She's not a teenage boy.

I look down at her for a few moments, then walk to my car, and move away from the entrance to the driveway. She reverses out and is on her way. Her car is gone from sight by the time I get to the end of her street.

47

Debbie Rosco plays on my mind as I head south. A couple of times, near the start of the drive, I wonder if it's her car I see ahead of me. A red Peugeot, at this distance practically unidentifiable from any other red, saloon car, but it could be her. Why would she be heading south on the A9?

I feel like I'm letting something go. There's so much involved in this case, so many people. There's always something else, there has to be. You make a call on where to draw the circle, and you concentrate on what's inside. As for what's on the outside, you end up forgetting it or willfully ignoring it, and all you can do is hope that your judgement was correct in the first place.

I pull into a lay-by a little north of Drumochter. Call Sutherland. Another phone call from the road. It feels sloppy, like I should be on top of everything, handing out timely orders, rather than constantly playing catch-up.

'Hey, sorry, got something else. Maybe you could ask Fisher.'

'Sure,' he says.

I don't ask what he's doing now. If it's important, he'll tell me.

'Mrs Rosco,' I say. 'Just had a quick word with her, but didn't really have time to talk. I'm going to interview her tomorrow. Get me some more background. See what you can dig up. Anything. I mean, absolutely anything.'

'Sure.'

'OK, thanks. I'll call when I'm heading back.'

He hangs up. I lay the phone down and stare along the road for a few moments. There's a great wave of dark cloud coming in from the west, contrasting with the high, white cloud overhead.

I look over my shoulder, and then ease the car back out onto the road.

★ ★ ★

Words dry up.

Sitting with Baden on the M9 between Glasgow and Perth. I realise he looks a little better every time I see him. Decent sleep, decent meals. I presume he didn't get to stay in the Dorchester last night, but he won't have been stuck in a stinking cell in the basement of Scotland Yard either.

DCI Meadows of the Specialist Crime Division wasn't too excited about me taking Baden off for a couple of hours, but he felt some imperative from my official calling in of the favour he owes me for saving his backside on the Revel kidnapping case three years ago.

Still, he asked that I didn't question Baden. On the face of it, that's a counter-intuitive request, because I have him alone and it's a perfect opportunity for conversation to arise, and things to be said. However, now that Mr. Baden has employed a legal team, there's really no point. The slightest hint that I've been treating him as a suspect, or even a witness, and they'll be screaming about police abuse, harassment, and inappropriate procedures.

So, here we are, driving in silence, and I'm wondering why I made the trip down from Dingwall. I needed to see Baden with his mother, I needed it confirmed. I needed to see that woman look into his eyes, the look on her face when she sees her son for the first time in well over a decade.

But things have been falling into place. We know the body that washed up in the lake wasn't Baden, we know how Rosco engineered the cover-up. There isn't any doubt that this is the real Baden sitting beside me.

Yet, I had to come. It felt right to come. This is where the investigation goes, this is how it progresses. Me and Baden sitting in a car, travelling to see his mother.

The phone goes. On the motorway there's nowhere to pull over, so I lift it. DHM Tallinn. Haven't heard from him in a while.

'Kenneth, hey,' I say.

'Inspector,' he says. 'Anything to report?'

'We're getting there. A few things happening. Can't really talk at the moment, sorry.'

Slight pause.

'All right, of course. I just wanted to let you know that there's going to be a service for Dorothy next week in London. I know it might be a stretch for you, and it'll depend on what's going on work-wise…'

'No, I should try to be there. Definitely. What day?'

'Thursday.'

'E-mail me the details. What about you?'

'Sorry, can't. Ambassador's away all week.'

'Welded to your desk?'

'Something like that.'

'Anything to report from your end?'

'The Estonians... they've just closed up shop. It's not our business any more. I mean, they're usually great, great working relationship. But now they're in this mode, it's like, it's an internal matter. You know, thanks for your help, but we'll handle it from now on. And you know, we've got our guy back, what exactly is it we'd want from them anyway?'

I think I might have a few more questions for them. I can see their point. Britain has done enough sticking its nose into other people's business, you can understand why anyone would turn their back on it. But it's hard not to think that someone at that end is still complicit in what's going on over here. For these murders to start when they did, someone in Estonia contacted someone in Scotland.

I glance at Baden. It was either someone from the authorities, or it was this guy sitting here.

'I'll call you tomorrow,' I say.

'Sure.'

'Thanks for letting me know about Dorothy. I'll try to be there.'

We hang up. Just placing the phone back down when it rings again. Sutherland. Around three o'clock. No need for headlights yet; we'll get the full complement of daylight.

'Yep?'

'Boss,' he says. 'Sitting down?'

Almost smile at that. The first time he said it to me I thought something big was coming. Now he's overused it. He'll say it on a Saturday afternoon when County haven't lost.

'Driving, so yes.'

'Emily King isn't dead.'

Sitting in the inside lane travelling at sixty-seven miles per hour. Car in front, a white Audi A3, behind me a Toyota pulling a caravan that I passed while talking to the DHM. Pale blue skies up above.

'What d'you mean?'

As he says it, I realise I'm not surprised. Not at all surprised. Emily King isn't dead? Of course she's not dead, you idiot!

'Emily King married DS Rosco.'

'What?'

'Can you talk?'

'No, I can't, but you can.'

Glance at the side of the road. Contemplate just pulling over, so that I can get out the car and talk in peace. But then, I'd be talking beside a motorway and I'd barely hear anything, so there'd be little point. Contemplate postponing the conversation until we're in Perth, and maybe I'll wait until then to get more detail. However, I need the full gist of it now.

'So, I was chasing down Mrs Rosco, and it was kind of weird, because the woman's life appears to have started when she married him. Got into Rosco's things, copy of the marriage licence etc. Everything pertaining to the two of them. This woman did not exist before she got married. Seriously. There's nothing. Deborah Geddes. That was the name on the license. There's nothing about her on record, any record. Not this Deborah Geddes. And you know what that means.'

'Keep talking.'

There's never *nothing* on record about people. Not now. Not for a long time.

'Out of nowhere she appeared, a month or two after Emily King returned from Estonia, and she married Rosco. That's the first time she's recorded as existing.'

'But how...?'

Stop myself asking the question.

'It's her. I'm looking at photographs. The old one on the board of Emily, the one of her from university we got from Gibson's house, and one, only one, that we found among Rosco's things of him and Debbie on his wedding day. Like the woman didn't want her photograph taken. But it's the same woman, sir. Looking at the picture on her driving licence, there's something different about her now, like she lost something since she married Rosco...'

I can see his brow creased, see his head shaking slightly.

'It's hard to explain. I'll show you when you get back up.'

'We need more than that.'

He'd been so definite in his declaration, his big announcement, that I presumed he was going to have more. Yet, the concept does not surprise me. In fact, suddenly everything falls into place. Everything would make sense, if DI Rosco was married to Emily King. It just wouldn't make sense that it was his ex-wife whom I'd spoken to earlier today, and that she'd also been murdered last week.

And then the thought strikes me. This whole thing started out with the possibility of there being two John Badens. Perhaps, it would transpire, that the real mystery was that there were two Emily Kings. Nevertheless, that possibility is no less incredible now than it was a few days ago.

'I know,' he says, 'maybe they were sisters or something, but all it comes down to is that her hair's different, there's a thinness about the face, she's wearing those thick-rimmed spectacles. I had someone down at SCC run the photographs of Emily King and Debbie Rosco through Ganymede, and they've come up with 97 per cent match. So, we're continuing to work on it, but if we could, somehow, get some DNA from his ex-wife. And we need to work out who this other person was in Anstruther.'

Ever the pragmatist, Sutherland. I immediately consider the possibility of there being two of the same woman, while Sutherland automatically assumes that one of them is someone else.

'Call Sergeant Edelman, have a word.'

'In Anstruther?'

'Yes.'

'Will do. Do you know where Mrs Rosco is now, sir?'

Shake my head. Had the damned car parked across the end of her driveway, and let her go. Visualising the two women. The old photographs of Emily King, and the woman I just spoke to today. Emily, young and dark-haired and attractive. Mrs Rosco, seemingly much older, more than twelve years older, hair dyed blonde, her glasses now chic and expensive. But there was the reason why I found her so unattractive; she'd had work done. It was a while ago – perhaps after the wedding photograph had been taken – her face had grown into it, but there was something not quite right which I hadn't placed at the time.

'Still in Aviemore. She was going to the doctor's. That's what she said, at any rate.'

'You want me to check that?'

'Sure, if you can get anywhere. And get her car registration number... no, no, not yet. Too early for that. Too early to be going all out. Keep doing what you're doing, come back to me if there's anything else significant.'

Hang up, phone back down, two hands on the steering wheel.

'Who were you talking about?'

I don't answer.

48

'How long has she been here?'

We pull into the car park. Late afternoon, sun low in the sky.

'Three years,' I say, as I turn off the engine. Out the car, close the door, and stand for a moment looking at the trees. The air is crisp and cold. It's going to be a beautifully clear, sharp evening.

'It's a nice place. She seems to be doing fine.'

He's staring around at the trees. The woods here are nothing compared to what he's just experienced, but I can't blame him for looking at them with some amount of fear.

'She seemed happy when I spoke to her last week,' I say.

'Did you tell her that I was still alive?'

'Didn't have to, she knew. She didn't doubt for a second that you were still alive.'

'The police in Estonia said that she'd identified my body.'

'That wasn't her. That was your aunt.'

He looks confused.

'Margaret?'

'Yes.'

'Why did she identify the body?'

I'm not going to get into explaining it at the moment, as that would undoubtedly lead to talk of Rosco. When we get into it with Baden on Rosco, it ought to be under strict interview conditions, so that we don't give his lawyer an excuse to strike off anything he tells us.

'Let's go and see your mum.'

He nods. Looks nervous. Wonder if he's going to start crying, even before he sees her. However wrong the things he was doing before he was taken prisoner, coming back here after twelve years must still be incredibly strange, verging on the traumatic.

We could probably stand there looking at the house until it gets dark, so I lead him off with a slight touch of the arm, and walk through the car park and up the front steps. There's a large front door, unlocked, and a small reception area inside.

Show my ID as I approach the woman at the desk.

'DI Westphall, I'm expected. Here to see Mrs Baden.'

'Of course,' she says. 'You've been here before?'

'Yes.'

'Shall I call someone to take you through, or do you know where you're going?'

'Is Mrs Baden in–?'

'–She'll be in her usual spot,' she says. 'By the window.'

'Thanks.'

I walk on, a glance behind to make sure Baden is following. He looks agitated, but I guess he's nervous about seeing her. I suddenly wonder if he's nervous about it because he's not actually John Baden. He's worried that she's going to call him out on it. Maybe he's worried she won't recognise him because he is her son, and that would be even worse.

The latter is more likely.

'Come on.'

We walk along the short corridor, hung with paintings of deer in the glens, through the small sitting room, leather chairs and shelves of books – they probably call it the library – where once again there is no one sitting, and then through to the large common area at the back of the house, where Mrs Baden spends her life.

She's not at the window as we come through, although her place is intact, a cup of tea on the small table beside her spot. There are a few others around – the word *inmates* comes unavoidably into my head – but no nursing staff. We walk over to the window and stand by her chair.

I can feel her presence, feel that she was here, but left a while ago. A peculiar feeling, and it's quickly gone. Not a feeling that I can place or recall or bring back. Came and it went. Look back around the room.

'Where is she?' he asks.

'I don't know. Gone to the bathroom, maybe.'

I look back around the room, and then outside. She hasn't just gone to the bathroom. It's more than that. I open the door by her seat, and take a step outside. Slightly colder back here than at the front of the house, with the lawn and trees in shadow. The cold immediately clutches at me, and I almost hear the voice from inside the house before it comes.

'Shut the door!'

Take a moment to look around, stare into the trees. Has she gone in search of her deer? I step back inside and close the door behind me. The warmth in the room, compared to outside, is quite noticeable.

''Bout bloody time.'

I ignore the mutter. Not even sure where it comes from.

'Where is she?'

Don't look at him, shake my head slightly. Step forward, positioning myself a little better. Look around the room. There are eight people here, mostly sitting on their own. Communal separation.

'Excuse me.'

Three of them look up.

'Excuse me,' I repeat, with a slightly raised voice.

Now I've got the attention of all but one of them.

'Mrs Baden, who usually sits by the window here. Does anyone know where she is?'

Greeted by largely blank stares, as though most of them hadn't realised that the same woman had been sitting by the window for the last few years.

'She left,' says one guy.

'When?'

He looks over his newspaper. A funny old guy, acerbic. I can read him. Of all of these people, the one you could sit and talk to. The one who would have the stories and opinions, all without sentimentality.

Shakes his head, sighs.

'Time in this place,' he says, and he makes a small gesture with his right hand, the corner of the newspaper folding over as he lets it go.

'Ballpark?'

'American are you?' he says.

'Ten minutes or two hours?'

He looks at the carpet for a moment, then lifts his gaze.

'One of them, or somewhere in-between I expect.'

'You're not helping.'

'I'm not trying to, son.'

He raises his paper and disappears behind it. The door opens, and one of the nursing staff comes in, pushing a tray. Tea and biscuits. A few pastries. They probably use an endless supply of food as one of the selling points of the place, even though by the time they get to this age, no one wants to eat all day. It will allow the company to charge fifteen times more than the cost of the food that no one eats.

'Can you tell me about Mrs Baden,' I say, indicating the window.

'What about her?'

'She's not in her spot. You know where she is?'

The nurse glances over at the window, although the emptiness of the place where she usually sits hardly needs to be looked at to be confirmed, and then she nods and smiles.

'She had a visitor.'

'Where did they go?'

'Might be in her room. Maybe they went off-site, although she should have checked in with the front desk.'

'Who was the visitor?'

'It was her daughter, I'm pretty sure.'

'She doesn't have a daughter.'

'You'll need to check at the front desk. Why don't you do that? The woman that was here, she's been before. We all know…'

'Describe her.'

She hesitates. With the raising of my tone, she suddenly realises she's being questioned. No one likes being questioned.

'I'm… why don't you speak to the front desk?'

I don't bother pursuing it. I know what I need to do.

'When was the last time you saw Mrs Baden sitting there?'

Another glance at the vacant spot.

'Might have been half an hour ago,' she says. 'Maybe longer.'

* * *

Go through the motions to confirm what I suddenly already know. The woman who was married to Rosco was also, somehow, Emily King. She came down here, ahead of me, to take Mrs Baden somewhere. And I had my car blocking her exit.

Perhaps she's never going home. Perhaps this is it. Her work done, and off she flies.

Another phone call to Sutherland. I get him to bring up the photo of Debbie Rosco from her driving licence and e-mail it to me. I get the picture on my phone, I show the picture to two of the nurses. They confirm that she was the visitor to Mrs Baden. Having already checked the car park, I know that her car is no longer here. We establish from CCTV that they left, together, forty-three minutes previously.

Forty-three minutes from Perth. Dundee, Stirling, Pitlochry, Dunfermline; any direction, from right in the middle of the country, north, east, south, west, and off she'd go.

Behind at every step of the way, not making the decisions when I needed to. Ignoring gut instinct, too flat-footed, too wedded to procedure, too afraid of lawyers.

Not willing enough to embrace the weird. The world is full of weird, and so often we miss it or we let it pass, because it's too hard to explain. This case has had weird written all over it from the beginning, from Baden's appearance to the strange tale of Dorothy. Was it ever going to be straightforward?

Baden has been sitting in the car while I established the timeline of what happened, such as it is. I haven't mentioned to him yet that the reason his mother isn't here any more is because Emily King has taken her.

I head back to the car park, after another call to Sutherland and a request to put out an APW for Mrs Rosco, and indicate for Baden to get out the car. Darkness beginning to fall, the air is perfect. Late autumn crispness, wonderful smell. Somewhere there's a log fire just getting going. Not the time to enjoy it.

Baden follows me back inside. I ask for the use of a private room for a few minutes, and they direct me to an office along the corridor. A small desk, one chair, no phone, a photocopier and a shredder, a couple of office cabinets and shelves with stationery.

We stand in the room for a moment, barely enough space for the two of us, and I close the door and show him to the chair behind the desk. He sits down, looking nervous for the first time since we drove back to the forest together.

'Is she dead?'

'Who?'

'My mum,' he says, annoyance and hurt in his voice.

Of course, I wasn't trying to be oblique, mind just flying everywhere at once. Need to eliminate everything, and ask straightforward questions, intrinsic questions, to try to get to the heart of this.

Before I was following the money. Now, regardless, I need to follow the weird.

'Sorry, no, she's not dead, not as far as I know.'

I place my phone, with the picture from Debbie Rosco's driving licence, on the desk. He looks at it, the surprise shows on his face.

'You recognise her?'

'That's Emily,' he says. 'I think it's Emily. She looks... different. Was this how she looked before she died?'

He looks up at me. His fingers are resting on the phone, so I reach down and slip it back into my pocket.

'Can I see it again?'

'No.'

'Emily's dead, right? You said, Emily was dead?'

'I need to know what happened when you were in Estonia.'

'I've told you everything.'

'No, you haven't. I doubt you've told me ten percent of it.'

He doesn't say anything, but I doubt he's even genuinely going to be able to deny the percentages.

'I shouldn't be interviewing you again. This was just about seeing your mum. But she's not here, we've moved on from that, and this can't wait for a courtroom, it can't wait for your lawyer, it can't wait for you to get taken back into custody. Talk to me.'

He exhales a long breath, a little shake of the head.

'I told you. Emily was bad. She was a bad person. She killed Solomon, she must have misidentified the body, just like we planned. That's all.'

'That was Emily's picture I just showed you?'

'Yes, I'm sure of it.'

'This is the woman who came today and took your mother away.'

'What? Why?'

'Well, we don't know why, do we? Emily King is alive and well and took your mother away from here today. We don't know where. And yet, strangely, Emily King died last week. Just like Waverley and Gibson and Rosco, since your return was announced.'

'What?'

He's looking confused, but there's always something. Maybe I'm looking for it, and people usually find what they're looking for, even if it takes some manipulation. For a moment, though, I think I see through the cracks. The John Baden on the other side.

'What?' he repeats, although this time there's a different quality to his voice.

'People have been dying, including Emily. And yet Emily was here, less than an hour ago. There are, it would appear, two Emilys.'

'That's absurd.'

'Mr Baden, you know, you're right. It is absurd. Give me another explanation.'

'I can't!'

'Not good enough. You and Emily went out to Estonia together. You died out there, your body was identified. Emily died last week. Murdered. And yet you and Emily still roam the Earth.'

'There was no body in Estonia. It was Solomon.'

'It was Solomon?'

'Yes. You know it was. We talked about this.'

'So that's a very straightforward explanation.'

'Yes.'

'So what's the straightforward explanation for the fact there are two Emilys?'

'I don't know.'

His voice has lost some conviction now. Staring at the desk, head dropped down an inch or two. Fight going, just for a moment. It will come back, it always does, but this is the vulnerable time.

'You appear back from the dead, and immediately everyone involved in the case starts dying. Waverley, Emily, Gibson, Rosco, they're all dead. And now, at last, we have a suspect. This woman, who looks like Emily, and by all reckoning is Emily, has potentially now killed four people. And she's just kidnapped your mother.'

'It can't be Emily,' he says.

'You just looked at that photograph and said it was Emily. Did your mother know Emily?'

'Of course.'

'Well, that would be one reason why she just walked out of here without making any fuss whatsoever.'

He sits back, face now a perfect picture of dejection. Lost. He came here, came back to the UK, feeling confident, and now it's begun to collapse all around him.

'Where might she have taken her, do you think?' I ask.

'I don't know.'

Lean on the table, try not to make it too much of a clichéd copper move.

'John, your mum's out there with a serial killer. She might not be your classic knife-wielding, random psycho that you get in the movies, but she's killed four people. She's not going to stop now if she's got more work to do, and she didn't just come here to take your mum out shopping.'

He swallows. Can't hold my gaze.

'Emily, Rosco, whoever she is, she's taking out people from the old days. People that are going to know you. Is it possible that she's going to kill your mother so she can't identify you?'

'That doesn't make sense.'

'Why?'

'There are lots of people that can identify me. I was at uni. I played football. There were guys at work, guys down the pub, ex-girlfriends. There must still be distant aunts and cousins.'

'So, what is it then?'

'Maybe she's clearing up loose ends, but that doesn't make any sense with Mum.'

'Why's she taken her then?'

'I don't know. Maybe just... I don't know.'

'Maybe just what?'

'Just doing it to get at me, to hurt me.'

'Why would she be doing that?'

'She… that Emily, she's a bitch. A total bitch.'

He shakes his head, still staring at the desk. I lean back against the wall, give him a moment. Even leaning back I'm still only a couple of yards away from him. I'm not worried about the time elapsing since the two women left. I have no idea where they went, and to be honest, I think the old woman is very possibly already dead.

'What do you mean, *that* Emily? That Emily, as opposed to the other Emily?'

'Yes.'

He spits out the answer, as though he resents admitting it.

'Then there are two Emilys?'

'There were the last time I looked. Aren't there two of everyone?'

'I don't think so.'

He scoffs as though I'd just denied the existence of alcohol.

'Tell me.'

'We need to find Mum.'

'I have no idea where she might have taken her.'

'Anstruther maybe.'

'Why?'

'You said that's where the other Emily was, the one who was killed.'

'Well why would she go back?'

'To meet me there. That's where I'm supposed to be going. She doesn't know I'm in police custody, does she?'

Take a moment, look at my watch. How long would it take to get to Anstruther? Dundee, cross the Tay Bridge, down through Fife, through St Andrews. Just over an hour, maybe longer at this time with traffic around Dundee.

What are my alternatives at this stage? Take Baden back to Gartcosh, head up the road and wait for word from around the country. Wait for some station somewhere to spot the car. That's it. There's nothing else positive to be done.

Sometimes, of course, that's all there is. Waiting for something to happen. But you have to try. I should be taking Baden back, and the Specialist Crime boys are going to be singularly unimpressed that I'm not.

Make the decision on what to do, and part of that is to not call this in. At some point DCI Meadows will get in touch, and then I can have the uncomfortable conversation. If I call it in now, it will quickly escalate, it'll be put through to Dingwall and Quinn will be bowing to the centre's wishes.

I walk back outside, not looking at the receptionist as we go. Lead Baden to the car, wait until the door is closed, and then call Sergeant Edelman in Anstruther. I run quickly through it. The car, the descriptions, the what-we-know and the what-we-don't. Ask her to check out the house, warn her to be careful. If there's anyone off duty, might be an idea to call them in. A couple of minutes, and then get in the car beside Baden.

'Right, we're going to Anstruther. It'll take about an hour, which is plenty of time for you to tell me how there came to be two Emily Kings.'

He holds my gaze for a moment and then looks away. Nervous.

Time to go. Into gear, reverse out of the parking space, and on our way.

49

I give him ten minutes. Fifteen. We're driving in silence, but it's not uncomfortable. The story is coming. Perhaps he's giving himself time to make something up, and I'm sitting here letting him do that. But I don't think so. He's about to tell a story that he's not told before. I'm used to them.

'You're not going to believe me,' he says finally. Somewhere along the A90, traffic busy, sitting in the outside lane at a steady seventy-five. Make speed while we can, because Dundee is going to be much slower.

'You'd be surprised,' I say.

Another pause. Almost there.

'It's sad.'

'I like sad.'

Is that true? Do I really like sad? Or have I just become so used to it? I've allowed it to find me, I let these stories in.

'You play chess, Inspector?'

His voice has lowered. Words come slowly.

'Occasionally.'

'This starts with chess. Emily grew up in Canada. She was a chess genius. Long before I met her. I mean, she was young, she was five, six-years-old, and she wasn't just beating adults... she couldn't find anyone to actually give her a game. She'd play several at a time. And, of course, with someone that young, and that much talent, it just defined who she was going to be. She was going to be the first woman to win the world chess championship. For a few years it was all she did. Didn't go out, didn't really have too many friends. She studied the game. She studied the great champions and their matches, she did what all these people do; learned hundreds, thousands of openings by rote. Her parents pushed her into it. They had a world champion on their hands, they weren't going to let that go. They'd get her a coach, and she'd suck him dry and spit him out in a matter of months, moving on to the next guy. By the age of ten, eleven, she was winning tournaments on a national level, by thirteen she was a grandmaster. She was a thing in the local news, a couple of times in the national news, although, of course, no one was that interested in chess. But it was coming.

'Then they get this guy in, a Russian. A Russian coach. He comes in all brusque and Slavic and rude, telling her she's nothing, more or less a rank amateur, but that he can turn her into something special. Her parents go for it. They've got some sponsorship by now, they sign her up with this guy. He wants to take her around, travel, broaden her horizons, much more than they have been doing. The parents accompany them at first, but they have jobs, they don't have limitless amounts of money. By the time she's fourteen, Emily is travelling to tournaments, outside Canada, alone with this guy, and by the time she's fourteen-and-a-half, he's fucking her.

'She doesn't like it at first, but then it becomes normal, it becomes what happens. And then it's not just him. And it's not just, you know, straight sex. She has men doing all sorts of things to her.

'That, really, was when Emily became two people. That was when it started. In her personality and in her head, I'm sure that was when it happened. She was this, well, not entirely normal fifteen-year-old girl, but innocent. She'd had this weird childhood, immersed in chess, and she'd missed everything. Boys, secret cigarettes, alcohol, normal teenage development. So there she was, quiet and shy, sweet and naïve, still had cuddly toys, still the little girl that her parents had always known. And then, there was the other Emily.'

He pauses for a moment. I give him the time. He's right, it is a sad story. I can feel it creeping into me, feel the melancholy and awfulness of it seep in through my head, pour through my body, infecting every part of me. The awfulness of human beings knows no boundary.

'Couldn't last, of course. These things always break. Her dad found out about it. She never told me the story of that, how it happened. He found out, and he did... he did what some dads would have done. He shut down her chess, he banned her from the tournaments, told everyone she was burnt out and wouldn't be playing, possibly ever again, and she was consigned to home. Now, it could be that that might have saved her. Might have. The dark side of her didn't like it, but the other side, the real Emily, she was relieved. Except her father...'

Shake my head in the dark of the car. Know what's coming.

'He thinks... who knows what he thinks? His little girl is lost to him. That person, the one living in the single bedroom in the house they've always lived in, is gone. Might as well be dead. Instead he's got this slut staying there, this young woman who'll sleep with anyone. It's barely his daughter. He sees it, there and then. There are two of her, and one of them isn't related to him.'

'So he sleeps with her.'

'Yes. Emily's mother… She likely didn't know the details of what Emily had been doing, but she's a mother, she's not naïve. Not in the way the dad had been. And she knows, knows as soon as it starts happening with the dad. She goes for it. Walks in on them, kills him in front of her. Right there. Beats his head in with an ornament, while Emily cowers in the corner draped in a sheet.

'Although, in fact, she told me, she didn't cower at all. She sat and watched, quite dispassionately.'

Watched and learned.

'So, the dad was dead, Emily is sixteen and alone. She has an aunt in Scotland. Inverness. She comes here. Emily, fucked up in all sorts of ways that no one knows about, comes to live in the Highlands to finish school, ending up at university in Aberdeen.'

'Which is where you met.'

'Yes.'

We hit traffic approaching Dundee. Still plenty of time for the rest of the story to unfold. I'm already infected by it. Already filled with the pain, already sensing the difference between these two characters, these two halves of the same person.

'She did all right for a while, I think. Maybe the two Emilys started to grow towards each other. The real Emily started to grow up, the other Emily was contained. Dr Jekyll and Mr Hyde began to meld into one, the former toughening up, the rough edges and bitterness being removed from the latter. We started a relationship, which was all right for a while. She was never going to stick to just me, we argued about that, but I had to accept that's who she was. And she didn't mind me… you know, that's the way it was. A lot of sex. There was a lot of sex. And then this Andrei guy arrives from Ukraine, and perhaps that's all it took. The Eastern European in him. That's what I thought at the time. She'd already told me about her life in Canada, and how it'd ended. I felt like I was trying to ease her through it, ease her into some kind of normal adulthood, then this guy walks in.

'I immediately started seeing more of the other woman. Her Mr Hyde. The slut. The witch. The conniver and liar.'

'You stayed with her, though.'

'Yeah, I did. Lovestruck fool, moth to the flame, name the cliché. Always thought I could… I don't know what… help her. Cure her. Instead I was just drawn further and further in. The other Emily won me over. And then we started this whole business with Andrei, and we were lost.'

Another pause. It's coming out though, it's flowing. He's started.

Doesn't mean he'll finish, but we're getting somewhere at last.

'The organisation ran as it did. Emily was never in charge, but she was the heart of it, you know. She ran a lot of the connections. There was Gibson and me and Waverley.'

'And Rosco.'

'And fucking Rosco.'

'You said he was a moth to the flame too.'

'He was. The dark half of her, that's what he was after, and she used him. It was good for the operation, I have to admit that. She was more or less living two lives by then. One with him, and one with me.'

I keep any more comments to myself. I don't think there's a fragility in his decision to talk, but I don't want to risk shutting him up by being glib or antagonistic.

'And then this thing with Solomon happened. Emily did her usual, you know, slept with him, but we were both sceptical about him joining the business. For a kick-off we didn't need him. And there was something about him. He was trying to be cool, but we could tell.

'We fixed up the Estonia trip, we made our plans, had it all sorted. Part of the plan was that Emily would kill Solomon. Her idea right from the start. She thought she'd stitched Solomon up. But she wasn't counting on one person...

'Her other self. Her good self. Emily might have been a slut, she might have been manipulative, but it was still a stretch to actually kill someone. And it wasn't like she turned up armed and dangerous. All along she was going to kill him with her bare hands. And some part of her just couldn't cope with that. This thing inside her, knowing it was wrong, screaming at her, trying to wrest control.'

A slight pause. Take a brief glance at him. He's staring at the dashboard, eyes are dead. Lost in the past.

'The two days before she killed Solomon were... insane. She was insane. Raving. Fighting, arguing with herself. Impossible to tell who she was. I couldn't talk to her. Literally. I was too scared, and she was completely unapproachable. This thing, I thought, this thing is just going to play out one way or the other.

'The original plan had me and Emily meeting Solomon, but in the end she didn't want me there. Said I'd get in the way. As she was leaving, she looked over her shoulder. This plaintive, pathetic, desperate glance, as though she was being led away by someone else, taken to do something she didn't want to do.

'I stayed in the hotel room. Waited all night. Emily's plan was that we'd spend the next day together in Tartu, being as normal as possible, and then I should go missing in the middle of the following night. And that was how it played out. She came back in the small hours of the morning. I hadn't slept, waiting for her.

'She walked in, like she'd just fired an unwanted employee. Composed, hair unruffled, very businesslike. Except... she'd dyed her hair. At least, I thought that's what it was. That it was dyed.

'She slept for, like, I don't know, two hours, and then she was up. We had to be seen in the town, looking normal. Normal tourists, doing normal tourist stuff. We ate breakfast, we walked around, we drank coffee, we went to churches and to see the river and so on. There's not a lot to do in that place, and we did it all.

'All day, I had this sense. You know, something. That something wasn't right, something weird had happened. Occasionally I'd catch a glimpse of something, but it was so wrong, so extraordinary, that it didn't make any sense.

'And then, I don't know, it was around two in the afternoon, we're sitting outside this little coffee place, and I see her. I'm sure of it. Emily – the old, normal Emily that I loved – across the other side of the square. Just a fleeting glance...'

He stops for a moment, and I leave him to the silence. He sounds convincing and involved in his story, but of course, the previous times I've questioned him, he's only told me what suited him, and regularly not told me the truth.

'And she was gone. And... maybe it wasn't her. It would be ridiculous if it was, after all. I mean, how could it be, she was sitting beside me at the time? Yet I realised. Whatever happened with Solomon, this woman who'd come back, this was the other Emily. My Emily had left her body. Banished for good, never coming back. Does it... is it possible that she had become someone completely different? That I really did see her across the town square?'

Another pause. At a standstill for a moment. Look at my watch. Almost at the Tay Bridge. Glance over at him. His head is down, his words have become less agitated.

'Maybe, in her head, that dark side won over. Won over completely. That's all.'

The traffic starts moving again, and this time we might actually get going. Decide to leave the questioning for the moment.

Why would I even entertain the possibility that there might physically be two Emilys? Would anyone else believe him? Would Sutherland or Quinn give him the benefit of any credulity? Would any police officer?

So why am I? Is it because I already handed my scepticism in at the door when I chose to believe Dorothy's tale? From that moment I started thinking that perhaps there were two different versions of Baden. That I now accept there aren't, doesn't really matter. It's still allowed me to give credence to the possibility that there are two of Emily.

That someone's mind can be split like that, that someone can have two distinct personalities, is well known to science, medicine, and the law. But what I'm allowing here, the possibility of it, would be universally considered preposterous. When it comes to writing this down and submitting a report, am I really going to give this as an explanation? Am I really going to try to justify this, and then expect to have a job as a detective inspector at the end of it?

If it's not this, then there must be something else. Yet the other possibilities, that it wasn't Emily King who died in Anstruther, that it's not Emily King who was married to Rosco, all of them, while being practical and possible, send us backwards in the investigation. Yet there must be something. Surely.

'So, you presume that Emily, dominated by her evil side, turned you in,' I ask, halfway across the bridge, the traffic surging forward into the night, towards Fife.

The question hangs in the car for a while. He's looking out at the reflection of lights in the water. The sky has clouded over, here on the east coast, not so far away from the clear skies of Perthshire. No moon, no stars.

'I really don't know,' he says eventually.

50

Drive into Anstruther from the back of the town, and down to the seafront. Back again for a second time within a few days, after having not been here in years. The place seems quiet, no obvious sign of police activity. Not that I'd been expecting it. Had they actually found Debbie Rosco and Baden's mother, I'd have received a call.

Drive past the harbour, no one out walking by the sea. A couple of teenagers standing in the car park, one with a skateboard, the other with a bike. One café is still open, and the pubs. A small supermarket, a woman just leaving, clumsily clutching a couple of overpacked shopping bags.

Along the front and then turn up towards Emily King's house. I have a feeling that's where we need to be, that Debbie Rosco will have gone back there. If there's no sign of anyone, then we will head for the police station. If there has been no sign at all of Rosco in the vicinity, then it looks like I'll need to head back to Gartcosh, drop off Baden, then drive north, mission unaccomplished.

That's not going to happen, though. *It finishes today.* However absurd it is that those words came to me, I know they're true. This finishes today, by one means or another.

The evening is well advanced. If it's going to finish, it had better get on with it.

The phone rings. I jump a little at the sharp sound, and realise how tense I've become. Need to relax. This is going to play out one way or another. Me being tense isn't going to make any difference to it.

Lift the phone. It's DCI Meadows. The call was bound to come. Possibly better now than in a few minutes' time. I'm not answering it. I'll give him a call shortly, when I've got a better idea of whether we're right to be here or not.

Round the corner, along the road from Emily King's house, and the confirmation is right there, beneath a dim, orange streetlight. There's a police car parked in the driveway, and parked across it, the red Peugeot belonging to Debbie Rosco.

I immediately slow and stop the car some thirty yards from the house. There are no lights on, which is odd, if there are three people, if not more, inside.

The street is on the edge of town, a row of neat, uninteresting houses down either side. Emily King's is one like any other.

'Close the door quietly when you get out,' I say.

Engine off, out the car, doors gently closed. Walk slowly towards the house, and as we do so, I realise that there is a dim light in the front room. Just a side light, the curtains closed.

It's an open driveway with no gate. Inside the house, more than likely, are Debbie Rosco, Mrs Baden, and at least Sergeant Edelman.

I've gone from nowhere this morning, to believing that Debbie Rosco is guilty of several murders, based on what I have to admit is absolutely no evidence whatsoever. It's all supposition. All of it. Her actions are questionable, and there's curiosity in what Sutherland reported, but even if she is Emily King – as I suddenly started taking for granted – there's no proof that she killed anyone. We don't have her at the scene of any crime, we don't have any fingerprints, we don't have DNA, we don't have any witnesses. We might even struggle with motive, once we've unravelled this as much as we can.

'You all right?' I say, my voice low, standing at the entrance to the drive.

'Sorry?'

'You're about to see your mum for the first time in twelve years, and Emily, who might have betrayed you. How are you?'

Giving myself time. Thinking out the permutations of how things are going to look in there. Do I call for backup, do I sneak round the back, do I ring the doorbell?

The front door is going to be unlocked. She needs us just to walk in.

'I don't know,' he says.

We glance at each other. He looks nervous, but not as bad as he did back in the Estonian forest.

Up the short driveway, hesitate for a second at the door, and then turn the handle. The door opens, the mechanism of the handle and the noise of the hinges both thunderous in the silence.

The kitchen to the right, unlit. To the left, the front room, the door open an inch, dim light around its edge. No longer hesitating. Quickly along the short corridor, open the door, step into the room, turning the main light on as I enter.

The mother isn't there. Sergeant Edelman is, tied to a chair, gagged, her police shirt ripped. Debbie Rosco is sitting behind her, leaning on Edelman's chair. In her hand is a six-inch kitchen knife, which she's balancing on her right index finger, letting the point of it bounce softly on the sergeant's exposed shoulder.

'Detective,' she says. 'You followed me all this way. Tomorrow couldn't come quickly enough for you?'

Edelman looks blankly back at me. No fear there. However this happened, she's going to be annoyed at herself.

I step forward into the room.

'Don't come any closer or she gets a knife in the neck.'

Edelman's eyes narrow. I know what she's saying. *Don't mind about me. My fault. Do what you have to do.*

A couple of footsteps behind me, and a smile comes to Rosco's face. Just a glance over my shoulder, however, then she looks back, keeping her eyes on me the whole time that she talks to him.

'John, you've changed. Lost a bit of weight. Looks good on you.'

'Emily...'

'Expect they told you I was dead.'

They can talk. Lovely reunion for them. I start to calculate. Three yards across the room. She'll never take the time to kill Edelman if I suddenly make a move. Her automatic reaction will be to fight me. Of course, she's the killer with the knife, so there's that to be taken into the calculations. As are the possibilities of making other distractions.

'Where's Mum?'

'She's fine, don't worry. Just like we planned.'

Edelman's eyes widen. I start to turn. Much too late. Don't even have time to feel stupid.

★ ★ ★

'Hey, it's been a while. What've you been up to? Still working on this Estonian case?'

Take a few moments to get my bearings. Motorway. Cars. Night-time. Outside lane, steady seventy-five. I'm driving, and although my hands are on the steering wheel – I can see them there – I can't actually feel them. I have no sensation of my hands touching anything.

I glance at Dorothy. Hold her gaze for a moment. There's a slight smile on her face, then I turn back to the road, even though I'm not sure I need to. Which is odd, because I'm definitely sitting in the driver's seat of a car in the outside lane of a motorway. It's normal in that situation to have to pay attention.

'Where are we going?' I ask.

'It's coming towards the end, so that's where, I guess. We're going to the end. It finishes today, remember?'

'What d'you mean, the end?'

'I'm not entirely sure. You just turned up here. What stage are you at with the case?'

I glance at her again. She had seemed so maudlin before. Almost as though there was a great chunk of her missing. She was half a person. It was inconceivable to think that she worked at the FCO. It didn't make sense. She was just a heartbroken young woman, wrapped up in her own tragedy.

'You seem different,' I say.

'Yes, I know.'

'You've found your family?'

'Of course… They're here somewhere.'

She's smiling, and looks around as though she might be able to see them, then stares forward again, a slightly detached look on her face, her eyes straight ahead.

'I'm sure I saw them earlier today. Expect they'll be in for dinner.'

Her voice drifts off, an uncomfortable edge to it, as though she's talking about something she doesn't want to, and then she's quickly back, positive and airy again.

'Hey, but we're here for you. Fill me in on the details. I mean, I know we never talked about it on our drive across Europe, but I knew the case, obviously. I'd done some work on it. Did you explain the mystery of how there managed to be two John Badens?'

OK, so that's why I'm here. Need to focus on the case. That makes sense. Need to gather my thoughts, try to lose that feeling of disconnection. It'll probably help if I just start talking. The focus will follow.

'Haven't quite pinned it down. I began to wonder if there might really be two of him…'

'Really? That doesn't make sense. How can there be two of anyone?'

I glance at her. Given her somewhat incredible story, I thought she might be more credulous, but I might as well be testing this theory out here, because I'll need to do it once I get back to Dingwall. *If* I get back to Dingwall. That seems to be in some doubt for the moment.

'Well, that's an interesting point. Anyway, in the case of Baden, we'd dismissed it. There was another person who was in on their deal – one of my old lot actually, I mean, security services – went missing out there and it was his body that Emily King identified as Baden's. It was all an insurance scam, which is sort of mundane really. She'd get the money, he'd sneak back into the country and off they'd go to live a happy life. Except, he got grabbed in the forest and held prisoner.'

'But wasn't the body identified back in the UK?'

'Yes, but the police officer, Rosco, was tied up in it. He manipulated things, made sure they happened correctly. His father inadvertently helped by not properly identifying the body. Made it easier for everyone.'

'What would Rosco have done if Baden's father had looked at the corpse and said, that's not him, as he surely would have expected him to do?'

'They were similar build, height, etcetera. Hair not so different. The body was bloated anyway, which helped his cause, then post mortem the face had been badly beaten. It was going to be hard to identify, even if his father had looked at it properly. So, Emily King saw the body prior to that disfiguration, but her father didn't. I don't know yet if Rosco had any help on the inside at the mortuary in the UK, or in Estonia, but that's for later. At the moment we just need to stop people getting killed.'

'People are being killed?'

'A couple from Baden's university days, Rosco – we think – and Emily King.'

'You *think* Rosco?'

'Drowned in his own vomit. Might have had his face held in it, might not...'

She nods. We continue along the outside lane. There doesn't appear to be anything on either inside lane for the moment, but I can't move the car, so I don't think about it. Maybe we would change lane if I did think about it. Logically I must be controlling this entire thing with my thoughts, so why wouldn't I be able to change lane?

'So, who do you think is killing all these people?' she asks.

'Emily King,' I say. 'Pretty sure.'

'I thought you said Emily King is dead.'

'She is.'

Dorothy smiles, and speaks in some bastardised version of a generic American accent.

'Well, Officer Dibble, either she's not, or you've been smoking some bad shit, you know what I'm saying?'

Give her a glance and then look back at the road.

'I know, it sounds weird, but I've begun to wonder if it's a possibility. That in some way... the Emily King of twelve years ago was schizophrenic, so is it possible, that at a time of extreme stress, when her two halves were, I don't know, feuding, tearing each other apart, tearing herself apart, that she somehow split in two?'

I glance at her again to see her reaction. She's staring straight ahead, face blank.

'There must be something else,' she says. 'That doesn't make sense.'

'The story you told me didn't make any sense,' I say.

'I don't remember the story.'

'So what else is there?' I say.

Troubled by this Dorothy, and the possibility that she doesn't remember the story she told me, troubled that I might have unsuitably lent her my credulity. Although shouldn't I be more troubled by the fact that I'm here with her now?

'If there are two people who are possibly Emily King, then simply put, one of them can't be. One of them must be someone else. You have to examine who these two people are. So start with the one who's still alive. Who is she?'

'She was married to DI Rosco.'

'Before this all started? Before twelve years ago? I thought she was with Baden?'

'No, we're not sure yet of her involvement with Rosco before the thing in Estonia. However, a few weeks after it, Rosco married a woman named Debbie Geddes. That's all we had. They divorced a few years later in the face of Rosco's drinking.'

'And where does Emily King fit in?'

'My Sergeant has done some digging around. We were curious because Debbie Geddes didn't seem to have any sort of background. Turns out, Emily King became Debbie Geddes. I should say that we have no proof at this stage, it's based on photographs. But it's what we're working to. And it certainly fits and makes sense.'

'Apart from the fact that Emily King is already dead.'

'Yes.'

'So, let's look at this other Emily King, the dead one. How do we know that this is Emily?'

A few seconds. Glance at her again. I keep looking to make sure she's there, because I know that at some point she's not going to be.

'She was living as Emily King. Everything was in her name. She had the history of Emily King in her paperwork. The house was in that name.'

'Did anyone ID the body?'

'No.'

'OK, that seems crucial.'

'There was no one to ID the body.'

'Did she look like Emily King?'

'Yes. Well, from photographs and what we could make out, given that again she was badly beaten.'

'There's a pattern emerging.'

'Hmm... yes, maybe there is.'

'So why did you take with such credulity that she was Emily King?'

'Had no reason not to. She lived this strange, solitary life. She had all this paperwork, she had the birth certificate, she had everything in the house. As far as we could make out, this was Emily King, slightly older and a little bit strange and lonely, which would tie in with her boyfriend having died and her never recovering. Had no reason to think otherwise.'

'OK, that's not unreasonable. Now, however, in light of the fact you think this Debbie woman is Emily King, don't you think it's reasonable, rather than assuming they were both Emily and some strange act of separation took place, that in fact the one who's dead isn't Emily at all.'

The car is now in the inside lane. How did that happen? Maybe it was because I wanted it to.

Think it through. There is a pattern, isn't there? The beating to disguise the doppelgänger, the use of the doppelgänger in the first place. It's not a far-fetched coincidence, it's a reuse of a tactic. And if Emily King and John Baden hatched a plan for him to disappear, perhaps they also hatched one for her to disappear.

'You sorting it out yet?' she asks. 'I can see you thinking.'

'Getting there.'

'So, you think she played a long game? Set up this other self, paid this person off to be her.'

'The other Emily, the now dead Emily, was receiving a thousand pounds a month, paid into an account.'

'That ties in. Maybe they just found some homeless junky, set her up, paid her to keep schtum.'

'That would fit.'

And makes more sense than there being two different Emily Kings.

'Although, it doesn't answer why,' I say. 'Why would she do it? And if she was waiting for Baden, why did she marry Rosco?'

'You think she killed four people already?'

'At least. I mean, who knows? There have been four murders

in the past week. And when we just turned up at the house in Anstruther, she was holding a police sergeant captive, with a knife at her neck. So that's confirmation, at least, of her criminal intent. She's who we're looking for, that's the first thing.'

'And what about Baden?'

I think about Baden and the last time I was with him. What happened? What was the last thing that happened?

He asked Debbie Rosco where his mum was, and she told him she was fine. *Just like we planned.*

Just like they planned.

'I think he hit me over the head. And he didn't seem surprised to see Emily as Debbie Rosco.'

'So you think they talked after he escaped.'

'That would make sense. Someone must have called her after he escaped in Estonia. I was wondering if it was someone on the inside in the police, but it would also make sense if it was him. He called her from Estonia. He explained what had happened and that he was coming home.'

'She must have been pretty shocked. I mean, if she hadn't known. How would she know he hadn't just been living it up in the Caribbean all this time?'

'You're right, who knows what was said? And how would he have known where to call her?'

'Hmm… This is getting complicated.'

'Yes.'

'Still, things are usually simple when you find out all the facts. Maybe you should just ask them.'

'What?'

'Just ask them.'

I glance at her. She's smiling. A sad smile. Suddenly, there's a look about her that reminds me of how she'd been before. The serenity that was there a while ago has gone.

'What about you?' I ask.

She stares at me, growing more melancholy before my eyes.

'It's not about me,' she says.

51

Same room, now tied to a chair. Wake up, head slumped forward. Feel sick, neck hurting from the position I've been sitting in, head screaming from the blow.

My first thought is of concussion. I must have concussion. How could I not? I shouldn't drive when I leave here.

I shouldn't drive when I leave here? Seriously? That's what you're thinking?

'You all right?'

The voice is right behind me.

'Dorothy?'

A pause. How can it be Dorothy? Why am I even thinking about Dorothy? She was in the car. We both were. But there wasn't a car. How could there have been? All there was, was me being an idiot, getting beaned over the head by Baden.

'Edelman.'

I look round as best I can, wincing at the movement. We're back to back in the chair, traditional style. You've seen it in the movies. I have this image of her passing me a paperclip, and me somehow using it to untie the knots that are cutting into my wrists. The image vanishes into the void of its own implausibility.

'Who's Dorothy?'

'Sorry, bang on the head.'

'I saw. Are you all right?'

'Not sure yet.'

Raise my head, try to ignore the pain, look around the room. Same room as we walked in on, just Edelman and I. No sign of Baden and Rosco.

'Nice to see you again,' I say, even though I can't really see her.

Yes, feeling light-headed.

'You too,' she says, almost laughing.

'Is it possible that they're about to release poison gas and we're going to have thirty seconds to get out of here?'

She laughs this time.

'I don't think they're that sophisticated,' she says. 'Although there's a lot more going on than we realised.'

'Yep.'

Close my eyes. Too soon for coherent thought.

'Maybe we could have dinner when all this is over,' I say.

'Seriously? You're hitting on me when we're tied to a chair and they're probably going to kill us? I think you might've been watching too many films.'

'Is that a yes?'

She laughs again.

'Smooth, Inspector. I can probably sue you for sexual harassment now, of course.'

'Maybe if you won't go out to dinner, our lawyers can go out to dinner together. We can have vicarious dinner.'

'You need to clear your head, Inspector.'

She's still laughing when the door opens. Emily King watches us for a moment, then enters the room, Baden behind her. I turn to look at them, but the sharpness of the pain makes me turn away again.

'Glad to see everyone's having fun,' says King. 'Now what?'

Eyes closed, deep breath through the noise. Exhale slowly. Same again. Let the head clear. I can feel it clearing. Forcing out the murk, forcing myself to think. Clear thoughts. Focus on something. Find a point, and home in on it. Clear everything else away, so it's a single clear thought. Expand from there.

You've just been in a car with Dorothy. How did that happen? Must have been dreaming. But we talked about the case. She said things that I hadn't been thinking, didn't she?

There are not two Emily Kings. This is Emily King standing here.

'Who was she?' I say.

Eyes still closed.

'What?'

Open my eyes, turn to King.

'The woman who was living in this house, pretending to be you? Who was she?'

King waves a desultory hand. If this was a real movie scene, she'd be holding a gun, but her hands are empty. Her hair is slightly more dishevelled than it was when I walked into the room, and I wonder if they've been having sex. Just the thought, or perhaps where it comes from, threatens to have the fug descend again, and I need to force my brain to remain clear.

'Just some tramp. Picked her up off the street, kept her happy, drugged up. Paid her an allowance. She never needed much. Cover, in case that lot from the east ever came looking for me. It would just have been some hitman with a name to go after, and there she was. Except they never bothered. Either way, I didn't really expect her to live this long. Didn't matter up until now.'

She turns to Baden, who's leaning back against a small table.

'Didn't do quite enough to persuade him that there were two of me, did you?'

He shrugs. She turns back, shaking her head.

'I'm going to have to kill you both,' she says.

Close my eyes again, turn away. Perhaps it would be better if my head was in a fug after all.

'Just haven't decided if here's the best place. Probably doesn't matter.'

'There's no point,' I say.

What's this? Negotiating for my life? Or negotiating for Edelman's life? I already lost Dorothy, I can't lose someone else.

'Interesting,' she says. 'Go on.'

'You're going to get caught...' I begin, pausing for a moment after she snorts, and Baden emits some low, dry laugh. 'It was my sergeant who worked out that Debbie Rosco and Emily King were the same person, it was him who put me onto you. Everyone's already looking for you. So, you're right, it doesn't matter where you kill us, just whether you actually do it. Everyone will know. Every police force, every border guard, every airport, every ferry port. So where exactly are you going to go? We don't know the full story, but we know you're guilty. Now, if you kill the sergeant and I, your crimes just get multiplied by a thousand. Some petty revenge or clearance operation from twelve years ago, involving holding someone's face in vomit and a hit-and-run? No one's interested. We might not even be able to prove that you did it. But cop killers? The media don't like cop killers. No one does. Sure, the life of a cop isn't actually worth more than the life of anyone else, but it's bigger news. And bigger news attracts bigger sentencing. That's just how it is.'

Have delivered this little speech staring at the carpet. An ugly carpet. The carpet of someone who didn't care about where she lived. Finally glance round. Head still screams with pain every time I move it, but I try to stay impassive. Disinterested, almost.

She's staring at me, head slightly lowered, eyes that tell it all. A woman who kills. Goading her is hardly likely to make her more reasonable. That's not usually how it works.

Time to extract the confession.

'Do you really want to go back to prison, John, having been held captive for–'

'–Ha!' she spits out. 'Call that captivity?

Baden isn't saying anything. Staring at her, thinking things through. Nervous eyes, coupled with a look of disdain at her casual disavowal of his twelve years in a basement. Trying to sort out their mess in my own messed up head, while having trouble enough putting one coherent thought in front of another.

'Let's just leave them and go,' he says.

'What?' she barks at him. From the look on his face, he actually seems to be hurt by the tone. It's the first argumentative note between them since they were reintroduced.

'Why did you marry Rosco?'

She turns her contemptuous look from Baden to me. I wonder what Edelman is thinking all this time. Working things out. Hopefully coming up with a plan, although I've no idea what it could be, to get us out of this. I'm stalling, right enough, because that's what one should do in this kind of situation, but I'm not sure what I'm stalling for. Are we expecting reinforcements?

Heavy sigh from King, followed by, 'Fuck's sake. Whatever. He was pathetic. Used to droop around me like some drunken, romantic poet. I thought John had just chosen to bugger off. I thought, you bastard. So I married Rosco. Suited me. I could keep an eye on him, and if John came back, it'd serve him right. Poor fucking Rosco. Just went to pieces when we were together. Couldn't handle it. But, God, it was shit. I stayed away most of the time, and Rosco turned into this abject drunk. Then I heard on the grapevine that John was still alive, holed up in some prison somewhere, and Rosco, pissed out his head one night, admitted that he'd landed him in it. Fucker. Said he did it to protect me. He was pathetic. So, I left him. He, at least, kept his mouth shut because he had as much to lose as the rest of us.'

'You didn't come and find me, though, did you?'

She looks sharply at Baden, and once again you can feel the increase in the tension. She turns back and I hold her gaze for a moment, before looking away. Stare back at the floor. And that's all there is. It was about money. Nothing else. Maybe sex. Money and sex.

I had managed to invent some romantic notion of the possibility of a person being able to split into two. An incredible notion. A criminal case that went beyond the mundane. Why had I wanted that to happen? Was the thought that there were two Emily Kings or two John Badens more about me than about the case?

'What about the chess story? Is that true?' I ask.

She glances at him, shakes her head.

'You told him the chess story? Nice. Sure, detective, I'm a chess genius. And I got fucked by just about everyone I ever met for my trouble, including dear old Daddy. Happy?'

'Let's just leave them and go,' says Baden again.

'No,' she replies, sharply.

He shakes his head.

'Look, either way, we need to get out of here. We need to go and get my mother, and be on the road.'

'Sure,' she says, her tone suddenly more flippant.

'Either we kill them before we go or not. But if he's telling the truth, and it's perfectly reasonable to assume that he talked about the case at some point in the last few days, then people are after us. This'll just make it worse. Let's leave them and get out.'

'How many people have you killed in the past week, John?' she asks.

I turn to see his face.

'How many?'

Voice with a bit more edge. He doesn't answer.

'Aye, there's the rub. You don't want to be associated with murder at all, do you, you fucking coward? I've been killing people to make this easier, and now you're like, "Oh I'm here, let's not kill anyone else!" Jesus!'

'Easier! You killed everyone I spoke to trying to track you down! I didn't ask you to do that.'

'You didn't have to ask me. God, you don't think those bastards out there, Andrei and his lot and whoever else is still running everything, you don't think they were going to be after you? We need to disappear, and everyone who knew you were coming back here to find me, has to be dead. You know they do. There have to be no loose ends. I did it *for us.*'

They share an angry stare, then she walks to his side, reaches round and picks up the knife that's lying on the table, the one she was holding to Edelman's neck when we arrived. She holds it out for him.

'On you go.'

He doesn't take it. His eyes are on it, but I suspect it's because he doesn't have the strength to hold her gaze any more.

'Take the fucking knife. It's time you got your hands dirty.'

'Jesus, seriously!'

Now he's looking at her.

'I've been living in a fucking forest in Estonia for the last twelve years.'

'It didn't sound so difficult the way you described it,' she says.

Her voice has lost the urgency, but now it's cold and harsh.

'And this isn't about the last twelve years, it's about the last week. Kill them. Do it. Now.'

She holds the knife towards him, blade forward, close to his stomach.

'Take it.'

Another long pause, then he takes the knife from her, the blade gingerly between his fingers, then turns it in his hand so he's holding the handle. He steps away from her, then looks at Edelman and me. I wonder if he's ever killed anyone before. He may be responsible for deaths by his actions or instructions, but it's a different thing to actually thrust that knife into someone and watch them die.

Not everyone has it. Clearly, Emily King has. John Baden, I'm not so sure. Or perhaps he's still weighing what I said about cop killers. I may have been stalling, but it was still entirely accurate. In general people don't like the police, until someone kills a police officer, and then everybody likes them, and the dislike is transferred to the killer.

When he moves it's fast, sudden, unexpected. A quick turn, and he drives the knife into Emily King's stomach. There's the noise of her being forced back against the table, her exhaled breath, the sound of the knife sucking on her internal organs as he pulls it quickly back out again.

She doesn't react, as though her body has been shocked into complete inaction, but the look on her face is not one of surprise. Just hatred.

He drives the knife in again. This time she falls backwards, the table pushed to the side, and as he stands still, the knife leaves her body again as she tumbles to the floor.

The gurgling has started in her throat. Eyes wide, she stares up at him, but there will be no insightful final words. Nothing thrown his way. Blood on her lips, and then dripping down her chin. Head slumps. Eyes remain half-open, head falls slightly forward.

Dead.

The sudden burst of activity and noise is swallowed up by the room. I felt Edelman straining behind me to see what was happening, and now she's turned back. I can just hear her breathing.

'I thought it was supposed to be the woman who killed the man after sex,' I say. Obviously still in action movie hero mode.

He doesn't even dignify the line with a glance. He places the knife on the table, steps back, still staring down at King, and then finally he turns, looks at me, holds my gaze for a few moments, and then walks quickly from the room.

52

'Have you got a plan?'

'Yes.'

I don't immediately elucidate the plan, because I'm still thinking about how likely it is that it'll actually work.

'Are you going to tell me the plan?' she says after a while.

'We shuffle the chairs over to the table,' I begin.

'We'll never be able to reach up.'

'We're not going to reach up. We're going to tip the table. The knife will fall off the table. Then, and I concede this isn't going to be great, we're going to have to tip ourselves over, try to land without banging our heads, then shuffle over beside the knife. Then one of us is going to have to try to pick it up, and then cut the ropes.'

I'm thinking it through. Visualising it. That's what you're supposed to do with plans. Playing it out in my head. It all sounds reasonably practical apart from the bit about cutting through the rope. Unless the knife is sharp and with a serrated edge, it will either be completely impossible, or will take a very long time. Better, I suppose, than sitting here until we rot.

'That's your plan?' she says after a while. I don't reply.

'I was hoping you might have a way to communicate with the emergency services,' she continues.

'It's all I've got.'

★ ★ ★

We shuffle around the room. There is a comically stupid tipping of the chair, followed by a very uncomfortable attempt at grasping the knife. All efforts at cutting the ropes are hampered by the knife being soaked in blood, and constantly slipping in my fingers. Finally, after two tense and frustrating hours, we are free. At that precise moment we hear the sound of vehicles outside, and immediately afterwards, before we have even lifted ourselves off the floor, the door is pounded in and the reinforcements from St Andrews arrive.

53

Sitting at my desk, Wednesday morning. Cup of coffee. Perfect strength, exactly the right temperature, just the right amount of milk. No sugar. A fleeting moment, of course. If one lingers over it, then it will cool down and will no longer be warm enough. So it has to be drunk quickly.

'So, you were tied together for more than two hours?'

I nod. It's nice to see that Sutherland is amused by the way I spent the previous evening.

'Did you talk to each other?'

'There was some conversation.'

He's smiling.

'What?'

'That's how romance develops,' he says. 'People thrown together in a crisis.'

Lower my eyes. Another drink of coffee. I think of my two hours tied together with Sergeant Edelman. It began jovially enough. Inevitably, however, the good humour gradually wore off. It was my fault. I was getting annoyed. She tried to make it light, but I was getting so frustrated with the bloody knife.

We didn't argue, nothing particularly pointed was said. We just waited patiently for me to cut the rope, so that we could split up. In my head I hear a phone call where I, after a period of a week or two, call her up to apologise for being stressed and taking it out on her – although I didn't really – and she's pleased to hear from me. It's an easy in. I have an apology to make, and there's an offer of dinner already on the table. Yet, sitting here, sadly contemplating the remains of a cup of coffee, I know I'll likely never make the call.

Perhaps tying up the case will draw us back together, put us in contact again.

The smile has gone from Sutherland's face, as he realises I'm not rising to the bait. As he sees that the thought of it ignites some sort of inner melancholy.

The door to the conference room opens and Quinn emerges, leaving the door open behind him. There was no one else in there. He was video conferencing with the suits at the Specialist Crime Division. I expected to be asked to sit in on it, but was quite happy that he chose to have the conversation without me.

'Walk with me,' he says, as he passes by our desk. 'Both of you,' he throws over his shoulder.

Given that he then walks into his office, which is no more than five yards away, there wasn't a lot of walking to be done. Walk with me, however, has become the ubiquitous phrase of the manager, summoning his staff in an act of self-aggrandisement. Or, at least, it was fifteen years ago, and this is Quinn just catching up.

We follow him into his office, close the door behind us, and then sit down across the desk at the command of his perfunctory wave.

'They've got him,' he says.

'Baden?'

'Yes. Trying to get on a boat to Belgium leaving from Hull this morning.'

'He has his mother with him?'

'Yes, of course.'

'Is she all right?'

'Fine,' he says, after a short pause, likely indicating that he's taking it for granted, or hadn't thought to ask.

'They're bringing him back up this afternoon,' he continues, 'and you won't be taking him out for any more day trips, Inspector.'

I have nothing to say to that.

'I spent most of my time in there getting my backside dragged over the coals for your act of cavalierism. You could at least have called them. Called somebody.'

'I called Anstruther.'

That even sounds weak to me. Decide that I probably ought to keep my mouth shut. Limit talking to answering specific questions, and nothing else.

'I didn't find that argument of much use to me,' he says dryly. 'You're going to spend the next couple of days putting together an airtight case here. I know the person you presume to have killed these others is now dead, and that Baden is in custody and at the very least, you and Sergeant Edelman are witness to him committing murder. But I want this thing nailed down. I want to know who was doing what to whom, when they did it, why they did it. I want the extent of the operation, I want details and dates and facts. I want money that changed hands. I want quotes. I want proof. More than anything, I want proof.

'This will be taken out of our hands, I'm quite sure. Well, that's fine, if that's what they want to do. But I don't want them looking at what we hand them and scoffing, throwing the damn thing out the window and starting all over again. If they're going to take it, then so be it, but I'm determined we're not going to look bad as a result.

With Natterson gone, and God knows how long it's going to be before we get a replacement, I can hardly afford for you two to be spending too long on this. But for now, for today, for the weekend, I don't want you doing anything else. Nail this thing down. And don't be thinking, the Super wants to look good in front of the Chief Constable. It's not about me, it's not about you. It's about this station and about doing a good job, and I don't think that's what's been done here so far.'

A pause, then he indicates the door with a nod, and Sutherland and I rise and walk quickly out the office. Half expect to get out there and find the entire place with their ears to the door listening. The office goes about its business, as it usually does, phone calls and reports and idle chatter and the sound of the photocopying machine.

We close the door behind us and stand for a moment. That turned into a bit more of a rebuke than I'd been expecting. In fact, if I'd known he was going to do that, I'd have insisted on Sutherland not being there.

Not, however, that I've got too much to complain about. The Specialist Crime suits are right to be annoyed at me. I just carted Baden off around the country, trusting him and trusting my own infallibility, and my ability to see the job through.

We glance at each other, not a lot to be said.

'Another cup of coffee and we'll start making a plan,' I say.

Sutherland nods and we walk back to our desks.

★ ★ ★

Work until nine thirty, head home, stopping at the supermarket to buy a tuna steak, a packet of salad, ciabatta and a bottle of wine. Into the house, choose to put on a jumper rather than turn up the heating at this time of night, some of the salad and bread on the plate, fry the steak for a minute on each side, pour a glass of wine and a glass of water, and then sit at the table. No music, no radio, no television. A long day, nice to have the quiet.

We can work at it for another few days, but I doubt we're ever going to have the kind of detailed proof that Quinn asked us for. Everybody's dead. The thought of that, sitting here in wonderful silence and low lighting, makes me smile for some reason. Everybody's dead.

There was an operation, run out of Eastern Europe, to harvest human bodies and sell the organs and blood illegally in the UK, and quite possibly around the rest of Europe. Emily King and John Baden were at the heart of this end of it. They hatched a plan, and it worked until the point when, if Emily is to be believed, Rosco saw a chance and landed Baden in it.

But Emily didn't exactly wait for him. Came home, sorted her own life out. Split herself into two, after a fashion, and lived out the life of the half who wasn't Emily King. And then, out of nowhere, John Baden appears and calls several people before actually getting hold of her. Must have done it before he turned up at the Embassy for the first time.

At that point, knowing he'll be coming home, she goes about tying up loose ends, planning right from the off, presumably, that she'll be jumping ship and moving on.

I doubt she needed to kill any of them. Perhaps she just wanted to. Enjoyed it.

The problem is still out there, of course. It looks like our murder case has been cleared up, but the harvesting of organs still goes on, and whatever route they use into the UK is likely unaffected. For the moment, though, we're putting together a case against someone who's already dead, dealt summary justice by her former boyfriend.

Work is done for the day, however. I can switch off, and concentrate on nothing other than the fact that I absolutely nailed this tuna steak. The only problem being, that when you cook a tuna steak to perfection, it's cold in about three minutes.

54

The first of December, an early snowfall in London. Standing in a small cemetery in Balham. Temperature around freezing, but not much wind. The snow was light, and it won't last. Just enough to give the ground a perfect covering, to make the cemetery attractive for the burial. As though it was planned.

Second burial in two days. Natterson yesterday. Still haven't recovered. Another train ride down to London, the thought of the anguish – Ellen and all of us at the station, and Natterson's broken parents travelling along with me.

By now, Jason Solomon's mother knows that her son, whose return she has awaited for twelve years, is long dead. More heartbreak, another memorial service, the ashes of his body finally in the hands of his family.

There aren't many people here. I guess Dorothy never made too many friends. Maybe she never saw the point, as she lived her life thinking that she was about to jump back into the old one at any moment. Perhaps she could think of nothing but the family she lost. Perhaps she was just an unhappy young woman who had constructed a story around herself that fitted the tragic narrative of the tragic person she needed to be.

I stand at the back and listen to the vicar. His words are heartfelt. Sad. He is brief, but he goes beyond the usual platitudes of the minister brought off the substitutes' bench because the deceased never actually attended church.

I wonder if she went to church in hope. She prayed for her life back, as though there was actually someone up there who might answer her call.

The sadness seeps up through my shoes, like the cold. It infects me as much as it infects everyone here. Most of the women are silently weeping. A couple of men too.

The brief few words are over, the public part of the burial is done. I take a further step back, as the small crowd around the grave begins to move away. There are a few who do not move.

How many times have I felt myself in Dorothy's company since she died? Three or four? Was she really there, or was it just my imagination, bringing someone back who I wished could still be there?

'Inspector Westphall?'

Come back from wherever it was that my mind was running. Had been staring straight ahead. Staring straight at the man before me, without seeing him.

'Yes, sorry. Miles away.'

He holds out his hand, and I take off my glove to shake it.

'Johnny Hughes, Dorothy's brother.'

'Hi. I'm sorry…'

'That's all right. She was… I don't think any of us were surprised. You were with her in the car from Tallinn?'

'Yes. I…'

Words run out. What can I possibly say?

'You were the last person to talk to her. Well, apart from the hotel receptionist, of course.'

'Yes.'

He turns and looks over his shoulder.

'We're just going back to Mum's for something. You know, the usual, tea and sandwiches. You can see, it won't be big. Wonder if you had the time to…'

'I don't know that…'

'Really, it's, you know, don't worry. No one's looking at you wondering what you said to her. It's been coming, for so long. We've seen it. We tried to get her to get help. And then in the last few weeks… we don't know what happened. Maybe you could have a word or two with Mum, when she's calmed down. She's not, you know, she's not looking at you wondering what happened. Maybe if you could just say a word or two, anything really, anything that might help.'

There are tears in his eyes. He looks strong, but suicide is so damned tough. Tougher than all the rest. It really is. Bad enough to lose a sibling to an accident or illness or murder, but with those there's usually nothing you could have done. But with suicide you're always left wondering. The phone call you never made, the argument you had, the visit you cancelled, the doctor's appointment you didn't do enough to make sure was kept.

'Of course.'

He shakes my hand again, and turns back to be with the family. I have no idea what I'm going to say.

★ ★ ★

Unusually, it seems everyone who was at the graveyard is now back at the house. What had seemed like a small crowd outdoors, now makes for a busy sitting room and kitchen.

Not a great deal of conversation, and what there is, barely audible. No one has much to say. Usually, once the burial or service is over, people will relax, conversation will be had. Relatives who only ever meet at funerals and weddings will catch up with all the news.

I don't see that happening here. The sense of loss, of confusion, in Dorothy's immediate family, seems to be infecting everyone. Even the few who I decide likely came down here from King Charles Street are saying little. Maybe there are some people from Vauxhall Cross too. The two organisations work so closely together, Dorothy might well have had friends over the river.

I don't know any of these people, but they stand out when you know what you're looking for.

That guy there, looking at his watch. Of course, he could be desperate to get back to any office in the city, but I feel like I know him. I feel like he's me, ten years ago. The same eyes, the same look cast around the room, the same look that we give to every room of people, searching for anyone who shouldn't be there, searching for anything out of the ordinary.

I get a cup of tea, help myself to a plate of food. Three small sandwiches, a piece of quiche, two sausage rolls. The food of the bereaved. I walk over to the side of the room and place the cup down on a mat at the edge of a sideboard. Take up my position on the periphery. The guy who doesn't really know anyone else there. The guy who feels slightly out of place. The guy who's thinking about leaving the minute he arrives.

What do I look like? An ex-boyfriend perhaps? Or a chancer who walked in off the street looking for a free sandwich? The funeral crasher.

'Hey, how you doing?'

Young guy. I knew it. One of my old lot. Trained to get information out of people at awkward social functions. Perhaps some of the low conversation was a few of them clustered together saying, who's the guy in the corner, we need to find out. Make sure he's supposed to be here. Hey, Matt, you've done the course, go and speak to him.

Like I might be one of those terrorists, subverting the western world by eating sandwiches to which he's not entitled.

'Good, thanks,' I say.

'So, how d'you know Dorothy?'

I take a bite of a sandwich so that he has to wait until I've finished my mouthful before getting an answer. He acknowledges my right to food and waits patiently, looking back over the small room.

Bright wallpaper, unusual abstract pictures. Colours and shapes, impossible to do anything other than interpret what they might be. I don't do art, so wouldn't even try.

Take some tea.

'We were friends,' I say. 'You?'

'We did some work together. So, how did...'

'Where?'

Slight pause. That's not how the interrogation is supposed to go. It's not supposed to be about him. It's about me.

'On an overseas development project. So...'

'You're DFID?'

Another pause, then, 'Yes, DFID. It...'

'You're not from Vauxhall Cross then?' I ask.

He gives me a look and then rolls his eyes, shakes his head.

'Didn't recognise you,' he says.

'I left while you were still at Oxford.'

'Durham,' he says quickly. 'I didn't think Dorothy knew too many of our lot.'

'Drove from Tallinn with her last week.'

Now there's recognition. He holds my gaze for a moment, let's his eyes drop, nods, touches my arm. Touches my arm...

'Right. Sorry. That must have been pretty tough for you.'

Looks back up, I answer with a slight movement of the head. He's still nodding.

'Right, OK, I should... yeah, good to meet you. Enjoy the, eh...' and he indicates the food and turns to retreat to his comrades.

Well that ended quickly once he'd learned who I was. I must be a thing. Someone they're talking about. The guy who took the last drive with Dorothy. The guy who, quite literally, drove her to suicide.

Alone again. Through the door I can see Dorothy's mother. Sitting at a table, her eyes glazed over. I'm here to talk to her, but it's not time yet. I'll need to wait until she's ready, although I doubt she will be today. There's someone sitting with her, but neither of them is talking.

I turn and look out the window. Grey December, not much snow lying out on the street. Some on the hedge across the road. There's a bookshelf to my right, and I do that thing that people in my situation do the world over. No one to talk to, so you try to stay busy, so that you're not just standing there, so you're not drawing attention to yourself by your isolation.

I could be talking to people if I wanted, you're saying, but right now I'm looking at these photographs, or this painting, or these books on the bookshelf.

There are two rows of books, all paperbacks, all with the spine broken in several places. Many of the usual suspects. *Wolf Hall. A Prayer for Owen Meany. The Great Gatsby. The Unbearable Lightness of Being. The Life of Pi. Midnight's Children. Kidnapped. Dance, Dance, Dance.* And then, there it is. Right in the middle. Waiting to be picked out. A thin paperback, one noticeable crease down the spine, the title of the book in red, the author's name in black.

The Song of the Dead by H Wakamoto.

I stand and look at it for a moment. There's a cup of tea in my left hand, a sandwich in my right. I put the sandwich into my mouth, but don't immediately reach out to lift the book. I remember a line now, now that I'm standing here looking at this, but I don't know where I've heard it before.

The voice that I recall saying the words, was it Dorothy or was it that other voice inside my head, the voice that spoke the words, *it finishes today*?

They creep up behind, to cut off my head,
And all I can hear, is the song of the dead…

Staring at the book, the cup of tea hovering just below my mouth, eating the last of the sandwich, I feel the hairs begin to stand on my neck. *The Song of the Dead.* This is her book. This is Melanie Waverley's book.

Melanie and my Dorothy, do they inhabit the same world? Yes! Of course they inhabit the same world! Don't we all inhabit the same world?

Someone taps me on the shoulder. Turning and taking a step away, I spill a little tea. Eyes wide with surprise, as though they've snuck up on me.

'Sorry,' says Dorothy's brother, 'didn't mean to frighten you. I wondered if you could come and talk to Mum now.'

I stare at him for a moment, then look back through the door into the next room. She's still sitting in the same position, her head down, her eyes staring blankly ahead. I wonder if the family has decided that it's time I speak to her, or whether she herself has asked.

'Of course,' I say.

'Thanks.'

He starts to walk through, and I follow him. I glance back over my shoulder at the bookshelf, but already I'm too far away to distinguish the writing on the spines of individual books.

I pause for a last look. I think it's still there. White, with red and black writing. On a bookshelf, where it ought to be.